PENGUIN

FLINT THE

Dragonlance® Preludes II, Volume Two

Mary Kirchoff has published widely with TSR, including ENDLESS QUEST® Books and *Portrait in Blood* for the AMAZING™ Stories book series. She is the author of the short story "Finding the Faith" for DRAGONLANCE® Tales; *The Magic of Krynn*; and *Kendermore*, Volume Two of the DRAGONLANCE® Preludes I Trilogy. She was the editor of *The Leaves from the Inn of the Last Home* and *The Art of the DRAGONLANCE Saga*.

She lives in a constantly renovated Victorian house with her husband, son and two Irish setters.

Douglas Niles is the author and game designer of more than fifty titles. These include the Moonshae Trilogy of FORGOTTEN REALMS™ novels, and board games based on Tom Clancy's novels, *The Hunt for Red October* and *Red Storm Rising*.

Formerly a teacher of speech and drama, he now lives and works at his home in the southern Wisconsin countryside. He and his wife, Christine, have two children, Allison and David. They are currently attempting to train an enthusiastic Bouvier named Kodiak.

FROM THE CREATORS OF
THE DRAGONLANCE® SAGA

The Art of the DRAGONLANCE Saga
Edited by Mary Kirchoff

The Atlas of the DRAGONLANCE Saga
by Karen Wynn Fonstad

DRAGONLANCE Tales:
The Magic of Krynn
Kender, Gully Dwarves, and Gnomes
Love and War
Edited by
Margaret Weis and Tracy Hickman

DRAGONLANCE Heroes
The Legend of Huma
Stormblade
Weasel's Luck

DRAGONLANCE Preludes
Darkness and Light
Kendermore
Brothers Majere

DRAGONLANCE Heroes II
Kaz, the Minotaur

DRAGONLANCE Preludes II
Riverwind, the Plainsman

DragonLance® Saga

PRELUDES II

VOLUME TWO

Flint
—the—
King

Mary Kirchoff and
Douglas Niles

Cover Art
CLYDE CALDWELL

Interior Illustrations
VALERIE VALUSEK

PENGUIN BOOKS
in association with TSR, Inc.

PENGUIN BOOKS

Published by the Penguin Group
Penguin Books Ltd, 27 Wrights Lane, London W8 5TZ, England
Viking Penguin, a division of Penguin Books USA Inc.
375 Hudson Street, New York, New York 10014, USA
Penguin Books Australia Ltd, Ringwood, Victoria, Australia
Penguin Books Canada Ltd, 2801 John Street, Markham, Ontario, Canada L3R 1B4
Penguin Books (NZ) Ltd, 182–190 Wairau Road, Auckland 10, New Zealand

Penguin Books Ltd, Registered Offices: Harmondsworth, Middlesex, England

First published in the USA by TSR, Inc. 1990
Distributed to the book trade in the USA by Random House, Inc.,
and in Canada by Random House of Canada Ltd
Distributed to the toy and hobby trade by regional distributors
Published in Penguin Books 1990
3 5 7 9 10 8 6 4 2

PRODUCTS OF YOUR IMAGINATIONTM

Printed in England by Clays Ltd, St Ives plc

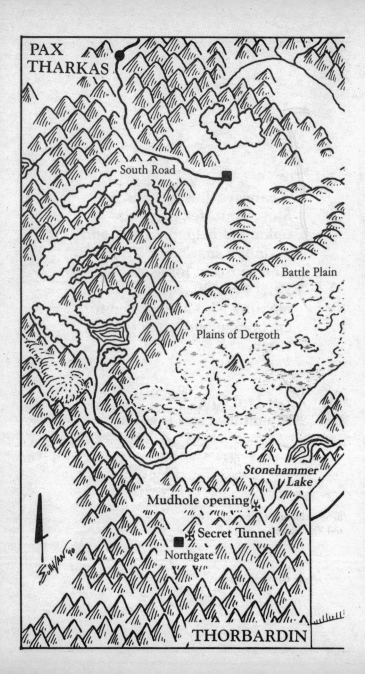

PAX
THARKAS

South Road

Battle Plain

Plains of Dergoth

Stonehammer
Lake

Mudhole opening

Secret Tunnel

Northgate

THORBARDIN

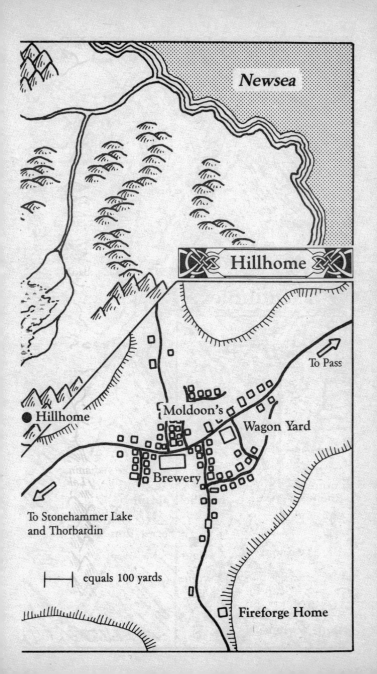

Newsea

Hillhome

To Pass

Hillhome

Moldoon's

Wagon Yard

Brewery

To Stonehammer Lake
and Thorbardin

⊢⊣ equals 100 yards

Fireforge Home

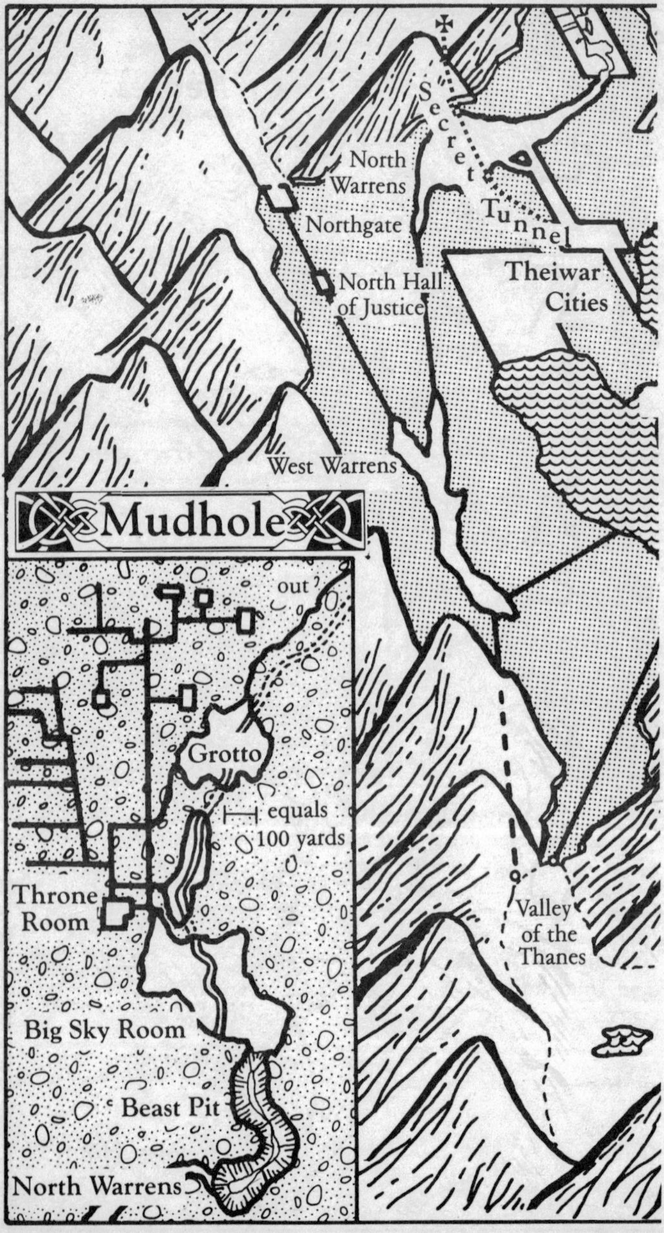

Mudhole

North
Warrens

Northgate

North Hall
of Justice

Secret Tunnel

Theiwar
Cities

West Warrens

Mudhole

out ?

Grotto

⊢—⊣ equals
100 yards

Throne
Room

Big Sky Room

Beast Pit

North Warrens

Valley
of the
Thanes

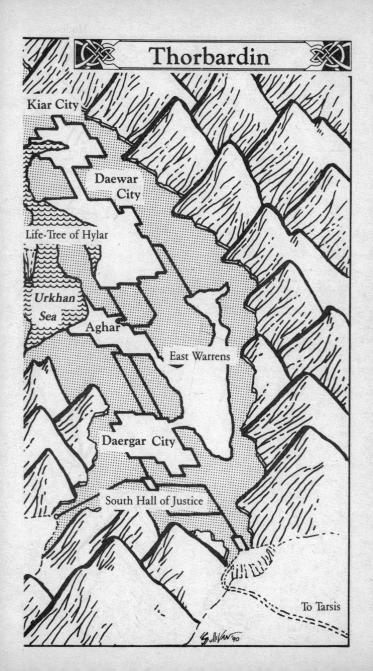

Thorbardin

Kiar City

Daewar City

Life-Tree of Hylar

Urkhan Sea

Aghar

East Warrens

Daergar City

South Hall of Justice

To Tarsis

PROLOGUE

The hammer fell rhythmically against the anvil, over and over, gradually returning the wheelrim to its circular shape. A sheen of perspiration glistened on the dwarven smith's skin when the fire rose, but then he fell into shadows as the blaze sank into the coals. The smithy around him was empty, dark but for the forge fire.

As the hill dwarf's body labored, so did his mind, frantically. He thought about the secret he had learned, scarce minutes before. Again and again his hammer fell on the rim as he pushed himself past the point of exhaustion. Sparks exploded from each contact, hissing through the air before settling to the earthen floor of the shed.

Indecision tormented him. Should he remain silent?

Should he speak out? The hammer continued pounding.

Immersed in his task, the dwarf did not see the grotesque figure moving through the shadowy doorway. For a moment the fire flared, outlining a black, misshapen figure shorter even than the dwarven smith.

This dark one shuffled forward, and again the blaze rose, revealing a hump of flesh that twisted the stunted body half sideways. Still the smith hammered, eyes focused on the wheel, unaware of the one who slowly limped toward him from behind.

The hunchbacked figure raised a hand to his chest and wrapped his blunt fingers around a small object that hung suspended from his neck by a chain.

Blue light glowed between those fingers as the amulet sparked to life. His other hand gestured toward the smith. Softly, the blue light spread outward, advancing slowly like an oily, penetrating mist. It reached forward in uneven tendrils, closer and closer to the smith.

For the first time, the hammer faltered slightly in its blow. Reflexively, the dwarf raised it again, ready to strike. Suddenly his face distorted in a grimace of unimaginable agony, and his body convulsed with a violent spasm. For a moment his movement ceased, as if he had been frozen in a grip of excruciating pain.

The hammer remained poised above him as his body stiffened, wracked within the blue glow that outlined him. The gentle, almost beautiful cocoon belied the supernatural grip of its power. Only the dwarf's eyes moved, growing wider and more desperate with the slowly increasing, inevitably fatal pressure of dark sorcery.

Abruptly the light vanished, and the hunchback shuffled backward, melting into the darkness.

The dwarven smith's hammer finally slid from his gloved hand with a loud clang to the anvil. Slowly, the corpse toppled forward, the stocky body splaying across the anvil and the nearly straightened wheel. It slipped silently to the cold ground.

Chapter I

Autumn Winds

Watching dead leaves swirl into his windows, Flint Fireforge threw back his mug and swallowed the last of his draught. A satisfied belch ruffled his thick mustache. For cheap ale, it wasn't half bad, he concluded. But it *was* gone. He held the empty bottle—his last—up to the light of the fire. The dwarf stroked his salt-and-pepper beard out of habit. After considering his empty larder, Flint decided that it was time to see if his ale order was in at the greengrocer's. He was going to have to leave the comfort of his home and fire for only the third time in the month since his friends had left the treetop village of Solace.

The dwarf and his companions—Tanis Half-Elven, Tasslehoff Burrfoot, Caramon and Raistlin Majere, Kitiara

Uth-Matar, and Sturm Brightblade—had parted ways to discover what they could of the rumors concerning the true clerics, agreeing to meet again in exactly five years. Flint had spent much of his time in the last few years adventuring with his much younger friends or traveling to fairs to sell his metalsmithing and woodcarvings. Truly he missed them, now that they were gone. But the truth of the matter was, at one hundred forty years, the middle-aged dwarf was just plain tired. So, being reclusive by nature, he had stayed at home and done little more than eat, drink, sleep, stoke the fire, and whittle in the month since their departure.

Flint's stomach rumbled. Patting the noisy complainer, he reluctantly eased his bulk from his overstuffed chair near the fire, brushing wood shavings from his lap as he stood. He pulled his woolly vest closer and looked about his home for his leather boots.

The house was small by the measure of the human-sized buildings up in the trees. But his home, built in the base of an old, hollowed-out vallenwood, was quite large by dwarven standards—opulent even, he reflected, with not a little pride. Sure, it didn't have the large nooks and crannies found in the caves-turned-houses of his native foothills near the Kharolis Mountains, nor was there the ever-present homey scent only a white-hot forge could produce. But he had carved every inch of the inside of his tree into shelves or friezes depicting vivid and nostalgic scenes from his homeland. These included a forging contest, dwarven miners at work, and the simple skyline of his boyhood village. Such carvings were not easily done on the stone walls of the homes of most hill dwarves.

The stroke of his knife over a firm piece of wood was Flint's greatest joy, though the gruff hill dwarf would never have admitted such a sentiment. Idly, he raised his hand to one of the friezes, touching his fingers to the carved crest of a jagged ridge, following the dips and summits. He dropped his hand to the carvings of the dark pine forests below the crest, admiring the precise bladework that had marked each tree in individual relief on the wall.

With a large, shuddering sigh, Flint took his heavy, well-worn leather boots from under a bench by the door and jammed them onto his thick feet. There was nothing to be done about it—he'd put off this errand as long as he could.

The massive vallenwood front door creaked as Flint opened it, causing the shutters on his windows to bang in the chill breeze, their hinges sagging like an old woman's stockings. They ought to be repaired—there were many such tasks to be done before the first snow fell.

Flint's home was one of the few in Solace at ground level, since he was one only of a handful of non-humans living in the town, including dwarves. While the view from up in the trees was quite lovely, Flint had no interest in living in a drafty, swaying house. Wooden walkways suspended by strong cords attached to high branches were the sidewalks of Solace. Probably they had provided a useful means of defense against the bandit armies that had once ranged across the plains of Abanasinia in the wake of the Cataclysm. Nowadays the trees served as an aesthetic delight, Solace's trademark. People came from many miles away simply to gaze on the city of vallenwood.

The day was cool but not cold, and warming sunshine cut through the thick trees in slanted white lines. The greengrocer's shop rose above the very center of the eastern edge of the town square, a short distance away. Flint set out for the nearest spiral stair leading to the bridgewalks overhead. By the time his short legs had pumped him to the top of the circling thirty-foot wooden ramp, his brow had broken out in beads of sweat. Flint plucked at the furry edges of his vest and wished he hadn't dressed so warmly; he slipped his arms from it and draped the leather and wool garment over one shoulder. He saw the grocer's, at the end of a long straightaway.

For the first time in quite a while, Flint truly noticed his surroundings. The village of Solace was washed in vivid fall colors. But unlike the maples or oaks of other areas, each large vallenwood leaf turned red, green, and gold in perfect, alternating angled stripes of about an inch wide. So instead of seeing blazing clumps of solid color, the landscape was a multicolored jumble. The bright sunlight cast the leaves in a shimmering iridescence that shifted in shade and intensity with each passing breeze.

The view from the bridgewalk allowed him to see quite a distance. He looked down at a smithy, where the blacksmith Theros Ironfeld toiled at shoeing the lively stallion of a robed human who was pacing with impatience.

A seeker, Flint thought sullenly, and his mood darkened. It seemed the seekers were everywhere these days. The sect had arisen from the ashes of the Cataclysm, which was itself caused by the old gods in reaction to the pride and misdirection of the most influential religious leader at the time, the Kingpriest of Istar. This group, calling themselves seekers, loudly proclaimed that the old gods had abandoned Krynn. They sought new gods, and sometime during the three centuries since, the seekers claimed to have found those gods. Many of the folk of Abanasinia had turned toward the flickering promise of the seekers' religion. Flint, and many others of a more pragmatic nature, saw the seekers' doctrine for the hollow bunk that it was.

They could be recognized by their brown and golden robes, these seeker missionaries who rode about the plains collecting steel coins for their coffers. Most of them at the missionary level were the young, bored malcontents who grew up in every town. The promise of money and power, if only over people desperate for a sign that gods existed, seemed to lure these spiritual bullies like a magnet. They were molded into persuasive salesmen by an intensive "training" session in the seeker capitol of nearby Haven, and they claimed to have converted thousands to their cause.

The seekers were as close as anything to the governing body of the plains. A body with muscle, of course: seeker followers were equally divided between the zealous acolytes who taught the words and ways of the new gods, and the men-at-arms who garrisoned the towns for no discernible purpose.

Unfortunately, groused the dwarf to himself, their concept of governing seems to involve little more than mooching off the towns and villages unlucky enough to host their temples and guardposts.

Flint's mood dipped even farther when he noticed a group of seekers hovering around the doorway to Jessab the Greengrocer's. He recognized this bunch as rude, belligerent, over-postulating phonies who couldn't cure a split finger any more than they could speak with their so-called gods. In one of the few times Flint had ventured from his home in the last month, he had come upon a villager choking on a bite of meat. This very group had been summoned to help, and after much desperate prodding from the small, gathered crowd, the leader of the three, a pimply young whelp, had sighed and gesticulated uselessly above his head as if casting a clerical spell. No miracle appeared. The villager had gasped his last before the other two could try to help him. The three had shrugged in unison and then headed into the nearest inn, unconcerned.

Flint could feel his face tighten with anger now as he considered the cluster around the doorway. Novices, he noted, from their coarse white robes edged with embroidered hemlock vine and the all-too-familiar emblem of a lighted torch on the left breast.

"Who are you staring at, little man?" one of them demanded, his arms crossed insolently.

Flint's eyes narrowed in irritation, but he let a shake of his head and a snort of disgust suffice to answer the question. Tipping his head slightly, he made to squeeze his way between them and into the greengrocer's.

A bony finger poked him in the shoulder, scarcely enough pressure for the dwarf even to notice. "I asked you a question, *gully* dwarf." The seeker's friends laughed at the insult.

Flint stopped but did not raise his eyes. "And I believe I gave you as much answer as your kind deserves."

Egged on by his friends, the young seeker pressed his point. "You've got an awfully smart mouth for an outnumbered old man," he growled, stepping fully in front of Flint. He reached down to grab the dwarf's lapels.

"Teach him a lesson, Gar," a crony purred in anticipation. Flint's irritation turned to fury. He looked into the face of his antagonist. What he saw was the glee-and-fear mixed expression of an animal who was closing on an easy victim. Or so the seeker thought.

Flint decided that the fellow needed a lesson in humility and manners. Moving like lightning, he drove his fist into the boy's belly. Stunned, the youth doubled over and clutched at his stomach. The dwarf's stubby fingers flew up to pull the seeker's droopy, coarse hood down over his red face. Flint quickly drew the strings tight and knotted the hood shut, until only the boy's pimply nose poked out. Flailing his arms desperately, the seeker let out a screech and tumbled to the planks of the bridgewalk.

Flint was dusting off his hands when his sharp dwarven ears picked up the familiar "whoosh" of blades being unsheathed. Whirling around with stunning quickness, the stocky dwarf knocked the small daggers from the other seekers' hands. The metal weapons glinted in the sun as they flew over opposite sides of the bridgewalk.

"Daggers! Look out below!" Flint called over the railing in case anyone stood beneath. Looking down, he saw a few villagers scatter without question, and the blades fall harmlessly, point down, into the earth.

When Flint looked up again, he saw the backs of the seekers as they fled, the two toadies pulling their still-hooded, stumbling leader after them.

"Run home to your mothers, you young whelps!" Flint was unable to resist shouting. My, but it's a fine day, he thought, looking up into the blue sky before stepping spiritedly into the greengrocer's.

Amos Cartney, a human of some fifty years, owned and ran Jessab the Greengrocer's. Flint could not enter the shop without remembering the time he, Tanis, and Tasslehoff had stopped in for some snacks to bring to a night of fellowship before Flint's hearth, shortly after Tasslehoff's arrival in Solace, some years ago.

"Hey, Amos, who is Jessab, anyway?" Tasslehoff had blurted out of the blue, plucking at items of interest on the candy counter. "Must be someone important, for you to name your store after him. I mean, your name is *Amos Cartney*, not *Jessab*."

Knowing the answer through local gossip, Flint had tried

desperately to clap a hand over the kender's big mouth. But the quick-footed imp had danced away. "Watch out, Flint! You nearly suffocated me," he had scolded the dwarf. "Your father, maybe?" he pressed, turning back to the suddenly pale shopkeeper. "Grandfather? Hmm?"

"The man who owned the store before me," had been Amos's quiet reply.

"That's it?" Tas squealed.

"Mind your own business, kender!" Flint had growled low in his throat.

But Amos waved away the dwarf's concern. "No, he stole my wife and left behind this shop. I leave his name up to remind me how fickle women can be, in case I'm ever tempted to trust one of them again."

The tender-hearted kender's eyes had filled with tears, and he came to Amos's side to pat the human's shoulder, treasures newly "found" in the shop dropping from his pockets in his haste. "I'm so sorry . . . I didn't know. . . ."

A slight, stoic smile had creased Amos Cartney's face as he gently slipped his hand from the anxious kender's. "And you know what else? I haven't been tempted, all these ten years."

Flint secretly agreed with Amos's evaluation of women— he'd had some bad experiences of his own—and from that time forward, the human and the dwarf were friends.

Seeing Flint in his doorway now, the greengrocer wiped his hands on his apron and waved the dwarf inside, a hearty grin on his face.

"Didn't bring that nosy kender with you, I see!" He snickered, continuing to wave Flint forward. "Hurry on in. I've been having some trouble with seekers hanging around the doorway, pestering my good customers. Can't seem to get rid of 'em." Amos shook his balding head wearily.

Flint patted his old friend on the back. "Tas has gone exploring for five years. And I don't think those seekers will be bothering anyone for a while, either."

Catching the glint in the dwarf's eye, Amos's smile was grateful, but it still held a hint of weariness. "My thanks, but they always come back. Maybe not the same troublemakers, but every day there are more seekers to take their places." Amos dug the heels of his palms into his eyes and rubbed.

Flint's good mood ebbed as he was forced to agree with the shopkeeper. Solace was not the same friendly village it had been before the seekers had encroached on it in the last few years.

"But what am I saying?" Amos forced his mood to brighten. "You didn't come here to listen to my woes. Where's your list? I'll rustle up your goods." Amos elbowed the dwarf conspiratorially in the ribs. "Got that bottle of malt rum you've been waiting for, too." Taking the scrap of parchment Flint held up in his hand, Amos cackled as he shuffled off to collect the dwarf's groceries.

"Thanks, Amos," Flint called softly, absently scanning the shelves around him.

He saw huge clay jars of pickled cucumbers, onions, and other vegetables. The smell of vinegar lingered thick around here, and Flint moved away. The dwarf passed a row of barrels, containing rye and wheat and oat flours, and then smaller bins with sugar and salt. Opposite these was a wall of spices, and he read their odd names with amused curiosity: absynt, bathis, cloyiv, tumeric. What made people add such bizarre things to their food? the dwarf wondered. What was wrong with a plain, sizzling haunch of meat?

Flint was looking at a tin of salted sea snails, a treat he hadn't had in years, when he heard someone beside him say in a gravelly voice, "So there *is* another hill dwarf in this town! I was beginning to feel like the proverbial hobgoblin at a kender Sunday picnic," boomed the stranger, clapping Flint on the back merrily. "Hanak's the name."

Flint took a small step sideways and looked at the speaker. He was nearly big nose to big nose with another dwarf, all right. Wild, carrot-red hair sprang from the other dwarf's head like tight metal coils, and between that and a poker-straight beard and mustache were eyes as clear blue as the sky. Flint tried to judge his age: the lines on his face were not too deep, but he was missing his two front teeth, though whether from aging or fighting Flint could not say.

The strange dwarf wore a tight chain mail shirt and a well-worn cap of smooth leather. His high boots were light, almost like moccasins, but showed the wear and stain of much travel. Hanak smacked his lips and rubbed his hands together as he looked at the shelves of food.

"You must be new to Solace," said Flint noncommitally.

Hanak shrugged. "Just passing through, actually; I'm headed for Haven. I hail from the hills south of here a good ways, almost down to the plains of Tarsis. Never been this far north before," he admitted.

Flint turned back to his shopping but then felt the other dwarf's eyes on him.

"You're from the south too, unless I miss my guess."

"You don't," Flint admitted, facing the stranger again. Hanak's inquisitive words made Flint uncomfortable.

"Not so far south as me, though—east hillcountry'd be my guess," the other hill dwarf said, tapping his chin in thought, squinting at Flint. "Perhaps just north of Thorbardin?"

"How did you know?" Flint asked brusquely. "I've never met anyone who could pinpoint someone's region so closely!"

"Well, now, it wasn't too difficult," the dwarf said, his tone implying anything but. "I travel for my living, selling leather work. I detected a slight accent and noticed the black in your hair—nearly every dwarf in my region has red or brown. And that long, loose, blue-green tunic and those baggy leather boots—you've been away from dwarves for some time, haven't you? I haven't seen anyone wearing that style in years, you know. Say, what village are you from, exactly?"

Flint was a little put off by the clothing comments—he'd gotten the boots as a gift from his mother a few decades before—but he decided the dwarf meant no offense. "I was raised in a little place called Hillhome, smack between Thorbardin and Skullcap."

"Hillhome! Why, I was there but twenty day ago. Was trading my boots and aprons. Not so little anymore, though. A shame what's happening there, isn't it?" he said sympathetically. "Still, you can't stop progress, now can you? Um, um, um," the dwarf muttered, shaking his head sadly.

"Progress? In Hillhome?" Flint snorted. "What did they do, raise the hems on the frawl's dresses by half an inch?"

"I'm talking about the *mountain dwarves!*" yelled Hanak. "Marchin' through town, drivin' their big wagons over the pass. They even stay at hill dwarf inns!"

"That pass was built by hill dwarf sweat, hill dwarf blood!" cried Flint, appalled at the news. "They'd never let the mountain dwarves use it!" No, *never*, Flint repeated vehemently to himself.

The history of the hill and mountain dwarves was a bitter one, at least during the centuries since the Cataclysm. At that time, when the heavens rained destruction upon Krynn, the mountain dwarves withdrew into their great underground kingdom of Thorbardin and sealed the gates, leaving their hill dwarf cousins to suffer the full force of the gods' punishment.

The hill dwarves had named the act the Great Betrayal, and Flint was only one of the multitudes who had inherited this legacy of hatred from his forefathers. Indeed, his father's father, Reghar Fireforge, had been a leader of the hill dwarf armies during the tragic, divisive Dwarfgate Wars. Flint could not believe that the dwarves of Hillhome would avert their eyes to the undying blood feud.

"I'm afraid they are," replied Hanak, his tone gentler. "Theiwar dwarves at that, the derro dwarves of Thorbardin."

"Derro? It can't be!" growled Flint. That was even worse. Indeed, the derro—the race of dwarves that comprised the bulk of the Theiwar clan—were known to be the most malicious of mountain dwarves. Their magic-using shamans had been the prime instigators of the Great Betrayal.

The other dwarf backed a step away this time and held up his hands defensively. "I only know what I saw, friend, and I saw derro strolling merrily among the dwarves of Hillhome—and not a one of the hill dwarves was spitting on 'em, either."

"I can't believe that," Flint muttered, shaking his head. "I can't believe my brothers would allow it. Our family used to carry some weight in the village. Maybe you heard our name—Fireforge? My brother's name is Aylmar Fireforge."

A shadow crossed the other dwarf's face fleetingly, and he seemed almost to nod, then think better of it. "No, it doesn't ring a bell," he said, then quickly added, "but I didn't stay long enough to get to know anyone so very well."

Flint ran a weary hand through his salt-and-pepper mop. Could Hanak be right about mountain dwarves infesting Hillhome?

Flint felt a strong hand squeeze his shoulder. "If *my* kinfolk were dealing with devils, I'd go have me a look," Hanak said kindly. "May Reorx guide you." With that, he strolled out the door of the grocery, leaving Flint to his troubled thoughts.

Amos slammed a brown, wrapped bundle onto the counter before him. "Salt, a bag of apples, four eggs, a slab of bacon, one jar of pickles, two loaves of day-old bread, four pounds of the richest Nordmaarian chicory root known to man—and dwarves—" He snickered "—a vial of tar to fix those creaky shutters before winter sets, and the long-awaited malt rum," he finished with satisfaction.

Flint reached into the pocket of the vest over his shoulder and said distractedly, "You can leave the tar. I won't be here to see winter reach Solace."

Noting the dark tone in the dwarf's voice, Amos looked at his friend with concern, but he knew better than to ask questions. The shopkeeper had never seen Flint so preoccupied, even when those young, troublemaking friends of his were in town. He took the money for Flint's purchases and wordlessly nodded good-bye.

Chapter 2

The Trail Home

Darken Wood. *The place certainly earns its name*, thought Flint. Tall pines, their needles a green that was almost black, towered over the forest floor. Huge, musty oaks, draped with thick vines and feathery moss, and even an occasional looming vallenwood trunk that rose to disappear among the foliage, prevented a single sunbeam from reaching the ground.

The forest was not huge, but Flint knew that it sheltered a number of dangerous denizens. Some years earlier, a small party of mercenaries had entered Solace bearing an unusual trophy—the head of a troll slain in these woods. Bands of hobgoblins and worse reputedly still dwelled among the ancient trunks of Darken Wood.

The feeling of potential danger brought Flint a keen sense of awareness even as his mind wandered. The narrow trail twisted among the tree trunks, enveloped by ferns and great, moist growths of mushrooms and other fungus. The scent of warm earth, heavy with decay, overwhelmed the dwarf with a thick, cloying presence.

Flint did not find the odor unpleasant. Indeed, after his long residence among humans, not to mention the constant presence of kender, elves, and other races, this dominance of nature refreshed his spirit and lightened his step. There was something joyful in this solitude, in this pastoral adventure, that brought a forgotten delight to Flint's soul.

For many hours he made slow progress, not from any sense of exhaustion, but instead because of the great ease within him. His hand stroked the smooth, worn haft of his axe. Absently, his ears and eyes probed the woods, alert, almost hoping for a sign of trouble.

The trail forked and he paused, stark still for a moment, listening, thinking. He sensed the earth, the twists and turns in the surrounding land—as only dwarves could—through his thick-soled boots. Soon he learned what he needed to know, and he chose a direction.

Toward the south for a while. Flint followed no map and needed no compass to maintain the route he had selected. It would lead him the length of the woods, and avoid both the lands of the Qualinesti elves to the south, and the seeker-ruled city of Haven to the northwest.

The seekers, he thought with a mental grimace, I would walk to the ends of the earth to avoid. Those pesky "prophets" had made life in Solace unpleasant enough. But in Haven—the city that was their capitol and the center of their arrogant worship—their presence was sure to be unbearable.

The region of Qualinesti was different, though. Flint had actually entertained thoughts of going there, into that nest of elves, to see his old—and unlikely—friend, the Speaker of the Suns. Flint remembered fondly the time he had spent in Qualinost some years back. He was still one of the few dwarves who had ever been invited into that elven

15

kingdom—and by the speaker himself! A visiting dignitary had acquired a silver and agate bracelet at a territory fair, which he then gave to the elven leader. The Speaker of the Suns had been so impressed by the metalsmith's craftsmanship that he had tracked down the smith, who was none other than Flint Fireforge of Solace, and extended an invitation for the dwarf to demonstrate his craft in the marble elven city.

It was during that first trip to Qualinost that Flint had met Tanis Half-Elven, the Speaker of the Sun's ward. Young Tanis had stood for hours watching the dwarf's demonstrations in the elven city, staying afterward to talk. Flint understood the boy, who seemed unhappy because of his mixed heritage, and the two spent many pleasant hours together whenever the business of selling his crafts brought Flint near Qualinesti.

The dwarf was tempted now to find the half-elf. On their last night together at the Inn of the Last Home, Tanis had said he was going to go on a quest that would bring him to terms with his heritage at last. Flint presumed Tanis meant he was going back to face the full-blooded elven relatives of his in the city of Qualinost who had never really accepted the half-elf. The dwarf was somewhat concerned about his friend, but he had shrugged off any misgivings. After all, the companions had agreed to separate for five years, and Flint would be damned if he'd be the one to break that agreement.

So he would give Qualinost a wide berth and follow the forest paths instead. He knew that if he kept a steady pace he would pass from the wood around nightfall.

Flint began to wonder now, in the quiet of Darken Wood, if he hadn't been fanciful, believing even half of what the dwarf back at Jessab's had said. Mountain dwarves—much less the replusive derro—in Hillhome! Yet why would Hanak have invented such a tale? Flint pushed the question away for the time being. The answer would be made clear soon enough.

He had been getting lazy in Solace—and bored, if the truth be known—without his young friends around. He had been at rest too long. Unconsciously he hefted his axe.

Flint found himself thinking about Aylmar and wondering how long it had been since he had seen his older brother. Oh, fifteen, maybe twenty years, he decided with a frown. Then a smile dotted his face as he recalled the escapades they had had together, the nick-of-time victories, the grand treasures.

In particular he remembered the grandest treasure of them all—the Tharkan Axe. His older brother Aylmar and he had stumbled upon the axe on one of his earliest treasure-hunting forays into the foothills of the Kharolis Mountains, near Pax Tharkas, to be exact, which was why the brothers had so named it. Typical dwarven greed had driven the two Fireforge brothers into the deepest recesses of a hobgoblin lair that was rumored to be filled with riches. Dispatching more than fifteen of the hairy-hided, six-foot monstrosities with blows to their red-skinned heads, Flint and Aylmar had made their way through the last of five interconnected caves to the hobgoblins' treasure chamber. There, atop a four-foot-high pile of coins and glittering gems, the beautiful axe gleamed like a beacon. Aylmar had snatched it up first while Flint stuffed his pockets and pouches with other riches, then the two had run from the lair before any more hobgoblins appeared.

Many years later Aylmar, his heart already showing the weakness that would soon force him to retire from the adventuring life, presented the weapon to Flint on his Fullbeard Day—the dwarven coming-of-age celebration. Smirking, and using the teasing tone that he knew got Flint's dander up, Aylmar had said, "Considering the girlish way you fight, boy, you need this a lot more'n me!" That had been more than forty years ago.

The dwarf remembered, with a touch of gruff sentimentality, the times he had wielded that Tharkan Axe on his travels. The magnificent weapon had gleamed, cutting a silver arc around Flint in battle. For several good years the weapon had served him. It served to remind him of Aylmar as well.

His brow furrowed at the memory of the barrow mounds

where he had lost the axe while on yet another treasure hunt. Amid heaps of coins, a scattering of gems, and the bare skeletons of a dozen ancient chieftains, a figure of cold, sucking blackness had lurked. A wraith of death, it had seized Flint's soul with its terrible grip. A deadly chill had settled in his bones, and he had staggered to his knees, hopeless to resist.

The Tharkan Axe had flashed, then, with a white-hot light that drove the wraith backward and gave Flint the strength to stand. With a mighty heave, the dwarf had buried the weapon in the shapeless yet substantial creature before him.

The wraith had twisted away, tearing the axe from Flint's grip. In terror, the dwarf had fled from the barrow, emptyhanded. Later he returned, but there had been no sign of treasure, wraith, or axe.

Flint looked forward the most to seeing his older brother again. Aylmar would be disappointed, though, to learn that his younger brother had lost the Tharkan Axe. Flint glanced with barely concealed scorn at the inferior, worn battle-axe now resting in his hands. The weapon bore only the most superficial resemblance to the great Tharkan Axe. Where that enchanted blade had shone with the glow of perfect steel, its edge ever sharp, his current weapon showed the pocks of corrosion. The wooden handle was thin and worn, long overdue for replacement.

Yes, it would feel good to see the rest of his family, as well, Flint had to admit. Aylmar had been patriarch of the clan since Flint was a youth, when their father had died of the Fireforge hereditary heart condition, leaving behind a wife and fourteen children. Flint's work-worn mother had passed on some twenty-odd years ago, which was the last time Flint had been to Hillhome, for the funeral.

Aylmar had a wife, Flint knew, though he could never remember her name. And at least one son, young Basalt. Flint remembered his nephew quite clearly. Basalt had been an enthusiastic youngster, somewhat of a hellion. Aylmar had grown dour with age and responsibilities, and he disapproved of his son's prolific time in the alehouse and gaming hall. As a consequence, Basalt had adopted Flint as his mentor.

Flint flashed on a collage of faces and names, his own younger brothers and sisters—*harrns* and *frawls*, as the dwarven sexes were noted. There was Ruberik, Bernhard, Thaxtil—or was that Tybalt? Quiet, demure Glynnis and brash Fidelia emerged from the faces of his sisters. He had left home before the seven youngest siblings had been much more than babes, and he had forgotten most of their names since his last visit.

It was not unusual for dwarves to loose track of their relatives, but Flint wondered now if perhaps he should have paid more attention to the younger children—they had been a good bunch, always eager to fetch things for their older brother, willing to give up the extra pastry or bite of meat for the brawny Flint. And there had never been that much to go around.

With a start, Flint realized that if he did not hurry now, the sun would set before he came to the edge of Darken Wood. He stepped up the pace. Even so, it was already early evening on his first day out of Solace when Flint at last came upon the White-rage River. Flint crossed the rushing stream on a high suspension bridge that reminded him of the village in the vallenwoods, and made camp on the eastern bank in the shelter of two red maples. The next day he followed the bank of the White-rage until he reached the Southway Road.

For a little more than one joyously uneventful week of nearly perfect blue skies, Flint advanced down the Southway Road, which formed the eastern fringes of Qualinesti, avoiding the rare habitations of the elves. On the morning of the eighth day he left the Southway Road, since it continued southwest to the ancient fortress of Pax Tharkas, and Hillhome lay to the southeast.

He blazed his own trail through the hillcountry, the thick forests and foothills east of that settlement. Here the vast slopes of dark fir trees surrounded barren chunks of sharp granite. A land of steep gorges and winding valleys, the hills did not achieve the height of true mountains, but their chaotic nature made the trail as rugged as any snowswept alpine ridge.

This was hill dwarf country, Flint's homeland, and the rough ground was like a smooth path under his feet. He spent the ninth night, a rainy one, in an isolated, warm, and nearly empty dwarven inn in the Hills of Blood, where he rinsed the dusty trail from his body and whetted his appetite for his impending reunion with his dwarven clan.

His mind lingered less on the rumors of mountain dwarves in Hillhome and more on memories of the village: the cozy stone houses lining the broad main street; the sheep and goats in the surrounding sloping fields; Delwar's forge, where Flint had first seen the shaping of metal by fire. He recalled the sense of safety and security that always seemed to linger like smoke around the kitchen hearth of his mother's home. And the scent of the thick-crusted, fresh-baked rolls he and his father would purchase each morning from Frawl Quartzen's bakery after the cows had been tended. They were good memories. . . .

Late in the cold afternoon of the eleventh day, Flint's trip was lengthened by a detour around the Plains of Dergoth. Prior to the Cataclysm nearly three hundred fifty years before, the plains held many water holes. When the Kingpriest of Istar brought the anger of the gods down upon Krynn, the face of the world was changed, and the land south of Pax Tharkas turned to desert. One hundred years later, during the Dwarfgate Wars—which were an attempt by the hill dwarves and their human allies to retake Thorbardin after the Great Betrayal—the magical fortress of Zhaman collapsed in the Plains under a powerful spell and formed the hideous skull-shaped mound known afterward as Skullcap. That same explosion tore apart the Plains of Dergoth once again, and marshes crept over the surrounding land.

Flint had no interest in wading through a swamp—his fear of water was legendary among his friends in Solace. So it was that he chose to climb through the low mountains to the northeast of the narrow pass that cut through the peaks to Hillhome. Flint took his time in finding a clearing just to the east of the pass and off the Passroad, then in collecting and igniting the right logs for a hot, long-lasting fire, and finally in sizzling the last of the fat slab of bacon he had brought with him from Solace. As darkness settled, Flint relaxed. I'll miss this solitude, he thought, sighing.

He looked at the Passroad, just a little below his camp. Deep ruts ran along its length. Whereas in the past it had borne only the traffic of sheep- and goat-herders, or the occasional farmer's cart, now the road was wide and well-worn.

Flint recalled the building of the Passroad from his childhood, though he had been too young to help with the work. The hill dwarves had labored for several years to smooth out the grades, lay a stone foundation over the swampy stretches, and create a route that could, someday, connect Hillhome to the not-so-distant shore of the Newsea.

The immediate purpose of the road had been to open up the valley adjacent to Hillhome to hill dwarf settlements, and this had occurred to a limited extent. Still, in retrospect, the road had not been very profitable, considering all the work.

Suddenly Flint's thick body tensed like a mandolin string. He was not alone.

The dwarf's first warning was a vague perception, not really sight but more sound, of something approaching from the southwest. Wooden wheels crunched over gravel. Flint turned from the low fire to the pass, and his infravision— the natural, temperature-sensing ability of dwarves that allowed them to see objects in the dark by the heat they radiate—quickly adjusted.

A heavy, broad-wheeled wagon, looking more like a huge rectangular box, rattled up the rutted Passroad from the direction of Hillhome. Who would be driving a wagon through the pass in the dark of night?

Flint stepped from his fire to the edge of the road. Hunkered over intently on the buckboard, the driver snapped a whip over the heads of the four-horse team that was laboring to pull the wagon up the steep incline toward the pass. The steeds snorted and strained, pulling an obviously heavy load. Flint could not determine whether the small figure of the driver was dwarven, human, or something worse. Now he could see two more forms standing several feet behind the buckboard in a guarding stance, holding onto the sides of the lurching wagon. As they drew closer, Flint caught sight of three sets of unnaturally large eyes.

Derro dwarves. That explained why they were willing to drive through the mountains at night, Flint realized.

Derro were a degenerate race of dwarves who lived primarily underground. They hated light and suffered from nausea when in the sun, though they were known to venture from their subterranean homes at night. While normal dwarves looked much like humans, only differently proportioned, derro dwarves tended toward the grotesque. Their hair was pale tan or yellow, their skin very white with a bluish undertone, and their large eyes were almost entirely pupil.

And they were reputedly so evil and malicious that they made hobgoblins seem like good neighbors.

Flint thought about dashing behind an outcropping, but it was already too late to hide: he had been spotted along the roadside. He was more than curious, anyway, remembering Hanak's sighting of derro mountain dwarves in Hillhome. The driver's hideous eyes bore into Flint's from about fifty feet away, and the derro stopped the wagon at the crest of the pass with a violent tug on the reins.

"What are you doing here at this time of night, hill dwarf?" The driver's voice was raspy, and though he spoke Common, the words came to him slowly, as if the language were not totally familiar. The derro on the sides of the wagon dropped to the ground, and one circled around the horses to stand protectively below the driver still on the buckboard. Each held a shiny steel-bladed battle-axe casually in his hands.

"Since when do derro claim rights over Hillhome's pass?" Flint was not the least bit frightened. He watched the armed guards, whose eyes were focused on the axe hanging from Flint's belt. The two derro wore dark metal breastplates and heavy leather gauntlets. They carried themselves with the cocksure attitude of veteran warriors. The driver, who was unarmed and unarmored, held the reins and watched.

"You hill dwarves know the agreement," the driver growled deep in his throat. "Now get back to the village before we are forced to report you as a spy . . . or worse," he added. The guards took a step toward Flint, gripping their weapons with purpose.

"Spy!" sputtered Flint, almost amused, and yet his hand moved to his axe. "Great Reorx, why would I be doing that? Speak up, dwarf!"

The horses pranced impatiently on the Passroad, snorting misty breath into the chilly night air. The driver stilled them with a jerk on the reins, then clenched his fists at Flint. "I'm warning you—get out of the way and go back to the village," the driver hissed.

Flint knew he would get no answers from these derro. He forced his voice to remain level. "You've already caused me to burn my bacon with your nonsensical questions, so pass if you must and I'll return to my charred dinner."

Flint saw the two armed derro separate as they neared him. Each held his battle-axe at the ready, and Flint looked at the weapons with momentary envy, thinking of his own, trail-worn blade.

With growing annoyance, Flint hefted his axe. His body tingled with energy, anticipating battle. Though he did not seek a fight with these mountain dwarves, he would be cursed by Reorx before he'd back down from his hereditary enemies.

"Can you prove you're not a spy?" asked one, taunting.

Flint stepped to the side, away from the fire. "I could if I thought enough of such wide-eyed derro scum to be bothered with it," he snapped, his patience gone.

The nearest derro flung himself at Flint, his axe whistling through the air. The hill dwarf darted backward in time to also avoid the second derro, who charged in low. The two mountain dwarves' axes met with a sharp clang of steel.

A sublime sense of heightened awareness possessed Flint as he turned to parry a blow from his first attacker, then sent the second derro reeling back with a series of sharp blows. Hacking viciously, he knocked the fellow's weapon to the ground just as the other one leaped back toward him.

Whirling away, Flint raised his own axe in a sharp parry. The two blades clashed together, but the hill dwarf stared in dismay as the haft of his axe cracked, carrying the head to the ground. Suddenly Flint was holding only the haft of his battle-axe. He stood there, defenseless, as if naked.

The second guard's pale, blue-tinged face split into a grotesque grin at Flint's predicament. A sinister light entered his eyes as he raised his axe, ready to crush the hill dwarf's skull.

Flint moved with all the quickness his years of battle experience could muster. He thrust the axe handle forward, using it to stab like a sword. The splintered ends of wood struck the derro's nose, and the Theiwar dwarf cried out in agony, blinking away blood.

Flint struck again, smashing the wooden stick over the derro's knuckles, which gripped his axe. Crying out again, the guard dropped his weapon, stumbling blindly from his bloody nose and eyes. Flint quickly snatched the axe up and swung menacingly at the suddenly retreating derro. He turned on the one who was sprawled on the ground, urging him along as well.

The two disarmed Theiwar sprang onto the wagon as the driver lashed the horses. Whinnying with fear and snorting white clouds of breath into the night air, the massive beasts struggled to get the heavy wagon rolling. In moments it lurched through the pass and started on the downhill trek to the east and Newsea. As they rumbled away, the hill dwarf got a good look at their pale, wide eyes staring back at him around the side of the wagon, their glares full of hatred, and not a little fear.

Thoroughly disgusted with the needless fight, Flint stomped back to his fire and snatched the pan of burned bacon, tossing the blackened remains into the scrub. No longer hungry, he sat with his back to the flames and pondered the strange encounter.

His mind was a jumble of burning questions. What sort of "agreement" with these evil dwarves could have caused the hill dwarves to forget centuries of hatred and forced poverty because of the Great Betrayal? And what did the derro have to hide that they were concerned about spies?

Thorbardin, ancient home of the mountain dwarves, lay some twenty miles to the southwest, past Stonehammer Lake. Flint knew that the derro belonged to the Theiwar, one of five clans in the politically divided underground dwarven city. Mountain dwarves as a whole were notoriously clannish, concerned only with their mining and their metalcraft. So of all the clans, why would the derro come to the surface, since they were ones the most sensitive to light?

Flint examined the axe his attacker had left behind. It was a weapon of exceptional workmanship, hard steel with a silver shine and a razor-honed edge. He would have guessed the axe to be of dwarven origin, except that the customary engraving that marked every dwarven blade was missing from the steel.

Flint shivered, whether from cold or apprehension, he could not be sure. Still, it reminded him the fire needed stoking. Tossing two small logs onto the coals, he stared into the flames until the fire's mesmerizing effects made his eyelids heavy.

These mysteries he would take to sleep, unresolved. He moved away from the fire to where he could keep an eye on the camp yet remain concealed. But nothing disturbed him again that night.

* * * * *

Flint awoke at first light and at once headed east through the pass toward Hillhome. He stayed with the rutted, mud-slick road until he came to the last low ridge before the village, just a quarter-mile away. There he stopped to relish the view.

He had made the journey in less than two weeks, a refreshing enough adventure until the derro skirmish the previous night. But now he felt a peculiar emotion choke his heart as he looked down at the winding, paved road, the expanse of stone buildings, the blockhouse that was the forge in the village of his youth.

The rugged valley stretched east to the pass and west to Stonehammer Lake, broadening into a grassy vale around

Hillhome. Several side canyons twisted back into the hills to the north and south.

Flint's warm feeling chilled somewhat when he realized that a low haze hung in the valley where before the air had been impeccably clear. Of course, there had always been a little smoke from the town forge. . . .

The town forge! Flint realized the barn beside it was three times or more the size it had been twenty years ago. A great, muddy yard surrounded it, containing several parked wagons. The wagons, Flint realized with a jolt, were just like the one he had encountered the previous night at the pass.

And where once a single stack had emitted the smoke of the small forge, now four squat chimneys belched black clouds into the sky. The town itself seemed to have doubled in proportion, stretching farther to the west toward Stonehammer Lake. Indeed, the sleepy village of Flint's memory now bustled with a size and energy the dwarf found unnerving. Main Street, which once had been paved with sturdy stone, was now practically churned to mud by the traffic of crowds and vehicles.

Flint anxiously made his way down the Passroad until it became Main Street. He slowed his steps to search for familiar faces—familiar anything!—but he recognized not a one, nor did any of the busy dwarves look up from their hurried pace. He paused to get his bearings.

For a moment he wondered if he had come to the right place. Up close, Hillhome looked even less like the town in his memory than it had from the ridge. The same large buildings—the mayor's mansion, the trading barn, the brewery—still dominated the central area. But around them clustered a mass of lesser structures, tightly packed, as if each was trying to shoulder the other aside.

Most of these newer buildings were made of wood, and many showed signs of uncharacteristically hasty construction and shoddy workmanship. The town square was still a wide open space, but where it had once been a tree-shaded park, now it was a brown and barren place.

Flint's eyes came to rest on Moldoon's Tavern across the street. A happy sight at last! A young frawl was standing at the back of an ale wagon parked out front, hefting two half-kegs onto her shoulders. She struggled her way up the two wooden steps and into the inn, the door of which was held open by a large, middle-aged dwarf.

Flint well remembered the rugged human, Moldoon, who had opened his inn in quiet Hillhome. The man had been a hard-drinking mercenary who had retired from fighting and carousing. His small alehouse had become a comfortable club for many adult dwarves, including Flint and Aylmar. Flint wondered if the human were still about.

With a sense of relief he started toward the familiar doorway. He made his way around the ruts in the street and shouldered his way through the thick crowd in Moldoon's. The hill dwarf's eyes rapidly adjusted to the darkness, and he saw with relief that the place had not changed all that much.

When designing his saloon, Moldoon had realized that most of his patrons would be short-statured dwarves, yet he wanted a place that was comfortable for himself as well. He neither made it human-sized (though other people would have gotten sport out of watching dwarves scrabbling for doorknobs and seats), nor did he make it dwarf-sized (he, himself, would look silly on a too-small chair). What he did do was make all tables and chairs adjustable with just a turn of the top; all doors had two knobs on each side. The bar itself had two levels: the right side to the patrons was dwarf-height, and the left was human-height. The ceiling was high enough to accommodate all.

Right now, a haze of greasy smoke hung just below the stained ceiling beams. The spattering of the grill—Moldoon always seemed to get the most succulent cuts of meat—and the familiar low rumble of conversation sounded like the same talk in any tavern in Ansalon.

Flint saw an old man behind the lower section of the bar. White bearded, with an equally full, platinum mane of hair, he stooped slightly with age, but revealed a frame that had once been broad and lanky.

"Moldoon?" Flint asked in disbelief, his face alight with expectation. The dwarf stepped over to the bar and spun the

27

nearest stool top to his level.

Recognition dawning, the man's face broke into a crooked grin. "Flint Fireforge, as I live and breath!" With amazing alacrity the man vaulted the bar and gathered up the stout dwarf in an awkward bear hug.

"How long have you been in town, you old scut?" he asked, shaking the dwarf by the shoulders.

"First stop." Flint grinned broadly, his whiskers tickling his nose. The human seized Flint up again, and after much back-thumping and hand-pumping, he grabbed a pitcher and personally overfilled a mug for the dwarf, scraping the foam away with a knife.

"It's good to see you again, old friend," said Flint sincerely, raising his mug and taking a long pull. He wiped his foamy mouth with the back of his hand and said happily, "None better!"

"Not Flint Fireforge!"

Flint heard a frawl's voice coming from around Moldoon's right arm. She stepped around to the innkeeper's side, and Flint recognized her as the one he had seen lugging kegs from the wagon outside. Indeed, as Moldoon drew her forward, Flint noticed that she still held one on her left shoulder. Staring unabashedly at Flint, she lowered it to the ground. Her hair was the yellow-orange color of overripe corn, and she wore it in long braids on either side of her full, rose-red cheeks. She wore tight leather pants and a red tunic, belted tight, revealing an unusually tiny waist for a frawl.

Flint gave her a friendly, almost apologetic smile. "Yes, I am, but I'm sorry, I don't remember you."

Moldoon threw an arm down around her shoulders. "Sure you do! This is Hildy, Brewmaster Bowlderston's daughter. She's taken over his business since he's been ill."

Hildy thrust her hand forward over the bar and gripped Flint's firmly. "I've heard a lot about you, Flint. I'm a . . . um, friend of your nephew, Basalt." She blushed.

Flint slapped his thigh. "*That's* why you looked familiar! Haven't you two been friends since you were both in nappies?" He winked and gave her an approving glance under raised eyebrows. "Although you've grown up some since then."

She smiled and blushed again, lowering her eyes. "I wish *Basalt* would take notice," she began, but her smile faded. "Of course he's not aware of much else but drink these days, though, what with the tragedy and all." She reached out gingerly and squeezed his arm sympathetically.

"Tragedy?" Flint's mug of ale froze halfway to his mouth. His eyes traveled from the frawl's blue eyes to the innkeeper's rheumy ones and back.

Suddenly the sound of shattering glass rent the air. Startled, Flint turned toward the left end of the bar, where he saw the harrn who had held the door for Hildy. This same dwarf was staring at Flint, his face a mask of terror.

The dwarf seemed stupefied, and he began gesturing wildly at Flint. Flint was stunned.

"You're dead! Go away! Leave me alone! You're d-d—!" The screaming dwarf struggled to get the last of the word out, then finally quit in frustration. He covered his eyes with his arms and sobbed.

"Garth!" Hildy cried, coming to his side to uncover his eyes. "It's OK. That's not who you think it is!" The big dwarf resisted at first, then slowly allowed one eye to emerge from above his folded limbs:

Garth was unusually large, well over four and a half feet, and none of it was muscle. His rounded belly poked out below his tunic, which was too small at every opening: the neck was too tight, and his wrists hung at least an inch below the cuffs.

"What's going on here?" Flint demanded, both irritated and embarrassed by the strange incident.

Moldoon looked red-faced as well. "Garth does odd jobs about town for almost everyone. He's a little simple—most people call him the village idiot—and well, you two *did* look quite a lot alike," Moldoon finished, his voice coming faster.

"What two? What are talking about? Spit it out, man!" Flint was just angry now.

"The tragedy," Hildy said dully.

Moldoon wrung his hands and finally said, "I'm sorry, Flint. Garth was the one who found Aylmar dead at the forge one month ago."

Chapter 3

The Terms

The general looked over the smoldering city below. He saw the seaport of Sanction, wracked by forces both geological and mystical. Its people were being driven away, the very earth beneath it changed by volcanic eruptions and the rivers of lava flowing down to the Newsea.

He also saw what the tortured city would become: the heart of an evil empire embracing all of Krynn. Sanction would protect the nerve center of that empire with a barrier of arms and with the awesome barrier formed by the Lords of Doom. These three towering volcanoes stood at three points of the general's view, spewing ash and lava, gradually changing the shape of the city and the valley. Active for the past few years, the smoking peaks dominated Sanction and the surrounding chaos of steep mountains.

The brown waters of the port, and the Newsea beyond, marked the fourth direction, to the west. The Lords smoldered, oozing rockfire and slowly wracking the city below. The Newsea beckoned placidly, a route that one day the general's armies would follow on their path to conquering the west. Clasping his heavy gauntlets to his hips, the general peered through the narrow eyeholes in his mask, pleased by the destruction below.

The general wore ceremonial armor of black, etched in red. Tall boots of polished leather protected his feet and muscular legs. A breastplate of deepest blue-black reflected darkly across his torso, while several large rubies winked crimson around the edges of the plate.

His face lay entirely concealed behind the grotesque dark helm. A scarlet plume, rising from the crest of the helmet and then trailing below and behind him, enhanced his height even more than his already impressive natural size. Heavy, curved plates of the same black steel as his breastplate covered his shoulders and accentuated his imposing physique.

Now he paced alone, atop a blocky, black-walled tower just south of the city—one of two such prominences on the black fortress known as the Temple of Duerghast. This huge, walled structure squatted low on the slopes of the smallest of the Lords of Doom, Duerghast Mountain. The towers of the temple provided a splendid view of Sanction, and the mountains and sea beyond.

The Temple of Duerghast was, in fact, more of a fortress than a place of worship. The high black wall surrounded the entire structure. It provided space for barracks, troop training, and even an arena for gladiatorial combat.

The temple and the entire city, now as always, lay under a leaden, overcast sky. The gray blanket was caused by the smoke and ash that spewed from its surrounding summits, and because the valley of Sanction was a windtrap, terminus of the Newsea.

A river of steaming lava, glowing cherry red in the eternally twilit valley, cut through the center of Sanction. Another finger of flaming rock trickled toward it by a different path. Soon the two boiling streams would meet, forming a lava moat around the other temple.

The general's gaze lingered on that great construction—now a pile of rock, slowly being given form by the lava and ash. The Temple of Luerkhisis, that one was called, after the second of the Lords of Doom. The temple held the keys to so much of the future, for in its bowels were kept the precious eggs of the good dragons. Those gold, silver, brass, and bronze orbs would—when the time was right—force the neutrality of good dragonkind, allowing the empire of darkness to be born.

But there was much to be done before that could happen. An army had yet to be raised, equipped, and trained. Plans would be drawn, powers marshaled. All of this would take time. But he knew how to put that time to good use.

The general had begun to organize his forces. Already, thousands of mercenaries had gathered in the scarred city below him, replacing the huge numbers of refugees who had fled to safer lands when the volcanoes first rumbled to life. The general had agents crossing the wildest lands of Ansalon, gathering tribes of hobgoblins and ogres, bribing them with promises of plunder and war. And across the valley, in the temple taking shape over the hiding places of the good dragons' eggs, the spearhead of his army was even now being created. Draconians.

It was the equipping of his massive army that brought the general to this meeting today.

A great, crackling rumble suddenly reverberated through the valley, like an impossibly loud peal of thunder. The peak of Duerghast, south of the general's temple, pitched monstrous boulders from its cauldera. Idly, the masked figure watched the house-sized pieces of rock crash to earth, tumbling down the mountainsides and adding to the destruction as they fell. The helmet blocked the general's peripheral vision, but all of a sudden he detected a presence off to his left. He whirled around and saw the new arrival unconsciously finger the steel ring that had allowed him to be teleported here.

"You are late," said the general, his voice a deep, rasping complaint.

The newcomer, a dwarf, ignored the rebuke and shuffled toward the figure towering before him. The general's height accented the small stature of this one. When the dwarf threw back his hood, his grotesque face suddenly came into view, a fitting image to counter the general's mask, though the dwarf's features were his own.

Milky, pale skin covered the dwarf's body, with a bluish cast vaguely reminiscent of a corpse. His eyes were pale, and very, very wide. Now, even under the deep overcast, he squinted against the daylight. A shock of yellow hair on the dwarf's head shot in all directions, bristly and uncontrolled. His mouth was concealed by a tangled beard that, despite its length, grew only in sparse, ugly patches from his cheeks, chin, and neck.

The dwarf was a derro, a race of less pure stock than the hill dwarf or Hylar mountain dwarves, since it reputedly resulted from an ancient intermixture of human and dwarven blood. Still a mountain dwarf, he was a member of the Theiwar clan.

He came directly from Thorbardin, the great underground realm of the mountain dwarves, where he served as the adviser to Thane Realgar, ruler of the Theiwar. The Theiwar was the only clan of derro, and they competed jealously with their rivals of the Hylar, Daergar, and other clans.

In addition to his derro race, this dwarf differed from the typical mountain dwarf in another important way: he was a magic-using savant. Though all dwarves were resistant to magic, few were able actually to cast spells. Among these, the savants of the derro were most potent; and of these savants, Pitrick, adviser to the thane, was the most feared.

Pitrick moved awkwardly, partially dragging his right foot. He leaned forward in an unnatural stance, his body distorted by the large hump of flesh that deformed his back and right shoulder.

"You summoned me, and I came," said the dwarf. "Is that not the important thing?" Craning his neck, he looked up at the general. The masked human turned away silently. His expression pensive, the dwarf studied the general's straight, well-armored back.

"I see you wear my present," the general said, though he looked out over the smoldering city of Sanction. He had given the little derro the amulet, iron forged into the likenesses of five writhing dragon heads, as a token for closing the weapons shipment arrangements. The general himself had received it from his Dark Queen, and he half hoped that Her presence in it would further influence the weasely adviser to his cause.

"It has proved quite useful already," Pitrick said offhandedly, yet he offered no thanks. "But to business. My journey, though fast, is not without risk," observed the dwarf, ignoring the general's shrug. "Should the other clans of Thorbardin gain wind of our transaction, I need not tell you that your source of arms would vanish."

The general said nothing. The vast horde of men gathering in the valley below would be nothing more than an angry mob until outfitted with weapons. Excellent, razor-sharp steel blades—the kind made by the Theiwar mountain dwarves of Thorbardin.

"That is why we meet today," said the human. "To discuss the shipments."

"I trust that you have not been dissatisfied with our craftsmanship," remarked the dwarf, his tone smugly confident.

The general ignored the question. They both knew no answer was required, for dwarven weaponsmiths were the most talented crafters of steel on all of Krynn. Nowhere else could a soldier gain arms of such strength and quality.

"I shall require an increase in the amount of all types of weapons." The general's voice was a harsh rasp through the mask. "A doubling, to be precise."

The hunchbacked dwarf turned away, placing a hand to his chin as if deep in thought. The hand concealed a thin smile of pleasure as the dwarf's mind immediately began counting the additional coinage that would flow quickly into his, and his clan's, coffers. That meant more power for the Theiwar, more power to the thane's adviser.

"Of course, if you should need to speak to your thane about this matter. . . ." The general's tone made it clear that such a delay would be regarded as a major nuisance.

"Certainly not!" huffed the dwarf. "I am fully empowered to make such a decision. And make it I shall, though of course there are some problems to be worked out."

The general stood mute, arms crossed at his chest. He looked down at the diminutive derro.

"The details are manifold," explained the dwarf, turning to pace about the platform atop the tower. He moved awkwardly, dragging his twisted right foot, but the impediment did not seem to slow him down. He spoke slowly, as if deep in thought.

"Our materials, particularly coal, are in short supply. We can find more, but it will be costly, and, naturally, our price must reflect this. We will be forced to *triple* the fee."

The general chuckled, deep within the enclosing confines of his armor and helm. "An amusing thought." The laughter abruptly ceased. "Our fee will be doubled, as the work is doubled. No more."

After a discreet pause the dwarf nodded his acceptance. Still in profile to the general, his hand surreptitiously slipped around the iron amulet that hung at his neck. Eyes shifting, he soundlessly mouthed a word and a soft blue glow suddenly gleamed between his fingers. Turning back to the general, Pitrick raised his other hand in a mysterious gesture. His wide, pale eyes sought the general's through the holes in the human's mask. Mustering his courage, the dwarf began to intone.

Suddenly, the dwarf felt something strike him, hard, along the right side of his head. He cried out in pain and surprise as he sprawled to the wooden platform, tumbling to lie in the shelter of the parapet wall. He rubbed his cheek, already feeling a large welt developing there. The derro struggled to his feet and looked around; there was nothing material that could have struck him. He looked at the general with new respect. Then he felt an unfamiliar sensation: fear.

The general stood unmoving, watching the dwarf.

"An amusing diversion, magic," the human said. "I trust

you will not attempt to use your pathetic tricks on me again. This time, I leave you your life. Next time . . ."

"An honest mistake, I assure you," said the dwarf, biting back his anger. No one had bested or humiliated him in decades. "A doubling of the fee will be quite satisfactory."

"These shipments must be increased immediately," instructed the general. "I will have extra ships in the bay within the month, and I want them loaded quickly."

Pitrick nodded. "It shall be done. The arrangement with the loathesome hill dwarves remains, but I am taking steps toward a more satisfactory solution.

"Because they built the road through the pass, they think they can control us! True, the road is our only passage from Thorbardin to Newsea, but we pay them well for its use. Yet they complain when we stay in their town! They charge exorbitant prices for goods. If they learned the true nature of our shipments, there would be no end to their extortion!

"I was forced to kill one of them already, for spying," the derro said, almost in passing. "Fortunately, I was there at the time and was able to strike him down before he had the chance to tell anyone what he'd discovered. The fools think he died of a heart attack!"

"The hill dwarves are your problem. You are the one who insists the trade remains a secret." The general's tone was disinterested, unsympathetic. He turned away, looking over his smoking, smoldering city. Clearly, he had no curiosity about the petty squabbles that frequently occurred among dwarves.

The derro fumed at the human's disdain and sought to regain some measure of his dignity and pride. "Your weapons will be waiting on the shore!" he said stiffly. "Even if I must obliterate Hillhome to get them there!"

Instinctively bowing to the general, as he would to his thane, the derro once again fondled his steel ring of teleportation. The circlet of metal was formed by two rings woven together and split at the top, the rough ends bent outward. It softly illuminated the dwarf's entire body. Then, a bright spark jumped from one edge of the ring to another. In the space of a blink, the hunchbacked Theiwar was gone.

Chapter 4

An Uneasy Reunion

"That was Aylmar's favorite chair," sighed Bertina,
wiping a tear as she gestured to the overstuffed seat in which
Flint sat. Aylmar's widow drew another mug from the ale
keg, sniffling as she passed the foaming goblet to Flint.

Many a reverent mug had already been raised to Aylmar's
memory. And to "good old Flint," and an assortment of
other things, as the hour grew late and the guests at this impromptu party grew increasingly besotted.

"It's a disgrace that my dead brother is dishonored by a
night of mourning like this!" Ruberik grumbled disdainfully.
Third Fireforge son—Aylmar and Flint were first and
second—Ruberik stood by the hearth, stiff in his black
waistcoat and too-tight tie. He turned up his nose at the mug

of ale Bertina held toward him and frowned disapprovingly at the newly empty keg, the pools of ale on the floor, and the sleeping dwarves throughout the large room.

"Oh, Ruberik," scolded Fidelia, one of the older Fireforge sisters, "don't burst a vein." A buxom, bawdy lass, she tossed back the contents of her mug and held it out for refilling. "We're not so much mourning Aylmar—we've done that for a month—as celebrating Flint's return."

Ruberik's work-roughened hand reached out to snatch the mug from her waiting lips. "If you have no respect for your elders, young woman, at least try to summon a bit for the dead!"

"We grieve differently, that's all," his sister said, used to his pompous outbursts. Hitching her leather skirt to a height improper enough to make her puritanical brother fume, she fetched another drink undisturbed.

Plain, heavy-set Glynnis, next in line after Ruberik and not the brightest under the best of conditions, giggled suddenly, oblivious to the tension in the room. Letting loose a loud hiccup, she smirked at her older brother. "Fidel is right, Rubie. Flint only comesh home onesh every twenty years! And when he does, I'm . . . I'm . . ." Glynnis squinted in concentration. She hiccupped again, and then her head fell forward. In a second she snored, face down in a pool of ale. Ruberik rolled his eyes, as if to say, "There she goes again."

"His favorite chair," cut in Bertina, continuing as though unaware anyone else had spoken. "He'd sit there for hours." She looked wistfully at Flint in the large, wood-framed chair with fluffy, goose-down cushions.

Flint already felt uncomfortable enough, listening to the squabbles of his family. But his sister-in-law's look made him squirm. He wanted to get up, to sit somewhere else in the room, but virtually every surface—table, chair, or floor—already held a sleeping Fireforge. Flint winced at the thought of the hangover that would fill the house on the morrow.

He sat back in Aylmar's favorite chair and sighed, his mood maudlin. This was not the homecoming he'd expected; he felt disloyal, but he could not shake the thought that his friends back in Solace felt more like family than this gathering of strangers.

His reception had started out well enough. Indeed, Flint's homecoming had provided the Fireforge clan with a much-needed cause for celebration. Cousins and siblings and old neighbors all gathered at the family home within minutes of his arrival. The large house, home to Flint's parents before their deaths, was now occupied by Aylmar's family and Ruberik, who was a bachelor.

Set into the hillside, which was common in Hillhome, the house was large by dwarven standards, and it felt spacious. The family was now gathered in the "front room," which had a high ceiling and tall doorways to accommodate human visitors, which the Fireforge family had more of than the average dwarven family because of their adventuring ways. The walls were of stone, reinforced by dark oak beams. The only room with windows, its two round openings were now double-shuttered against the autumn chill. A large, spotless hearth was the room's focal point, and the furniture was a dozen or so chairs and a large rectangular table, for meals were taken here.

The rest of the house spread out behind the front room. Five other chambers had been carved into the hillside and shored up with perfectly matched and cut stone, so that not a speck of earth could be seen between cracks. Two rooms had been added to the east side nearest the barn for Ruberik, who made his living as a farmer.

Glynnis was a housefrawl; Fidelia worked at the grain mill; the next oldest brothers, Tybalt and Bernhard, constable and carpenter respectively. They and the remaining seven siblings all lived nearby, having grown up and moved out. To tonight's party they had brought a tumbling mass of nieces and nephews, many of whom had been born since Flint's departure, and brothers- and sisters-in-law who seemed to outnumber his siblings.

Yet Flint wondered about his favorite nephew, Aylmar's eldest son, Basalt, who was conspicuous by his absence. It seemed odd that the boy was not at his mother's side during her time of grief. On the other hand, Basalt's brothers and sisters—Aylmar and Bertina had had more than half a dozen children, by Flint's best reckoning—had been struggling to outdo each other in offering comforts to their notorious Uncle Flint. He could neither smoke nor drink fast enough to keep up with the refills they offered him. A seemingly endless stream of plates, each loaded with an unusual treat, was placed before him by a niece or nephew. He sampled spiced goose eggs, cream cakes and fruit pies, bits of succulent meat, fish larvae, and other exotic delights.

A pair of geese had been butchered and an impromptu feast prepared. Flint tore off a bite from a drumstick now and decided to engage Ruberik in a discussion more suited to his brother's somber mood.

Taking a handkerchief from his pocket, Flint scrubbed the grease from his mustache and beard. "Please tell me," he began, "what you know of our brother's untimely death."

Ruberick grew grimmer still. "Aylmar had been laboring at his trade, blacksmithing, and his heart gave out on him." The dwarf shook his head sadly. "It's as simple as that."

"We told him not to work so hard!" exclaimed Bernhard, who was seated next to Flint in a hard wooden chair. The seventh Fireforge sibling, his soft black hair prematurely balding, leaned forward and knotted his thick, calloused hands. "But that is one of the reasons why he was the best at his craft."

"The money was just too much temptation," interrupted Ruberik. "He couldn't resist the offer to work for the derro."

"Yeah," Bernhard said vacantly. "Anyway, Aylmar was called to the forge in the derro's camp—they've taken over Delwar's forge—to fix a wheel late one morning."

Flint found it difficult to believe that the Aylmar he'd known would have had anything to do with derro, but he *had* been gone a long time. . . . Flint remembered the walled yard near the town smithy.

"That place has become a blighthole filled with evil derro!" interjected Ruberik again. "A blemish on the face of our hills!"

Bernhard rocked his chair onto its back legs. "You don't think it's such a blemish when you take your cheese there to sell," he commented wryly, "nor when you build an addition to your abode with the profits." He squinted up through one eye to glimpse his brother's angry, red face.

"That's business! Mind your elders!" was Ruberik's stern reply.

Bernhard rolled his eyes and lowered his chair to the floor with a bang. "Anyway, Aylmar went to the yard that day, 'an emergency,' they said. Any smith would've taken the job—these derro panic at the thought of missing a night on the road, so they pay real good for day work and such—"

"And Aylmar, the damned fool, had to take on this one job too many," Ruberick interrupted yet again, unable to conceal his anguish. "He died beside his forge, among strangers, what is worse."

"Garth, the dimwit, found him there all blue," finished Bernhard matter-of-factly.

Bertina gasped, and Fidelia elbowed her brother in the head. "Have a care, will you?"

"Uh, sorry, Berti," the carpenter said limply, making a hasty exit to help with the tapping of a new keg.

"But if these are mountain dwarves," interjected Flint, "why isn't there a smith among them who can fix their wagons?"

"I can explain that," said Tybalt, stepping away from the fire to join the circle. He was a stocky, unsmiling dwarf who had inherited all of the worst Fireforge features: the bulbous nose, their mother's weight, and their father's slight chin. Even when off duty, he wore his constable uniform—shiny leather breastplate and shoulder protectors hardened in boiling oil and dyed blue, gray tunic beneath that to his knees, gray leg wraps, and thick-soled leather shoes. He removed it only once a week to bathe.

"Mayor Holden wisely made it a condition of the agreement that the mountain dwarves use the services of the hill dwarves when in Hillhome—extra money for our craftsmen." Tybalt brushed a piece of string from his breastplate. "Besides, the derro hate light so much that they would never station a smith above ground so far from Thorbardin. If it weren't for Hillhome, they'd have to bring a smith along on every trip just in case of breakdowns, which would be exceedingly costly." Tybalt struck a ramrod pose. "Everyone says Mayor Holden drove an excellent bargain with the Theiwar."

Fidelia snorted indelicately and ruffled Tybalt's dark hair as she strolled by him. "*You* tell that to anyone who will listen because you're bucking for a promotion, Brother!" She took another pull on her mug of ale.

Hearing an opening to the question that had brought him here, Flint leaned forward intently, his elbows on his knees as his eyes scanned the group. "I came all the way from Solace to find out why Hillhome is dealing with mountain dwarves at all, let alone derro! Can someone give me a good answer?"

Everyone began talking at once, and Flint was forced to wave his arms above his head and whistle for silence. He looked at his brother the constable. "*You* seem to know the details of this 'agreement,' Tybalt. Why don't you explain it to me."

Looking flattered at his older brother's attention, Tybalt cleared his throat. "It started about a year ago, them using the pass. They leave Thorbardin and meet up with the Passroad somewhere around the western shore of Stonehammer Lake. They're taking their cargo to the coast at Newsea. We hear they've got a jetty set up in some cove, where they meet ships from the north and transfer their goods."

"So, how did it all start?"

Tybalt paused and scratched his chin. "One day, a short one of these derro, kind of bent over like, showed up and met with the mayor and a bunch of the elders. Offered to pay twenty steel pieces a wagon—*twenty steel*, mind you—if we'd let them come over our pass.

"Course there was still some, like Aylmar, who wanted nothing to do with them. But the deal was struck. Then, the wagons started comin' through," Tybalt said, punching his hand for emphasis. "They make the run to the coast, and on the way back the derro stock up on grain, beer, cheese, all manner of stuff you can't get where there's no sun. Pay in good steel coin, twice or more what anybody could charge before. It started out with only one wagon a day coming and going, a few derro on each. They must be doing twice or more than that, now."

"And always derro, the Theiwar?" asked Flint.

"Yup. Some stay with their wagons, but most sleep at the inns in town during the day. They don't mix much with townfolk. There's been a few fights and such, but they don't try to cause too much trouble . . . usually.

"The town's never had so much in its treasury, and all of us're doing better than we ever thought possible," Tybalt concluded defensively.

"So what you're saying is, Hillhome is allowing mountain dwarves in the village strictly for the profit," Flint concluded numbly.

"Can you think of a better reason?" Bernhard asked innocently.

Flint's temper exploded as he jumped to his feet. "I can't think of *any* reason to have dealings with mountain dwarves!" He glared angrily into each and every face. "Has everyone here forgotten the Great Betrayal? Or the Dwarfgate Wars, in which Grandfather Reghar gave up his life trying to take back the hill dwarves' place in Thorbardin—our birthright!—from the mountain dwarves who stole it? Have you forgotten, Tybalt?"

Tybalt straightened self-righteously, "I haven't forgotten, but I don't make the laws. I'm sworn to uphold them. For that matter, I'd toss a hill dwarf in jail as soon as I would a mountain dwarf!"

Flint scowled and turned on Bernhard. "How about you?"

His younger brother shrank under his gaze. "I'm just a carpenter . . ." He tugged on his beard self-consciously, afraid to look at his eldest brother as he struggled with some inner thought. "You can't forget what you never knew, Flint!" he blurted at last. "I never heard the stories like you did, not from Father. And all that was over three hundred years ago!" Bernhard seemed almost relieved to have said it. Flint's expression softened somewhat.

Fidelia did not wait for her brother to get around to her.

"Frankly, I'm for whatever makes me money," she said, sensually running her hands down her tailored leather apron, a far cry from the coarse cloth their mother had been accustomed to wearing. "I like to think that we're getting back from Thorbardin a little of what's been owed us—payment for all these years of poverty."

Flint rubbed his face wearily. It was obvious that he did not know his family at all. He looked at his closest sibling. "And how about you, Ruberik? At least *you* don't seem to think much of derro."

Ruberik appeared to be giving the discussion great thought. "No, I don't, and I haven't forgotten the Great Betrayal either, Flint. I would not have approved the agreement if asked, but I wasn't. The council, with the support of the majority of the citizens, made the decision." He had dropped his usual stuffy tone. "But now that they're here, I'm not adverse to making a little profit—just so we're comfortable. I'm not greedy like some others in town," he added defensively.

Flint rubbed his face wearily. "These wagons," he said, changing the subject slightly. "What do they haul? And where are they going?"

Tybalt spoke up again. "Mayor Holden says that they carry mostly raw iron. Sometimes tools—plows, forges, stuff like that. They cover the twenty or so miles from Thorbardin in one night, arrive before sunup, spend the day in town or sleeping, then set out at night for a dock at Newsea. Usually two days later, they return to Hillhome, and then continue on back to Thorbardin."

Flint picked up his pipe from the fireplace mantle, relit it, and took a long draw, squinting through the smoke at his three brothers. "Does *anyone* know where they're taking so many farm implements?" he asked suspiciously.

His brothers looked at each other, puzzled. "Why should we care where they go after Newsea?" Tybalt exclaimed. "The derro pay us in steel—the most valuable commodity on Krynn. And for what?—promising them clearance through the pass and selling them our goods at a slightly elevated price."

"It's almost like free money!" added Bernhard.

But instead of persuading their brother, their comments made Flint even more irritated. "Nothing is ever free," he growled softly. Ruberik remained silent, frowning.

A strange silence crept over the room, taking with it the last drop of the spirit of celebration. One by one, the Fireforge family dispersed. Ruberik finally shuffled off to his private chamber, and only Bertina stayed behind in the main chamber with Flint.

At last Flint got up and moved to the wooden bench Ruberik had vacated, both to sit closer to Bertina and to—finally—leave Aylmar's favorite chair.

"I'm sorry that I didn't get back sooner, Berti." Flint forced the words out awkwardly. Even with a bellyful of ale, he could not make himself tell her of his feelings of guilt. But he sensed that she understood.

"It's enough to have you home now," she said, patting his thick hand. "This is just what the family needed."

Flint's hands curled into fists. "But maybe I could have helped him . . . done something!"

Bertina squeezed her brother-in-law's arm reassuringly and shook her head. "We went there as soon as we heard, Rubie and me." Her eyes were far away. "You mustn't blame yourself."

Suddenly the front door slammed back against the stone wall. "Isn't it just like 'Uncle Flint' to worry about his family?" a new voice snarled sarcastically from the door. Flint recognized it before he even looked up: Basalt. Their eyes met. His nephew was no longer a youth of fifty. He had a full beard, darker than his bright red hair, and a preponderance of freckles beneath his sea-green eyes. Basalt was tall for a dwarf, but it was more than height that gave him an appearance of haughtiness.

"Basalt!" cried Bertina, rousing herself to leap to her feet, smiling happily for the first time that evening. "Flint's here! Your Uncle Flint's come home!" Flint, too, rose and stepped toward his nephew, smiling warmly.

"I know." Something in Basalt's voice cast a pall over the room. "I heard a few hours ago, down at Moldoon's."

Basalt's green eyes fixed Flint with a cold stare. Bertina coughed, embarrassed. And Flint felt himself shrinking under that gaze. Though he did not know how he could have done otherwise, Flint realized that he had let the boy down by being elsewhere when Aylmar had died. Though he knew he should, he could not bring himself to rebuke the rudeness of his brother's son.

"It's good to see you, Basalt," Flint said at last. "I'm sorry about your father."

"Me, too!" the young dwarf snapped, grabbing someone's half-finished mug of ale from the table and tossing the contents down his throat. It was not his first of the night, Flint realized. "Nice of you to make it back, *Uncle*, although your brother's been cold in the ground for nearly a month!"

"Basalt!" Bertina gasped, finally finding her voice.

"Let the boy—let Basalt speak his mind," Flint corrected himself, giving his nephew a pained look. Normally a young dwarf who spoke that way to an older relative would suffer a severe reprimand, if not a punch in the nose or a brief banishment. But somehow, Flint could only feel sorry for Basalt. And angry at himself for his long neglect of his family.

"I have nothing to say," Basalt said softly, sorrow, ale, and anger making his eyes flash. "The subject bores me." With that, he disappeared into the shadows that cloaked the house beyond the firelight.

Bertina stood clutching her apron, looking with anguish from Flint to where Basalt had retreated. "He doesn't mean it, Flint," she said. "He's just not been the same since . . . since . . . It's the drink talking." With a soft moan, she hurried after her son.

Flint watched her go, then leaned back in his seat before the fire, deep in morose reflection. A last bit of burning log dropped through the fire grate and rolled forward; Flint stood and jabbed it back into the fireplace with his toe, then watched sparks fly, burning from red to gray, long into the night.

*   *   *   *   *

Clumping through the cold room in his heavy farming boots at first light, Ruberik brought Flint to his senses the next morning. The older dwarf did not remember having fallen asleep. Someone had covered him with a rough wool blanket during the night, which tumbled to the ground as he jumped up.

"No place to make hot chicory in my new rooms," Ruberik grumbled by way of apology. Pots banged and kettles clanged while he clumsily heated water over the fire, then poured it through a length of coarse netting that held some fresh ground, roasted root. Taking a sip of the brew he shivered. "Nice and bitter," he concluded, looking as pleased as Ruberik ever did. With that he pulled on a heavy leather coat and grumbled his way into the dawn, slamming the door behind him. A current of damp, cold air rushed through the room and fanned the fire in the grate.

Flint chuckled at his brother's ill humor despite his own fatigue. He dug his hairy fists into his eye sockets, stretched, and smacked his lips. Hoping to douse the sour taste in his mouth, he took the water kettle from the fireside and made his way to the kitchen, across the room from the front door. The area was small but well organized. Using Ruberik's netting, Flint managed to rustle up his own pot of brew. Bertina kept the cream in the same place his mother had: against the back of a low cupboard along the cold north wall, where it stayed fresh longer.

When he'd downed enough chicory to feel his senses straighten, Flint looked about and noticed that the house sounded empty, its usual occupants apparently having already gone about their day. He decided to give Ruberik a hand in the barn.

Helping himself to two big hunks of bread and cheese, Flint slipped his boots on and stepped outside into a bright but brisk morning. He picked his way along the narrow, muddy path that led from the small front yard to the barn far off to the right of the house. He stopped at the well to rinse himself, letting the brisk autumn air dry his cheeks and beard and refresh his tired soul.

Swallowing the last of his bread in one big bite, Flint covered the remaining distance to the barn.

Pausing at the massive door, Flint grasped the thick, brass ring that served as a handle. It was polished and smooth from centuries of use. He remembered the times when, as a child, he had strained and hauled on that ring with all his strength without ever budging the massive door. Now he gave it a tug and the heavy timbers swung out.

Even before his eyes had adjusted to the dim light inside the barn, its odors washed over him. The hay, animals, manure, rope, stone, and beams blended together into a smell that was unique, yet each odor could be separated from the others and identified individually. Flint paused there for a moment, savoring that aroma.

Chickens roamed throughout, flapping from beam to beam, picking at the grain mixed in with the fresh straw scattered across the floor. Three cows tethered in tidy stalls raised their heads from an oat-filled trough to eye Flint disinterestedly. At the rear of the barn, six goats jostled and clambered over each other to get to the two buckets of water Ruberick had set inside their pen. A pair of swallows swooped down from the rafters and out the open door, passing inches above Flint's scruffy hair. The dwarf ducked reflexively, then chuckled at his reaction.

Ruberik stomped into the light from the depths at the back of the barn, a shiny milking pail in each hand. He saw Flint, looked surprised, then seemed about to grumble some insult. He thrust a pail into Flint's hands.

"Let's see if you remember how to milk a cow, city boy," Ruberik said, his tone unexpectedly light.

"Solace is hardly a city," Flint scoffed, then rose to the challenge. "I've been milking cows since before you even knew what one was, baby brother." Hitching up his leather pantlegs, he lowered himself onto a three-legged wooden stool next to a brown-spotted cow.

"Make sure your hands aren't cold. Daisyeye hates that— won't give you a drop," warned Ruberik.

Flint just glared at him, then rubbed his hands together furiously. He reached out quickly and began tugging; in seconds, he had milk streaming into the pail. Daisyeye chewed contentedly.

"Not bad," Ruberik said, nodding as he looked over Flint's shoulder, "for a woodcarver."

Flint ignored the jibe, handing his brother the full pail of creamy milk. "You know," he said, wiping his damp hands on his vest, "I'd forgotten how much the smell of a barn reminds me of Father." He inhaled deeply, and his mind wandered back to other mornings, when he had been dragged from his warm bed at the crack of dawn to work in this place. He had hated it at the time. . . .

"You're lucky to have any memories of him," Ruberik said enviously. "He died before I was really of any use to him. Aylmar had his smith—and then one day you were gone, too. Had to teach myself to run a dairy farm," he finished, using his cupped hands to scoop more oats into the feeding trough.

Flint's hands froze under Daisyeye in mid-milking stroke. He'd left Hillhome those many years ago, never thinking how it might make his siblings feel. He felt compelled to say something—to offer some explanation—and he tried. "Uh, well, I—" And then he stopped, unable to think of anything. He stole a glance at Ruberik.

His younger brother moved about the barn, whistling softly, oblivious to Flint and his halting response.

Ruberik finished feeding the animals and clapped his hands to remove grain chaff. "I've got to stir some cheese vats," he said, finally aware of Flint again. "Care to help?"

"Uh, no thanks," Flint gulped; he hated the overpoweringly sour smell of fermenting cheese. He took the bucket out from under Daisyeye, handing it to his brother. "I'll finish up the chores in here, if you'd like me to."

"You would?" Ruberik said, surprised. Flint nodded, and Ruberik listed the remaining morning tasks. With that, he left through a door at the far right of the barn, the scent of cheese billowing in after him.

Flint covered his nose and began milking his second cow in many decades.

* * * * *

He finished the chores by late morning. Ruberik had left to deliver cheese, so Flint sat at the edge of the well and looked opposite his family's homestead, through the multi-colored autumn foliage and steady green conifers at Hillhome below. The Fireforge house was about midway up the south rim of the valley that surrounded the village—the notch known simply as the Pass cut into the eastern end of the valley; the Passroad continued through the town and down the valley to the eastern shore of Stonehammer Lake.

Flint could see the town beginning to bustle with the activity of a new day, and without really deciding to do so, he found himself walking on the road that snaked down to the center of the village. The stroll stretched his stiff joints and freshened his spirits. He passed many houses like his family's, since most of the buildings here were set into the hills, made of big stone blocks, with timbered roofs and small, round windows.

The village proper was more or less level, and thus had many wooden structures, certainly more now than Flint ever remembered. As he came around a bend in the road, bringing him within sight of the village, he was again surprised at the extent of the changes in Hillhome.

The great wagon yard and forge seemed to serve as a central gathering place for work on the heavy, iron-wheeled freight wagons. The trade route ran east and west, straight through Hillhome on the Passroad. His view of the yard was blocked by a high stone fence. New buildings stood crowded together along the Passroad, extending the town past the brewery building, which Flint remembered as once marking the town's western border. Off Main Street, there were still the neat, stone houses with yards; narrow, smooth streets; little shops. But the pace of life seemed frantic.

That busyness nettled Flint, for reasons he could not even explain to himself. He had intended to explore Hillhome, to see the new sights, but instead he found himself resenting the changes and heading toward the safety of Moldoon's once again to enjoy the comfortable familiarity of the place.

"Welcome, my friend!" Moldoon greeted the dwarf pleasantly, wiping his hands on his apron front before he took

Flint's arm and drew him forward. At this time of day, the place was virtually empty, just a table of three humans in the center of the room before the fire, and a pair of derro drinking quietly at another.

"Have you a glass of milk for an old dwarf's touchy stomach?" Flint asked, spinning a stool at the bar to his height. He slipped onto it easily, propping his chin up in his hand.

Moldoon raised his eyebrows and grinned knowingly. "Don't you mean a touchy old dwarf's stomach?" He reached under the bar for a frosty pewter pitcher and poured Flint a mug of the creamy liquid. Flint tossed back half of it in one gulp.

"I heard your family got together last night," said the bartender, topping Flint's glass again. "You cost me half my customers!"

The dwarf smiled wryly, shuffling the mug between his hands on the bar. Then he remembered the one family member who had remained at Moldoon's rather than greet his uncle. "Not Basalt," he said to the barkeep. "He didn't seem any too glad to see me . . . when he finally got home."

Moldoon sighed as he filled two mugs with ale. "Aylmar's death really hit him hard, Flint. I don't think it's got anything to do with you. He blames himself—he was his father's apprentice. But he was here, not at home, when Aylmar went off to the wagon camp."

"I know how he feels," grumbled Flint into the last of his milk.

"Barkeep, do we have to wait all day?" A scruffy-looking derro at the table behind Flint waved two empty mugs over his greasy yellow head, smacking his lips and glaring at Moldoon.

Moldoon held up the overflowing mugs in his hands, splitting an apologetic look between the derro and Flint. "Right away," he called sheepishly, muttering, "Be back in a moment," to Flint before hurrying to the table.

"Wagondrivers," he breathed as he returned to the bar. The dwarf stared as his old friend absently popped two steel pieces into his cash box.

"For two mugs?" Flint asked in amazement.

Moldoon nodded, looking both incredulous and a bit ashamed. "That's the price to *them* anyway. Apparently they don't get much good ale in Thorbardin, so most of the crews load up on it late in the afternoon before their night-time run." He mopped at a sweat ring on the bar. "Business has never been better—for every business in town. Most of us merchants think the return is worth putting up with a few rowdies, now and then." With that, Moldoon excused himself and shuffled into the kitchen to settle a dispute with the village butcher, who had called angrily from the back door.

Flint walked around the end of the bar and helped himself to a mug of ale. He dropped one steel piece onto the bar. Suddenly cold, he shivered and headed for the fire, desperate to return some warmth to his old bones.

When the fire failed to lift his spirit, Flint pulled from his belt pouch his sharp whittling knife and a small, rough piece of wood he'd been saving. Sometimes, when ale failed to ease his mind, only carving would help. He would forget everything except the feel of the wood in his hands as he worked life into it. Think of the wood, he told himself as he sat in front of the fire.

Like most dwarves, Flint was not much given to expressing his feelings. Not like his emotional friend Tanis, who was always tormenting himself about something. For Flint, things either were or they weren't, and there was no point worrying either way. But every now and then something could get under his skin, like the uncomfortable feelings he'd had since returning to Hillhome. Flint shivered inwardly and drew his mind back to the wood. He stayed the afternoon at Moldoon's, slowly, painstakingly shaping his lifeless piece of lumber into the delicate likeness of a hummingbird. Moldoon refilled his mug now and then, and soon all was forgotten in the joy of his creation.

The tavern filled steadily with more hill dwarves, and more wagondrivers replaced the previous group. Flint scarcely noticed much beyond his sphere, though, so engrossed was he in the finishing details of his bird.

"So, it's good old Uncle Flint."

Flint nearly sliced off one of the hummingbird's intri-

cately detailed wings. The sarcastic voice at his shoulder
sounded like animated ice. Basalt. Flint slowly looked up.
His nephew loomed, glaring at him with a humorless half
smile on his red-bearded jaw. "It's a bit early for drink, isn't
it?" Flint asked, wishing he could bite his tongue off the second the patronizing words left his mouth.

Basalt eyed Flint's own mug. "That's not milk you're
drinking, either."

Flint set down his tools and sighed, swallowing the irritation he felt because of his ruined good mood. "Look, pup,
I've always had a soft spot for you." Flint eyed him squarely
now. "But if you keep using that tone of voice with me, I'm
going to forget you're family."

Basalt shrugged, taking an empty chair near his uncle's. "I
thought you already had."

Flint had never struck someone for telling the truth, and
he was not of a mind to start now. Instead, he grabbed Basalt by the shoulders and shook him, hard.

"Look, I feel terrible about your father," he began, searching his nephew's freckled face. "I'm not one for wishing, but
I'd give anything to have been here, anything to have
known. But I wasn't and I didn't, and that's what *is*, Bas."

Trying hard to look unperturbed, Basalt rolled his eyes in
disbelief and looked away. "Don't call me that," he whispered, referring to the affectionate nickname Flint had let
slip.

Flint had seldom seen such suffering as he noted in his
nephew's face, and he had felt it only once: after his own father's death. "Aylmar was my big brother—my friend—just
like you and I were before I left."

"You're nothing like my father."

Flint ran a hand through his hair. "Nor would I try to be. I
just wanted you to know I feel his loss, too."

"Sorry, old man. No consolation." Basalt turned his back
on his uncle.

Flint was getting angry. "I'm still young enough to whip
the smartmouthedness out of you, harrn."

But Flint could see by his nephew's reaction that he no
longer heard him. Basalt strutted before his uncle, wearing a

patronizing smirk. "I can't blame you for coming back now, you know, when there's *real money* to be made." He did not even try to keep the bitterness out of his voice.

It was Flint's turn to poke at his nephew, his thick index finger within an inch of Basalt's bulbous Fireforge nose. "I've had about all I'll take from you today. You want someone to be angry at, and you've chosen me, when the two people you're really hopping mad at are your father and yourself!"

Basalt's ample cheeks burned scarlet, and suddenly his right fist flew out toward Flint's jaw. His uncle quickly blocked the punch, landing a right jab of his own squarely on Basalt's chin. The younger Fireforge's head jerked back, his eyes bulged, and he slithered to the floor.

Basalt wiped his lip and discovered blood on the back of his hand; he looked up at his uncle at the bar in astonishment and shame. Flint turned back sourly to his mug, and in a moment Basalt got to his feet and left the inn.

Flint dropped his care-worn face into his hands. He had fought wolves and zombies, and they'd taken less of a toll on him than the confrontations he'd endured in the last day. The clamor of noise surrounded him; the smell of greasy, unwashed bodies began to fill the tavern. These familiar things seemed less comforting and enveloping than before. *Nothing* about Hillhome seemed the same. He resolved at that moment to make his hasty good-byes in the morning and get back to the life he understood in Solace.

At that moment a party of pale blue-skinned derro dwarves noisily entered Moldoon's. Turning his back to them in disgust, Flint tried to ignore the bustle around him. He knew no one in the tavern except Moldoon. And though the barkeep had been joined around dusk by two matronly barmaids, he was too busy with the throng of customers to talk.

It might have been the ale, his fight with Basalt, or the whole unsettling day combined, but Flint grew suddenly annoyed with the presence of the derro in Moldoon's. Now that it was dusk, a pair of the fair, big-eyed dwarves, already drunk, sat down beside the agitated dwarf and rudely bellowed at Moldoon for more ale.

"Don't they teach you manners in that cave of a city you come from?" demanded Flint, all of a sudden swinging around on his stool to face the two mountain dwarves.

"It's a grander town than you can claim," sneered one, lurching unsteadily to his feet.

Flint rose from his stool too, his fists clenching. The second derro stepped up to his companion, and the hill dwarf saw him reach for the haft of a thin dagger. Flint's own knife was in his belt, but he let it be for now. Despite his anger, he sought no fight to the death with two drunks.

At that moment, luckily, Garth clumped in, carrying a sack of potatoes, and headed for the door to the kitchen behind the bar. He took one look at Flint's angry face nose-to-nose with the derro and he let out a loud, plaintive wail that caused everything else to fall silent. Moldoon looked up from where he was serving patrons across the inn. Garth was alternately pointing at Flint and the derro, babbling, and holding his head and sobbing. The gray-haired innkeeper covered the distance in four strides. Instructing a barmaid to lead Garth into the kitchen to calm down, he planted himself between Flint and the derro.

"What's the problem here, boys? You're not thinking of rearranging my inn, are you?" Moldoon was looking only at the derro.

"He insulted us!" one of them claimed, shaking his fist at Flint.

Flint pushed the pale fingers away. "Your presence insults everyone in this bar," he muttered.

"You see!" the derro exclaimed self-righteously.

Moldoon took the two derro by their elbows and propelled the startled dwarves toward the door. "I see that you two need to leave my establishment immediately."

At the door the derro wrenched away from his grip and turned as if to attack Moldoon, hands on the weapons at their waists. Moldoon stared them down, until at last they dropped their hands and left. Shaking his head, the innkeeper slammed the door behind them and then strolled toward Flint at the bar.

Flint sank his face into his ale and gulped half the mug down. "I don't need anyone to fight my battles for me," he grumbled angrily into the foam.

"And I don't need anyone breaking up my inn!" countered Moldoon. He laughed unexpectedly, the lines in his face drawing up. "Gods, you're just like Aylmar was! No wonder Garth went crazy when he saw you about to take a swing at those derro. Probably thought it was Aylmar back from the dead for one more fight."

Flint looked up intently from his ale. "What are you talking about? Aylmar had a set-to with some derro?"

Moldoon nodded. "At least one that I know of." Moldoon looked puzzled. "Why are you surprised? You, of all people, must have guessed that he detested their presence in Hillhome."

"Do you remember when the fight was? And what it was about?"

"Oh I remember all right! It was the day he died, sadly enough. Aylmar didn't frequent here much himself, but he came looking for Basalt. They got into their usual fight about Basalt's drinking and 'working for derro scum,' as Aylmar put it, and then the pup stormed out."

Flint leaned across the bar on his elbows. "But what about the fight with the derro?"

"I'm getting to that," Moldoon said, refilling Flint's mug. "After Basalt left, Aylmar stewed for a bit here, watching the derro get louder and louder. And he just cracked— launched himself right at three of them, unarmed. They swatted him away like a fly, laughing at 'the old dwarf.' "

Flint hung his head, and his heart lurched as he imagined his brother's humiliation.

"Indeed, this conversation makes me remember something," Moldoon added suddenly. Flint looked up half-heartedly. The bartender's face looked uncharacteristically clouded.

"Aylmar told me after the fight that he had taken a small smithing job with the derro. Naturally I was surprised. Aylmar had leaned forward and whispered—" Moldoon's voice dropped "—that he was suspicious of the derro and had taken the job so that he could get into their walled yard to look into a wagon. He asked what I knew of their security measures, and I told him that I'd overheard that each crew of three slept during the day in shifts, one of them guarding their wagon at all times."

Flint's interest was piqued. "Why do they need to guard farm implements so closely?"

"That's just what Aylmar asked," Moldoon said softly, then sighed. "I guess he never found the answer, or if he did, it died with him, since his heart gave out at the forge that same night." He clapped Flint on the shoulder and shook his head sadly, then turned to wait on another customer.

Flint sat thinking for several minutes before he worked his way through the crowd and left the smoky tavern. The sun was low in the sky. He stood on the stoop outside Moldoon's, but instead of crossing the street and walking back up the south side of the valley to the Fireforge home, the hill dwarf set his sights down Main Street to the east, just sixty yards or so, toward the walled wagon yard.

Chapter 5

The Break-in

In Flint's youth, the wagon yard had been the black-smithing shop of a crusty old dwarf named Delwar. While most dwarves, racially inclined toward smithing, made their own weapons, nails, hinges, and other simple objects, Delwar had provided the villagers with wagon wheels, large tools and weapons, and other more complicated metal designs.

Flint had learned a lot of what he knew about blacksmithing from the old craftsman, whose burn-scarred arms and chest had both frightened and fascinated the young hill dwarf. Flint and other harrns would sit in the grassy yard outside Delwar's shop and barn to watch the smith through the open end of his three-sided stone shed; Flint enjoyed the

59

smell of smoke and sweat as Delwar hammered hot metal almost as much as he liked the taffy treats and cool apple drinks the smith's robust wife would bring out to them.

But Delwar and his wife had long since passed away, and a menacing, seven-foot high stone wall had been built around that once-friendly spot. Someone had told him— Tybalt perhaps—that a "modern" forge had been built on the western edge of town, and Delmar's had been long abandoned until the mountain dwarves had bought the rights to its yard and forge as part of their agreement with Hillhome. The derro had built the wall, which Flint estimated enclosed a thirty-by-twenty-yard area. There was one entrance into the yard: a sturdy, wooden ten-foot gate stretched across the southern edge along Main Street. Flint saw no guard posted on the outside, but one surely supervised the gate from the inside.

Flint strolled nonchalantly down the road, passing by the walled yard with scarcely a look, focusing instead on the ducks hanging so invitingly across the street in the butcher's window. After twenty or so yards the wall turned a corner. A narrow alley, no wider than would allow two dwarves abreast, ran the length of the eastern wall and the opposite building. Flint continued his unhurried pace until he was out of sight of Main Street. He covered the last ten yards to the northeast corner in a sprint, since the sun was dropping lower. He could not waste another moment of light.

The newly built wall had no toeholds of any kind. Flint went around the corner to the northern wall, but the stone continued on for only five feet before the wall joined with and became Delwar's fifteen-foot-tall barn and blacksmith shop.

A skinny oak sapling had somehow rooted itself in the small alley. Flint knew it would not support his weight. He looked about the alley desperately, and farther down his eyes came upon a discarded old rain barrel, several of its slats missing. He clomped up to it and turned it on its side, testing its strength; not so good, but the bottom was still solid and there were probably enough slats left to support him for a minute or so.

Flint dragged the barrel to the corner near the sapling and stood it on its open top. End to end, the barrel was nearly as tall as he and more than half the height of the wall. Reaching nearly above his head, he grabbed both sides of the barrel's metal rim and tried to haul himself up. The rotted barrel creaked and rocked dangerously toward him. He could get no leverage.

Frowning, Flint considered the sapling again. Perhaps its lower branches were sufficient to support him just long enough to spring onto the barrel. He pushed the barrel so that it stood on his right, between the sapling and the wall. Hitching up his leather pant legs, he gingerly raised his right foot to rest on the strongest of the limbs, about two feet off the ground. Flint took a deep breath, grabbed the trunk of the sapling with both hands, and thrust himself upward. It held him for a split second, and then he slid down the scrawny trunk of the tree, snapping every little twig on the way to the ground.

Frustrated, Flint stroked his beard while he thought. He tested the flexibility of the sapling's trunk and decided that its green wood might bend. Taking it firmly in his left hand, he pushed it toward the ground until it was low enough for him to step on. Counting to three, he launched himself off the doubled-over tree, hearing it snap and tear just as his hands closed around the top of the barrel and he was able to pull himself up. With one more quick spring, he was atop the stone wall. Flint dropped the seven feet to the ground, landing alongside the barn and in six inches of mud with a "splooch!"

"You leave now!"

Flint nearly jumped out of his boots, which were stuck fast in the mud. He looked up in the late-afternoon light and espied a big dwarf standing a few paces away. His face was a mask of fear, and he appeared to be dragging a sack full of black coal.

"Garth!" Flint hissed, both relieved and dismayed. He tried to wrestle his booted feet from the mud, but the boots would not budge. He stopped struggling and looked up at Garth pleadingly.

"Leave me alone!" Garth said fearfully, turning away. "Why are you haunting me?"

"Garth," Flint began, trying to calm the harrn before he drew attention, "I'm not the dwarf you found by the forge—that was my brother, Aylmar. You needn't be afraid of me. I'm Flint Fireforge, your friend."

Garth looked at him suspiciously out of the corners of his eyes, hugging himself protectively. "You promise to stay out of my dreams now? I didn't hurt you." He shook his head vigorously. "The humped one sent the blue smoke, not me. I just found you."

"Garth, it wasn't me—what blue smoke?" Flint asked, suddenly curious.

"The blue smoke from the stone around his neck!"

"Whose neck? A derro?"

"Yes! You were there, why are you asking me?" Garth said, angry and flustered by this line of questioning. "I have to go to work now. Get out of here, or he'll use his magic, wherever he is!"

With that warning, Garth hefted the sack, but Flint reached out to stop him. "Garth, you mustn't tell your bosses I was here again. Promise me, or I'll—I'll give you more bad dreams!" Flint winced at using such a cruel trick on the terrified harrn. Eyes wide with dread, face paler than death, Garth only nodded as he lumbered away around the corner of the barn.

Flint tried to sort through Garth's strange mutterings. Was he merely spouting dreams he'd had, ones caused by finding Aylmar's body, or had he been the only witness to some horrible deed?

The hill dwarf moved to take a step and remembered with a soft groan that he was still stuck in the mud. Flint curled his toes and tugged upward, but his boots were buried so well that his feet pulled out instead. Wiggling the high-topped leather boots back and forth with his hands, he finally managed to wrench them out with a loud sucking sound. Each one had to weigh over fifteen pounds now, and he had neither water nor cloth nor grass to clean them with, since the entire yard was churned to mud. He would move as quietly as a squad of ogres with these on. Hardly the barefoot type, Flint reluctantly set them down along the fence anyway, where he could grab them on his way out.

Flint poked his head around the corner of the barn and stole a glance at the wagon yard. It was crisscrossed with deep, muddy ruts. Two of the flat-bed mountain dwarf wagons were standing side-by-side, their buckboards pointed toward Flint; he saw no guards. Tybalt had said that one wagon was always coming from Thorbardin while another was returning, never in tandem. So which wagon was full of cargo and on its way to Newsea, and which one was returning to the mountain dwarf kingdom? Flint knew he had little time before the derro crew awoke or returned from the taverns, and no time to choose wrongly.

Suddenly he saw a derro emerge from the open side of the blacksmithing shop in the middle of the north wall, some ten yards to his right. The derro guard circled both wagons, bending down to look under the one on the left, farthest from the shop.

"We should be getting on the road within the hour," the derro called toward the building. "I'm anxious to get back to Thorbardin. Did Berl or Sithus tell you when they'd return?"

"They always stagger back at the last minute," an unconcerned voice said from the depths of the shop. "You worry too much. Come on back and catch a few more minutes of sleep before the long haul."

"You're right," said the derro by the wagons, striding toward the darkened shed. "Everything looks OK out here, anyway. That idiot brought the coal for the forge, I see, so at least tomorrow's crews won't run short. These mountain roads cause the wagons to break down too often."

Flint could barely make out their conversation as it continued in the shop for a few more minutes, then died away. Soon he heard snoring.

The guard had looked under only one wagon; Flint locked his gaze on the other one, farthest from the shop. Taking a cautious step around the barn, Flint's tender feet touched a deep, cold mud puddle, and he recoiled. Shaking globs from his feet, he decided to circle around to the left, where there were less ruts. His approach would be hidden by the wagons.

Forging through the mud, he came at last to the side of the wagon. The sturdy wooden conveyance rolled on four spoked iron wheels that were as tall as the cargo box between them, at least six feet off the ground, and certainly way above the stubby dwarf's head. The cargo box had wooden sides reinforced with thick bands of iron.

The dwarf grabbed onto the front right wheel and began pulling himself up from one spoke to the next, until he stood halfway up the massive iron ring. His chin just crested the box, and he saw that the thick, dirty canvas was stretched tight over the top of the wagon. He struggled to untie a corner of the canvas, and finally he pulled enough away to climb further up the spokes and crawl inside the box. It was surprisingly cramped, he noted as he looked around.

Plows! By Reorx, the mountain dwarves were indeed going to great lengths to ship plows! And cheap ones at that! Flint mouthed his astonishment silently. The interior of the wagon held five huge iron plow-blades. Each of the blades looked uncorroded, as if it had been freshly forged, but the metal was pitted and rough from imperfections of casting. They *should* be embarrassed to have anyone see such shoddy workmanship!

This was not what Flint had expected to find. Who cared if the mountain dwarves' notorious greed allowed them to lower their smithing standards? Flint was curled into a painful ball to keep his head from bulging the canvas, but he shifted onto his knees now and hunkered down to think. Suddenly, his aching back produced a most unexpected thought.

Why was he bent double in a box that was at least as tall as he? Unless it was two boxes, not one, he concluded excitedly. He examined the floor of the wagon and was frustrated in his attempt to find secret compartments.

Flint poked his head out of the canvas and looked and listened; the yard was still quiet. He lowered a foot around the wheel and onto a spoke, then slipped down.

Flint dropped from the wheel and crawled under the wagon, struggling to balance in the deep, muddy ruts as he slowly inspected the underside of the box. Brushing mud away with his fingertips, Flint probed each crack with his carving knife.

He missed it the first time, but as he doubled back he found the concealed panel. Mounted between the axles was a long rectangle made from two of the wagon's floorboards.

Quickly Flint pried at the door, seeking a latch. His fingers probed and prodded, and then he felt the mechanism, hidden in a knothole. After a push of his blade, he felt the catch release; the narrow panel swung downward.

He was so close!

Praying that the shadows under the wagon would conceal him a few moments longer, Flint raised his head into the cavity the panel had revealed. Spotting several long wooden crates, he wasted no time in prying the nearest lid off, snapping the tip of his knife.

But he paid no attention to his weapon as the wooden lid fell away. Instead he stared at a pair of steel longswords—weapons of exceptional quality, he could tell at a glance; these were not like the pitted plows above. He snapped another box open, finding a dozen steel spearheads, razor sharp and wickedly barbed. He did not have time to check any more boxes, but he knew that there was no need.

Weapons! And not just any weapons, but blades of superior craftsmanship, excellent quality. The steel gleamed with purity, proving it to be expensive and rare.

But they were without craftsman's marks, no artist's signature. Wherever the arms were headed, the mountain dwarves wanted their origin to remain a secret. Nearly every day for at least a year, a wagon full of weapons had left Thorbardin for some unknown shore. What nation on Krynn needed so many weapons?

Only war required such numbers.

The answers Flint had sought left only more questions. Had Aylmar learned of this before he died? Flint swallowed a lump in his throat as he remembered Garth's mutterings of a "humped one and magical blue smoke." Had Aylmar died because of what he had stumbled upon?

Heart pounding, Flint dropped back to the ground and was preparing to dash for the south wall when a heavy boot crushed his left hand into the mud.

"You didn't know half-derro could see in daylight, eh?" Flint looked up slowly from under the wagon and saw a derro standing above him, leering. Flint shifted his eyes and saw that, for now, the guard was alone. Desperate, he grabbed the derro's ankle with his free hand and tugged with all his might. The surprised mountain dwarf slid in the mud and dropped, hard, on his back, knocking the wind from his lungs. Flint could get no traction, so he pulled himself up by the other one's elbows and pierced the thrashing derro's windpipe with one quick slash of his carving knife. The derro stopped struggling.

Flint looked around quickly, then back under the wagon toward the shop. He could see one figure shifting uneasily in the shadows, calling out the dead derro's name. He would come looking for his friend any minute.

Flint looked at the surrounding walls bathed in twilight, including where he had entered the yard and his boots still lay. He had no barrel and sapling to help him over the seven-foot barrier now. He looked to the vast wooden gate, directly opposite the shop, the wagons obscuring his view. Though closed, the gate was made of closely spaced rails. His boots would never have fit in the spaces, but his bare toes might . . . He had to make the fifteen-yard dash to that gate.

Keeping low, Flint ran as fast as he could, keeping his eyes on the ruts that threatened to trip him. He hurled himself at the gate and jammed his toes into the spaces between the rails.

"Hey!"

The cry came from behind him. Heart pumping wildly, Flint hauled himself up the gate by sheer desperation. Balanced on his stomach across the top of the gate, he was swinging his right leg up to prepare to leap off when the gate underneath him swept open. Flint looked down anxiously and saw that two of the guards were returning from the taverns, staggering and laughing, oblivious to Flint clinging to the top of the gate above them.

But the guard from the shop was yelling a warning as he ran to the gate. His cohorts looked up in time to see the hill dwarf's exhilarated expression as he threw himself from the top of the gate and crashed into them. Their bodies broke his fall, and they were scattered like bowling pins, taking the other guard down with them. Flint jumped to his feet unhurt. The stunned derro could only shake their foggy heads as the barefoot hill dwarf cut left on Main Street and tore down the road and out of sight.

Chapter 6

Hasty Departure

Flint deliberately avoided the village, leading his muddy trail away from the Fireforge home. He would not be able to explain his appearance to his family—from his head to his toes he was mud-caked and spattered with blood. His mind was in a tumult, and he needed to think things out before he could face anyone with his suspicions.

His tender bare feet cold and sore, Flint set out into the eastern hills just south of the pass. Using steel and flint, he made a fire in the seclusion of a small cave that had a mountain stream trickling past it. He stripped off every stitch of his dirty clothing and washed it by hand in the ice-cold water, laying it out to dry on rocks around the fire. The tired old hill dwarf splashed his face, scrubbed the mud from his hair, and then, unclothed, he returned to sit by the fire, staring without thoughts into the flames for a very long time.

Flint's blue-green cotton tunic dried quickly, and when he slipped it over his head, he was glad for the long hem that dropped to his knees. His leather pants would take much more time to dry. And he dearly missed his boots.

His stomach rumbled now, reminding him that he had not eaten since that morning. Noticing fish in the shallow stream, he knelt beside the water and pushed up his sleeve. He dipped his hand in, slowly herding an unsuspecting rainbow trout to where he could raise his hand quickly and flip the fish onto the shore. It took him four painstaking tries, but finally a small trout, yet a good seven inches long, was flopping around on the sandy cave floor. Flint quickly slit its silvery belly with his carving knife, cleaned it, then skewered the fish on a sharpened stick. He remembered seeing some berries on his way to the cave, and while the fish was roasting over the flames, he picked two handfuls of red raspberries by the light of the waxing moon.

Only after his stomach was full of succulent fish and sweet berries did he feel capable of thinking at all. Though he had only the ramblings of a simpleton to support the belief, Flint knew in his gut that Aylmar must have been murdered, and likely because he knew the true contents of the mountain dwarves' wagons. He had killed one of the derro on instinct—but on what evidence? The word of the village idiot? Though his family might believe him, he would still be imprisoned, causing great humiliation and the ruination of the Fireforge name in Hillhome. What bothered Flint more, though, was that from jail he would be unable to discover Aylmar's killer and avenge his brother's death.

Flint was determined to do both, or die trying. He would keep his suspicions to himself, until he had evidence no one could refute.

* * * * *

"This is a fine example you set for the family!" grumbled a harsh voice from the barn door when Flint arrived on the front lawn the next morning. He had spent a fitful night sleeping in the cave before setting out at dawn, circling around the south side of the village to reach the family home. Ruberik was in a huff, his milking pail in hand. "Disappear all night and then come staggering home—a disgrace, that's what it is!"

Flint's feet were blistered and cold, and he had no patience left. "Listen, Brother," he growled, fixing Ruberik with a glare that halted him in his tracks. "I don't know what branch of the family could produce such a tight-faced, sneering, pompous sourpuss of a hill dwarf as yourself!"

Ruberik's eyes bugged out of his head, and he was too astonished to reply before Flint continued. "Whatever quirk of nature made you my brother, you are my *younger* brother and you've taken too much advantage of my good nature. Now, I've had enough of your self-important proclamations. You have no idea where I've been or what I've been doing, so I'll expect you to keep your opinions to yourself and show some respect to your elders!"

Ruberick's ruddy face turned ruddier still, and he spun about on his heel, clanging his milking can against the barn door's frame in his haste to leave. Sighing heavily, Flint stepped into the house and was thinking about grinding some chicory root to make a hot morning cup when Bertina scurried out from the depths of the house and set about the task herself.

She gave Flint an appraising glance, but kept her opinions to herself. "Out a bit late, weren't you?" She glanced down at his bare, red feet. "I'll bet Aylmar's old boots would fit you if you're needing a pair," she offered tactfully. She was unfazed. Without waiting for an answer, she fetched a pair of boots very like his own lost ones from the depths of the house.

Flint slipped them on gratefully. They were a little big, which was good now, considering his swollen feet. "Thanks Berti," he said softly, "for the boots . . . and for not asking."

His sister-in-law knew what he meant and nodded, beating some eggs in a bowl. They ate a breakfast of scrambled eggs, buttered bread with jam, and pungent chicory. Flint was about to offer to help clean up when the front door burst open and Tybalt stormed in, holding a pair of mud-caked boots under his arm.

The young dwarf was clearly agitated as he approached Flint. "You recognize these?" he asked, holding the muddy boots up. He looked at Flint's feet. "Those are Aylmar's old ones! I knew these were yours!"

"Good morning to you, too, Brother," Flint said, trying hard to sound nonchalant. He had not thought about being traced by his boots! He took a sip of hot chicory and tried to keep his hand from shaking.

"Don't 'good morning' me!" Tybalt cried, slamming his fist to the table. "What were you up to, anyway? And what possessed you to leave your boots behind?" Tybalt was working himself into a frenzy.

"What in heavens are you talking about, Tybalt?" asked Bertina, handing him a cup of the hot drink.

He waved it away in exasperation. "It seems our visiting brother took a trip through the mountain dwarves' wagon yard yesterday. They found his muddy boots by the barn."

Tybalt began to pace before Flint. "That's not the worst of it. When I showed up at the constabulary for work this morning, I was told a derro had been stabbed to death and that the murderer had left behind his boots! I began to laugh, but then I nearly choked when I saw them," he snarled, his hands clenching into fists.

Tybalt squinted at Flint. "They have a good description of you, too! The guards you jumped got a good look at your face before you fled. Of course, the description could match practically anyone—except for the boots."

He resumed pacing, his hands behind his uniformed back. "And then there's Garth . . . he heard the description and began jabbering some nonsense about Aylmar being back from the dead to give him bad dreams. Fortunately, the derro don't pay much attention to the village idiot, but there's some folk who know that he's got you all confused with our late eldest brother!"

"Tybalt! I won't have you calling that poor harrn such things in this house," Bertina scolded him. "Garth is perfectly pleasant. He just got caught between the hammer and the anvil once too often, is all," she finished softly.

"Bertina, who cares about Garth?" Tybalt shouted. "Flint murdered a derro in the wagon yard!"

"Aren't you convicting me without even asking if I did it?" asked Flint.

"Well, *did* you?" a hesitant Tybalt demanded.

"Would it matter?" Flint asked cagily.

"Of course it would!" Tybalt sank into a chair and tugged at his beard in agitation. "Don't you see the position you're putting me in—and me with my promotion coming up! I should hand you over to Mayor Holden. I should, and I just might!"

Flint looked at him squarely. "Do what you must, but you said yourself that the description could fit practically any dwarf in Hillhome. Why don't you just pretend you've never seen those particular boots before?"

Tybalt looked like he was being pulled in two pieces. "I can't do that! *I* know those boots are yours, and I'm sworn to uphold the law, no matter who breaks it!"

"Who says the killer wore those boots?" Flint suggested. "Perhaps they were thrown into the wagon yard by some cruel young harrns playing a trick on an old dwarf sleeping off an excess of spirits."

"Is that what happened?" Tybalt asked eagerly, sitting up straight.

"Do you really want to know, Tybalt?"

Tybalt's eyes closed, and he shook his head quickly. He combed the fingers of both hands through his thinning dark hair. "I shouldn't even *think* of doing this," he began through gritted teeth, "but if you leave town, at least until this blows over, I'll forget about the boots." He frowned into Flint's face. "You don't seem to care about your own fate, but please consider that the rest of us chose to live in Hillhome, even if you don't think our lives are very interesting or worthwhile!"

"Stop it!" snapped Bertina to Tybalt, as the muscles in Flint's jaw tightened. "Are you a human or a dwarf? I declare, sometimes you and your ambitions embarrass me, Tybalt!"

"Thanks, Berti," Flint said faintly, a hand on her fleshy arm, "but Tybalt's right—I don't want to bring shame down on the family. I'll leave right away." He fetched his pack and axe from a small storage room behind the kitchen.

Smiling in relief, Tybalt stepped up to Flint as the old dwarf adjusted his backpack. "I'm sorry about this, really. It's nothing personal. No hard feelings?" he said, thrusting his hand toward Flint.

His brother considered the beefy hand with its stubby fingers, then turned away. "You're a hypocrite, Tybalt Fireforge, and the worst kind for asking me to help you pretend you're being saintly instead of selfish."

Tybalt leaped back as if struck. "But you said I was right about you leaving!"

Flint gave him a pitying smile. "You are, but not for the reasons you think." He shook his head and then turned to Bertina, anxious to be done with Tybalt. He could hear his brother rushing out of the house behind him.

Flint's sister-in-law stood mute, tears filling her eyes. Her face glowed a bright crimson that paled all her previous blushes. "You can tell me, Flint. Why would you do such a terrible thing?" she asked, but there was no harsh judgment in her voice.

Flint felt he owed her, wife of his murdered brother, as much of the truth as he dared. "It was self-defense," he said vaguely, measuring his words.

Bertina brightened through her tears. "Then why don't you stay and tell the mayor that? He'll take your word over those of the derro!"

"Do you think so, if it meant he would lose the mountain dwarves' trade?" Flint shook his head. "No, it's not that simple, Berti." He hugged her awkwardly and headed for the door.

"Where are you going?"

"I don't know," Flint said evasively. "But don't worry, Bertina, I'll be back some day. . . . Soon. Say good-bye to everyone for me." She slipped a sack full of food into his hands, brushed a kiss across his bristly cheek, then fled into her room at the back of the house.

Flint stood in the sorrowful silence a moment and looked around his family's home one last time. He wished he could have settled things with Basalt, said good-bye to Bernhard and his sisters—the saucy Fidelia, and naive Glynnis—but they were at work in the town. Ruberik was out in the barn, he knew, but he could not bring himself to offer an explanation for his departure and face the inevitable tongue-lashings. So, he tucked his shiny axe into his belt and walked out the door.

Flint did not notice the small shadow that cut across his path. Nor did he see that anyone was following him as he stomped through the hills to the southwest of Hillhome.

The hill dwarf was too preoccupied with finding his brother's murderer to notice anything, for he was on his way to the vast dwarven city of Thorbardin.

Chapter 7

A Kingdom of Darkness

The Kharolis Mountains were not the tallest range upon the face of Krynn, nor the most extensive. They did not contain smoldering volcanoes such as the Lords of Doom in Sanction to the north, or the great glaciers found in the Icewall range. The ruggedness of the range's individual valleys and peaks, however, could be surpassed nowhere on the continent of Ansalon.

Sheer canyon walls dropped thousands of feet into narrow, twisting gorges. Streams poured with chaotic abandon from the heights, slashing their way deeper and deeper into jagged channels of rock, engraving their mark with each passing day. Trees survived only on the lower slopes and valleys; most of the Kharolis range was too rough or too high to support anything more than sparse patches of moss and lichen.

The crests of the range never lost their snowcaps, the hanging teeth of which descended as glaciers into the circular basins of the heights. These twisted and turned in every direction before finally coming to rest in the frigid blue-green waters of the high lakes.

The landscape of the Kharolis Mountains, inhospitable in the extreme, was the home of a populous kingdom and thriving culture that dwelled there quite comfortably, since its members rarely saw the landscape above them.

They were the dwarves of Thorbardin.

Thorbardin was a powerful dwarven stronghold, containing seven teeming cities and an extensive network of roads and subterranean farming warrens. The whole of Thorbardin covered an area more than twenty miles long and fourteen miles wide.

Toiling in their vast underground domain, the dwarves paid little attention to occurrences on the surface world. They had enough space and enough intrigue in their subterranean lairs to last them many centuries.

At the heart of Thorbardin lay the Urkhan Sea. Not a sea at all, it was actually an underground lake some five miles long. Cable-drawn boats crisscrossed the lake in an intricate network, linking most of the cities of the dwarven realm. In the center of the sea was the most amazing city of all: the Life Tree of the Hylar. Twenty-eight levels of dwarven city were carved within a huge stalactite that hung from the cavern roof to dip below the surface of the sea.

Thorbardin drew its food supply from three great warrens. These massive caverns devoted to sunless agriculture were capable of producing huge crops of fungus and mold-based food. Each warren was shared by several cities, but individual food plots were jealously guarded.

Despite its size, Thorbardin was historically connected to the surface world by only two gates, at the north and south boundaries of the kingdom. The Northgate had been destroyed by the Cataclysm. The dwarves had withdrawn into their underground domain, sealed the Southgate against every form of attack they could imagine, and turned their backs on the world.

Although considered one kingdom by outsiders, the mountain dwarves of Thorbardin actually consisted of no less than four identifiable clans, or nations: the Hylar, the Theiwar, Daewar, and the Daergar. Each of these was ruled by a thane, and each had its own interests, goals, even racial tendencies.

Thorbardin's schisms were aggravated by the absence of one true monarch to rule the kingdom as a whole. According to ancient legend, Thorbardin would become truly united only when one thane obtained the Hammer of Kharas. That ancient artifact, named for the greatest of dwarven heroes, had been missing for centuries. Untold effort, treasure, and lives had been expended, fruitlessly, in attempts to locate it.

Without the hammer to unite them, the nations of the dwarven kingdom struggled against each other. Spies were sent to observe the activities of rival thanes. Treasure stores were jealously watched, because riches—particularly steel and gems—were a traditional measure of dwarven status.

The Hylar, the eldest of the mountain dwarf races, were the traditional masters of Thorbardin. Their might had been severely taxed by the Dwarfgate Wars, however, allowing other nations to gain increased prominence. Most notable among these was the Theiwar clan, made up of derro dwarves and controlled by their magic-using savants.

The derro, paler complected and of slightly larger stature than their Hylar cousins, lived in the northern portion of Thorbardin. They practiced dark magic and were regarded with superstitious awe by other dwarves. They had a well-earned reputation for treachery, betrayal, and sorcerous manipulation. Other mountain dwarves regarded them with fear and extreme distrust.

It was the derro Theiwar who had excavated a new, secret exit from northern Thorbardin, allowing them to send their wagons of weapons to the sea without the knowledge of the other clans. Wealth was power, and the Theiwar intended to be very powerful, indeed.

* * * * *

The great throne room gave an impression of unlimited space, like a wide clearing beneath a silent, nighttime sky. Tall columns stood around the periphery of the chamber, rising into the darkness like massive tree trunks. Low torches flickered in a hundred locations, cloaking the chamber in a warm, yellow light.

The vast chamber, nevertheless, lay more than a thousand feet below the surface of Krynn. Great halls, shielded by massive steel-and-gold doors, led from the throne room to all parts of Theiwar City. A hundred dwarves stood alert at the various doors, clad in gleaming plate mail and armed with axes or crossbows.

Now one of these doors swung slowly open, and a hunchbacked dwarf entered the chamber. His long, bronze-colored robe rustled along the floor behind him. He hastened toward the center of the room.

There, Thane Realgar rested quite comfortably in the massive throne, his boots extended and crossed before him. The ruler was an old dwarf, with white streaking his yellow beard and long, loose-flowing hair. He had ruled the Theiwar clan for many decades. Most of the routine matters of the clan were handled by his chief adviser, so that Realgar could devote his own energies to the search for the Hammer of Kharas. He regarded any business not relating to that hammer as bothersome.

Realgar's personal bodyguards stood to either side of him: a pair of hideous gargoyles poised like watching statues. They perched, absolutely motionless except for their eyes, which followed the hunchbacked derro as he advanced. The gargoyles' skin was a rough-hewn gray, indistinguishable from stone. Their leathery wings, of the same color, spread like menacing, clawed hands behind the throne. Their faces were vaguely human, accented with sharp fangs, tiny, wicked eyes, and a pair of twisted horns growing from their foreheads.

The hunchback reached the throne, and the gargoyles suddenly hissed. They flapped their wings once and sprang forward to stand to the left and right of the thane. Extending clawed fingers before them and noiselessly working their jaws, they stood in mute warning as the hunchbacked dwarf bowed obsequiously.

"Ah, Pitrick, it is good of you to return to my city," said the thane of the Theiwar.

"How did you fare at the council of thanes?" inquired the adviser.

"Bah!" The thane clapped his fist into his palm. "It was one Hylar treachery after another! They seek to entangle the Daewar in an alliance, and always to cut us out!" Realgar leaned forward then, a conspiratorial smile upon his lips. He lowered his voice. "But, my dear adviser, I think they are beginning to fear us!" The leader of the Theiwar placed a stubby finger to his bearded lips. "Now, tell me how things fared in my short absence?"

"You will be pleased," Pitrick offered eagerly. "Production has nearly doubled and promises to further improve. So it is, too, with the number of wagons running. We have very nearly reached the desired levels of transport."

"Splendid." The thane turned his attention to a scroll in his lap, signaling Pitrick's dismissal.

The adviser coughed slightly. "There is one other matter, Excellency." The thane looked up in surprise and gestured for him to continue.

Pitrick shifted uncomfortably, nagged by the pain in his crippled foot. "It seems that one of our drivers was slain in Hillhome. The murderer, a hill dwarf, escaped." Pitrick took a breath. "We have reason to believe that this dwarf broke into the wagons and discovered the nature of our shipments."

"When did this happen?" The thane's voice was quiet, almost bored.

"Several days ago. I received word from one of the drivers not two hours past."

Gold chains clinked slightly, their heavy links sliding as the thane leaned forward. Realgar's sacklike robe of deep blue ponderously swathed the throne around him. Indeed, whenever he chose to walk he required several attendants to carry the massive train.

"Solve the problem quickly," said the thane, his voice still lazy and bored. "You have opened the route for us, and it is your responsibility to keep it both open, *and secret.*"

"Of course, Excellency," Pitrick bowed deeply, using the gesture to hide the smile that creased his thin lips. By the time he straightened, his expression was again a featureless mask. "I shall see to the task at once. I have but one favor to ask of Your Greatness."

"And what is that?" Realgar asked absently.

"We must strengthen the guard at the tunnel," explained Pitrick. "Increase both the number and the quality of the troops we have there."

"Specifically?"

"The Thane's Guard," Pitrick supplied quickly. "They are the most reliable of your troops, and they will perform the task alertly. I'll need two dozen of your guard and a good captain. . . ."

The thane squinted. "You would have a captain in mind, of course?"

Pitrick smiled thinly. "Indeed, Excellency. I believe Perian Cyprium is just the officer for the task."

"There wouldn't be another reason you have selected her?" asked the thane.

Pitrick coughed again, bowing his head modestly. Staring at his adviser's bristling yellow hair, the thane pondered for a moment. Perian was a good, loyal captain, one of his best. Both of her parents had served him well before their deaths. She would not be happy with the assignment—her disgust for the adviser was as well known as Pitrick's lust for her. The thane himself found Pitrick distasteful, but he keenly appreciated the savant's power and insight.

Besides which, Pitrick was the architect of the arrangement with Sanction. His diplomatic and magical skills could prove the key to all of the Theiwar's future grandeur. The thane considered him indispensable if the nation was to achieve the glory that was its rightful destiny. Thus it was that Realgar had no real difficulty assessing Pitrick's request.

"Very well. I shall put Captain Cyprium under your orders, effective immediately. We will double the guard, for now.

"And as for Hillhome," concluded the thane, "that will require some thought. The hill dwarves' ungrateful attitude and perpetual greed are beginning to annoy me."

Pitrick bowed to conceal his smile.

*   *   *   *   *

Perian marched purposefully through the second level of the city, preparing to climb to the third level, where she knew she would find Pitrick, the thane's hunchbacked adviser. In her gut she fought a crawling sensation that threatened to overwhelm her with disgust.

She had been fending off Pitrick's odious advances for several years, but a summons that required her to call upon the adviser in his apartments put her at a distinct disadvantage. Still, the thane had ordered her to see the adviser, and her duty was to obey.

The only child of her generation in a long line of dwarven warriors, Perian had buckled on armor and taken up the sword when it was her turn to follow in the family tradition. Her father, mother—until Perian's birth—and uncles had all served with merit in the thane's House Guard. That elite legion, dedicated to the racial supremacy of the derro, comprised the most trusted of the Theiwar troops.

Perian had proven adept both at the physical aspects of combat and at the mental challenges of command, rising quickly through the ranks of the thane's personal bodyguard. Now she commanded the House Guard, proudly taking her place with the four or five highest ranking officers in the thane's service.

Thane Realgar, she knew, was the most powerful king in all Thorbardin, mainly because the magical abilities many Theiwar possessed gave him an edge. Vicariously, she ought to take some pride in that status. Instead, she admitted only to herself, she felt a slight tinge of guilt and discomfort.

Perhaps it was because, unlike most of the Theiwar dwarves—the inhabitants of Thane Realgar's two cities—

she was only half derro. Full derro always found a savage glee in the dark side of things. But the other half of her dwarven ancestry could be traced to the Hylar dwarves, and Perian often wondered if that aspect did not dominate her private personality.

She was innately distrustful of magic, and Pitrick was the most powerful savant, or mage, among the Theiwar: grotesque, malicious, and deceitful. His undeniable magic power was just the surface manifestation of many unpleasant features. There was also the matter of his leering and rude sexual proposals, stopping just short of brute force.

Unfortunately, she could not afford to be entirely indifferent to him. She reflected, with her usual frustration, on the tangled hold Pitrick had over her life.

Perian's father and mother had also been loyal, decorated soldiers in the thane's troop of Huscarles, or House Guards. When Perian was born, her mother retired from active duty and devoted herself to raising her only child. She had been indulgent to Perian, and often wistful around the child. Perian's father, on the other hand, had been emotionally distant from both of them—a proper dwarf soldier, Perian had always thought. Given her family, she had encountered no difficulty joining the House Guard—about ten percent of its troopers were female—or rising quickly to the rank of sergeant. That was when Pitrick, the oily adviser to the thane, had first entered her life.

He had confronted her with evidence of her true origin, in the form of letters from her mother to a Hylar soldier—her mother's secret lover. According to Pitrick, that illicit union had produced Perian. As far as she was aware, no one but her, her mother, and Pitrick knew that she was neither a fullblooded derro nor the daughter of the bold warrior whose reputation was known far and wide. It was true that Perian's ruddy skin and auburn hair were slightly unusual for a fullblooded derro. It was equally true that the House Guard of the Theiwar required its members to be racially pure. Perian dreaded the day Pitrick would use his information as the ultimate blackmail. Perian had no way to confirm her circumstances of birth. But she had to admit the sample of her mother's handwriting was genuine and, as the rank of captain loomed before her, this information had placed her in Pitrick's power. So far, she had always managed to call the adviser's bluff without goading him into action, but he was too unstable and dangerous to be taken for granted.

Many times Perian had wondered whether her father was naturally distant, or whether he had suspected the truth. She wished her mother had never written those letters, had not been so foolish, just as she often pondered how powerful an emotion love could be, to make someone like her mother risk everything.

Eventually she reached the lift that would take her into the noble's quarters, high in the upper level of the city. Pitrick was no noble by birth, but as adviser to the thane he was considered the second most important dwarf in the Theiwar city. An iron cage descended to meet her now, and she stepped inside. With a steady clanking, the chain-and-pulley mechanism carried her up for a hundred feet through a hollow column in the mountain.

When it stopped she stepped onto the terrace of the noble's plaza. Perian ignored the view over the wall, where much of the underground Theiwar city could be seen in its splendor—the neatly squared streets, high walls, thick columns, houses and shops, blanketing the floor of the cavern. She strode to the doors and was instantly admitted.

She was greeted by a disfigured, cloaked servant, but his master quickly came into the antechamber and viciously sent the servant scurrying away. As always, the hunchback's stare discomforted her.

"Good news," said Pitrick, clapping his hands delightedly together. "You are assigned to me, now—I am your commander!"

Perian felt a chill of apprehension shiver along her spine. "In what capacity?" she asked, forcing her voice to remain level.

"We are increasing the guards at the mouth of the wagon tunnel! Come now, don't pretend surprise. You know of its existence. You will be placed in command." Pitrick's sparse beard could not hide his leer. The hump on his back forced him to bend forward, and thus he was always looking up at her.

"I prefer to remain with my old billet, the training of the guard," she objected.

Pitrick leaned closer, his dank breath moist against her face. "I grow tired of your game, my dear. Keep in mind that I could have you ruined with a single word!"

"Then do it!" Perian shot back.

With a sneer, Pitrick stepped away and looked her up and down. "You know me too well, dear girl. Still, perhaps I shall, someday. Perhaps I shall, if you continue baiting me this way," Perian noted, his hand clasping the iron amulet that always hung from his neck. Blue light began seeping between his fingers.

"You will do good work for me," the hunchback said softly. Perian's head grew light, and she was surprised at the musical pleasantness of his voice. Perhaps she had misjudged him.

The blue light grew stronger, occluding her vision until only Pitrick's face loomed. She felt his hot breath against her face. Her soldier's training told her, dimly, that she should resist. She felt Pitrick's hand reach around to the back of her mail shirt. His breath, heavy with nut fungus, pressed moist and smelly around her face.

Suddenly her head jerked upward. Her left hand shot forward, knocking the amulet from Pitrick's grasp, as she wrapped her right hand around the small axe at her waist. She clenched her teeth as her head cleared.

"Wait," Pitrick urged, his voice still soft.

But the spell was broken. Perian's hateful gaze brought the hunchback up short.

"If you ever try to magic me again, I'll kill you," she growled.

Pitrick looked at her, his moment of surprise quickly turning to amusement. "It's time for you to go down to your new post now," he instructed. "Have a look around, establish your guards. I'll be down soon to inspect your position.

"If there is any sign of intrusion, or even the hint of a hill dwarf anywhere around there, I want you to tell me person-

Chapter 8

Unexpected Company

*The prominent nostrils twitched, tickled by an un*familiar, yet tantalizing odor. One great eye, bloodshot and sunk deep within its socket, opened. The lid, of green, leathery skin, blinked several times, and then its counterpart opened. Once again the long green nose moved, seeking confirmation of the scent.

The body that slowly rose to a sitting position was humanoid, though perhaps half again as tall as a man. But its features were hideous in the extreme.

Gangly arms, each as long as a man was tall, hung from the creature's shoulders. Though they were proportionately slender, a wiry cord of muscle showed beneath the mottled green skin, promising great strength. The creature's legs, too, were revealed as long and thin, but they had no difficulty supporting the monster as it rose to stand.

Its hands and feet each bore three wicked claws, with fingers partially webbed. Blotchy skin, the color of dark moss, covered its whole body. In places it was smooth, but in others the skin lay wrinkled, a rough, warty surface.

Atop the creature's head was a thicket of black, stiff-standing hair. Its mouth opened slightly and revealed upper and lower rows of pointed, needle-sharp teeth. Above its mouth, extending more like a tree limb than a nasal aperture, was the creature's long, pointed nose.

It was this sensitive proboscis that had caused the monster to awaken, and now it probed the air, sniffing and snuffling for clues. What was that tantalizing scent? Where did it come from?

The creature's lair was a cave, and a slight breeze wafted into the cave mouth from the valley below. The source of the scent, obviously, was outside the lair.

Moving through the dingy cave, the monster passed numerous scattered, well-gnawed bones of previous meals. Skulls of deer, bear, hobgoblin, human, and other victims stood along the wall of the cave, making a crude trophy mound. But now the creature ignored all of these mementos, moving toward the fresh air in search of new food, perhaps a new skull.

The creature emerged to discover twilight settling over the high valley. The spoor came more clearly now, and the great beast licked its lips with a black, moist tongue. Its dark eyes, almost hidden in the deep recesses of its black sockets, squinted into the darkness, searching for the source of the tantalizing odor.

An odor, the troll knew, that could only emanate from one of its favorite foods: dwarf.

*   *   *   *   *

Flint's destination, the mountain dwarves' kingdom, was twenty or so miles southwest of Hillhome. The wagons' shipments must have come from there, and Garth had also said the derro he saw was a magic-user; it was common knowledge that only one type of dwarf could muster more than simple spells. That was the Theiwar clan of Thorbardin.

Flint suspected his older brother had discovered the secret of the derro, and he was determined to make whoever was responsible for his death pay with his life.

His burning vengeance, he had to admit, was colored by the legacy of bitterness and hatred left by the Dwarfgate Wars, when another Fireforge, the respected dwarven leader Reghar Fireforge, had died at the hands of the mountain dwarves. Those epic conflicts had opened schisms in the dwarven races that seemed likely never to heal.

Flint had no clear explanation for these arms shipments of the derro, but he knew the reasons must be sinister indeed. Why else would a race that was known for its pride of craftsmanship not sign its work?

Flint was following the Passroad west. Traveling in daylight, he felt fairly secure that he would not encounter any derro. The road hugged the northern shore of Stonehammer Lake, whose cold water looked dull gray-green on this overcast late-autumn day. Most of the leaves in this distant arm of the Kharolis Mountains, in the corridor between Thorbardin and the Plains of Dergoth, had already turned brown and scattered across the flat lands, leaving only the olive-colored firs to cover the spiny mountain ridges.

The terrain grew considerably rougher as the slopes and crests of the southern hillcountry tumbled around Flint. The elevations soared steeply from the valley bottoms, climbing to narrow ridges and fringed with levels of sheer cliffs, bare rock faces, and dark forests of pine. In places, looming knobs of granite overlooked grass-filled valleys, often giving Flint the impression of huge, serene faces looking across the hillcountry. The Passroad twisted around like a snake, never running straight for more than a mile or two.

Flint had never been to Thorbardin—they didn't exactly embrace hill dwarves there—but his father had once told him something that was tugging at his mind now. The dwarven capitol city had two entrances: Northgate and Southgate. Originally, a wide, walled ledge edged the mountainside at the entrances, but the Cataclysm had destroyed most of the northern ledge, leaving only a five-foot remnant towering one thousand feet above the valley.

The Passroad seemed to be leading him toward the northern entrance, and unless his father had been mistaken, that gate into the great city would soar one thousand feet above him. But how could that be? How could the huge, lumbering freight wagons enter Thorbardin from the north?

Unless the Passroad continued past Northgate and circled the expansive realm to enter at Southgate . . . If that were the case, Flint had a long walk ahead of him, since the city stretched more than twenty miles in circumference.

But that didn't make sense either. The heart of the Kharolis Mountains stood between here and there, and no wagon could cross that tumultuous landscape. It was a puzzle to him.

Flint had walked nearly a full day before his keen dwarven senses raised the hair on the back of his neck; someone or something was following him. He wasn't terribly surprised, since he had expected to be pursued. Still whomever it was seemed in no hurry to catch him, nor even to be concerned about being detected. Once he even caught sight of a distant figure trudging through the grassy vale which Flint had passed through a short time earlier.

Flint continued to look behind him at regular intervals, but never again spotted the figure. Could it have been some hill farmer, going about his business? Flint had been too far away to distinguish if the figure was a human or a dwarf. Still, his trail sense nagged him, warning him to stay on guard.

His second afternoon out of Hillhome was damp and cold. Flint stopped to rest at the crest of a rocky ridge, and to eat the last of the cold meat sandwiches, rock cheese, and dried apples Bertina had slipped into his hands as he'd left the family house. Shoulders of bare granite loomed around him, and several caves dotted the side of this steep slope. He had discovered a makeshift trail in the base of a narrow ravine and veered off the Passroad to lose his pursuer. Now, at the crest, he looked behind and saw for the second time the stalwart figure on his trail.

There was just a flash of movement before his pursuer disappeared into a wide belt of pines fringing the base of the ridge. But the glimpse had been enough to convince the crusty dwarf that his suspicions had been well-founded. Flint resolved to wait for whomever followed him, forcing a confrontation on his own terms.

Flint crept back into the narrow ravine, retracing his steps for a dozen yards down the side of the ridge. He wiped his sleeve across his sweaty brow as he found a sheltered ledge with a fine view of the ravine below. There he sprawled. Withdrawing his axe from his belt, he laid the weapon beside him on the rock.

His elevation, coupled with the steepness of the ridge, gave him a significant vantage. He gathered an assortment of rocks, some as big as his head, so that he could lob them using both hands, and some fist-sized stones that he could easily pitch with one hand. Finally, he settled down to wait.

Long minutes passed with no sign of movement from below, but this did not surprise the dwarf. The belt of forest below the ridge was wide and tangled, and it would take even the fastest of pursuers the better part of an hour to climb the slope.

Suddenly he tensed, seeing movement below, and very close to him. He grasped his axe, then swallowed a gasp. There was neither human nor dwarf below him, but something ten times worse, for, creeping into the ravine was a mottled-green, wart-covered, large-as-an-ogre troll. He had never fought one before, never even seen one, but he recognized it nonetheless. And he knew their malevolent, ravenous reputation.

He was momentarily relieved but surprised to see that the troll's attention was not directed up at him. Indeed, the monster as well, seemed to be staring down the ravine, from a position one hundred feet below Flint. The creature moved its long limbs in a deliberately rigid gait that reminded Flint of a crab—a giant, vicious crab, to be sure.

The wind, soaring up the ravine, brought the pungent, vaguely fishlike odor of the beast clearly to Flint's nose. The

troll's wicked claws, on hands and feet alike, grasped out-
crops of rock as it held itself against an expanse of cliff, leering outward with those black, emotionless eyes.

Then Flint almost laughed out loud as he realized the creature's intent. It was laying an ambush for something that
crept up the ravine below them—perhaps the same pursuer
that Flint had intended to confront!

Now that's what I call fair, he thought to himself. Someone follows me through the hills for a few days, and then
gets eaten by a troll.

Still, the nearness of the monster gave Flint some cause
for alarm. He resolved to wait, quietly and patiently, for the
little drama below to run its course. Then, when the troll
was absorbed with its victim, Flint would make a fast and
easy escape.

A clatter of rocks abruptly drew the dwarf's attention farther down the steep ravine. He could see no movement, but
something was obviously charging upward. Whoever's following me moves with no mind for caution, Flint mused as
his pursuer scrambled and scratched up the ridge.

Another clatter told the dwarf—and the troll, too, no
doubt—that the chaser had climbed higher still. Perhaps
whomever it was had already come into sight of the troll,
for Flint watched the beast grow taut in its rocky niche, preparing to spring. Indeed, he saw movement in the ravine finally and determined that it was a short human or dwarf
who was climbing so steadily.

A brown hood covered the fellow's head, so Flint could
not see his face. He could, in fact, tell little about him. Flint's
pursuer stopped to catch his breath; he peered upward
along the ravine that stretched to the top of the ridge, measuring the distance. At last, even in the gathering darkness,
Flint got a good look at his young, red-bearded face.

Flint's pursuer was not a derro spy, or a human. The
dwarf below him, in imminent danger of being attacked by
a hungry troll, was none other that Flint's nephew Basalt.

"Reorx thump you!" hissed Flint, astonished. He didn't
know what the silly pup was doing here, but the dwarf
probed his mind desperately for a way to warn his nephew

about the deadly ambush.

Flint seized one of his smaller rocks and pitched it down the ravine at the monster, watching with satisfaction as it whacked the troll squarely in the back of its grotesque head.

"Basalt, look out!" Flint cried, springing to his feet. Moaning piteously and rubbing its head, the troll spun to look upward, its jaws widespread in a malicious grimace. Even in the dim light, Flint could see the creature's long, pointed teeth.

The troll leaped upward, astonishing Flint with its prodigious bounds. The dwarf sent a large boulder skittering down the chute, but the rock ricochetted past the troll's head, narrowly missing Basalt, who had begun to scramble up the ravine behind the speedily climbing troll.

Flint hefted another of his large rocks, holding it over his head as the troll closed in. The creature's wide, black eye sockets stared at him in a way that was all the more terrifying for their complete lack of expression. Aiming carefully, the dwarf pitched the boulder when the troll was some thirty feet below him. The heavy rock, its momentum aided by the muscles of Flint's broad shoulders, struck the troll a crushing blow on its left leg.

"Take that, you ugly, green-bellied goblin-eater!" A taunt worthy of Tasslehoff, Flint thought with satisfaction. He hooted with joy as the monster's leg snapped from the force of the blow. The troll uttered a sound—a low, cold hiss of dull pain—and tumbled backward. Its leg twisted and flopped.

Now, for the kill, Flint hoped. Grabbing his axe, the hill dwarf bounded down from his ledge. He raised the blade over his head and closed on the troll as the beast fell between two rocks. Its leg hung to the side, useless.

But before Flint could reach the brute, the charging hill dwarf halted in astonishment. The monster's leg twitched slightly, and Flint heard a strange, grating sound, like two jagged rocks scraping together. The troll took its lower leg in both huge, warty hands and arranged it into a proper alignment. Horrified yet fascinated, Flint unconsciously moved closer to watch; the troll looked up through red-veined eyes and hissed at him, slashing out with a jagged claw. Flint drew back only slightly, but the troll returned its attention to its wounded leg.

Amid the gruesome scraping sound, bubbles and bulges could be seen forming under the troll's thick, green warty skin. Slowly, the bulges flattened out, and the spine-chilling sound ceased. Before Flint could comprehend the meaning of the macabre scene, the troll became aware of him again. Its eyes locked onto Flint as it leaped to its feet. Dropping to a fighting crouch, the creature danced toward Flint on two good legs! The limb, crushed to bonemeal a moment before, had somehow grown firm and again supported the beast's weight.

"Holy gods of old—you can regenerate!" Flint cried, flabbergasted. The troll slashed with its viciously clawed hand again, but Flint came out of his stupor long enough to knock the digits away with his axe. Striking quickly, he lopped the troll's hand off. It made a sickening spraying sound, thick green blood spurting in a steady stream. Flint cast an anxious eye down the slope for Basalt. His nephew was vaulting upward as quickly as he could, panting with exertion, short sword extended. But he was still some distance below.

The monster seemed more stunned than tortured at the loss of its hand. Flint pressed the advantage, hacking with his axe, driving the monster back. Although the beast was more than twice Flint's height, the dwarf stood above him in the steep ravine. Flint had the initiative, striking, dodging, and striking again.

Once more his advantage proved illusory. The troll dodged away from him while it held the oozing stump of its hand. Not the squeamish type, even Flint was repulsed as three tiny claws sprouted from the bloody wound with a loud popping sound. He heard the green skin stretch, and the claws grew impossibly fast, revealing fingers and then, in moments, a completely new taloned hand. Fully regrown, the creature made a gurgling-regurgitating sound in the back of its throat—Flint swore it was snickering—and then the troll crept toward the hill dwarf.

Flint scrambled backward up the steep chute, struggling

to keep his balance in the loose rock. A fall would slide him, helpless, into the slashing maelstrom of tooth and claw below.

"Uncle Flint!" cried Basalt.

Flint did not even stop to see where Basalt was. "This is no picnic, Basalt! Run, you hare-brained numbskull!" If the troll turned on his inexperienced nephew, the boy would be devoured before he could raise his blade.

"I can help!" Basalt gasped, slipping on loose rock as he scrambled closer. Now the troll did turn.

Powered by fear, Flint sprang forward, hacking the sharp blade of his axe into the monster's back. The blow sent sticky, gelatinous, pea-green blood showering onto Flint, who gagged and spat furiously. Nearly cleaved in two, the monster writhed away as best it could, hissing in pain and rage, giving Basalt enough time to slip past it.

"Stay back!" shouted Flint to his nephew, then bounded forward with another swing of his axe.

But Basalt had a mind of his own, and he delivered a sharp jab with his short sword into the troll's belly. The monster had begun to regenerate again, but the new blows doubled it over, sending it twisting and rolling down the ravine. Grinning proudly, his right arm covered in green blood, Basalt prepared to leap after it.

"No!" ordered Flint, grasping his nephew's shoulder. "You've got to learn when to retreat, harrn."

"But we've got the advantage now!" objected Basalt, looking longingly down the ravine.

Flint jerked on Basalt's collar. "Only until it grows back together." He chuckled suddenly, then pretended to frown. "Never mind that! What are you doing here in the first place? I'd like to know."

Basalt began a clumsy explanation, but Flint cut him short with a poke in the chest. "Not now, pup! There's a troll growing below us! You've got a lot to learn about adventuring!"

Flint leading the way, they raced up the ravine as fast as they could, reaching the top of the ridge in a minute. The troll was out of sight below them, having fallen around a bend in the ravine.

Basalt followed the older dwarf at a steady trot. Night closed around them, and still the two dwarves maintained a fast pace. They scrambled down the far side of the troll's ridge and hastened across the valley floor.

Finally they collapsed, exhausted, in a small clearing among the dark pines. Though it was pitch black, they dared not make a fire.

In the dim light, Flint leveled his gaze at his nephew. "You've got some explaining to do, son. Why don't you start by telling me what you're doing here?"

Basalt fixed him with a sullen glare. "You've got some explaining to do yourself, like where do you think you're going?"

Flint's mouth became a tight-lipped line. "I owe answers to no one, least of all a smart-mouthed boy of a dwarf like yourself."

"I'm not a boy anymore! You'd know that if you ever came home, or stayed more than a day!" For a moment Basalt gave Flint a look that was so belligerent, so full of Fireforge stubbornness, that Flint's hands curled involuntarily into fists. But in another moment the older dwarf laughed out loud, clutching his paunch in mirth.

Puzzled, and a little insulted, Basalt demanded, "What are you laughing about?"

"You!" said Flint, his laughter slowing to a chuckle. "Aye, pup—you're a Fireforge, that's for sure! And what a pair we make!"

"What do you mean by that?" Basalt growled, unwilling to be teased out of his bad humor.

"Well, you're stubborn like me, for starters." Flint crossed his arms and squinted at his nephew, considering him. "You're not afraid of standing up to your elders either. You even tell 'em off once in a while, though you'd best watch so that doesn't become a habit! And you didn't hesitate one whit before jumping into battle with an honest to goodness troll."

Flint looked at his nephew with affection. "And you didn't come out here to spy on me, anyway, did you?"

"No!" Basalt said quickly, sitting up. "You were right, Uncle Flint," the young dwarf said softly. "What you said about me being mad at my dad and at myself was true. I knew it when I threw that punch at Moldoon's—" He looked away sheepishly "—but I guess I didn't much like you being the one to point it out."

Basalt plucked nervously at his bootlaces. "I didn't like leaving things the way they were between us." He looked up now, clearing his throat gruffly. "I've done that once before, and it will haunt me for the rest of my days." Basalt's voice broke, and he hung his head. Flint sat quietly while his nephew composed himself.

"Even Ma doesn't know this," he began again, his eyes looking far away into the night now, "but Dad and I had a fight the night he died. She wouldn't be surprised, though— me and Dad argued almost every night. Always about the same thing, too. 'Stop drinking and get a decent job,' he'd say."

Basalt looked squarely at Flint. "The thing that always stuck in my craw was that, in addition to apprenticing to him, I *had* a job. He just didn't like me hauling feed for the derro's horses, that's all." Basalt heaved a huge sigh and shook his head sadly. "He tracked me down at Moldoon's that night and started up the old argument again, said the derro were up to no good and he would prove it. I told him to stay out of my business, and then I left him at the bar." Basalt's eyes misted over as he looked into the dark distance again, focusing on nothing in particular.

Basalt's expression turned unexpectedly to puzzlement. "There's just one thing I don't understand. Dad said he hated that the village was working with the mountain dwarves, said he'd never lift a finger to help a derro dying in the street." Basalt stroked his beard thoughtfully. "So what was he doing smithing for them the day his heart gave out? Why that day?" Basalt turned his face to the heavens.

Flint heard his nephew's grief and was wracked with indecision about the secret suspicions he harbored over Aylmar's death. Basalt's account of the fight with his father only bolstered his hunch. Could he trust Basalt? He squeezed his nephew's shoulder.

"Basalt, I don't think your father's death was an accident," he said.

Flint's nephew looked at him strangely. "Are you talking about 'fate' or some such hooey?"

"I wish I were," Flint said sadly. "No, I think Aylmar was murdered by a derro mage's spell."

"That's going too far!" Basalt said angrily. "I've heard Garth's mutterings, and I know my father thought the derro were evil. But why would they want to kill him? It doesn't make sense!"

"It does if he discovered they were selling and transporting weapons, not farm implements, and enough to start a war!" When Basalt still looked confused, Flint pressed on, telling Basalt how he had searched a derro wagon and what he had found there. He left nothing out, none of his worst imaginings, and he told him about the derro he killed. "Seemed like I had no choice," he added.

Basalt struggled to absorb the news. "You knew all this and yet you didn't *tell* anybody? You just *left*?" Basalt asked, smoldering.

Flint snorted at the irony. "As Tybalt aptly put it, 'Who would believe the village idiot?' That's all the proof I have so far, Bas: Garth's 'mutterings' and what I saw with my own eyes in that wagon. And when they tie me into that derro I killed, Mayor Holden won't be likely to order a search of the wagons or a murder investigation on *my* say-so, either." He shrugged. "Since these derro come from Thorbardin, there was nothing else I could do but go to the mountain dwarves myself and find the derro scum who killed Aylmar."

Basalt no longer looked skeptical. "How are you going to find this one derro, when there must be hundreds of magic-using derro there."

Flint gave a devilish grin. "Ah, but how many of them are hunchbacked? Garth, bless his simple heart, kept calling the derro he saw 'the humped one.' That's my only clue, but it's a good one."

Basalt jumped to his feet. "Well, what are we waiting for?

Let's go find the Reorx-cursed derro who killed my father!"

Flint patted the harrn's hand. "You're a true Fireforge, like I said. But *we* aren't going anywhere in the dark." He sighed. "I'm not sure that I want any help, but you can't go back the way you came—a clumsy pup like you'd be troll food for sure," he teased. "I guess you'll have to come along, but we'll leave in the morning."

Basalt smiled eagerly. "You won't be sorry, Uncle Flint!"

I'm not so sure about that, Flint thought inwardly. What would he do with Basalt when he got to Thorbardin?

A cold drizzle fell, then turned to light snow. They looked for an overhanging shelf of rock well off the Passroad, since a wagon or two was bound to pass in the dark, and made a crude camp. Uncle and nephew talked long into the night, about Basalt's father and Flint's brother, and even Flint's father, too. Though he hated to see their conversation end, Flint knew they would pay for their indulgences with exhaustion in the morning.

* * * * *

By late afternoon the next day, a snowy one, the road curved into a narrow valley and began climbing steeply. Flint and Basalt wondered at the difficulty of maneuvering heavy wagons up and down these switchbacks, but the rutted state of the road proved that it did carry steady traffic.

They were closer to the heart of the Kharolis Mountains now, and the surrounding hills had gained sharp definition. The slopes towered thousands of feet in the air, with jagged precipices of bare rock exposed to the wind.

Flint groaned and struggled up the heights made all the more arduous by heavy snow. He cursed the sedentary life that had led him into this physical decline. He knew—or at least convinced himself—that this would have been no trouble for him a short twenty years ago.

But the hills brought him a sense of exhilaration as well. The view of jagged crests stretching for a hundred miles, capped by the snows of autumn; the sweeping grandeur of the valleys and the inexorable crushing force of the mountain rivers—all of these returned a joy to his old heart that he hadn't even been aware he was missing.

The sun was dropping over their right shoulders when the road abruptly ended at a shallow stream, as if a giant broom had descended and swept the rutted trail away. The bank rose steeply on the opposite side, unmarked by a single rut or hoofprint, while the two-foot-deep stream, so clear and cold Flint could see the gravel bottom, teemed across their path. Big, fluffy snowflakes plopped into the stream and melted into the steady current. Flint smiled to himself; hiding a trail in a riverbed was one of the oldest tricks in an adventurer's book.

Flint looked downstream, then upstream to the right. Kneeling near the edge of the water, he saw an almost imperceptible curve to the right in the tracks leading to the stream. "See these, Bas?" he said, pointing to the ruts. "I think the wagons are turning off right here, where they enter the water. They follow it upstream."

Basalt peered closely, then smacked his thigh in astonishment. "Why, you're right! Let's go!" The young dwarf took a step toward the stream. Flint's hand flew out to stop him.

Water. Water that was over half as tall as Flint's four-foot frame. Flint shivered involuntarily, considering the rapid icy flow. The stream had no bank to speak of, what with the severe pitch of the canyon walls that shaped it. It was twenty or thirty feet at its widest point.

"What's wrong, Flint?" Basalt asked. "Aren't we going to follow the stream?"

Flint struggled to keep the color from draining from his face. He couldn't let Basalt learn that his uncle's aversion to water went beyond normal dwarven distaste, to cold, blinding fear. Flint didn't even like admitting it to himself. It wasn't his fault, after all. It was that damned lummox, Caramon Majere.

One fine day not many years before, when Flint had been waiting in Solace for Tanis to return from a trip to Qualinesti, Tasslehoff Burrfoot proposed that Sturm, Raistlin, Caramon, and Flint take a ride on Crystalmir Lake in a boat the kender had "found." They set out on the lake, and everyone was having a grand time until Caramon tried to catch a fish by hand. He leaned out too far, tilting the boat and sending everyone into the water.

Raistlin, always the clever one, had bobbed up beneath the overturned boat and was quite safe in the air pocket it formed. His oafish twin brother did not fare so well, sinking like a stone. Sturm and Tas, both fearless, strong swimmers, soon righted the boat and Raistlin with it, while it was left to Flint to try to rescue Caramon.

The three in the boat waited eagerly for Flint and Caramon, but all they saw was a immense amount of splashing and gurgling, and then the water became ominously silent. Frightened, both Tas and Sturm plunged back into the water; the knight hauled Caramon, coughing, into the boat. It was Tas who found the dwarf, half-drowned and hysterical; all four of his friends had to help drag him into the boat, where he lay shivering, vowing to never set foot on water again.

"Uncle Flint?"

"What? Oh, yes. I'm thinking!" he snapped. If he wanted to avenge Aylmar, he had no choice but to venture into the stream.

"Oh, all right!" he snarled at last, hitching up his belt, willing his right foot to take a step into the stream. Only it would not move.

"What's the matter, are you afraid of water?" Basalt asked incredulously.

That did it. Setting his chin firmly, Flint clomped two steps into the swiftly flowing stream, barely suppressing a scream as melted mountain snow flowed over the tops of his leather climbing boots. He bit his lip until it nearly bled. Suddenly a strong eddy grabbed his legs and sent him sliding off the uneven, slimy rocks under his feet.

"Whoa!" Basalt's strong arm reached out; he caught his uncle by the collar and held tight before the dwarf fell face-first into the frigid water. Flint's axe clattered against the rocks on the narrow bank, and he nonchalantly wiped water droplets from the weapon's shiny surface while he gathered the courage to make another move.

"Let go of me—I mean, you can let go of me now, Bas," he

finished more calmly, twisting his damp tunic back into place. He had one goal now that overshadowed all others: he wanted only to get to the end of this stream-road as quickly as possible without falling. And if he should fall, he prayed that Reorx would take him quickly.

Flint set off slowly, concentrating so intently on his feet that his head began to ache with the strain. His toes were numb, as were his legs beneath his soaked leather pants. Sharp rocks jabbed at the souls of his feet through his boots.

They had progressed perhaps one hundred feet upstream when Flint heard the sound, though at first he thought it was only the blood banging through his temples. No, he decided, it sounds like wagon wheels. But why would a wagon be coming through now? It was only early evening, just heading toward dusk. The hill dwarf held up a hand to warn Basalt, and he concentrated on the approaching noise. It was coming from behind them, he determined, probably an empty wagon returning after a run through Hillhome to Newsea.

The hill dwarves couldn't backtrack and they couldn't outrun the wagon. They had to hide! But where? Flint tore his gaze from his feet and spotted some aspen branches hanging over the stream from the right side of the tiny bank. They would just have to duck low and hope the branches covered them.

Quickly he slogged the ten feet to the branches, waving Basalt to follow. Flint instinctively held his breath before dropping to his knees on the rocky stream bed, letting the cold mountain water lap at his shoulders and tear at his jangled nerve endings till he thought he could endure it no more. He felt Basalt stiffen at his side.

Hurry, damn you! he screamed inwardly at the approaching wagon. Oh, how I wish I were on that dry wagon and the derro were in this wretched water, thought Flint. That image gave him an idea.

"Bas," he whispered, no louder than a breath, "Wait for me in the brush back where the road turns to river. Two days, no more. Then go home."

"What? I'm going with you!" Basalt hissed quickly, then

he saw the determined look on his uncle's gray-bearded face. "You need me—"

"Look, Bas, I'm not even sure *I* can get in this way," Flint began almost apologetically, "but two of us are sure to get nailed. Two days, no more! I'll be OK!"

The wagon was almost upon them. Approaching their home base, the guards obviously did not fear an attack and were asleep on the buckboard, and the driver nearly dozed from the tedium, too. The four horses pulled the wagon steadily up the stream bed through the knee-high water. Flint mentally measured the distance and timed the rotation of the huge wooden wheels with their iron spokes.

Flint broke his concentration just long enough to hold Basalt's gaze. "Watch yourself, son."

The wagon was smack in front of them now, the four horses churning the water with their big hooves. Flint launched himself between the bone-crushing wheels and caught the bottom of the cargo box with just three of the thick fingers of his right hand. He quickly swung himself monkey-style until his left hand connected with the axle brace of the right front wheel. Wrapping his arms and legs around it, he held on for dear life and dangled beneath the wagon and just above the water, waiting for some large, pointed rock to impale him from below.

The wagon stopped abruptly, and he heard animated conversation.

"*You* clear the tunnel," someone said.

It's *your* turn!" another said in a sleepy voice. "I had to clear those boulders out of the way by that ridge a few days ago."

"Oh, *all right!*" the first one said.

The front end of the wagon bounced slightly as one of the derro sprang to the ground and landed in the water with a splash.

Flint hugged the axle and made himself as small as possible. Lowering his head just slightly, he looked under the front of the wagon and saw that thick brush blocked the bank of the stream beside them. The hill dwarf saw only branches, water, and the mountain dwarf's waist at water level until the fellow moved the tree limbs to either side of the wagon, forming an opening in the steep stream bed.

Deep ruts that led out of the stream were revealed where the branches had been. With an oath, the driver coaxed the horses through a turn to the left, and the poor creatures laboriously hauled the heavy wagon out of the stream and onto the concealed portion of the road.

The driver did not stop the wagon as both guards dropped to replace the brush pile, then climbed back onto the rear of the wagon, where Flint could hear them crawl over the hollow wooden cargo hold and take their places at the front again.

They rolled a short distance, and the sounds of the stream fell behind. It suddenly grew dark, and Flint knew they had entered a tunnel. His arms began to ache so that he could no longer hold onto the bouncing axle brace. Unclenching his stiff hands, arms, and legs, he dropped to the sandy ground, being careful to avoid the enormous iron wheels. He crouched in the darkness, waiting until the wagon had rumbled out of earshot. His heat-sensing infravision responded only dimly in the cold tunnel, outlining the walls in faint red.

Flint took two short steps, his boots crunching softly on the tunnel floor. Then he froze. A second click, following the sound of his own footstep, came from the right. Then another, from higher up, and another even higher. When he heard something snap directly overhead, Flint twisted desperately and threw himself to the left, but it was too late. A cage of iron bars slammed down around him, and he crashed into its side. Furiously Flint grasped the bars with both hands and pushed, pulled, lifted, and rattled them, but the cage was too heavy to budge. He dropped to his knees and scraped at the tunnel floor. Aside from a thin layer of loose gravel, it was solid rock.

The dwarf leaned back against the bars. "Damn!"

Chapter 9

A Parting of the Ways

*They took his axe immediately—Flint felt naked with-*out it. Still angered by the ease with which he had been captured, the hill dwarf seethed under the watchful eyes of
eight guards while a detachment proceeded to alert their
commander. The sentries in the tunnel were derro dwarves,
white-skinned and wide-eyed. They wore polished black
plate armor with long purple plumes trailing from their
helms.

Although the cage had been raised so that he was no
longer imprisoned by bars, the derro guards made Flint sit in
a stone recess in the tunnel wall. As they waited, the derro
played some kind of betting game with pebbles on the
smooth, stone floor at the mouth of the cramped alcove. Es-

cape, for the moment anyway, was clearly out of the question. He could only sit and fidget as time crawled by.

"Who's in charge here, anyway?" Flint asked once, after more than an hour had passed.

One of the derro guards looked up from the game with a cold gaze. His large, pale eyes showed almost as much emotion as the stare of a dead fish, Flint thought. "Shuddup," was the fellow's only reply.

Sometime later Flint heard the step of several pairs of heavy boots. The guards hastily put away their stones and jumped to their feet, standing rigidly. The footsteps tromped closer, but Flint could not see whoever approached through the narrow opening of his niche.

"Column, halt!" The command, spoken in a harsh yet undeniably female voice, brought the march to a stop. "The prisoner?" he heard the same voice inquire.

"In here, Captain."

Two derro hauled Flint roughly to his feet and pulled him from the alcove. He found himself facing a frawl mountain dwarf, leading a fresh detachment of guards. She carried a small hand axe, unlike the battle-axes hoisted by the rest of the guards, and she wore the golden epaulets of command on her shoulders.

Her smooth face and warm hazel eyes set her immediately apart from the others, all of whom were male. She wore the same helmet as her men, with its trailing purple plume, but wild copper curls escaped its confines and danced across her shoulders every time she moved her head. Her chain mail sleeves revealed arms of sinewy muscle, but the steel breastplate she wore suggested an undeniably feminine fullness of shape.

"Why am I being held prisoner?" Flint blurted. "I demand—" He stopped suddenly, cut off by the slap of a guard's meaty hand across his face.

"Prisoners have no rights here," the frawl said coldly. "You may speak when given permission. Otherwise, keep your tongue still. You'll be given ample opportunity to confess your crimes of spying on the Theiwar. Come along."

The detachment surrounded him. In silence they tromped

back the way they had come, deeper into the tunnel, toward Thorbardin. Flint noted that the passageway had only recently been widened, or perhaps created anew; jagged outcroppings of rock still remained on the walls revealing, in places on the floor, fresh chisel cuts. Wagon tracks were visible, but had not yet scarred the rock floor.

Eventually the tunnel swung to the left and before long opened into a vast cavern. A pall of smoke hung in the air, and the clash of heavy iron tools rang constantly, echoing around the stone chamber with a reverberating din. Before Flint stood huge mounds of coal, forming a black ridge some twenty feet high. This pile blocked his view of the rest of the cavern.

"Looks like a pretty big operation," suggested Flint artlessly. "Making some farming tools?"

The businesslike frawl seemed not to hear him at first. Then she turned and eyed him sarcastically. "It's strange— you don't seem unintelligent . . ."

"Thank you—" he interrupted.

". . . just foolhardy," she finished, as if he had not spoken. "You would be well advised to curb your curious nature, and your clever tongue, if you don't care to lose both."

He studied her profile curiously. What manner of dwarf was this commander? She did not fit his mental picture of a mountain dwarf, and her eyes and hair did not seem to match the derro around her. Yet she was obviously a leader, and her rank indicated that she'd been recognized and rewarded for that ability.

They left the huge cavern and entered a maze of tunnel-like streets. Uncountable side streets led away from the avenue, and mountain dwarves moved quickly and quietly along them. Overhead, perhaps twenty feet above, the street was capped by a stone ceiling. The buildings to either side extended from floor to ceiling. Counting the windows, Flint guessed that most of them contained three or even four interior floors. Some of these buildings appeared to be built from stone and brick, while others seemed to be carved from the solid mountain. All of them, however, were decorated with the heavy, brooding stonework that characterized derro cities. All dwarven architecture tended to be intricately carved and sculpted, but the derro favored a style that seemed almost oppressive, palpably dark, to Flint.

As they wound along the rows of stone buildings, Flint counted mostly shops and houses. He heard the unmistakable noise of rowdy drinking from taverns, the sounds of households preparing for the day, the rumble of manufacturing houses and craft shops—all the bustle of a major city.

"So this is Thorbardin," he said, his wonder almost overshadowing his predicament.

"*One* of the cities of Thorbardin," his escort corrected him. "City of the Theiwar of Thane Realgar."

They marched down a wide avenue in almost total darkness, the only light coming from small wall torches, and shed by fires in hearths and cookstoves glowing in the buildings. Flint had no trouble seeing in the dark, and he suspected that the derro were even more at home in it than he was. This city was as large as any Flint had ever been in, and it was only one of many! For the first time Flint began to grasp the enormity of the mountain dwarf kingdom.

Finally they turned off the avenue into what looked like a side street. A clanking of metal suddenly drew Flint's eyes upward in alarm, fresh with the memory of the cage that had snared him earlier. The noise did come from a cage of sorts, but this one was an enclosure of metal bars suspended from a heavy chain. With a crash the contraption settled into a square frame of metal that stood before them. The frawl stepped forward and opened the cage.

"What's this?" growled Flint. "An underground cell isn't good enough?" A derro prodded him forward sharply while the captain looked at him in surprise. "It's a lift. You really are a barbarian, aren't you? Step in. We're riding to level three, for an . . . interview." She and two guards joined him in the cage.

"Then what?" Flint scowled, trying to cover his nervousness as the cage suddenly lurched upward. The mountain dwarves seemed to be indifferent to the gently swaying movement.

"That's up to Pitrick." She looked into his face for the first time. "You should have anticipated the consequences of your actions," she added angrily.

"Who is 'Pitrick?' "

"Chief adviser to Thane Realgar."

They rode upward in silence for a few moments. The cage passed into a hollow cylinder in the bedrock, then emerged onto a flat platform, perfectly square and approximately a hundred feet on each side. The ceiling was quite high, nearly at the limit of Flint's vision in the darkness. It appeared to be a natural cavern roof, not an excavated ceiling, though how it came to be suspended atop four square walls puzzled Flint. Each of the walls held a sturdy gate, and each gate was guarded by a pair of derro wearing the same purple plumage as the sentries in the tunnel.

The cage lurched to a halt, and one of the derro swung the gate open. "Out, now," ordered the captain. She and the guards stepped behind Flint. The captain approached one of the doors, but stopped when Flint called to her.

"Wait!" the hill dwarf shouted.

The frawl turned and looked at him curiously. He noticed that several of her coppery curls had fallen over one of her eyes. Impatiently, she pushed the offending locks away.

"What is it?" she asked.

"Might I know your name?" Flint felt compelled to ask the question.

She hesitated a moment, and Flint thought her face softened in the bare light.

"You might," she said, turning on a polished heel. She marched to a gate in one of the walls, which the derro guards hastily opened. They just as hastily closed it behind her, and she disappeared from Flint's sight.

* * * * *

"Captain Cyprium to see you, my lord," intoned the burly derro sergeant who guarded Pitrick's door.

"Send her in." The voice, from within the apartment, sounded to Perian like the rasp of a reptile. She stepped through the door, and it was quickly closed behind her.

"Do you have news, or is this a visit for pleasure?" Pitrick inquired. Sitting in a hard granite armchair, wearing a robe of golden silk, the adviser looked up with interest at the captain's entrance.

"We've captured a hill dwarf at the tunnel," she reported flatly.

Pitrick sprang to his feet, his grotesque frame moving with surprising agility. "Excellent!" he cried, clapping his hands in delight.

"He seems pretty harmless," Perian added.

"Your opinion is of no interest to me," sneered Pitrick. "I will decide his status, and his fate."

"Shouldn't you take him to the thane?"

The hunchback limped over and looked up at her with a cruel grin. Now Pitrick's face pressed close to hers, and the stench of his breath brought the usual revulsion. "His Excellency has given me control of *all* matters relating to the tunnel and the trade route. I have no need to consult him. And need I remind you, my warrior pet, that 'matters relating to the tunnel' now include you."

Pitrick turned away from her. "I will see the prisoner, but not here. Take him to the tunnel beyond the North Warrens—you know the place." Perian felt sick to her stomach. Yes, she knew the place.

"Oh," added Pitrick, twisting to face her again. His grin had eroded to a thin, sly smile. "Catch one of those Aghar that forever raid the garbage dump. Bring him along with the hill dwarf. Have them all at the tunnel in four hours."

"A gully dwarf? Why?" The Aghar, or gully dwarves, were common pests in Thorbardin. They were the lowest form of dwarf, so dirty, smelly, and stupid that few of the other dwarves could tolerate their presence. The Aghar lived in secret lairs and often emerged to rummage through garbage dumps and refuse piles, seizing "treasures" that they would hasten back to their lairs. But they're harmless little creatures, Perian thought.

"Never mind why!" barked Pitrick, startling her with his vehemence. "You will obey me! Or—" His voice dropped ominously "—or you will pay the price for insubordination."

The sudden glow in his wild eyes left no doubt in Perian's mind as to what that price would be.

*   *   *   *   *

Flint was startled by the look on the Theiwar captain's face as she emerged from the gate and stomped back to the cage. She would neither meet the hill dwarf's eyes nor answer any of his questions, except one.

"My name is Perian Cyprium," she told him.

"Flint Fireforge," he said simply.

The cage took them back to the street level, where they marched down the avenue, around a corner, and along several smaller streets. Everywhere Flint saw busy derro, moving quickly and silently about their business. Never had he seen a place that was so populous, yet seemed so exceptionally ominous and grim.

They came to a barracks building where several platoons of purple-plumed guards stood or lounged about a courtyard. Here Flint was thrown into a cell, where he sat idly and undisturbed for several hours.

When a pair of derro guards eventually pulled him out and prodded him into the street, he was greeted by Perian and a half-dozen guardsmen. The latter, he saw, held in tow a miserable-looking gully dwarf. The little fellow's nose was running and his wide, staring eyes were red and bloodshot. He looked fearfully from one mountain dwarf to another.

Flint was surprised to see an Aghar here, but no sooner had Flint joined the gully dwarf than Perian barked, "Follow me," leaving no room for questions. She led them on a long march, but stayed well to the front so Flint had no chance to talk to her.

The only sound other than the cadence of their march was the sniffling of the gully dwarf, which persisted even after one of the derro ordered him to stop, slapping his face for emphasis. They left the great cavern of the city to enter the narrow tunnel again, back in the direction where Flint had entered. He had no illusions that they meant to release him, however.

This thought was confirmed when the silent march turned

abruptly into a narrow, forbidding cavern that branched off of the main tunnel.

You've been in worse predicaments than this, Flint told himself, although he was at a loss to remember one.

The captain stopped at the lip of a dark, yawning chasm. The edge of the pit was stony, like the floor, and dropped away suddenly. Flint wondered briefly what had caused the curious scratches around the lip, but the answers that occurred to him quickly made him drop that line of thinking. The pit opening was quite large, he noted, the far side being hard to distinguish in the darkness, even with his dwarven vision. The sides looked gravelly and crumbly—impossible to climb, Flint concluded. The vertical sides angled slightly, forming a rough chute.

The derro guards were arrayed in a semicircle around the Aghar and Flint. Perian stood several paces away. Flint got the distinct feeling that she was waiting for something.

Before long they heard the sound of another approach, though it could hardly be called a march. A footfall was followed by a scraping sound. This pattern was repeated, over and over. Finally, Flint saw why.

The dwarf who entered the cavern was the most repulsive example of the derro race Flint had ever seen. This grotesqueness came from far more than the derro's distorted posture, or his thin lips seemingly fixed in a permanent, cruel sneer. It was more than the straggly beard or thin, oily hair.

It was the eyes.

Those horrid orbs locked onto Flint, opened wide in a white stare of almost insectlike detachment. But when they flashed with hatred, their intensity blasted Flint like air across a furnace.

"You are the hill dwarf," the creature spat, the last two words sounding like a curse.

Flint maintained his composure, though he knew he could not conceal his revulsion. "And you must be Pitrick," said Flint.

The derro guards stepped back, creating a path for Pitrick to Flint. Though the hill dwarf was certain he had never seen this derro before, there was something about the medallion that hung around his neck . . .

The humped one sent the blue smoke . . .

What had Garth said in the wagon yard?

. . . the blue smoke from the stone around his neck.

The realization struck Flint. It burned in his gut and raced along his limbs like fire. Here was the dwarf who killed Aylmar, the mysterious "humped one" mentioned by Garth! Deliberately, Flint tensed his muscles. He noted the positions of the guards to either side, knowing this might be the only chance he would ever get for vengeance, and that he would have only an instant to make his charge.

That he would have only moments to kill.

Uneasily, Pitrick scuttled to the side and two brawny derro stepped between Flint and his enemy. *Did he suspect? He's obviously magical, but can he read my mind?* wondered Flint. But Flint saw no fear in his face, only pride and hate. The hill dwarf held his anger in check and resolved to wait for another chance, though every instinct urged him to propel himself forward in a berserk attack.

The derro stared at Flint for some moments before finally speaking. "I am about to ask you several questions. You must answer them. I have arranged a demonstration, a preview of the future's potential, shall we say, to ensure that I have your attention." Pitrick looked to the derro nearest the Aghar and nodded slightly. Sickened, Flint guessed what was coming.

The guard pitched the little dwarf off the lip of the chasm. Flint heard the Aghar scream and cry, saw him desperately scraping at the steep sides of the pit as he slid downward. Rocks and rubble slipped down with him, bouncing and tumbling along the steep, mud-streaked wall into the darkness below.

Suddenly, against all odds, the Aghar managed to halt his fall, barely within Flint's view. The hill dwarf saw the fellow's stubby fingers grasp a knob of rock. Slowly, the terrified Aghar pulled himself upward. Adjusting his grip, he braced a foot against the cliff and tried lifting himself ever higher.

The doomed figure's brave struggles only seemed to amuse Pitrick, who chortled over each frantic scramble as he toyed with the medallion around his neck. Taking a cue from their leader, the guards, too, seemed greatly amused by the Aghar's plight. Flint glanced toward Perian and noticed that she alone was not even watching. Her back was toward the pit, her eyes fastened on the floor.

Something moving in the darkness below wrenched Flint's attention back to the grisly drama in the pit. A huge, black, undefinable shape moved beneath the gully dwarf. Up from that shape lashed what looked like a living, thrashing rope. It groped upward, striking the Aghar's back, then quickly encircled his waist.

The gully dwarf shrieked as the thing yanked him backward down the chute. "Noooooooooo!" he bawled, scratching and grasping desperately at the loose rocks. His frantic eyes met Flint's for one long, painful moment, then he disappeared into the darkness.

The scream that rose from the depths was the sound of pure, primeval terror. It reverberated along the chasm, echoing and amplifying in the stone chamber. Flint closed his eyes and gritted his teeth against the horrid cry. Abruptly it ceased. To Flint's horror, what followed was even worse. A snapping, crunching sound rose from the pit. Then, as quickly as they had come, the sounds died away.

When Flint opened his eyes, Pitrick was standing scant feet in front of him. "You have one chance to answer each of my questions," he hissed. "Fail to satisfy my curiosity and . . . I'm sure you can imagine."

Flint saw his chance. Bursting between two of the derro guards, he clamped his powerful hands around the hunchback's throat and both of them tumbled to the ground, rolling to the brink of the pit.

Flint was startled by the strength in Pitrick's shriveled arms. Madly they wrestled from side to side, Flint's grip tightening as Pitrick fought to pry his knotted arms loose. The derro's jagged nails bit into the flesh of Flint's arms until blood flowed down his wrists and spread across the adviser's throat. Flint twisted and rolled across the rock-strewn

113

floor, inches from the precipice, trying to avoid the guards who scrambled back and forth in their attempts to separate the two combatants. Yet every time he tried to roll the squirming derro over the edge, the creature managed to twist away.

Many hands pulled at Flint's arms and legs. Something cracked against the back of his head, and Flint nearly blacked out. In that moment he was dragged from Pitrick's body and flung against the cavern wall, where two derro stood over him with axes, ready to dismember him if he so much as moved.

Pitrick flopped and writhed on the ground, gagging, his jaw opening and closing wordlessly. At last he rolled over onto his elbows and knees, massaging his throat. Two of the guards bent to help him up, but the savant drove them away with a livid snarl. He stayed like that for several minutes, panting, reveling in the simple sensation of breathing, of blood circulating.

Eventually Pitrick climbed unsteadily back to his feet, bracing himself on the cavern wall. He wiped Flint's blood from his neck with the sleeve of his battered bronze-colored robe and nonchalantly examined the medallion hanging there. At last Pitrick hobbled toward Flint, who was still propped up against the cavern wall.

Pitrick motioned to one of the guards, who slipped off an iron gauntlet and then helped the adviser fasten it on. The last strap was only partially buckled when the derro spun and savagely struck Flint across the face. He struck again and again. Flint could no longer see anything very clearly. Pitrick's arm was drawn back for another blow when Flint was surprised to hear Perian's voice.

She had stepped between them. It was evident in her tone that she knew the danger she was risking. "Adviser, this is my prisoner," she said stiffly. "He was brought here for questioning, not to be murdered!"

Pitrick's face distorted monstrously with the fury that consumed him. His pale eyes nearly popped from his skull as he shifted his attention from one to the other. He didn't strike Perian, however. The insane rage melted slowly from the adviser's face, to be replaced by a cruel, cunning smile.

"Yes, the questions." He turned back to the prisoner, who was sprawled half against the wall, half on the floor at the derro's feet. Flint's eyelids were puffed up, and blood ran from a dozen cuts on his forehead, cheeks, and lips.

"You are an interesting case, and vaguely familiar," mused Pitrick. "Such a ferocious assault had to be triggered by something more than the death of one gully dwarf. Who are you? Have we met before?"

Flint spat through his swollen lips, then croaked, "You killed my brother, you maggot meat."

"Your brother . . ." mused Pitrick. "But I'm sure I've killed so many brothers—and sisters, too. Can't you be more specific?" Pitrick asked.

"Given your busy schedule, how many hill dwarf smiths have you struck down with magic lately?" Flint growled bitterly.

"The smith!" Pitrick's face spread in an evil grin of recognition. "How delightful! Yes, I can see your resemblance to that smith now. But you must understand, the hill dwarf was a spy. He poked into places where he didn't belong. I did the only thing I could. And I was quite pleased with the effect—you should be happy to hear that he became very colorful toward the end, though the smell was unpleasant."

"Murdering animal!" choked Flint, twisting helplessly between two guards. Gradually his wits were returning, though he still had trouble seeing. He found he could force his eyelids up with a manageable amount of pain.

"So are you here purely on a mission of vengeance, or are you a spy, too?" Pitrick allowed that question to linger for a moment, then cut it off. "That needs no answer—of course you are. No one but a spy could have penetrated our defenses. Are you a murderer as well?"

"I don't know what you're talking about," Flint growled.

"Oh, please." Pitrick sounded mildly amused. "I'm certain it was you who knifed one of my wagon drivers in Hillhome just days ago. Or if it wasn't you, you certainly know who it was." Pitrick bent close to Flint's ear and whispered, "Give me the murderer's name, and I shall be merciful. I can be, you know."

"I've seen your mercy," sputtered Flint.

Pitrick struck him across the face again, grinning. "Not the full extent of it, dear harrn. And isn't it fortunate for me that whatever tidbits of knowledge you have about our exports will die with you?"

"You just keep believing that," Flint croaked. "You really think I kept such knowledge to myself? By now, half of Hillhome knows that you're exporting weapons, not plows." Flint watched with satisfaction as the hunchback's eyes widened in alarm at his lie. "The Hylar will know about it soon, and then all of Thorbardin!"

"Liar!" shrieked Pitrick. "You will die for this!"

The mad derro grabbed Flint by his jerkin and began dragging him toward the pit. Flint lunged toward Pitrick's throat, but immediately two guards pinned his arms and helped bring him to the ledge. Pitrick quickly jumped away, out of range of Flint's burly arms.

"Throw him in!"

"Stop!" Perian's order froze the guards to their spots; they held Flint poised on the lip of the pit.

"Throw him in!" screamed Pitrick. "I command you to throw him in, now!"

"You are under my command, you take your orders from me," Perian noted coldly.

The guards looked from Perian to Pitrick, unsure who to obey and afraid to take sides.

With a hiss, Pitrick clutched his amulet. Blue light lanced out between his fingers. In a low voice, he snarled, "Your officer is a traitor. Throw her in with the hill dwarf. Throw them both in!"

Under the influence of the savant's charm spell, the guards did not hesitate to comply with the command. The one holding Flint gave him a terrific shove that he could not counter. Dragging his feet along the gravelly ledge, Flint sailed, head first, over the edge. An astonished Perian was hurled over the side, immediately after him.

The sound of laughter echoed from the walls of the cave.

Chapter 10

The Pit

It was late afternoon, and Basalt continued to crouch in the shadow of the great mountain, waiting for his Uncle Flint. That is all he had been doing for the last two days. Every once in a while he would stretch his limbs and peer down the stream toward the tunnel mouth that was obscured by branches, five hundred paces away, hoping for a glimpse of the older dwarf. Each night he had seen one heavy wagon lumber out of the cave shortly after sunset and continue up the road to Hillhome. Before dawn, another one would pass by on its way into the opening.

Afternoon stretched into another cold evening. Bored as he was, Basalt dared not leave the niche to explore the surrounding area. Nor could he risk lighting a fire when night in the Kharolis Mountains descended around him. At least he had some food left in the sack Flint had passed to him. He opened the sack now, finding one ripe red apple, a dry butter sandwich, and a roasted goose drumstick. He gnawed on the succulent leg while he pondered what to do.

Shivering, Basalt wondered when his uncle might emerge. The moon rose, and still there was no sign. The sky above him was velvet black and starry, and the air bitterly cold. The mountains rose so steeply that he could not even look forward to daylight warming this place. The young Fireforge clapped his hands to his arms and trotted in place to keep his blood moving.

Basalt knew he should have left for Hillhome before dark, for he had passed the two-day limit his uncle had set. If I wait just one more hour, he kept telling himself, maybe Flint will return. But Basalt grew more anxious by the minute. Again he looked down the stream at the tunnel mouth. From it he thought he heard the sound of a wagon approaching—it was about time for one to leave for Hillhome—but the noise grew louder and unfamiliar. Puzzled, Basalt cocked his head to listen closely. It was not the steady rolling rhythm of the wheels, but more like clomping feet. Many feet.

A chill of terror ran up his spine as from the mouth of the tunnel marched no less than one hundred mountain dwarves in full regalia. Each wore a steel breastplate, a helmet topped with a bright red plume, and sharp axes and daggers at their waists. After a word from the leader at their head, the mountain dwarves fanned out in all directions. Basalt watched as a detachment of twenty armed dwarves approached, wading through the two-foot stream, right in his direction!

Petrified, the young dwarf threw himself to the ground and curled into a small ball. What should I do? he groaned to himself. Should I run? Should I hide? Is this just a routine patrol, or are they looking for something? Or someone? Maybe they found and tortured Uncle Flint until he told them an accomplice was waiting outside! Even in his frantic state, Basalt knew that that was ridiculous. But with so many dwarves, they were sure to find him. Will they kill me like they did my father? Uncle Flint! Where are you?

Basalt bit at his knuckles, feeling like he was about to jump out of his skin. He couldn't just sit there and wait for them to stumble on him. He turned and scrambled quickly up the narrow gully at the back of his hiding place. A few rocks tumbled down behind him, but he bit his lip and prayed to Reorx that the mountain dwarves would not notice.

"You there! Halt!"

Basalt heard the frantic call behind him, but he just kicked his legs higher and drove himself faster up the twisting gully. He was a good climber, and he knew he had some chance of outrunning them over the steep, craggy slopes.

A loud whistle blew. "The intruder! Get him!"

Basalt did not stop to look back. In the darkness, he was concentrating on finding hand- and toeholds in the dirt and rock, scarcely aware of anything else but his own labored breathing.

He reached a twist in the gully, but instead of following it, he spotted a ledge just above his head that flattened out for a short distance and led into the protection of some man-sized rocks. If he could just get to those rocks, he might have a chance of losing the patrol.

Drawing on strength he did not ordinarily have, Basalt flung himself up and onto the ledge. He broke into a run across the flat, gritty limestone shelf. Legs pumping wildly, he closed with the boulders and threw himself behind one to catch his breath for just a moment. He peered back down to where he had come from and saw no signs of pursuit. Hope blossomed in his heart, but he could not stop yet.

Keeping low, he zigzagged his way through the boulders and on up the mountain. The rocks gave way to a thick grove of pine trees, and he plunged headlong through them over a carpet of dried needles, uncaring of the low, stiff branches that slapped his face, leaving scratches on his cheeks. He could hear nothing but his own footsteps crunching brown needles and his heart pounding in his ears. The stand of trees ended abruptly, and Basalt ran headlong into a moonlit clearing. He skidded to a halt in the dewy grass, looked around, and then all hope died.

He had burst into a gathering of mountain dwarves.

The armed derro were equally surprised to see a hill dwarf in their midst, but they recovered quickly and surrounded him. Basalt counted eight—a smaller patrol than the one he'd dodged below—but, weaponless himself, he knew even one derro guard was more than he could hope to over-power.

"What have we here?" said one of them, stepping out of the circle toward Basalt. The derro's corn-yellow hair stuck out at odd angles, and his unnaturally large eyes reminded Basalt of two pieces of cold black onyx. But the mountain dwarf's skin was what was most disconcerting; its blue pale-ness looked translucent in moonlight.

"Well?" The derro poked Basalt in the chest with the point of a spear. "You're obviously a hill dwarf," he said, taking in Basalt's freckle-tanned face, thin leather vest, and muddy old boots. "We don't like finding hill dwarves near Thor-bardin. What are you doing way out here?"

Basalt willed his knees to stop shaking as he ransacked his mind for a response. "I, uh, I was hunting!" he finished quickly, latching onto the idea. "I'm near Thorbardin?" He let his eyes go wide with innocence. "I guess I got so carried away that I didn't notice where I'd wandered off to."

"What are you hunting at night? You hill dwarves don't see *that* well in darkness," the derro said, eyeing Basalt skep-tically. "And no weapons?"

"Raccoon," the young hill dwarf supplied hastily. "You have to trap 'coon at night, because that's when they come out of their nests."

The derro appeared to be considering Basalt's answer, rocking back on his heels, searching the hill dwarf's face for deception. All he detected was fear.

The soldier's eyes narrowed. "I saw your expression when you came through those trees; something was after you."

Basalt nodded. "I was tracking a raccoon when I saw—" He thought about making up another lie about a bear, but decided to stay close to the truth so he didn't slip up. "I saw another, bigger patrol of dwarves coming my way, and I panicked and ran."

"He's lying, Sergeant Dolbin!" said a voice from behind Basalt.

"Who cares? Let's just kill the hill scum and move on!" said another.

"Yeah, we've got a lot of ground to cover tonight!"

Basalt could sense the circle drawing tighter around him. Suddenly, someone pushed him from behind. The startled hill dwarf stumbled forward only to have the butt of someone's spear jammed into the pit of his stomach. He doubled over, unable to breathe, and another spear shaft thudded across the back of his neck. Gasping, he fell to the ground.

The ring of mountain dwarves erupted in laughter and taunts. "Look out, farm boy, the raccoons are after you!"

"Oooh, here comes one now!" Basalt saw a shape step forward and then felt his rib cage crack as the mountain dwarf's heavy boot crashed into him. The force of the blow rolled him over in the damp grass.

"Get him up," growled another. "I want to knock him down again." Basalt's head cleared for a moment as two pairs of hands lifted him to his feet. Someone slapped his face. He looked up just in time to see a hairy fist smash into his nose. Excruciating pain exploded in his skull as he tumbled over backward, landing in a heap on his left shoulder. The grass was cool and moist, but he also felt something warm and thick running across his ravaged face.

Basalt drew up his knees in an effort to stand, when something forced him back to the ground. A muddy, hobnailed boot pressed down on the back of his neck, grinding the side of his face into the earth. The night sky swam with colors before Basalt's eyes as the dwarves pelted him with kicks and hammered his back and legs with the shafts of their spears. He bit his lip to still his screams, but he could not keep from squirming as the blows only increased. And then, suddenly, they halted.

Basalt felt someone grab him by the armpit and jerk him to his feet. He looked up through the blood streaming down his throbbing face and saw that it was the first derro who had questioned him, Dolbin.

"Now that my men have taught you what happens when you wander where you're not wanted," the sergeant said, holding fast to Basalt's arm, "we're going to have some *real* fun."

Basalt slumped against Dolbin in defeat; he hoped they would kill him quickly, for he had no strength or will to fight left.

Dolbin forced him to stand, then smiled condescendingly. "You'll like my game—I'm going to give you a chance to get away!" Basalt perked up slightly, which was the response the derro sought. "Good, now you're ready to listen.

"The rules are very simple," he began. "We let you go, and then we try to catch you again. We'll give you a one minute lead, of course, to make it sporting."

Basalt's right eye was swollen shut, but he looked up through his good one. "And if you catch me?" he wheezed, agonizing stabs of pain shooting through him from his bruised ribs.

The sergeant shook his head sadly and clucked his tongue. "You really shouldn't dwell on ugly thoughts. But I will tell you what happened to a hill dwarf spy who got caught in Thorbardin just two days ago."

Basalt's heart lurched, and he felt near to fainting from his wounds. But he forced himself to listen to Dolbin's next words.

"How shall I say it?" Dolbin tapped his chin in a mock-sympathetic way. "I've got it! He's been relieved of the burden of being a hill dwarf!" His men hooted with laughter.

Flint's dead. Dolbin could only be speaking of Flint. The news dashed Basalt's last flickering hope and left him more numb than the pounding he'd just taken. He was distantly aware that Dolbin was addressing him.

"—won't ruin the game by giving up already, will you? We'd make death doubly painful for a poor sport," he warned. The derro roughly shoved Basalt through the circle of dwarven soldiers. The hill dwarf fell, struggling again to his feet while the soldiers kicked and jeered at him. Dolbin squeezed Basalt's right shoulder hard and pointed him to the edge of the clearing opposite where he'd burst in.

"Go!"

Basalt felt his legs moving with a will of their own, and he found himself half-staggering, half-running toward the trees.

"Remember, we'll be right behind you!" Dolbin yelled, and his men broke into laughter again.

Basalt stumbled past the edge of the clearing and barely avoided tripping on an overgrown log. He rushed forward, heedless of his path, and more than once crashed into a shadowy tree or lost his feet in a tangle of creepers. Desperately he wanted to stop and rest, or stop and listen for sounds of his pursuers, but he knew he could not—if he stopped, he might never move again. He also knew that he would never hear anything over the sound of his own lungs heaving against his bruised ribs or the blood pounding in his ears.

He ran blindly and nearly senseless, until suddenly the ground gave way beneath him. He stepped out into nothing, and silvery blackness rushed past him. Less than a heartbeat later, Basalt splashed into an ice-cold stream. His throat wanted to scream even while his mind fought to keep control. His chest felt as if it were wrapped in iron bands.

In panic Basalt clawed his way up the muddy bank and lay there shivering, his courage spent. The tiny bit of strength that remained was completely occupied in keeping Basalt from weeping openly. But he swore he would not cry, not even if the derro found him there and chopped him to bits on the spot.

"I know Flint wouldn't cry," he sputtered through clenched teeth. But he could not stop the tears from flowing, for his agony, for his fear and desperation. For his Uncle Flint.

After a few minutes, Basalt hiccupped to a stop. He could hear the sounds of the forest again. His teeth stopped chattering, and the ringing subsided in his ears. He crawled a few yards away from the stream and toward a thicket. There he lay, waiting for the pursuing derro.

Basalt listened for several minutes, but heard nothing.

Could they have lost my trail? he wondered. But he knew that made no sense. Used to life underground, the derro could see even better than him in the dark, and they weren't frightened out of their wits either. He had certainly left a trail that even a child could follow. So where were they?

Either they are toying with me, or . . . or they didn't follow me at all, Basalt thought. Strangely, the first possibility did not frighten him, but the second made him angry. Basalt reflected on the humiliating beating, remembered his bruises and shattered bones, and felt the cuts and scrapes suffered during his wild flight through the forest. He was nothing but a joke to these derro, first a punching bag and then a frightened rabbit to be chased off.

The shame was almost more than he could bear. Exhausted beyond endurance, broken in body and spirit, Basalt lapsed gratefully into unconsciousness.

* * * * *

Flint plunged down the steeply angled, rocky chute, tumbling head over heels, slamming from side to side. He fought to gain some control over the plummet, but could barely discern up from down. Jagged edges of granite tore at his flesh and clothing as his hands groped desperately for anything to grip. Suddenly his short fingers slapped against something long, thin, and hard, and instantly they locked around it. The dwarf growled in pain as his hand slid along the knobby shaft. Dirt and rock rained down on his head as the sudden weight on his handhold loosened sections of the wall. Daring to glance up, Flint saw he had caught an ancient tree root, half buried in the wall of the pit. He clamped his fist around it tighter and clung to the exposed root with all his might and desperation.

His feet met a rocky outcropping as he came to a stop. Expecting the rock beneath him to tear lose under the impact, Flint tightened his grip on the root as he tested the size of the ledge with his toes. To his alarm, it was only six inches deep, albeit three times his girth in width. He pressed his back against the wall and tried to think as he caught his breath.

What now?

That thought was barely formed in his head when something heavy crashed down around his shoulders, flailing and thrashing.

"Help me!"

Stunned and knocked off balance by the weight, Flint nearly lost his grip and tumbled over the edge, but blind instinct locked his fingers around the tree root. In spite of its tone of terror, he recognized the voice of the dwarven frawl guard, although he didn't dare budge an inch to look up.

"I can't hang on—" she squealed as she began to tumble off of Flint's shoulders, windmilling her arms.

"Get your feet on the ledge!" Flint hissed. "Hug the wall!" Flattening himself even more, he grabbed her flapping arms in one hand and held them tightly while she scrambled for footing next to him. Flint guided her hands to the root and together they clung to it, panting from fear and exertion.

After a moment's rest, Flint peered at the frawl. "What are you doing here?" he asked bluntly as he pressed his bleeding cheek to his shoulder. "Trip?" He coughed violently on the dirt in his throat.

"Hardly!" Perian shot back, not daring to move. "I was pushed in behind you by that swine-son, Pitrick. He'll roast on a slow spit for this."

"That's assuming we get unspitted ourselves," Flint responded. "Do you have any idea how far down the bottom is, or how to get out, or what exactly is *at* the bottom?"

"Of course not!" Perian snapped. "It's a beast pit. No one comes down here exploring. No one comes down here at all with any hope of getting out."

A noise from below froze her in place. Her eyes locked onto Flint's.

"I heard it, too." Flint shifted his position to get a better look down into the pit. The old mine shaft twisted and bent as it descended. After a few moments his eyes focused on what he thought must be the earthen floor approximately thirty feet below. As Flint strained to pick out any additional details, the noise—a sort of scuffling, he thought— came again. And a shadow passed below.

Still peering down, Flint asked, "What in the name of

Reorx is that?"

"A killer," Perian replied. "Beyond that, I couldn't say. And I really don't want to find out. I want to wait for my hands to stop shaking and then climb back out of here."

"I don't think that's too likely," Flint said, now scanning the tunnel above. "The sides of this pit are rough but crumbling. Trying to climb out is likely to send you plunging even sooner to the bottom. If we had something to dig handholds with, maybe we could work our way . . ."

Flint's idea was cut off by a scraping sound from below, as if something of great bulk was being dragged across damp rocks. Perian released the root with one hand to clutch Flint's shoulder instead. "I can see it—or something—moving down there," she whispered. "There it is again!"

Flint blinked, trying to focus on the small patch of floor at the bottom of the twisting shaft. He could hear the sound plainly now. It was a dragging, sloshing sort of noise, punctuated with numerous clicks and slaps. Though vaguely familiar, he couldn't quite identify it.

Until the smell reached them. With sickening thickness, the stench of rot and waste rose around them, filling the tunnel. Perian shrank back to the wall as Flint spat, trying to clear the taste from his mouth. "What is it?" groaned the frawl.

"Carrion crawler," answered the hill dwarf. "They eat most anything, as long as it's dead. If it's not, all the better, they have fun killing it. They can climb, too, so I expect it will be coming up." As if on cue, a section of pink and purple flesh passed across the pit floor. A moment later, an enormous green eye stared up at the pair. Glistening tentacles, each more than five feet long, circled a gnashing mouth filled with hundreds of grinding teeth. The head swayed back and forth, into view and then out again. All the while, the stench grew stronger and the noise louder.

"Look for big rocks, maybe we can drive it off," advised Flint frantically, releasing his grip on the root to grope across the ledge and wall. Moments later he had a small pile of fist-sized stones at his feet. "It's not much, but we might slow it down. Aim for its eyes. And whatever you do, don't let those tentacles touch your skin."

"What happens if they do?" whispered Perian, staring at the bobbing head.

"Its venom will paralyze you so it can dine at leisure later. Be careful!"

Flint hefted a pair of rocks. Holding them in one hand, he pried Perian's right hand from the tree root with his other and forced a rock into it. "When I say, give it a taste of stone!"

The feel of the rock in her hand gave Perian something to focus on. She hefted it, turned it over in her palm. A good shot from this could split a steel helmet, the frawl thought. She turned back to the pit, the rock poised above her head.

At that moment the carrion crawler burst into view from behind a twist in the tunnel, its tentacles flashing and writhing toward the ledge. Flint could see most of its segmented body now, twisting along the contours of the wall. A pair of short but thick legs, white and slime-covered, extended from each segment. Each leg ended in a pair of suction cups as big as the dwarf's head. Shreds of rotted flesh from past meals clung to the beast. Bile rose in Flint's throat as revulsion gripped him. The creature was far larger than any other carrion crawler the dwarf had ever seen, or even heard of; it was the grandaddy of all carrion crawlers. Swallowing hard, Flint tightened his grip on the root and hurled the stone. With a crack, it caromed off the shiny head and sailed down the tunnel, unnoticed by its target.

Instantly, Perian's arm snapped forward. The stone plunged straight into the crawler's mouth, disappearing in a tiny shower of tooth fragments. It was impossible to tell whether the beast felt any pain, but the repulsive head made a sort of roar and swung abruptly away from Perian. Though the beast was still at least six feet below them, three tentacles lashed out and wrapped around Flint's right boot. Instantly the leather steamed and hissed, and blisters formed around the ankle. Though protected from real damage by the leather, Flint howled with pain. He snatched up another rock and smashed at the thin, straining appendages. First one, then another, were severed by his ferocious blows. Blue ichor stained the rock ledge beneath Flint's foot.

Perian fired a second stone at the beast, hitting just at the rim of one of its eyes. Enraged, the carrion crawler swung its head out from the wall, dragging Flint's foot from the ledge. Desperately he clung with one hand to the root, groping for any sort of hold with the other. Perian grabbed him by the shoulders just as the monster reared again, and both of them flew off the ledge and out into space. The remaining tentacle around Flint's foot tightened, then snapped in two. Still clutching each other, Flint and Perian bounced and skidded down the length of the beast's segmented back, finally crashing onto a pile of bones on the ground.

Flint groaned as he scrambled to his feet. He seemed unhurt, but his foot, with the fragments of tentacle still wrapped around the boot, seemed to be growing numb.

He glanced around and saw that they were in a cul-de-sac. He could not see how far that cavern extended, but it was the only direction out.

"Quick, we need a weapon of some sort," Flint shouted to the prone frawl. "Don't you have a knife—some weapon?" he gasped.

"I did," she said in a small voice. "But I dropped it."

"You dropped it?" he groaned in disbelief.

"It must have slipped out as I was falling down the chute," she retorted defensively, struggling to her feet.

"Maybe we can find it down here, or anything else. We haven't got much—" Flint's gaze shot up to the wall where the carrion crawler should have been, but the monster had already turned around and was moving toward them "—time! Come on!" He grabbed Perian by the wrist and jerked her into motion.

Scanning the floor as they ran, Flint's eye caught the glint of metal among the rocks and scattered bones littering the carrion crawler's lair. With a kick he churned up a rusty but still solid blade about ten inches long. With his free hand, he snatched it on the run.

"It's gaining!" shrieked Perian. "How fast can that thing move?"

"Faster than us," Flint snorted, glancing backward at their

pursuer. He was horrified to see the creature a scant ten feet behind, and charging fast! In spite of its bulk, the beast moved with alarming grace and fluidity, its numerous legs rippling along its flanks. Then, as Flint watched horrified, the whiplike tentacles shot out and wrapped around Perian's throat from behind, jerking her to a dead stop.

"Gods!" swore the dwarf, skidding into the cavern wall. "Let her go, you stinking worm!" Brandishing the rusty blade, he spun around and stumbled toward the retreating monstrosity. With one hand he grabbed a fistful of Perian's jacket and with the other he slashed across the dripping, rubbery tentacles. Gobs of venom and thick, blue blood hissed through the air, thrown from the thrashing limb. It took a third lightning cut by the tarnished knife before the frawl was released. Flint flung the paralyzed but still conscious mountain dwarf over his shoulder and retreated, moving backward to keep his face toward the beast. It seemed momentarily stunned by its injury, though Flint knew it had too little brain to yield to any opponent.

But for the moment, it had something else to think about. Food, in the form of its own tentacles, had fallen at its feet. Flint gazed in disbelief as the horror gulped down the grisly bounty of itself. The hill dwarf turned and bolted once more into the cavern, only too aware that so far only luck was keeping him alive.

This might be the last thing I ever do, Flint caught himself thinking as he raced through the darkness. And I'm not doing it very well, he added as his benumbed ankle crumpled beneath the combined weight of him and Perian. Frantically he pulled himself up on the wall and, dragging both Perian and his own foot, continued deeper into the lair of the creature.

Or he would have, had the cavern not abruptly narrowed to a point and then stopped completely. His escape route blocked by solid rock, Flint dropped Perian to the floor. Her eyes, peering helplessly at him, were filled with unaccustomed terror. Flint looked away, then readied the humble blade he'd picked up. With a rueful chuckle he said aloud, "I'm naming you Happenstance, little knife, for whatever it's worth. You stand between us and perdition. I hope you're up to it."

As he turned to face the approaching carrion crawler, a flash of light from a fissure in the wall caught Flint's eye. With no hesitation, he hefted Perian's limp form and crammed her head first into the crack in the rock, wherever it led. He pushed her forward as far as possible, but then she wedged in and Flint could not budge her. "Forgive me, Perian," he muttered as he put his shoulder to her ample seat and heaved with all his might. The frawl inched forward, and then suddenly, as if something ahead was tugging on the other end, she zipped forward and out of sight. Startled, Flint tried to twist his neck up for a look through the hole, but a pair of hands grabbed him by the red trim on his tunic and dragged him, too, through the breach in the wall.

Flint crawled to his knees and saw Perian laying on the ground before him. He looked up.

Sporting an idiotic grin and a self-important posture was the filthiest pot-bellied creature the hill dwarf had seen in a long time.

"I'll be hanged!" Flint exclaimed. "A gully dwarf!"

"What you doing there? Monster get you," the gully dwarf said simply, scolding them with a click of his tongue.

"No kidding," chuckled Flint. "Where are we now?"

The gully dwarf beamed proudly. "You in Mudhole!"

Chapter 11

Mudhole

WHEN HE CREATED THE WORLD, REORX THE FORGE, A GOD
of neutrality who strove for balance between good and evil,
needed men to help Him with His work in this new land. For
many years the humans worked happily under the loving
guidance of Reorx, the master of creation and invention.
But the men became proud of their skills, as men will, and
they used them for their own ends. Early in the Age of Light,
four thousand years before the Cataclysm forever altered
the face of Krynn, Reorx became angered by this and trans-
formed some men into a new race. He took from them the
crafts He, upon the anvil of His immortal forge, had taught,
leaving only their burning desire to tinker and build, invent
and construct. He made the stature of this new race, known

as gnomes, as small as their goals.

The evil Hiddukel, the patron god of greedy men, was pleased by this because He knew the forging god had worked long and hard to make order out of chaos, and now the balance of god and evil was not being maintained. Hiddukel went to another of the neutral gods, Chislev, and, seeking to make mischief, He convinced Him that neutrality could not be maintained since evil was losing position. Their only hope, He said, was for neutrality to seize control. To that end, Hiddukel persuaded Chislev, who in turn persuaded His fellow neutral god, Reorx, to forge a gem that would anchor neutrality to the world of Krynn. A large, clear gray stone of many facets, it was designed to hold and radiate the essence of Lunitari, the red moon of neutral magic. And on that same moon it was placed.

Reorx, although still angry at the gnomes, loved them and could see how they might yet serve Him. He presented to them a plan for a Great Invention that would be powered by a magical stone: the gray gemstone. As only the gnomes could, they built a mechanical ladder that lifted itself into the sky and to the red moon itself. With a magical net given to him by Reorx, a gnome appointed by Reorx climbed to the top of the ladder and captured the Graygem for the Great Invention. But when he returned to Krynn and opened the net, the stone leaped into the air and floated quickly off to the west. Fascinated, most of the gnomes packed up their belongings and followed it to their western shores and beyond. The gem's passing caused new animals and plants to spring up and old ones to alter form overnight. Instead of anchoring neutrality, the gem made the pendulum of good and evil swing more rapidly than before. That is when Reorx knew He and Chislev had been tricked.

During many years of searching for the gem, the gnomes split into two armies. Both armies' searches led them to a barbarian prince named Gargath, who, seeing it as a gift from his gods, had plucked the marvelous gem from the air and placed it in a high tower for safekeeping. Gargath refused the groups' demands for the gem, so they both declared war on the barbarian prince.

After many abortive siege attempts, the gnomes finally penetrated Gargath's fortress. Both sides were amazed to see the gem's steel gray light suddenly fill the area with unbearable brightness. When anyone could see again, the two factions of gnomes were fighting each other. One side was filled with lust for the gem, the other side was curious about it.

Under the power of the gem, the gnomes changed. Those who coveted wealth became dwarves. Those who were curious became the first kender. These new races spread quickly throughout Ansalon.

As their mountain and hill dwarf cousins were always quick to point out, gully dwarves were the result of intermarriage between dwarves and gnomes. Unfortunately, the members of this new race lacked all the better qualities of their ancestors.

Seeing the result, dwarven and gnomish societies banned this sort of intermarriage, and members of the new race were driven out, most vehemently by dwarves. Forced to grub for existence among abandoned ruins and the refuse piles of cities abandoned after the Cataclysm, the gully dwarves were free to develop their own culture—or lack of it. Named Aghar, or "anguished," humans later nicknamed them "gully dwarves," noting their poor living conditions and the general disgust felt toward them by nearly every other race on Krynn.

Such was the lot of some three hundred Aghar living in Mudhole. Before the Cataclysm, Mudhole had been a thriving, productive mine, supplying the forges of Thorbardin above with rich iron. But that continental catastrophe had sent sheets of rock crashing into the shafts, cutting off all but one long tunnel that led back into Thorbardin. Even that one was pitched so that it was now nearly vertical and impossible to climb: it was this that the derro called it the Beast Pit.

But some good came of the Cataclysm, at least for the Aghar of Mudhole. Most of the dwarven-dug tunnels remained intact, and in some places actually intersected with stunningly beautiful organic caverns cut by centuries of water that ran through the mountains of Thorbardin.

The three hundred gully dwarves that inhabited Mudhole were broken down into family units; they lived in the ends of abandoned, dead-end shafts, but shared the four natural caverns as common space. They had "decorated" their homes with family heirlooms, such as petrified animals, and other bits of treasure garnered from the garbage piles of Thorbardin above. Thus, Mudhole was at once a natural wonder and an appalling pigsty.

*　*　*　*　*

"They can't really expect us to sleep in here, can they?" Perian moaned, pacing anxiously.

Nomscul, the gully dwarf who had rescued them from the Beast Pit, had led them here and left them, saying he would return shortly with food and some friends. Perian fingered the tattered edges of the filthy woolen blanket that was draped over a legless wooden chair. She disdainfully nudged an old bone on the dirty stone floor with a toe of her boot. Shivering, the mountain dwarf hugged herself and looked around in despair for someplace suitable to sit.

The perfectly square chamber had two doorways and was perhaps twenty feet square. It had been chipped out of solid granite, for the bites the pick-axes had taken could still be seen in the cold, gray-green stone walls. Thick, moldy old support beams crisscrossed the ceiling in no apparent pattern, or perhaps a few had been removed by the gully dwarves for other purposes. Indeed, some chairs and small tables looked to be hastily constructed of the same stout beams. Small rugs; worn, hairless animal skins; and the occasional piece of fine silk or rich but filthy lace, all but covered the floor.

Broken stoneware pots, sundry rodent skeletons, rusty weapons in various states of ill-repair, dozens of candles burned to an inch, bent utensils, one half of a hand-held fire bellows, a canoe filled with holes, a stringless lute, and a dwarf-high pile of unmatched shoes and boots rounded out the adornments.

Reclining on the big, soft bed of burlap-covered moss, Flint picked at his teeth absently with a splinter of wood. He chuckled at Perian's discomfiture. "I've slept in worse."

He watched her flit about the room apprehensively, virtually tearing off the whites of her nails. "Can't you relax for one moment?" he asked, putting down his toothpick. "I'll admit the accommodations aren't the best, but they're only temporary. Not ten minutes ago I was carrying you and limping for our lives from—well, you know what from. At least we're safe until I can get someone to show us the way out of here."

The first thing Flint intended to do after that was to let his nephew, whom he'd left waiting outside Thorbardin, know he was all right. Basalt would be plenty worried by now.

Perian whirled about, perspiration alluringly curling the ends of her coppery hair. She fixed him with an icy glare. "And what's that supposed to mean?" The mountain dwarf chewed the end of another nail off with her teeth, her eyes, like daggers, piercing his. "You think just because I suffered a little temporary fright paralysis I can't take care of myself?"

"A *little* paralysis? You were like a sack of flour!" Flint caught the embarrassed look in her eyes and held up his hands in mock surrender. He laughed. "Sorry if I assumed command. I forgot I was talking to a soldier. I'm used to ordering around youths and barmaids," he explained, thinking of his friends in Solace. He coughed uncomfortably when he saw her bemused face. "I didn't mean that the way it sounded! I have these friends—oh, never mind!" he exclaimed, unused to explaining himself. He rubbed his face, turned onto his side, curled up into the moss bed, and closed his eyes.

"You aren't going to sleep, are you?"

He opened one eye. "I thought I might until that Aghar brought some food, yes." He closed his eye again.

"But how can you sleep after what we've just been through?" she squealed, her fists clenched tight at her sides.

Flint sighed heavily, sat up, and looked at her through half-lidded eyes. "That's precisely why I need the sleep. I'm exhausted! In the last few days I've been pushed and punched and kicked and chased and dropped down a pit.

Every muscle and bone aches; the only thing holding me together is my skin! Do you think my face usually looks like this?" he asked, holding a cracked and swollen hand to his puffy lips, nose, and black eye. "Adventures always drag me out." He covered a yawn with the back of his thick, callused hand.

Perian looked astounded. "You mean you've had this sort of thing happen to you before?"

He blinked. "Sure, though the situation has become considerably more complicated than your average dungeon crawl. Don't tell me you haven't?"

"I'm the captain of the thane's guard, for Reorx's sake!" she said despondently. "I train troops for parade maneuvers and theoretical fighting, and I live in the plushest barrack on the richest level of Thorbardin! I am not accustomed to this!" she said, indicating the cluttered room with a wave of her hand.

He scowled. "So *that's* all it is." Flint punched his fluffy moss pillow and dropped his bushy gray head onto it. "Lay down, take a load off your feet! Mark my words, this place won't look so bad after you've had a good rest."

Perian stopped her fidgeting long enough to run a hand through her damp hair. "That's just it! I can't rest here!" She frowned and looked away, then mumbled, "If you must know, I'm dying for a rolled mossweed!" She resumed pacing.

"I'm sure the gully dwarves have some sort of weed you can smoke if you must," the hill dwarf said in exasperation, his tone telling her what he thought of the habit of smoking dried moss. With that, he turned over again. But he could hear her mumbling behind him.

"I know it's a disgusting habit, but it's the only one—well, one of the only ones I have!" She chewed nervously on a wild hank of her hair. "Some sort of weed, hmm? I'm used to the best dwarven mix from the north warren farms in Thorbardin, and you expect me to smoke any old dried thing?"

Flint yawned. "I don't expect you to do anything on my account but be quiet."

Perian had a retort prepared, when suddenly, from the

doorway straight ahead came the sound of clattering glass and metal and some other unidentifiable noises as well. The mountain dwarf whirled around in surprise, and the hill dwarf shot up angrily.

"What in the—?"

"Nomscul back with eats!" The Aghar popped up in front of Flint, the mud-streaked skin above his scruffy, unshaven chin spread in his usual eager grin.

Nomscul, they had learned, was Mudhole's shaman, the keeper of the clan's relics and lore. He served as its healer and wise man, and was widely regarded as its best cook. He was kind of its beloved leader, more for the cooking than the wisdom perhaps. Nomscul now wore a ratty, smelly wool vest that hung to his knees and was lined with pockets of differing sizes and fabrics. From his belt dangled a red cloth bag cinched with a twine. In his hands was a steaming bowl of something gray and stringy, which he shoved right under the old dwarf's big nose.

Though annoyed at first, Flint was drawn in by the rich, meaty aroma. He took another deep, satisfied breath and accepted the bent spoon Nomscul offered him. "Wonderful!" Flint sighed, barely pausing to speak between mouthfuls. "What is it?"

"Grotto grubs in mushroom mash," Nomscul answered proudly. Flint's spooning rhythm slowed for just a moment. He looked over and saw Perian leaning against a table, first mouthful poised near her waiting lips. Her eyes wide circles of disbelief, she set the spoon down and stared into the bowl.

"You like?" the anxious gully dwarf asked Flint.

The hill dwarf set his bowl down on a table, wiped his mouth on his sleeve, and hopped from the mossy bed. "Yes, Nomscul, it's, uh, very tasty."

Pleased, the gully dwarf patted the potbelly that bulged below his plain, dingy shirt. He bounded for the door. "I get more!"

"Wait!" Flint cried. The gully dwarf stopped and turned around, and Flint came to his side. "Look, Nomscul," he began, searching for the right words, "thanks for, you know, saving us and all, but I really need to be going now."

Perian stepped up next to Flint quickly. "*I'd* like to leave, as well." She scowled at the hill dwarf.

Nomscul's fleshy cheeks bunched up in a full smile. "King and queen want two leaf? Stay here, I be right back!" Nodding to himself, he dashed into the darkness of the stone tunnel beyond.

"Strangely pleasant little fellow," Flint commented. "Probably went to get an escort for us."

"What was that 'king and queen' stuff?" Perian asked, staring after the gully dwarf.

Flint shrugged. "I don't know, probably Mudhole's honorary title for guests." Perian nodded absently.

As they waited for Nomscul to return, Flint circled the room, looking into corners, picking up and examining little bits of gully dwarf treasure. He handed Perian a dirty, broken-toothed tortoise shell comb.

Sitting on the edge of the bed, the frawl dragged the comb's six remaining teeth through her matted hair. "Ouch!" she snarled after one particularly stubborn rat's nest. "I can't wait until I get out of these mud-caked clothes—I can barely bend my knees in these pants!"

Flint raised his eyebrows as a thought struck him. "Say, where do you think you'll be heading when we get out of here?"

"Home, of course," Perian said quickly, picking the dried mud from her pants. "What a question. Where else. . . ?" Abruptly she stopped, sucked in her breath, and clapped a hand to her mouth. "I see what you mean! I can't go back to Thorbardin—Pitrick thinks I'm dead! He'd never let me live now, after what happened at the pit!"

She fell back on the bed in despair. "But where will I go?" she moaned. "Thorbardin is my home, the Theiwar are my clan—I doubt that any other group there would take me! And I don't know how to live anywhere but underground!" She bit off the end of another nail.

Watching her torment, Flint smashed his hand down on a table. "But why would you want to live among such cutthroats, liars, and murderers?"

Perian bristled. "Not everyone in Theiwar City is like Pitrick, you know," she said. "There are more good half-derro dwarves like me, and even many a fine full-blooded Hylar."

"Yeah, the Great Betrayal is a testament to the charity of the blue-blooded Hylar and mountain dwarves in general!" Flint sneered, kicking at a broken pottery shard, sending shattered pieces into the air.

Perian sat up and chuckled without humor. "You think the mountain dwarves were all snug and warm after the Cataclysm? Thousands of dwarves starved to death in Thorbardin, including my grandparents! At least the hill dwarves, used to being above-ground, could forage for food!" She gave a patronizing laugh. "You hill dwarves are such ignorant bigots!"

"At least our people have *something* in common," said Flint evenly. The chamber fell uncomfortably silent.

Perian broke the silence at last, standing up, looking vanquished. "None of that matters anyway, since I can't go back there."

"Don't worry, Perian." Flint clapped her on the back, then felt awkward. He cleared his throat. "You'll probably fit in above-ground better than you think. You aren't like the other Theiwar I've met."

"You don't know the first thing about Theiwar," Perian accused, her eyes blazing with fire again.

"I know one thing—you're a half-derro. You don't look like a derro, or even other Theiwar," he shot back. He crossed his arms smugly. "And I know that no one who thought like a Theiwar would have defended a hill dwarf at the Beast Pit." His eyes narrowed. "Why *did* you do that, anyway?"

Perian squirmed under his scrutiny. "I don't know. For years I've stood by and watched Pitrick abuse everything from Aghar to . . . to me, all for his own twisted amusement. I guess something inside me just snapped today, when I heard what he did to your brother, when I saw that frightened Aghar go over the edge . . . I just couldn't stand by and let something happen one more time."

She snorted. "Frankly, it never occurred to me that he

would push *me* in." Her hands clenched into fists. "Pitrick deserves a long, slow, torturous death."

"He'll get it, the black-hearted bast—" Red-faced, Flint glanced up at Perian. "He'll pay for what he's done to all of us, but especially for Aylmar." Flint snapped a piece of pottery between his thumb and forefinger.

"Who's Aylmar?" Perian asked.

Bitterly, Flint told the tale of his brother's murder. His anger flared, fueled by the frustration of their forced inaction. "Where is that Bonehead fellow?" he roared impatiently.

"Nomscul," Perian reminded him.

"Whatever!" Flint marched to the door and poked his head out.

The little imp abruptly sprang from a corridor to the left, staggering under the weight of a large wooden box. Nomscul elbowed his way past the barrel-chested dwarf and dropped his heavy load unceremoniously onto the dirt floor.

Flint looked in disgust at the box. "What in the Abyss is that?" he bellowed, nearly bowling the smaller dwarf over.

"That two leafs king and queen want!" Nomscul pronounced, happily waving a dirt-caked hand toward the box. Flint and Perian squinted at the container and saw that it did, indeed, contain a sloppy pile of dirty, wet, decomposing leaves. "King find good grubs in there for queen to eat!" Nomscul winked conspiratorially at the hill dwarf.

Flint could see Perian gulp down her disgust. It was with the greatest drain on his limited patience that Flint managed to growl, "We don't want leaves. We want to *go away*, to *get out of here*. Please lead us—or if you're too busy collecting leaves—get an escort to take us to the surface."

"King want a skirt for queen now?" Nomscul was obviously puzzled by this new request. His queen looked dirty enough. Shrugging, he spread his hands wide to measure her thick waist, resolving to find one of the skirts that helped differentiate Aghar frawls from harrns.

"Of course, we don't want a skirt, you ridiculous little worm!" the hill dwarf exploded.

Perian put a hand on Flint's shoulder. "He doesn't understand." Turning to Nomscul, she asked, "How many ways out of Mudhole are there?"

The Aghar wiped his nose with his sleeve. "There one way—" He held up three fingers "—to get out of Mudhole. Beast Pit, garbage run, and big crackingrotto," he said.

"Garbage run?" Perian asked, with a sinking feeling.

"Up in warrens," Nomscul told her. "Get good food from weird-eyed dwarves." The Aghar forced his eyelids open wide with his fingers, then crossed them and giggled.

Seeing Flint's puzzled look, Perian explained. "The gully dwarves raid Theiwar City's dumps and warehouses in the north warrens all the time."

Flint nodded in understanding. "What is the 'big crackingrotto,' and where does it lead, Nomscul?"

"There big crack in wall of grotto, and it go out," the gully dwarf said simply. Nomscul picked a bug from his scalp, inspected it closely, then popped it into his mouth.

"Where is the grotto?" Flint demanded.

"That way." Nomscul chucked a thumb toward the corridor beyond the room. "Past bedrooms of Aghar—lots of Aghar in Mudhole!"

"That's good enough for me," Flint said, taking Perian's arm and pulling her toward the door. "We'll just explore around until we find something that looks like a grotto; Mudhole can't be that big. Come on, Perian."

"Where we go?" Nomscul asked, bouncing at their sides.

Flint did not stop to look at him. "I don't know where you're going, but Perian and I are gonna look for the cracking grotto."

Nomscul looked crushed. He fumbled in a pocket on his right side and pulled out a carved wooden whistle. Placing it between his thick lips, the gully dwarf blew so hard on it that his face turned red. Both Perian and Flint jumped at the unexpected shrill noise. Before either could turn or question, though, they were stampeded from both doorways by running, screaming, jumping Aghar, all talking at once.

"You can tell he king. He got big nose!"

"That your real hair, Queen? Hair not usually come that color!"

"Two chairs for king and queen! Hip-hop hurry! Hip-hop hurry!"

The teeming masses of Aghar flooded in endlessly from the corridors, tearing the astonished Flint from Perian's side. Where were they all coming from? the hill dwarf wondered as he tried to make his way to the door again. On every grubby face was an adoring smile, and each one he squeezed past reached up to touch his hair, her hem. What on Krynn did they all want?

"King getting away!" Nomscul shouted. Suddenly every gully dwarf within ten feet launched himself into the air and onto Flint's back and head, hugging him, squeezing his arms and cheeks as he was crushed to the floor. Someone poked him in his black eye, but the right side of his face was pressed into the cold stone floor and he couldn't even move his mouth to swear at the perpetrator.

"What is going on here?" Perian screamed over the din. Though she had not been knocked to the ground, ten gully dwarves clung to her legs and arms.

The Aghar atop Flint rolled off into a mound of wiggling, flailing limbs, as the hill dwarf struggled to his feet, shaking his head. His face was hot with anger, and he swung about in a wide circle, his fists raised and ready.

"King and queen must stay in Mudhole!" Nomscul announced, standing on top one of the tables to be seen. "The property say so!"

"Pro-per-ty! Pro-per-ty! Pro-per-ty!" The gully dwarves chanted, dancing and whooping and gibbering around their stunned dwarven visitors.

"What are you talking about?" Perian demanded. "What 'property?' "

That all-too-familiar puzzled look crossed Nomscul's face again. Suddenly his eyes narrowed suspiciously. "You testing Shaman Nomscul to see if *he* know!" The gully dwarf squinted in concentration, his eyes sinking into his skull as if he would find the answers there. At last he began to recite in an irritating, singsong falsetto.

King and Queen descend from mud,
Land in Beast Pit with a thud.
Aghar crown them, dance and sing,
And they be king and queen forever.

Nomscul began to hop up and down happily at having passed the test. "That what property say!" The gaggle of gully dwarves once again whooped, gibbered, and bounced around its newly acclaimed monarchs.

"That's terrible!" moaned Perian. "It doesn't even rhyme! And he must mean prophecy, not property."

Flint cast her a stony glance.

"We touch king! We touch queen!" the Aghar chanted, drawing a sloppy circle around the two.

Flint batted away their groping hands. "Stay back!" he growled. "Keep your disgusting paws off of me!" He made one last lunge for the door, but the press of bodies was too thick, and they brought him down again.

"Tie king up!" Nomscul commanded. Dozens of hands lifted Flint from the floor and stuffed him into a rickety chair made of beams. Eight dwarves sat on his thrashing form while Nomscul and a frawl the shaman called Fester ran circles around the chair with two lengths of thick rope.

"Untie me this minute, you miserable dirt-eaters!" Flint flung himself from side to side, sending the chair pitching and making the gully dwarves who clung to him hoot with glee. But the chair did not break, the Aghar did not lose their grips, and Flint remained tied up.

Arms behind his back, Nomscul leaned toward Flint and smiled right into the hill dwarf's scowling face. "*Queen* not running away," he said. Perian stood at the far corner of the room, relatively ignored by the Aghar since she offered no resistance. Her arms were crossed and her hazel eyes regarded Flint expectantly, a small smile about her lips. "Promise to be king, and we cut you loose," Nomscul offered affably in a singsong voice.

Flint hung his head over the arm of the chair and spat on the ground. "Me? King of the gully dwarves? I'd sooner drown!"

Chapter 12

A Cold Domain

Pitrick's twisted foot ailed him mightily; he had been on it far too long today, without the benefit of numbing goldroot salve. The day's events had piled up unexpectedly, leaving him with no time to perform a preventative spell or even to think to use his teleportation ring.

Dragging the clubbed foot behind him even more than usual, the adviser to Thane Realgar was relieved to see the iron door to his apartments, with its gleaming brass hinges and its embossed image of a huge, leering face, looming ahead in the dim torchlight. He hated all torchlight—hated the policy of low-burning flares on all of the public roads and levels in Theiwar City. Through meditation and heightened magic, he was able to see even better without it than most derro. On impulse, he mumbled a single word, "*shival!*" and waved his arm impatiently. For as far as he could see—more than one hundred feet—torches were instantly extinguished, trailing smoke and hissing.

Pitrick's eyes quickly adjusted to the comfortable total darkness. His soft, callus-free, blue-white hand came upon the multifaceted diamond doorknob and, as always, its cool, perfect surface gave him a feeling of tremendous security. A magical blast of lightning struck dead anyone but himself or of his choice who touched the knob. Pitrick had many enemies in Theiwar City and in the neighboring clans who would pay great sums to bring about the savant's demise. A number of them had already died hideous deaths at that very juncture.

But even those fond memories could not lift his foul mood. He stepped into his lightless antechamber and bellowed for his harrnservant.

"Legaer? Damn you, why aren't you waiting at the door for me?" The hunchback shifted his weight to his good foot and counted the seconds before his servant's shadow scurried up to him.

Pitrick backhanded Legaer's face, the points of his teleport ring leaving a bloody trail on the other mountain dwarf's already scarred cheek. "Five seconds delay! I must think of a punishment for such a lazy servant!" Pitrick paused to peer closely at Legaer. "I thought I told you to keep that veil on—it makes me sick to see your deformed face!" The savant wrenched his cape off and tossed it at the servant. "You are lucky to have such a tolerant master, for no one else would suffer your hideous presence!" Pitrick stormed past the dwarf and into his apartment.

Legaer had Pitrick to thank for his repulsiveness. Recruited shortly after the untimely suicide of Pitrick's twenty-third harrnservant, Legaer had felt honored to be asked to serve as important a person as the thane's savant. It was no coincidence that Pitrick always chose as his new servant the most physically appealing of the forgeworkers. Pitrick kept them prisoner in his apartments, using them as slaves and subjects in his magical experiments. If his experiments did not succeed in "accidentally" destroying their appearance, eventually they would be killed or maimed as punishment for some misdeed. They never lasted long; Pitrick grew bored with them once he'd broken their spirit.

"Fetch me a mug of mulled mushale," he ordered the cowed servant who dogged his heels. "And it had better be exactly room temperature this time, or you know the penalty!" Legaer bolted into the darkness. Pitrick made a mental note to think of a new torture, since there was little left to destroy of Legaer's face, and his ears had already been sliced from his head.

Pitrick threw himself onto a stone bench before the unlit hearth in the center of the main chamber. In the peace and total darkness, he began to relax.

He loved his home. It came as near to meeting his high standards as anything in his life ever had, though it had not been without cost. Two decades before, when he had come into power, he had chosen the location of its construction for its seclusion—the third level had not been so popular then—and for the charcoal-gray hue of the granite in that part of Thorbardin. For five years a crew of fifty craftsharrn had chipped and carved the granite to Pitrick's exact specifications; a sleeping chamber, a small galley, an antechamber leading into the main room, and several steps above that an efficient study and laboratory. All furniture—the circular hearth, his bed, the benches in the central chamber, the desk and chair in the study, even the support pillars—were painstakingly carved from the bedrock left intact, so there were no lines or joints to mar the fluidity of the space.

Another crew of fifty had spent ten years working their fingers to the bone, sanding and polishing every inch of granite so that it looked like marble and felt like glass.

Pitrick reminded himself that there was one occasion where he liked light: when the hearth was lit for heat, the orange-yellow flames sent eerie shadows dancing across every shiny surface in his home. Pitrick snapped his fingers and flames instantly licked at the charcoal in the hearth; he kept the blaze just low enough to cast phantom shapes on the walls.

Legaer crept in at last with the mulled drink, his head bent as he held the mushale out to his master. Pitrick snatched it from his servant's hands and then dismissed him with a wave. He was not in a mood to enjoy terrifying the pathetic dwarf today.

Pitrick absently sipped the tepid brew made from distilled balick mushrooms, waiting for its slight hallucinogenic affects to begin. The hunchback believed mushale heightened his senses and allowed him to focus beyond petty distractions and achieve a level of true meditation. Legaer had to be summoned to bring three mugs of the tasteless brew before Pitrick reached the ethereal state that just one usually accomplished.

Pitrick reflected on the possible reasons for this. He knew that it had little to do with his physical exhaustion. If anything, he should require less in his weakened condition. No, he realized, the cause was depression. The spark had somehow gone out of his life, his quest for power suddenly seemed less vital. With a start, he pinpointed the cause.

He had been goaded into pushing Perian Cyprium into the Beast Pit. Everyone else—including the thane, it seemed—bent his will to Pitrick's own so easily. He had clawed his way from his lowly heritage in the bowels of Theiwar City to the exalted position of the thane's adviser. No one had ever liked him, but he was feared and respected for his power, and he found fear and power to be the best tools. Except on Perian.

She alone had resisted him, had, in a sense, bested him.

The hunchback had tried everything he could think of to conquer her—physical abuse, magic, blackmail. But the frawl soldier was stronger than he, and she told him repeatedly that she would rather die than suffer his touch. She was heavily resistant to magic, perhaps because of her Hylar blood; to have her by sorcery would have been a shallow victory anyway.

He had been certain she would succumb to his threats to reveal her half-derro heritage to the thane, for she cherished her position as captain of the guard. But she had called Pitrick's bluff time and again; she sensed her value to him, and knew that he would not seek her banishment from the clan, because it would take her from his grasp. The secret of her power over him only fanned the flames of his desire to master her.

Pitrick had never doubted he would win her, nor realized how much he had lived only for that day. The derro's mushale-laden mind was overcome by an unfamiliar sensation. He had heard others speak of it as regret. He had never lamented a single action in his life, but he was astounded to admit to himself that he actually regretted being forced to push Perian into the pit and out of his life.

The responsibility lay entirely with the odious hill dwarf, and with Perian herself for going too far and being foolish enough to defend him. The look of admiration she'd given the other dwarf, when she'd never viewed Pitrick with anything but thinly disguised loathing, had driven the savant to the brink of insanity. Surely it was all her fault. But for once blame seemed less important to Pitrick than the fact that Perian was dead, beyond his sphere of domination. He would never possess her, never see her shivering at his feet as Legaer did. And never was a long, long time.

Just then the servant stole into the room with another mug of spirits. The disfigured dwarf treasured these times of meditation, strove to lengthen them with drink, because only then did the persecution of logic cease. Afterward . . . the old pleasures always returned with vigor.

Legaer quickly placed the mug under his master's hand, careful not to disturb the trance nor to signal his activity in any way.

But Pitrick did sense his loathsome harrnservant's presence, and it gave him an idea. A brilliantly heinous idea. His hand flew out to grab the petrified servant by the throat. Mushale heightened Pitrick's strength, and he easily lifted the dwarf off the ground, as easily as if he were a bug.

"Perhaps there is still a way to get Perian back. Yes! I have the solution. And she could be my servant. Of course, that position is already filled."

Legaer's eyes bulged from his head in terror. Pitrick smiled as he twisted the dwarf's neck until it snapped and the eyes rolled closed.

"But now it's vacant."

The savant casually dropped the dead dwarf onto the polished floor, stood, and stepped around the body. He picked up the filled mug, then set it back on the table again; any more ale and he might have difficulty concentrating on a spell to raise Perian from the dead.

*　*　*　*　*

Nomscul took the bag from his belt and slapped it in Flint's face, sending a cloud of dust up the hill dwarf's nose. Flint coughed and sputtered and cursed. "What are you trying to do, you darn fool, choke me with dirt?"

Mudhole's shaman looked surprised. "That not dirt, that magic! Why you not be spellstruck like Aghar?" He thought about that for a moment. "I know, that prove you king! Nomscul no can magic king!"

Flint considered Nomscul's stubbornly resolved expression with exasperation. "You can't *force* someone to be your king!" He strained futilely against his bonds.

But the gully dwarf's square jaw remained set. "It not I. It property. It fate. You must give in."

"But it's not *my* fate," Flint insisted, "because your prophecy is not my concern!"

Nomscul suddenly looked crestfallen. "You mean you no want to be our king? It great honor. We wait long time for you to come—since before Nomscul be Nomscul!"

Lower lip quivering, Nomscul pulled the rusted blade from a hiltless dagger and a mold-encrusted pendant from the pockets inside his furry vest and held them toward Flint. "If you not king, who get treasures Aghar save since Kittyclawsem? Who be our saver?" The room erupted into a symphony of wailing, moaning, sobbing, and shrieking gully dwarves, who threw themselves to their knees and pounded the ground in despair.

"Oh, for crying out loud, stop that infernal screeching!" Flint yelled. The room fell instantly quiet, and all eyes turned to him.

Including Perian's. Flint had all but forgot her in his desperation to escape. Suddenly the hill dwarf saw himself as she must see him, strapped to the chair, and he felt more foolish than angry. Enough was enough.

Flint regarded Nomscul, who was tapping his chin. "I have an idea. It's so much fun to be your king, that I've decided I'd like you to have the fun, too. I'm going to make *you* king for a day."

But instead of whooping with joy, the gully dwarf looked insulted. "Property no work that way," he said solemnly. "I no drop from mud chute with queen."

Flint would have rubbed his own face in frustration if he could have reached it. He considered his options. He could stay tied to the chair and try to outlast their attention spans. However, these Aghar seemed a tenacious lot, and patience was not one of his virtues. Why can't I be their king for just a while? he asked himself. He had no burning commitments, except to avenge Aylmar's death. It would take some planning to infiltrate Thorbardin and reach Pitrick; maybe these insufferable Aghar could be some help.

Was it truly fate that he and Perian had fulfilled the Aghar's prophecy? It was certainly one weird coincidence.

"Let me loose," he growled suddenly, his voice barely above a whisper. "I'll be your king."

"Huh?" said Nomscul, blinking in surprise.

"I said, I'll be your king," Flint repeated more loudly.

Nomscul looked suspicious. "You promise? You won't run away?"

Flint rolled his eyes. "I promise on my honor as a Fireforge that I will be your king and not run away."

Nomscul squinted in concentration. "For how long?"

Flint sighed. "A promise is a promise! For as long as you need me."

"And I'll be your queen," Perian said, stepping forward, smiling at Flint with a twinkle in her eye. He gave her a wink.

A cheer went up in the room and spread to the rest of the Aghar waiting in the hall.

"Get crown! Get crown!" Flint saw the crowd passing something forward, until the object was placed in Nomscul's hands. The gully dwarf shaman held forth a jagged metal crown and placed it proudly on Flint's sweat-soaked gray hair. The cold metal ring immediately slipped over the hill dwarf's eyes, forward off of his face, and fell with a "tink!" to the dirt floor. Nomscul quickly replaced it, and just as quickly it slid down Flint's head again, bounced off the arm of the chair, and flew through the air.

"Gee, a game! Crowntoss!" Nomscul giggled into Flint's face. "You one fun king!" He jammed the crown back on his king's head.

Flint screamed. "Not points down, you moron!" Nomscul hastily yanked it off and righted it.

Not a bad fit. Looked okay too, Flint decided. "Now, untie me!" The room was a flurry of gully dwarves trying to comply with Flint's wishes, some pulling on the ropes, a fair number trying to gnaw through them with their teeth. At last the bonds fell away and Flint stood up, rubbing his wrists and legs.

The Aghar were in a delirious frenzy; their "saver" had arrived. Nomscul whistled for attention. "Shudduuuuub!" he screamed, but no one was listening. Frowning in irritation, the shaman snatched the red bag from his belt and clapped it hard, sending a cloud of dust over the gully dwarves, who fell silent, as if under a spell. "See," he said, giving Flint a smug look. "I told you it magic."

He turned back to the gathering. "We plan crownation party for—" His eyes shifted from left to right as he searched his mind. "What your names?" he whispered to Flint and Perian. They quickly told him. "Party someday soon in Big Sky Room for King Flunk II, and Queen Furryend! I cook big food and everyone dance!" Most of the gully dwarves streamed like lemmings from the room to begin the preparations for the upcoming festivities.

Though even Perian had to laugh at Nomscul's mangling of her name, her face fell at the mention of his cooking. She quickly pulled Flint to the side. "Let's tell him to send Aghar up to the north warrens for some *decent* food, not the garbage pile they usually raid. I can tell them exactly what to get and where to get it." Her face brightened further. "Say, they could even get some mossweed, couldn't they?"

"Isn't a raid into Thorbardin risky?" asked Flint.

"The Aghar do it all the time," replied Perian. "I'll just tell them to be a bit more selective."

Flint decided her suggestion was a good one and had Nomscul dispatch two gully dwarves to the warrens with Perian's specific instructions in hand.

It was such a good idea, in fact, that Flint decided to send two more Aghar out, this time through the "big crackin-grotto," as Nomscul pronounced it, to resolve his most pressing concern: Basalt. His nephew must surely have returned to Hillhome by how, and probably thought his uncle was a goner. From Nomscul, Flint had a rough idea of where the "big crackingrotto" emerged from Mudhole into the Kharolis range; probably about a stone's throw from the western tip of Stonehammer Lake. Flint personally selected two young harrns named Cainker and Garf, and gave them his best guess for directions to Hillhome, as well as a thorough description of Basalt.

Flint stuffed a hastily scrawled note into the pocket of Cainker's vest. "Bring this to my nephew," he instructed as he sent them on their way. "It will tell him I'm safe." He had no real hope that they would succeed, but it was worth a try.

Thrilled at the prospect of some mossweed, Perian had allowed herself to be swept away by some frawls, who wanted to gussy her up for the festivities. Thus, Flint, his first kingly duties attended to, and left alone, finally fell to undisturbed sleep.

* * * * *

Beads of perspiration joined the streaks that flowed down Pitrick's temples, pooling above his lips. His thick tongue licked the sweat away unconsciously, since he was intent on the heavy, leather-bound tome beneath his eyes. The savant was seated behind the burnished granite desk that rose out of the floor in his cozy study to the right and three steps above the main chamber. To his left and flank were floor-to-ceiling shelves filled with heavy, bound books, faded scroll cases, a beaker of teeth, patches of fur, a harpy skull, an ivory ogre tusk, quill pens and ink bottles, ground toenails, a flask containing the breath of seven babies, and other assorted dried ingredients. The shelves to his right were reserved for bottles filled with raw components of every imaginable color, odor, and viscosity, including frog glands in phosphorescent swamp water, golden griffon blood, red-hot lava, the sweat glands of a bugbear, mercury, giant slug spittle, and rendered virgin rattlesnake.

Pitrick scanned the last page of the spellbook, the soft, fleshy tip of his index finger tracing the words. Frowning, he slapped the book shut on its front and looked up to stare into the flames in the hearth.

He would have to use his wish scroll. The spells to animate the dead, resurrect a corpse, or clone someone all required the *dead body*, or at least part of it. The savant also considered forcing Perian to reincarnate, but there was no way to control or predict the subject's new form, and Pitrick had no use for Perian as an insect. Besides, it, too, required *the body*.

A half-day's research had led the derro to choose one of the most simple spells there were. No bulky, disgusting, or hard-to-find components, no long incantations to memorize, no pyrotechnics to awe observers. Wishes seldom failed to be incarnated—*something* always happened—though casters often did not get what they thought they'd asked for. That was because the exact meaning of their words was always carried out, and they had not paused to consider the precision of their language.

A wish also carried a heavy price: it instantly aged the caster five years, whether he chose to summon a bowl of gruel or a copper-haired frawl back from non-existence. But that was a small price to pay for someone with a dwarf's long life expectancy.

The savant turned to his shelves and sorted through the piles of scrolls until he found the one he wanted: a fragile roll of parchment edged with faded red ink. It was the greatest treasure he had discovered among his mentor's belongings after he had poisoned the old wizard many years before. Pitrick had been saving it for a special occasion, and his fingers hesitated before he tugged the ends of the satin ribbon that held it closed. He had to carefully phrase his wish before he opened the scroll and unleashed its power.

Slipping it under his arm, he paced around the narrow space surrounding his desk to position himself in front of the hearth, the pain of his foot momentarily forgotten.

"What exactly do I want?" he said aloud. "I want her alive, my prisoner, and as beautiful as she was before she was devoured by the beast." He stopped, and his eyebrows raised with a fanciful notion. "I could bring her back submissive, or even adoring of me!" He shook his head. "No, that would not be Perian, and I would not have the challenge of taming her, nor enjoy her hatred of my power over her. And that is everything!"

Pitrick stepped around a support pillar and over the dead body of his former servant to pick up the mug filled with mushale. He took a only a sip to rinse his mouth, then spat the distilled brew into the fire. Tongues of flame shot up, nearly licking the ceiling vent, sending more shadows dancing in the smooth chamber. Now the formidable derro savant was ready.

Taking the scroll from under his arm, he untied the strings and gently unfurled the parchment. This was a momentous occasion, and Pitrick stood as straight as his hunched back would allow. Holding the scroll open before him, he closed his eyes and mouthed the phrase he had practiced in his mind.

"I wish Perian Cyprium to be raised from the dead, restored to her former beauty, here before me, powerless to leave my apartments, and unable to kill herself or me. That is my wish." Pitrick opened his eyes.

A howling wind arose from nowhere and swept through the flawlessly polished rooms, dashing papers from the desk, dousing flames, sucking the parchment from his hands. Pitrick clung to a nearby support column and waited for the spell's effects to subside.

Slowly, very slowly, the wail of the wind dropped to a gentle breeze. And then the air became as still and as cold as death. Then, nothing.

The savant did not need to look for Perian in the other rooms of his apartment. He could sense—knew with chilling certainty—that Perian was not there. He stood rooted to the spot, his fists clenched, fingernails slicing the flesh of his palms.

Somehow Pitrick knew that he was indeed five years older.

But for some strange reason that he could not fathom, the spell had failed.

Chapter 13

Death of a Friend

"Gimme another one," Basalt mumbled, sliding his empty mug toward Moldoon. The young dwarf smacked his lips and reflected that the ale didn't taste as sweet as it once had. But no matter.

The human reluctantly filled the heavy tankard, but cast a sad, pained looked at Basalt as the dwarf raised it to his lips and chugged noisily, ignoring the foam splashing onto his beard. Basalt set the mug down heavily, disappointed that somehow the draught did not bring him more pleasure.

"Take it easy with that," cautioned Moldoon.

The man's normally genial tone carried an undertone of genuine rebuke when he spoke to Basalt these days. Moldoon grew more and more concerned by the behavior of the young hill dwarf. Moody and irresponsible after his father's death, the youth had grown sullen beyond compare in the weeks since his Uncle Flint had left town.

Since his return from the Theiwar tunnel, Basalt had spent all his time drowning himself in self-pity. A new hatred of the mountain dwarves for the murder of his father and uncle, combined with a hopeless feeling of inadequacy, had left him feeling trapped. He did not feel he could trust anyone and he knew that no one would believe him, with his cockeyed story of Flint's disappearance and Aylmar's murder. He was, and always would be, an abject drunk.

"Say," ventured the innkeeper, as Basalt started on the last half of his mug. "Hildy's got to make her deliveries this evening. I happen to know she could use some help. . . ."

"Hah! She'd have nuthin' to do with me!" The scorn in Basalt's voice, Moldoon sensed, was directed inward, at the dwarf himself.

"Well, she sure won't if you keep treating her as badly as you do yourself! And neither will I!" snapped Moldoon. He turned to take the orders of other customers while Basalt watched the foam melt along the inside of his mug.

Finally he got up and shuffled to the door, stepping outside to look at the long, brown strip of the Passroad. Snow, colored red and purple by the fading twilight, covered the surrounding hills in a pristine blanket that contrasted sharply with the muddy blotch of Hillhome.

Once the dwarven community might have slumbered peacefully under winter's cloak, its residents content to await the coming of spring. But now it was just past the early winter sunset, and the town churned with energy in the chill darkness. Hammers pounded at forges, horses hauled their wagons through deep, sticky mud, merchants eagerly readied their wares for sale to the derro preparing to return to Thorbardin.

Basalt thought about going home, but the picture of his stern Uncle Ruberik stopped him. Ruberik never ceased berating Basalt about drinking. In fact, the ruder the young dwarf got, the more persistent the elder became about nagging. The family home, a guilt-ridden shell since his father's death, seemed like a nest of enemies now, and Basalt couldn't face it.

So Basalt sat on the wide steps of Moldoon's, mindless of the icy wind that blew through the valley. In a way, given his bleak mood, the chill wind almost seemed a friend, sharing his troubles and misery.

As Basalt sat with his chin in his hands, staring down the street, he saw a small, familiar wagon churning up the muddy lane. As Moldoon had predicted, Hildy was bringing more kegs from the brewery. For a brief second his mood brightened at the sight of the frawl, but then he sullenly reminded himself of Hildy's subtle hints and not-too-subtle encouragements to apply himself to some endeavor—any endeavor, to use her own words—more useful than sitting at Moldoon's bar. Feeling positively childish, Basalt got up from the steps and ducked around the corner so that he would not be seen.

His humiliation told him to slip down the alley and keep walking, but his heart told him something else, something that held his stride in midstep. Closing his eyes, Basalt leaned against the nearest wall and wondered, through his cloud of ale, why he wanted to flee in panic from someone he had known and been friends with all his life. Indeed, he remembered with a twisted smile, Hildy had given him his first—and only—kiss.

"Reorx curse it!" he growled, scowling at the darkness of the world. Shaking his head to clear it, he stepped back around the corner just as Hildy reined in the horses before Moldoon's.

"Hello, fair brewer's daughter," he said with a gallant bow. Straightening into his best cocky pose, he smiled up at her on the buckboard. "Can I give you a hand?"

Hildy reached out and let him lift her down from the wagon. "Excuse my staring," she teased, "but I once knew someone like you. And a fine fellow he was—or should I say, is?" She gave him a wink. "I'd appreciate the help. Let me just run inside and check Moldoon's order."

Basalt watched her pass through the doors. Now he was suddenly happier than he would have believed possible a few minutes earlier. Whistling absently, he prepared to unload the heavy barrels. Two long planks in the wagon served as a ramp, and he lowered one of these, anchoring its base firmly in the muddy street. As he dragged the other plank out the back of the wagon, his fingers slipped and it dropped to the ground, splashing mud and a wave of brown water across his boots and pants. But Hildy's reaction to him had so lifted Basalt's spirits that he just chuckled at his own clumsiness.

Someone else on the street was not in such a generous mood.

"Hey! Hill dwarf!"

Basalt looked up, surprised, into the snarling face of a derro guard. His straw-colored hair stuck out of his head at sharp angles, and his pale skin showed a blue vein flexing in his forehead.

"You clumsy sot! You splashed your stinking Hillhome muck all over my boots!" accused the Theiwar.

Basalt straightened, ready to bluster an insult at the belligerent dwarf when he remembered that Hildy would emerge from Moldoon's in another moment. Wanting nothing more than to avoid trouble and impress Hildy, he muttered, "I'm sorry. It was an accident." The apology caught in his throat, but at least it was done.

Basalt turned back to the wagon only to be yanked around by a heavy hand on his shoulder. "Accident!" bellowed the derro. "You're a liar! I saw you take deliberate aim at my boots. Now, you can clean them!"

The derro was stocky and well built, as tall as Basalt and wearing a chain mail shirt, heavy, iron-knuckled gauntlets, and a helmet. A short sword was girded to his waist. By contrast, the hill dwarf was weaponless and unarmored. He knew that the Theiwar, if provoked, could and would slay him with a single thrust.

His face burning, Basalt considered his options. Out of the corner of his eye he saw Hildy and Moldoon step from the inn, drawn by the commotion.

"You heard me—clean them!" growled the mountain dwarf.

"Get your mother the hobgoblin to do it!" Hildy piped in, her eyes smoldering with indignation as she stomped toward them.

By now, a small group of dwarves had gathered on the street, watching the confrontation warily.

Basalt saw the derro's mad, glaring eyes swing toward the young frawl. Suddenly, the most frightening thing in the world was not the threat to himself but the fear that Hildy might step between them, humiliating him beyond all capacity for endurance. Or, even worse, that she might get hurt.

"Not even a mother hobgoblin would claim this lump of flesh," Basalt growled, commanding the derro's attention again. Their gazes met, full of hate, and locked like horns.

"A hobgoblin wouldn't let a woman do his fighting for him, either," sneered the derro. "Though this one looks like she could distract me for a couple of hours, with the right enticement."

The derro's leering face was more than Basalt could stomach. With an animal growl he leaped at the mountain dwarf, his fingers clutching for the arrogant Theiwar's throat. The derro reacted quickly, crashing his mailed fist into Basalt's face. The hill dwarf dropped to the street, slumping down in the muddy ruts. His cheek throbbed, and when he pressed a hand to his face it came away covered with blood.

Choking on his rage and frustration, Basalt jumped to his feet and charged the derro again. He lowered his head and drove it into the derro's gut. The Theiwar stumbled back slightly, surprised by the force of the blow. But then he laughed as Basalt staggered away, clapping his hands to his throbbing scalp where he had just collided with the chain links of the derro's armor.

"Now get on your knees, hill dwarf, and clean my boots!" cackled the derro, stepping forward.

But the tall figure of Moldoon moved between them.

"That's more than enough." The human stared down at the Theiwar, an expression of loathing and anger working across his face.

"What're you doing, old man?" demanded the derro,

stepping backward and glaring.

"Get out of here, before this goes too far," warned Moldoon. He raised his hands, as if to push the derro away from the fallen Basalt.

But the mountain dwarf's eyes grew even larger as the man came toward him. In a flash he drew his sword, shouting, "I will decide how far this goes! I will show you how the Theiwar gain respect!"

The keen tip of the short sword shot forward, slicing through the innkeeper's apron and shirt and punching neatly, deeply between his ribs. Moldoon stepped backward, his hand clutched to his chest. He looked down in disbelief as a crimson flower blossomed on his apron, spreading its life-colored petals beneath his clenched fingers.

Basalt, still reeling from the blow to his head, watched in a daze as Moldoon wobbled, then collapsed with a splash into the muddy street. Hildy cried out and leaped to his side, cradling the stricken human's head in her lap.

Seeing Moldoon lying in a heap, his unfocused eyes staring into the sky, his mouth moving without making any sound, turned Basalt's blood to ice. Snatching up the heavy plank that had set off the whole encounter, he swung it with more strength than he normally possessed. The derro, still holding the steel blade slick with blood, tried to twist away but the board caught him on the hip and sent him sprawling. The short sword sailed from his hand and landed pointdown in the muck, with the handle above the water. Basalt dove toward it. But before he could reach it, a heavy body slammed into him from the side and pushed him back down to the street.

"Stop it!" snarled Tybalt, inches from his nephew's face as Basalt struggled in the mud beneath him. "There's been enough killing in this town—we don't need a hanging on top of it all."

Basalt writhed desperately, still reaching for the leering derro as other hill dwarves helped Tybalt restrain him. He lunged again, spitting sounds that did not resemble words.

"That's enough!" growled his uncle more firmly. Three

other dwarves held Basalt so tightly he could barely move at all, however much he struggled.

The constable turned back to the derro, who was standing again with his hand on the hatchet at his belt. "You're coming with me," he said, "as soon as you hand over that weapon. You'll be staying, courtesy of the town."

Tybalt indicated the town hall, half a block away, which included Hillhome's single jail cell.

The derro started to object but, apparently, something in Tybalt's eyes stopped him. Also, by that time the crowd around them had grown to several dozen or more onlookers, all hill dwarves. Some of them clucked with dismay at the sight of Moldoon's lifeless body, though none stepped forward to offer comfort to the weeping Hildy.

With a shrug, the Theiwar dwarf picked up his short sword, wiped off the blood, and sheathed his blade. Unbuckling his belt, he handed it to the constable.

"But he . . . Moldoon . . ." Basalt choked on the words through his outrage, watching the derro swagger down the street with one of the constables. "By Reorx," cried Basalt, "give me your axe, let me finish it here!" His voice was a wail of despair.

"Let the law handle it," Tybalt said curtly. "It was a fight on the street, with plenty of witnesses. A fight that might have been avoided . . ."

Tybalt didn't finish the thought, but Basalt understood his meaning. He looked at the crowd, desperately searching for an understanding face, but saw only horror and pity. He looked toward Hildy, saw her cradling Moldoon's lifeless head and looking up at him with tear-filled eyes.

Suddenly Basalt could not face these dwarves of Hillhome.

Twisting free of the crowd, he sprinted away, around a corner and down a side street. He turned again, stumbling into an alley, not at all sure where he was going. Blinded by his own tears, he stumbled around another corner, still fleeing with no direction. Finally, his weakened knees and straining lungs forced him to slow, then stop. Gasping for breath, he leaned against a shed for support.

Suddenly he heard giggling, children's laughter. Had they witnessed the whole, shameful event and followed him from the inn to mock him? No, it couldn't be—they must just be playing in the alley. Still, Basalt found their gaiety infuriating. "Go away, you brats!" he hissed through clenched teeth, not turning around.

But that only brought more cruel, haunting giggles.

Basalt whirled, half-crazed and ready to scare the wits out of the little fiends. From the depths of the shadows, two of the ugliest, dirtiest children he had ever seen rushed toward him. They broke into a run, waving twine, thong, and rope over their heads as they charged the startled hill dwarf.

They were on him instantly like rats, wrapping him in the rope and twine even as they scampered around him. One of them charged up his back, knocking him down. His head, still throbbing from the derro's chain mail, smacked into the packed earth, and the alley, his attackers, and even the ground began to spin uncontrollably.

And then he caught the scent of his assailants. Before he passed out, Basalt knew they were neither children nor rats, but something much worse.

As he lost consciousness, he wondered why he had been kidnapped by gully dwarves.

Chapter 14

A Curious Theft

A cloudy, silty puddle of mushale remained at the bottom of the mug. Pitrick swished it one way, then sloshed it back toward the other, watching its rhythmic, symmetrical motion. He watched the sediment, inevitable in mushale no matter how much it was strained, travel to and fro with the tiny tide. He found little solace in its simple spectacle. The fact that this was his sixth mug in half as many hours was both comforting and galling. For if Pitrick utilized mushale as a transcendental aid, as a step toward relaxation and deeper understanding, rarely did he allow himself to get so completely lost in its more addictive charms. Overuse was an abuse.

The savant was already addicted to power. To become de-

pendent on anything else, to develop an intimacy with anything else like he had with the concept of power, would only
serve as a distraction.

Yet, something had already diverted his attention. Perian
Cyprium, the flame-haired officer of the thane's House
Guard, was consuming his thoughts. Pitrick swished the
mushale dregs around the cup once more, listening for the
soft murmur of the liquid. In frustration he dashed the contents into the fire, then smashed the cup on the andiron. The
low flame turned bright blue as the fermented potion blazed
to life. Swelling not unlike the flame, Pitrick's melancholy
grew to anger.

She had humbugged him, by the gods! He did not know
how, or why, but somehow she had conspired with the fates
to cheat him. One of his most powerful and potent devices,
the "wish" scroll that he had held in reserve for so many
years, was gone, shriveled to ashes and blown away by its
own magical wind. Its power was unquestionable, un-
doubtable, but still it had failed. Pitrick had left no loop-
holes for the mystical powers. Yet the scroll was consumed,
the toll on his life span taken, and Perian was most defin-
itely *not* at his side.

"I have been a fool!" moaned Pitrick aloud in his empty
chamber. "And worse, I have been a blind, manipulated
fool. I have squandered one of the most potent magics
known and gained nothing.

"How could I allow this to happen? How could this frawl
become such an obsession?" With his face buried in his
hands, Pitrick limped around the chiseled and polished desk
and up several steps toward the chamber in the right corner
of the room. His gaze was falling on another place, another
time, perhaps another world. He didn't need to see
anything—the details of the room were clearly and perfectly
fixed in his mind. Without as much as glancing at his surroundings, he stopped and collapsed into the seat by the
hearth, propping his elbows on his knees.

"I loathe her, and yet I must have her. Every denial, every
move away only increases my desire. Does fate conspire
against me, does the magical fabric of this world seek to

frustrate me?" Pitrick's head snapped back and he howled, "How could it fail me? I made *no mistake!*"

The sound of rapping at his door stiffened Pitrick in the granite seat. He looked all around the room, at first confused by the sound, until it came again. The cloud of mushale and anguish in his mind cleared away as his focus returned to more immediate surroundings.

Along with the scroll, I have prematurely disposed of Legaer, as well, he mused. The memory of the hapless servant's soft neck beneath Pitrick's fingers brought a wry smile to his lips as he stood. Still, a replacement was needed immediately.

The knocking at the door resumed. Pitrick clumped irritably across the room, thoroughly annoyed by the intrusion. He paused, debating whether to answer it at all, but decided a fresh face might be diverting.

"What is it?" he demanded as he yanked open the heavy door, surprising the black-armored harrn of the House Guard who was standing there. The startled soldier snapped to attention, then just stood in the doorway, unsure of what to do next.

Pitrick reached toward his five-headed amulet but then stopped and withdrew his hand. This guard was here for a reason, after all.

"Have you a message, clod?" Pitrick snapped. He could feel a chill draft blowing across his feet, and knew that his cozy rooms would quickly grow cold.

"I was sent from the North Warren, Excellency. The duty officer there requests that you come at your earliest convenience."

This is unusual, Pitrick thought. "For what reason?"

"We captured an Aghar, Excellency. The duty officer felt that you should see him." Pitrick could tell from the dwarf's tone that he was frightened, probably thinking that bearing such a trivial request to the thane's unpredictable adviser was flirting with death.

Pitrick enjoyed that part of his reputation. "Why bother me with this? I am not concerned with the comings and goings of thieving gully dwarves. Deal with him in the usual manner and be done with it . . . unless there's something more to it that you haven't told me?"

The messenger was sweating now, rivulets coursing down his neck beneath his close-fitting armor. "Yes, Excellency," he stammered, "I have yet to tell you that he was stealing something of yours. He was trying to break into your personal warrens."

Pitrick was puzzled. This incident was of small consequence by any account. The warrens were Thorbardin's major food production area, and Aghar sneaked in to steal things from time to time. They took garbage, mostly, so stealing food was unusual, but it hardly required his personal attention.

Yet his chambers were growing cold, and his mind was wandering. A bit of sport with an Aghar might be uplifting, Pitrick thought. "You may go," he said to the guard and slammed the door in his face.

Taking a deep breath, Pitrick touched his ring while picturing the guardpost at the edge of the North Warren. By the time he exhaled, he stood at that very guardpost.

"Well? Where is the duty officer?" Several startled guards stepped backward, away from the sudden apparition, and snatched up their weapons. Immediately afterward, they recognized the thane's adviser and snapped to attention. A sergeant stepped forward and waved his hand speechlessly, indicating the direction to the duty officer. Without a nod and dragging his foot, Pitrick advanced down the tunnel.

The warrens were a gigantic labyrinth of passageways and grottoes wherein huge fields of fungus and mold, the staple foods of the subterranean dwarf, grew in great abundance. The warrens also boasted large pools containing trout and other cold-water fish. Various sorts of compost hills were dispersed throughout the area, providing nutrients for the thin soil. Eternally wrapped in darkness, the warrens were heavy with fetid air, carrying within them a sense of the power and limitless wealth of the earth, in all its living forms.

Within moments, Pitrick sighted the helpless prisoner bound and laying on the cavern floor.

"We caught him breaking into one of your rooms, Excellency," volunteered one of the derro guards.

Pitrick cut him off. "I know that! Are you the duty officer? If not, summon him here!"

The guard scurried away and around a corner of the tunnel. Pitrick nonchalantly eyed the frightened Aghar on the ground. He circled around the prisoner, whose gaze followed him like a bird's. As Pitrick was completing his circuit, the duty officer approached and saluted smartly.

"Tell me what is so important about this pathetic creature," Pitrick commanded.

The duty officer was admirably unshaken. "We caught him trying to get into one of your warrens, Excellency. Normally we wouldn't think much about catching a gully dwarf, but this one seemed almost to be looking for something *specific*. Usually they stick to the garbage piles and compost heaps deep in the warrens, and almost never come in this close."

Pitrick glared at the Aghar prisoner, inspecting the fellow's ragged garments. The gully dwarf offered a tentative, gap-toothed smile, prompting Pitrick to slap him across the face.

"You have done well," the hunchback said to the guard. The derro reacted to the adviser's praise, if not with pleasure, at least with a noticeable sense of relief. "Tell me more. What is in that warren."

"Mossweed, Excellency. North Warren Blue, specifically. Your personal stock. Him being here in the first place was odd enough, but that he'd try to steal smoke weed instead of food—it just doesn't add up. That's why I called you, Excellency. I thought you should know."

"Indeed." Pitrick fixed his eyes on the Aghar and watched the color drain from the little fellow's face. Why *would* a gully dwarf try to steal smoke weed? And why this particular smoke weed? Pitrick's North Warren Blue was renowned as the best in Thorbardin, but only among those aficionados familiar with the finer points of the weed.

The Aghar groaned and squirmed, looking around for a friendly face. When Pitrick spoke, his voice came out silky smooth, soothing the trembling gully dwarf.

"So you want some smoke weed, hmmm?" Pitrick smiled. It was more of a grimace, but it was the best he could do. "It is such a pleasure to find a gully dwarf with refined taste. Why do you enjoy it so?"

The Aghar squinted at him in fright, trying hard to understand the question. "Enjoy what so?" he finally inquired.

"The North Warren mossweed, of course," said Pitrick, pretending mild surprise. "You *do* smoke it, don't you?" The derro's mind seethed. He pictured his hands wrapping around the helpless gully dwarf's throat and squeezing, slowly, as the thing squirmed. He imagined a dozen delicious ends for the useless creature and wondered briefly which he would choose. When the time came, he knew, the answer would provide itself.

The gap-toothed Aghar looked at him in confusion for a moment longer. Then, like the sun emerging from a dense overcast, a smile of understanding illuminated his features. "Oh," he chuckled. "Mossweed not for Too-thee!"

"Oh?" Pitrick's eyes narrowed. "Who, then?"

"Mossweed for queen! New queen of Mudhole like *good* smoke!" the Aghar proclaimed, proudly. "Choose me, Too-thee, to get for her!"

Mudhole, Pitrick assumed, was one of the pathetic gully dwarf lairs on the fringes of Thorbardin. His outrage grew at the thought of some Aghar sow enjoying his smoke . . . But why? Why would a gully dwarf, who dined on worms and garbage, be concerned about the quality of her smoke weed?

"Tell me about this new queen of Mudhole," prompted Pitrick smoothly. "After all, I represent the thane—the king of the Theiwar. Perhaps he would be interested in meeting your queen."

"No, no. Queen already have king. But thane could visit! We throw big party for Queen Furryend and King Flunk and thane!"

"Have Furryend and Flunk been your rulers for a long time?"

"Oh, yes! Two days! Maybe more! King and queen, they

descend from mud, just like in property! They come down to Mudhole two days ago!" The Aghar spoke freely now, happy to pour out his knowledge for these Theiwar who knew so little.

"Tell me what Queen Furryend looks like," Pitrick snapped. His eyes narrowed to tiny slits. "Is she enormously fat, or covered with warts?"

"Oh, no, queen beautiful. She big pretty, with right size nose and red hair like iron rust." Too-thee looked up, hoping the explanation pleased the grotesque derro.

Pitrick turned away, his eyes bulging, his mind inflamed. The derro guards stepped back, frightened by the look on his face. The pieces of this puzzle were falling together. Queen Furryend—Perian it must be—descended to them two days ago, complete with a king—Flint—red hair, and a taste for North Warren Blue. She obviously thought it would be funny to steal his private stock, as if that would make a fool of him. Indeed, he understood why his wish spell had failed. His wording had been perfect. But he'd asked for Perian to be returned to life, and she'd never died! How they had survived he could not fathom, but he was certain that it was Perian who was queen to these gully dwarves.

Flecks of spittle trickled from the hunchback derro's twitching lips. He thought how that red-haired halfbreed wench must be laughing at his failure, and his rage became supreme. Pitrick turned back slowly, his unblinking eyes locked on the Aghar. Too-thee twisted and squirmed backward as the savant crept closer.

"I will kill you first," he hissed. "But you are just the beginning. Your entire thieving, conniving clan will be wiped out. I'll kill every one of them, one at a time, with my own hands if I must. But I will have her! I will have your queen, and she will suffer!"

Pitrick sprang forward, his powerful hands locking around the throat of the squirming Aghar. The derro guards nervously watched as the berserk savant vented his rage against the hapless prisoner.

Pitrick shook the Aghar like a rag doll, and then threw

the wailing dwarf aside. His hand grasped the medallion at his chest, his other rose to point an accusing finger at the gully dwarf.

A bolt of magical energy crackled from Pitrick's finger. It sparked through the air and struck the gully dwarf in the chest. The Aghar screamed and flopped over backward. Again and again, the magic hissed, sending forth crackling missiles that struck the little body with brute force. By the third missile, the Aghar was well and truly dead, its body smoking. Still Pitrick sent two more bolts into the pathetic corpse.

Appearing slightly calmer, Pitrick stepped back from his victim. "I have important matters to tend to," he snapped, compelling the attention of the assembled derro of the House Guard. They stood in a nervous circle, listening very carefully indeed. "This incident is not to be reported to anyone. I shall be monitoring this situation personally, and I guarantee that if even the slightest word of this leaks out, I will see to it that all of you—*all* of you—will pay for that slip of the tongue."

"You can count on our discretion, Excellency!" exclaimed the duty officer. "No one will know—no one at all!"

"Very good. Return to your posts, and forget today's event."

Pitrick touched the steel ring on his finger, as he pictured in his mind the chasm where he had last seen Perian and Flint. With the slightest blink, the ring performed its magic, and the hunchbacked derro disappeared from the North Warrens.

In the same instant, he materialized at the lip of the Beast Pit. His eyes narrowed as he gazed into the deep, dark chasm. Was it possible that both victims had actually survived their plummet into this dank hole? He tended to believe the tale of the dead Aghar. The new king and queen of the gully dwarves had to be the harrn and frawl that Pitrick had presumed dead.

If so, their new lease on life is about to expire, he thought with some measure of humor.

Pitrick studied the pit from above. Obviously there must

be a connection or passage of some sort that allowed them to escape to "Mudhole." Pitrick grinned at the name. Perhaps Perian would show him gratitude for being rescued from such a place! As for the hill dwarf, any number of spells would see to his permanent disposal.

But first, Pitrick needed to find the passage that had led them to temporary safety, and that meant exploring the Beast Pit. His teleportation ring, while perfectly suited for moving about Thorbardin and even carrying him to distant places such as Sanction, was of no use here. It could only take him to places that he had already seen. If he tried to teleport into Mudhole without knowing its exact location, he could materialize in the midst of the mountain somewhere, or worse. For this task he needed some other channel of movement.

And his spells could provide it. Pitrick reached into his belt pouch and withdrew a small feather. He twisted it between his fingers as he mouthed the words to a simple spell. Then, he stepped into the chasm.

Spreading his arms, Pitrick thrilled to the motion and power of his spell of flying. He swooped down, then darted back up, turning again to dive into the depths of the pit. Below him he saw a black cesspool of mud and slime. Something stirred there, and he knew it was the lair of the beast.

Curving away, Pitrick darted through the air, along the twisting channel that was the floor of the pit. Somewhere in this cavern was the passage to the gully dwarves' lair. Pitrick swore he would not rest until he found it.

A soft, unfamiliar sound came from behind him, and Pitrick paused, hovering for a moment as he looked back toward the mouth of the pit. He saw movement in the depths, and for a moment his heart froze as he got his first good look at the monstrous size of the beast.

It oozed toward him, pushing part of its segmented form forward, then trailing its other half after. Like a gigantic slug, reaching ahead of itself with those long, lashing tentacles, the beast came on.

If it were chasing me, I would run this way, Pitrick reasoned. If Perian and Flint found an exit, it should be here, near the furthest extent of the cavern, since this is where they would have had the time to examine the walls. But the flying savant saw nothing.

Then an idea struck him. His enemies weren't flying, they were on the ground. Their perspective was different. Pitrick settled to the cavern floor. And there, directly ahead of him, was a crack of light. It was nearly concealed by an overhanging boulder. Approaching it more closely, he could see that it led somewhere. He could even hear, faintly, sounds from the other side.

This is how they escaped me! he crowed to himself. Leaning closer to listen, the Theiwar could distinguish sounds of cheering and clapping.

"I'll give them something to shout about," he chuckled, flying upward twenty or thirty feet and hovering while he thought. Which of his spells would be most effective? Foremost, he wanted to snatch Perian away, and after that make sure that the hill dwarf, Fireforge, never bothered anyone again. He considered changing Flint into a snail, or blasting him to pieces with a lightning bolt. The more he thought about it, the more he laughed, and as he laughed, the beast crept closer. By the time the bloblike form was beneath him, Pitrick positively howled with glee.

He would not attack Mudhole alone, when help was so readily at hand.

The beast's tentacles lashed upward, and Pitrick shrieked as one dragged across his foot. Quickly darting higher, he examined the cave wall of the Beast Pit. Somewhere beyond that wall, he knew, lay Mudhole and his quarry. The tiny tunnel was the only connecting conduit between the Beast Pit and Mudhole now, but Pitrick could easily expand that.

Below him the beast lurched again. Its tentacles flailed blindly. Some groped upward while others searched through the tunnel.

"Allow me," hissed the deformed dwarf, still hovering. His right hand closed around the amulet at his neck while his eyes stared at the great wall of rock, the wall that divided the beast from the gully dwarves.

"*Gro-ath goe Kratsch-yill!*" He barked the magic spell, his voice suddenly firm. The familiar blue glow surged from the amulet, seeping between his fingers.

Pitrick raised his left hand, gesturing to the wall. The force of his magic reached out, penetrating the stone surface, altering and kneading that stone with the power of its enchantment.

Beads of moisture gathered on the rock and trickled down its quivering slope. Slowly the rock bulged and grew soft. Suddenly it gave way, splitting open like a tomato. Pitrick cackled as a torrent of mud and stone poured into this cavern and the one beyond. Then the beast, sensing dozens of vulnerable prey, rushed through the gurgling ooze into Mudhole.

Chapter 15

The "Crownation"

"MORE FUNGUS?" INQUIRED NOMSCUL, SHOVING a platter of the aromatic if chewy shapes under the noses of his newly crowned monarchs.

"I'm stuffed," Flint replied, holding up both hands and settling back on the soft cushion of moss. "What little room I have left I'm saving for those ribs you're cooking."

"Nomscul sorry about meat," the Aghar apologized, staring at his toes.

Across the great cavern, a huge steel spear rested over a low fire. Large ribs of pork were spitted on the spear, dripping juices into the fire with an appetizing sizzle, barely audible above the raucous noise of the great crownation festival. In his new, official, and royally appointed capacity as Mudhole's Best Cook and Chief Shaman (the longest, and therefore most important title in Mudhole) Nomscul had sorely neglected his duty when he forgot to light the cooking fire until the feast was well underway, a fact which had slowed the cooking of the meat significantly. It had also made him almost obnoxiously solicitous toward Flint and Perian.

At the moment, however, Flint didn't notice the absence of the meat—indeed, he couldn't have eaten another bite. All the food served during the ceremony had been quite good and, what's more, plentiful. Having lived above ground for all of his life, Flint never knew just how much variety there could be in subterranean dining. The food and drink had thus far included spiced mushrooms, raw and cooked fish, potatoes, and lichen leaves.

"This is the best I've felt since we got here," admitted the king of the gully dwarves, with a frank look at his queen.

"It was all right," Perian admitted. "I'm used to better, but most of this came from the Theiwar warrens anyway. Still, I'm surprised Nomscul did such a good job with it.

"I just wish Too-thee would get back with my mossweed. I wonder what's keeping him."

"He could still be here by the end of the meal," replied Flint, with a glance at the still raw pork ribs. "That gives him plenty of time."

Across the room they saw the low fire, with its sizzling rack of ribs impaled on a great, steel-shafted spear. Every few minutes Nomscul skipped over to the fire and rotated the pig slightly. His procedure was apparently mostly guesswork, but the meat sent a delightful aroma whispering around the assembled multitudes.

All of the approximately four hundred Aghar of Mudhole had assembled in the Big Sky Room for the great feast and celebration. By this point in the feast the chamber was pretty well ravaged, blanketed with litter, food and clothing scraps, and sleeping Aghar.

The cavern was divided by the shallow stream that flowed through so much of the gully dwarf lair. Here in the cavern the stream collected into a series of three deep, clear pools. Dozens of young Aghar splashed playfully in the chilly waters of these pools. Unlike virtually every other type of dwarf known to Flint and Perian, the gully dwarves of Mudhole actually liked the water. All of them seemed to be darned good swimmers. This fact amazed Flint, who didn't know a hill or mountain dwarf that knew how to keep his head above water.

Flint, Perian, and a dozen Aghar—their "court," which included Nomscul, Ooz, and Fester—sat on one side of the stream. A small, rugged stone footbridge crossed the waterway between two of the pools, connecting up with the larger portion of the cave where the rest of the gully dwarves were gathered.

Fester and Nomscul had been taking turns saluting and toasting their new rulers. Fester had become Perian's chief handmaiden and lady-in-waiting—or "weighty lady," as the gully dwarf referred to herself. Nomscul, in addition to his roles as healer, and Best Cook and Chief Shaman, had vowed to become the king's primary aide.

"You a real kingly king," said Nomscul, sloshing slightly as he offered yet another salute to his new monarch.

After Nomscul's toast, the air was filled with mushrooms, lichens, and fishheads flying back and forth. Several near-misses splashed into the water just feet from the king and queen, but a withering look from Nomscul, coupled with a menacing reach toward his magic bag, moved the game to a more comfortable distance.

"Say," commented Flint, "do you folks play any games down here: Kickball, stick-and-hoop, anything like that?"

Nomscul looked at him quizzically. "Stuck in hoop?"

"You know, sports," Flint persisted. "Athletic games. You get a bunch of—"

"Two," corrected Perian.

". . . two fellows on one side and two on the other, and they both try to hook a leather hoop over the others' post—that sort of thing. Or anything to watch that's more organized than this free-for-all."

"Agharpult!" yelped Nomscul, jumping up and down. "King wants en . . . entert . . . you watch this!"

The excited Aghar turned toward the crowd and shouted, "Agharpulters, get over here! Hurry, hurry, hurry!" Immediately the crowd turned into a shoving, pushing mass as gully dwarves from every corner of the room tried to converge in front of the bridge.

"You like this," beamed Nomscul. "We learn by watching Theiwar practice war."

Teams of gully dwarves suddenly began to form pyramids with rows of kneeling bodies, ten dwarves forming a four-tier pile. Other Aghar stood behind, squatting and preparing to charge the pyramids formed by their comrades.

At Nomscul's command, these others dashed forward, vaulting to the tops of the pyramids, whereupon all of the piled gully dwarves flung themselves face forward toward the floor. The momentum of the fall hurtled the topmost gully dwarf, at significant speed, across the room, eventually to crash into a crowd of gathered spectators.

Flint roared with laughter as the hapless gully dwarves tumbled over one another and sailed through the air, arms and legs flailing, usually screeching at the top of their lungs.

"Someone is going to get hurt doing this," muttered Perian.

"Oh, lighten up," retorted Flint. "These little guys have skulls thicker than the thane's best armor."

Indeed they must, concluded Perian as she watched a pair of them smack violently into the cavern wall, fall to the ground, and jump up beaming.

Between guffaws, Flint asked Nomscul, "Where did you say you learned this sport?"

Nomscul puffed out his chest. "We sneak teeny-tiny quiet into Big-Big Room and see Theiwar cracking walls with cattle-pult machines. It stupid name, since they fling rocks, not cattle. But it look like fun, so we do Agharpult."

"He's talking about the catapult range," Perian explained, amazed. "The thane's army trains with some of the heavy siege equipment in an enormous cavern on the second level. They practice hitting targets painted on the walls. I'm surprised any gully dwarf has ever seen it, though. That room is quite a distance from here." Flint thought he saw a glimmer of admiration in Perian's eyes as she studied Nomscul, who just grinned back at her ridiculously.

With tears of laughter rolling down his cheeks, Flint watched the beefiest Aghar he'd seen yet, launch off the top of an Agharpult and try to do a somersault in midair. Instead of tucking under, however, he wound up sailing across the room spread-eagled and upside-down, finally splashing against the far wall and sliding down into a pool of muck.

Splashing?

Suddenly alert, Flint peered at the opposite wall, squinting to make out details. Nudging Perian, he pointed and asked, "What's happening over there? The wall looks . . . squishy."

Perian followed his gesture and gasped. She saw the rock wall of the cave suddenly turned to mud and ooze slowly downward. The narrow tunnel to the Beast Pit gaped wider as its framework of rock melted away.

"It's collapsing!" She was instantly on her feet, shouting, "We've got to get everyone out of here now!"

The gully dwarves blithely continued Agharpulting around the room, oblivious to the danger.

Flint, too, sprang to his feet, and grabbed Perian's elbow, staring in disbelief. "That's no cave-in!" he growled. "The wall's turning to mud."

"The chamber connecting to the Beast Pit is behind that wall," whispered Perian. Her worried glance told Flint that they both were thinking the same, terrifying thought.

They watched, horror-struck, as the rock oozed onto the cave floor. Soon the narrow tunnel gaped wide, and they both knew that nothing blocked the carrion crawler's passage into Mudhole.

Then they saw white, flailing tentacles beyond the opening.

"Here it comes!" cried Perian. "These Aghar are helpless. We've got to clear the chamber and barricade this thing out of the rest of Mudhole!"

"Hey! Beast go home!" shouted Nomscul, leaping to his feet and scolding the horrifying creature from across the huge cave.

179

Other Aghar turned and shouted in annoyance, fear, or confusion, as the beast crept forward.

The carrion crawler's enormous bulk slithered through a round hole perhaps twelve feet in diameter as its tendrils lashed back and forth hungrily.

"If we don't get the Aghar out of here quickly, they'll stampede!" Instinctively Flint reached for the axe that would normally be at his waist, but found nothing. He cursed the fates that had placed him in this chamber without so much as Happenstance, the rusty dagger, to defend his "kingdom."

Screams and shouts rose through the Big Sky Room, and Aghar bolted in every direction. Some, by coincidence more than intent, actually headed toward the Thrown Room—which was the Aghar's new name for Flint's and Perian's quarters—or the rest of Mudhole. Most darted around blindly, screaming, waving their arms, or huddling on the ground, terrified by the approach of the monster.

"Follow me!" shouted Perian. An officer of the House Guard was trained to lead by example, not to mention expected to be followed. She grabbed a carving knife and started for the footbridge at a run, ready to cross it and confront the monster personally.

"Get to the Thrown Room!" Flint's voice was a thunderous bellow, but even that sound was washed away in the panic-stricken babble of hundreds of Aghar. A few of his closer subjects started toward the exits, but chaos reigned in the cavern. Flint snagged Fester, the nearest Aghar, by her collar. She held a large, bent roasting fork in her hand.

"Fester, look at me!" commanded Flint. "Tell everyone to get into the Thrown Room. Get everyone to the Thrown Room!"

The frawl stared at Flint dumbly for a moment, but he held her arms until he saw the fear fade from her eyes, and then she nodded vigorously. He took the fork from her hand and turned her loose, and immediately she began pushing Aghar toward the exits. One down, thought Flint.

Turning back to the action, Flint saw several Aghar run blindly into the beast, only to be struck and paralyzed by the flailing tentacles. The small forms tumbled to the ground, but thankfully the beast didn't stop to feed on them immediately. Flint hoped it wouldn't get a second chance later on.

But how could they stop it? He sprinted after Perian, seeing her reach the footbridge and start across with Nomscul at her heels. The roasting fork in his hand was a pathetic weapon, but anything was better than his bare hands against the huge, segmented monster.

More Aghar fell before the beast, and it crawled over the motionless forms, intent on the great mass of prey before it. Almost gleefully, it surged upward, stretching its bloated body a dozen feet in the air, still lashing with its tentacles.

Suddenly Perian stopped on the bridge and screamed. Nomscul, right behind the queen, ran into her and fell backward onto the approach to the bridge. Flint saw the hideous, hunchbacked figure of Pitrick soaring through the air over her head. The derro was flying straight for Perian!

Raising the long fork, undaunted by the incongruity of the gesture, Flint sprang toward the narrow footbridge. He saw the grotesque Theiwar land near Perian and seize her wrist in his right hand. The frawl twisted back, but Pitrick pinned her against the railing on the side of the bridge. The derro settled to the planks beside her and spoke a sharp word, cancelling his flying spell so that he could place his weight on the ground.

Nomscul climbed to his feet and charged forward, only to be kicked aside by one of Pitrick's heavy boots. Desperately, Perian pulled away. Flint charged as fast as he could, pushing his way through the Aghar.

"Your smoke weed will be a little delayed—but no worry. You will be leaving with me," hissed Pitrick to Perian, the thick odor of mushale heavy on his breath.

Pitrick gripped his amulet with one hand, staring into Perian's eyes. She twisted in his grasp but could not break away.

"*Kan-straithian!*" he barked. Instantly the blue light flashed. The savant released Perian and turned to face the charging hill dwarf. Nomscul, climbing to his feet behind

Perian, seemed momentarily forgotten.

Perian tried to run but her feet refused to move, as if they had been cemented to the bridge. She tried to turn, to open her mouth and speak, and found herself paralyzed by magic. Her eyes wild, she struggled against the spell, but Pitrick's magic had her frozen in place.

"Now for you," growled Pitrick, his huge eyes glaring insanely at Flint. The hunchback's fingers tightened around the amulet, and he raised his hand to point a bony finger at the charging dwarf. Flint knew that he would never reach Pitrick before the derro cast his spell.

"*Incinerus . . . Incinetoria . . .*" Pitrick began his spell, sneering at Flint, preparing to envelop him in an inferno of sorcerous fire. He did not notice Nomscul stepping around Perian's petrified form.

"In-sin-jin-fin-jin yourself!" challenged Nomscul, aping Pitrick's wizardly pose. He thrust his magic sack before himself and clapped it sharply between his hands, throwing a cloud of fine dust into the air.

Pitrick recoiled from the insidious powder, but too late to keep it from his nose, eyes, and throat. His fingers stabbed at his burning eyes, and then his whole body doubled over.

"Ah . . . uhhh . . . CHOO!" Pitrick's sneeze almost blasted Nomscul from the bridge.

"Maggot!" Pitrick hissed, stumbling away from the dust cloud. He delivered a vicious kick to Nomscul. The little shaman crashed through the railing of the bridge and splashed into the pool, gasping and wailing.

Then Flint reached the bridge, racing full-tilt toward the derro, his roasting fork poised above his head. Still struggling to regain his senses, Pitrick snatched a long, straight dagger from his belt.

Below them, Nomscul popped to the surface of the pool. "You got my magic stuff all wet!" he whined, paddling toward the bank.

The two dwarves came together. Flint's momentum carried Pitrick over backward. Locked together, each struggling for an advantage, they rolled over and over toward the shore. Each held his own weapon in one hand, his opponent's wrist in the other.

As they tumbled onto land, Pitrick thrust out his leg, pinning Flint below him. He threw all his weight behind his weapon, forcing the blade down toward Flint's unprotected chest. Caught off guard, the hill dwarf strove to straighten his arm, but Pitrick's blade inched closer. Desperately Flint kicked the derro away and rolled to the side. Both combatants jumped to their feet, stabbing and parrying as they scrambled momentarily to a safe range.

"You thought to escape me, hill dwarf?" cackled Pitrick, breathing heavily. "I admit you surprised me by surviving the Beast Pit."

Pitrick stabbed at him, but Flint skipped out of the way, driving his own long, pronged weapon into the derro's chest. As they jumped apart Flint expected to see blood on his enemy's robe, but instead he saw links of chain mail shining through the ripped fabric. Glancing at his weapon, he saw that the tines of the roasting fork had been bent and twisted—such a feeble weapon would never punch through the derro's armor.

"I'm full of surprises, too," taunted the Theiwar. "Here's another: when I finish with you, your whole town will be next to perish. You've shown me that Hillhome and all your sun-dwelling kin are too dangerous to my plans!"

"You should live so long," growled Flint, feinting toward Pitrick's left side. Nonetheless, the warning sent shivers along the hill dwarf's spine. Pitrick had to be stopped, now!

The evil derro sneered as he evaded the attack. "I shall, with Perian at my side. Together we shall destroy Hillhome and make slaves of its people."

The derro turned and darted along the side of the pool, moving with surprising speed. Flint raced after him. The hill dwarf knew his only hope was to press the derro so closely that he could not cast a spell.

Both figures turned suddenly when they heard Perian shout, "I'm free!" As the last effects of Pitrick's hold spell finally wore off, the frawl spun and started toward them. She snatched up a long, sharp cooking knife. Grinning, Flint turned back toward Pitrick.

But the savant surprised him. Instead of reaching for his amulet, Pitrick laughed defiantly and touched the ring on his left hand. Instantly the derro disappeared from sight.

Perian's scream drew Flint's attention back over his shoulder. Suddenly Pitrick was standing next to her, and the derro seized her left arm with both hands.

"I must leave now," he taunted Flint. "But I will be back, once I see that my property gets safely home." He leered at Perian, and icy daggers drove into Flint's heart.

Snarling, the hill dwarf dashed toward the bridge. He saw Pitrick reach toward the ring, even while holding tightly to Perian.

Neither Flint nor Pitrick could have anticipated Perian's next move. Just before the derro touched his ring and teleported them away, the frawl's right hand came around, still holding the carving knife which she had picked up earlier. The hunchback twisted his arm upward, blocking only a blow to his face. He realized too late that was not Perian's target.

Instead the knife slashed into Pitrick's hand, slicing through skin and bone. The Theiwar shaman screamed and pulled away, with blood streaming down his arm. Two fingers, sliced cleanly off, splashed into the water.

On one of them gleamed a small circlet of twisted wire.

Gagging and shrieking, Pitrick stumbled backward, cradling his mangled hand. Perian looked in shock at the blood streaking her robe.

The din in the cavern echoed around them. Some Aghar fled from the carrion crawler, while others attacked it with utensils. Their courage was worse than useless against the creature since the beast's tough hide turned aside their attacks. Its sticky tendrils lashed across the gully dwarves' skin, dropping them to the ground, helpless and paralyzed.

"Finish him!" shouted Flint, sprinting back onto the bridge, charging the howling derro.

Now Pitrick looked up with real fear in his eyes. He saw Flint charging, saw the murderous rage in the hill dwarf's eyes, and he staggered off the opposite side of the bridge, desperately fishing in his pouch for something.

Flint didn't slow down as he saw the Theiwar pull out a small, clear bottle. Pitrick raised the flask to his lips and swallowed the contents in one gulp, just as Flint launched himself toward him.

The hill dwarf plowed into Pitrick, driving him to the ground. Flint raised the fork, ready to plunge it into the squirming mage's neck.

But suddenly that neck was gone. As Flint watched in disbelief, Pitrick's entire body dissipated into a pale cloud of vapor. Flint slashed at it futilely with his makeshift weapon. But the cloud drifted away from him, and then passed through the hole in the cavern wall. In moments it disappeared from view entirely.

"Damnation!" hollered Flint, watching the gaseous form of his enemy slip away.

"We still have troubles," Perian barked urgently. "Look!"

Flint turned to see that the massive carrion crawler had reached the exit to the Thrown Room. He could trace the creature's path across the cavern by counting the fallen bodies of Aghar. Dozens lay in a twisted line across the cavern floor.

He heard Nomscul's voice, issuing orders.

"Hey, Agharpulters! Do it do it do it! Agharpult! Stomp that big ugly thing! Pult pult pult!"

Teams of gully dwarves were gathering before the beast. The Aghar formed their pyramids and launched themselves at the carrion crawler, heedless of the danger. What they hoped to accomplish was unclear. But the carrion crawler was clearly distracted by the spectacle of their bodies flying over its head and crashing into the walls behind.

Flint ran through the cavern, frantically encouraging the Agharpulters. If they could distract the beast long enough, he could. . . .

What *could* he do? He looked at the roasting fork in his hand, and then at the looming carrion crawler, and tossed the fork aside. At the same time, his eyes passed over the roasting meat, still sizzling on its steel-shafted spear.

Flint hesitated only for a moment. By Reorx, those ribs smelled good. And they were just about done, too. His mouth watered as he hoisted the red hot spear off the fire, then dropped it from his burning hands. He peeled off his robe and wound it round his hands, then grasped the spear again. Several dozen ribs weighted down the shaft, but pulling the meat off would take too many precious minutes.

"Jump! Faster!" He heard Perian commanding the gully dwarves, directing the erratic Agharpults toward their target. More and more of their subjects flew through the air with better aim this time, crashing into the rearing monster. They didn't harm the beast, but they fully occupied its attention.

Seeing Flint laboring with the heavy weapon, Perian raced to his side. The two of them lifted the spear between them and cautiously moved around to the monster's side. The thing's wormlike head remained fixed upon the shrieking, flying Aghar.

"Now!" Flint barked. The two of them rushed forward, holding the meat-laden spear at shoulder height. The steel tip struck the carrion crawler between two of its segments, a few feet back from its head.

Instantly it whirled, but the two dwarves, working smoothly, turned in the same direction, just avoiding those paralyzing tendrils.

"Push!" grunted Perian, and they shoved the spear deep into the monster's vile insides. Blue pus oozed from the wound, coating the meat that backed up along the shaft as the spear drove deeper and deeper into the monster.

The carrion crawler shivered and twitched, flopping to the ground as its legs collapsed. Its struggles grew weaker as Perian and Flint twisted and probed with the weapon, trying to strike a vital organ. Finally, with one last spasm, it ceased to move.

All around them lay gully dwarves paralyzed by the carrion crawler or stunned by their launch from an Agharpult. Flint was covered by scrapes and bruises from his fight with Pitrick, and by meat juices from the cooking spear. Perian's hands and robe were splotched red with Pitrick's blood. Exhausted, they stared at each other for a long moment.

"I was scared . . . when Pitrick grabbed you, I was scared

he'd take you away, and I wouldn't be able to stop him."
Flint glanced at the ground, then looked back into Perian's
face. "I'm so glad. . . ." He reached out and pulled her into
his arms, crushed her to his chest.

"I'm glad, too," she whispered, pulling his face to hers and
kissing him. Flint's heart thumped harder than it had when
Pitrick threatened his life.

And then Flint peeled Perian's arms loose and stepped
away. "We can't do this," he growled. "We're different, inside and out, and there's no hope for a match like ours."

"You can't know that," she cried, reaching after him.

But he stepped back again. "I know it."

Chapter 16

Misguided Mission

"Do you really think he'd do it?" Flint asked Perian.
He paced about the small Thrown Room several hours after
the magical battle with the derro savant during the "crownation" party. "He'd destroy a whole village of innocent hill
dwarves simply for revenge against me?"

Flint and Perian had helped the gully dwarves begin the
cleanup of the Big Sky Room, entombing the casualties of
Pitrick's magic in temporary vaults in the wall of a secluded
mine shaft. Fortunately only nine of the Aghar had suc-
cumbed to the assault. Those brave Aghar who had been
paralyzed by the carrion crawler's tentacles were slowly recovering in a makeshift infirmary under Shaman Nomscul's
care.

Next Flint had ordered the rebuilding of the hole in the wall to discourage any further attacks by Pitrick, piling rocks of all sizes before it. Another crew was assigned the grim task of dismembering the beast, since it was far too large to remove intact from Mudhole's narrow egress.

After he'd initiated these programs, Flint had returned, exhausted, to the Thrown Room, where Perian put salve and a bandage over a magic-inflicted burn on Flint's arm. They were both too wound up to sleep.

Sitting on the edge of the moss bed now, hunched over a small table, quill in hand, Perian nodded her copper head emphatically in answer to Flint's question. "Pitrick is the most insanely cruel and powerful dwarf I've ever known. Why, once I saw him—never mind," she amended, shaking away the story when she noted Flint's preoccupied look.

The hill dwarf smote his open palm angrily. "Blast my wicked temper! I never should have told him Hillhome knew anything about the weapons or Aylmar. It was a lie anyway!" He kicked the wall with the toe of his boot.

Perian shook her head. "You can't blame yourself for Pitrick's villainy! He's always hated hill dwarves—it was inevitable that his hatred would someday be turned against Hillhome."

Flint snorted and threw up his hands. "But now I've given Hillhome less of a chance! I only hope I get back before it's too late."

She glanced up from the notes she was making on an old scrap of parchment and shook her head. "But they wouldn't have had *any* chance otherwise, because they wouldn't have known an attack was coming. When you think about it that way, you've done them a favor!" She propped her head up with a hand on her cheek.

Flint frowned. "Thanks for saying that, but this is still my fault."

Perian pushed the curls on her forehead from her eyes and pursed her lips. "Pitrick's obsession with me hasn't helped matters." She shook her head fiercely. "I can't help but think that this would not have happened if I'd confronted him sooner, or even told the thane I thought he was crazy. Perhaps I should have just given him what he wanted!" She shuddered.

Flint shuddered, too. He had no difficulty imagining what Pitrick had desired from the frawl. He found himself looking beneath Perian's warm hazel eyes to her soft, fuzzy cheeks. He remembered the vision of her in Pitrick's grasp just a few hours ago, and his blood boiled. "You could not have given him that. It would have been worse than death."

Perian looked straight ahead without blinking. "No, I couldn't have done that."

Flint looked brightly at the paper beneath her hand on the rickety table. "What are you doing?"

She tapped her chin with the end of the quill. "Making a list of the things we'll need on the trail to Hillhome." She scratched a note. "How far do you figure it is to this little village of yours?"

Astounded, Flint could barely keep the smile from his face. "You mean you'd help me—I mean Hillhome?"

"Just try and stop me!" she said, setting her shoulders defiantly.

"But why? Why would you risk your life for strangers?"

"You're hardly a stranger," she laughed. "You've saved my life twice in the last, what—five days?"

Flint rolled his eyes. "Your life wouldn't have needed saving if it hadn't been for my bumbling in the first place."

Perian wrinkled her nose in disagreement. "We've been over that already. I was at the breaking point anyway. Something had to give." She hesitated, then quickly added, watching his expression, "—and then luckily you came along."

Uncomfortable with the direction of the conversation, the mountain dwarf decided to lighten it. "Does the king of the gully dwarves expect to leave his queen and subjects behind?"

Flint was stroking his beard and fingering the teleport ring Pitrick had left behind along with his fingers. He looked at Perian tentatively, chewing the edge of his mustache. "Please don't laugh," he said at last, "but I was actually thinking of taking them along. After all, I gave my vow not

to leave them. They're not the best fighters I ever saw—
actually, they're just about the worst—but I never saw any
braver. The way they went up against that carrion crawler,
well, it was purely noble. I don't imagine well-trained
mountain dwarves would intimidate them in the slightest."

Perian's eyebrows flew up, and she slapped the quill
down. "That's a great idea! How soon should we—"

Suddenly, there was a great commotion in the hall outside
their room. Expecting the worst, Flint and Perian shot each
other a look before leaping off the bed for the door.

"Cainker back! Garf back!" Nomscul shouted, running
down the dark tunnel toward them. He skidded to a stop
just short of Flint's nose. "Cainker and Garf, they bring
king's pop!" he explained out of breath, revealing that the
gully dwarves were not totally clear on the various branches
of the royal family tree.

Flint blinked. "My nephew? I can't believe those two
boneheads actually found their way to Hillhome, let alone
located my nephew. But you say they brought him here?
Why?"

"You bet they did, O kingly guy!" proclaimed Nomscul,
having misappropriated new words from his king and
queen. "You come see!" Nomscul frowned suddenly. "King's
father not real happy."

"Of course he's not! They were just supposed to give him
my note, not kidnap him!" Flint snarled, then sighed heavily. "Where is he?"

"In grotto," Nomscul explained. "They shove him
through crackingrotto. I magicked him," he said, holding up
the red bag dangling from his waist, "but he no will move."

Sighing again, the hill dwarf splashed his face with
strained puddle water from a basin by the door, drying it
with his sleeve. "You'd better take me to him right away." He
looked over his shoulder at Perian and winked. "Coming, O
queenly gal?" Smirking, she nodded.

"This way faster than through Big Sky," he explained as he
dashed ahead of them into a dark, narrow mine shaft. The
tunnel continued, straight as an arrow, for about six hundred feet, Flint noted, counting his steps by using an old

trick from his dungeon-crawling days. Neither he nor Perian had yet visited this part of Mudhole, and he wanted to make sure they could find their way out again.

Then the shaft dead-ended. Nomscul led them around a turn, and after another five hundred feet they came to another tunnel on their right, but Nomscul ignored it. "That go to Big Sky. We in Upper Tubes area now."

Two hundred fifty feet later the tunnel ahead narrowed by half, and another shaft turned sharply to the left.

"Have you noticed we seem to be heading downhill?" Perian called back to Flint, who was bringing up the rear.

"Yeah," Flint panted, winded by the walk. "And I'm glad of it, because it's the only thing that's keeping me going. How much farther?" he hollered ahead to Nomscul.

"Grotto right here!" Nomscul crowed unexpectedly, stopping so suddenly that Perian slammed into him, and Flint into her, his face buried in her russet curls. Without thinking, he closed his eyes and inhaled, his hands coming to rest on her upper arms. Flint jumped backward abruptly, flustered by his own reaction.

"Uh, Nomscul went down there," Perian said softly over her shoulder, pointing to the right.

Flint looked around the frawl. "Steps!" he said unhappily. Indeed, a very narrow stone stairway had been cut into the granite, curving and twisting downward so that it was impossible to tell where the bottom was. Flint followed Perian down the cramped stairs, counting out of habit.

"Eighty-eight, eight-nine!" he said out loud as his foot hit the last one. He could hear Perian draw in her breath ahead of him, and he looked up.

They stood on the threshold of a beautiful natural grotto, which was dimly lit by some source that Flint could not immediately identify. Though much smaller than the Big Sky Room, the ceiling of the underground cavern was just as high. A waterfall cascaded through a crack at the top of the far right wall, forming a clear pool, which in turn fed a stream that flowed out under the left wall. White, eyeless fish frolicked in the cold depths of the pool, disappearing beneath an overhanging shelf of rock above the water at the dwarves' approach. Draped in moss, stalactites and stalag-mites had formed here too, but so elaborately that they re-minded Flint of organpipes.

The ground before the pool was covered in a soft blanket of moss. In a moment Flint realized that it provided the source of the light in the grotto. Somehow alive with energy, the moss glowed slightly green and yellow and pink all at once. The effect was unbelievably soothing.

"Isn't it beautiful?" Perian breathed as she glided silently over the moss and headed for a natural stone bench nearer the pool.

"It is that," Flint agreed, unable to think of more appropri-ate or poetic words. He shook off the grotto's calming ef-fects to remember their purpose for coming here. "Nomscul, where's my nephew?"

Flint heard a groan behind him. Turning, the hill dwarf saw something move slightly in the shadows of the rock for-mations. He was not prepared for the sight of Basalt on his knees, a four-inch length of leash around his neck tying him to a stalactite, arms lashed to his sides by ribbons, belts, twine, and many other less identifiable materials. His face was swollen, caked with dried blood, and covered with Nomscul's "magical" dirt. His beard and hair were as stringy as a gully dwarf's.

"Basalt!" Flint cried, rushing forward to cut the length of twine that tied the young Fireforge like a dog to the lime-stone pillar. Nomscul bent over and began gnawing at a piece of twine on Basalt's wrist. "Not that way! Oh, never mind!" Flint slit the bonds himself.

The delirious Basalt dropped onto his face. Perian rushed to the pool, scooped some water up in her cupped hands, and splashed it on the young dwarf's puffy cheeks, causing the dirt to turn to muddy streaks.

Basalt slowly came around, shaking his head and spray-ing water. He rubbed his arms as his senses returned with the flow of his blood. Using the stalagtite for support, Basalt staggered to his feet and blinked furiously. His eyes focused first on the hill dwarf's expectant face.

"Uncle Flint?" He squinted. "But you're dead!"

Flint feigned annoyance. "First Garth, and now you! I wish people would stop saying that!" Laughing, he tried to gather his nephew up in a hug, though Basalt's bonds made that difficult. "You look like you've been dragged behind a wild horse, son, but you sure are a sight for my sore eyes. Garf and Cainker didn't do that to your face, did they?" He didn't wait for Basalt's reply.

"Nomscul!" he hollered, whirling on the shaman behind him. "Where are the two reprobates who kidnapped my nephew, hauled him here on his face, then tied him to a stake? As your king, I demand some answers!" Eyes wide with innocence, the gully dwarf shaman simply raised his thin shoulders and held his hands palm up in resignation.

"Now I know you're alive," Basalt said, his weary voice laced with happiness. "No one else bellows like that. Don't be too hard on the dirt-eaters, though the gods know I've sworn at them for dragging me through frozen streams and over mountain roads for eight-odd fun-filled hours. I tried not to make it too easy for them." He laughed, then coughed at the pain it inflicted on his sore face.

Suddenly his expression changed to puzzlement. "Say, did I hear you call yourself 'king?' Where are we?" He looked at Perian, standing behind Flint. "*Who* are we? What in the Abyss is going on here?"

Flint's eyes narrowed angrily. "I knew it was too much to hope that they would have given you my note. You see, they weren't supposed to bring you here, just tell you I was OK." Flint's face turned the color of raw beef. "I'll kill them with my bare teeth!" he stormed, hungrily looking about the room. But the gully dwarves were nowhere to be seen. Even Nomscul had skulked out of the room.

Flint saw the expectant expression on Basalt's face. The elder Fireforge ran his hand up his forehead and through his hair, and tried to think of how to explain this muddle to Basalt. He looked into his nephew's eyes, so like Aylmar's. "You heard me right: I'm king of this gully dwarf city, known as Mudhole."

"Did you lose a bet, or did you have to fight for the crown?" Basalt arched one eyebrow. "You *do* have a crown, don't you?" With that, Flint's nephew threw his head back and laughed without restraint, without concern for his bruises. He laughed so hard he held his sides. Flint rolled his eyes and waited patiently while his nephew got the hysterical laughter out of his system. But Basalt would wheeze to a stop, look at Flint as if about to speak, and then burst out laughing anew. Flint crossed his arms and waited. He twiddled his fingers. Finally he began laughing himself.

Suddenly they both were startled by the sound of someone clearing her throat loudly. The mountain dwarf thrust her hand between the two at the younger dwarf. "You must be Basalt. I'm Perian Cyprium."

"My queen," Flint added, his voice husky. Basalt gazed respectfully at the attractive frawl.

"You may as well know right off, Basalt, if you haven't already guessed it," Perian said, hooking her thumbs in her pants pockets in an almost challenging gesture. "I'm a mountain dwarf." She watched closely for his reaction.

As expected, Basalt's eyes narrowed suspiciously. "Now I'm *really* confused."

"I hope to remedy that immediately. Perian comes in a little later in the story." Flint took him by the arm and led him to the bench by the pool. "This is going to be a long one, so we may as well get comfortable."

Perian had found a small clay jug and fetched some water from the stream. She offered it to Basalt, who took it gratefully and gulped most of the water down, splashing the rest on his face to wash away the dried blood. The mountain dwarf sat on the moss near the hill dwarves, her arms linked around her knees, watching Flint as he prepared to tell his tale.

"I barely know where to begin," Flint said, and a tense muscle twitched in his cheek.

"You know why I went into Thorbardin—to find the dwarf who murdered your father." Flint's bright blue-gray eyes held Basalt's. "And now I'll tell you what happened after I stepped inside the Theiwar's secret tunnel and a cage fell and imprisoned me. . . ."

* * * * *

Flint returned to the bench beside Basalt, for the retelling of the events of the last week had agitated him so that he could not sit still and had begun to pace.

"How many days will it take Pitrick to organize the troops he'll take to Hillhome?" Flint asked Perian.

Filled with pent-up energy herself, the mountain dwarf had begun to pitch flat stones into the pool during Flint's story. She stopped now and considered the answer, chewing her lip, ticking thoughts off on her fingers.

"Pitrick will use my troops, the thane's personal guard, which are some five hundred strong," she began. "He'll want to keep the action secret and they are the only force loyal to the Theiwar throne. Besides being excellent soldiers, they are all derro, and a few of them are spell-casting savants like Pitrick. They'll leave at dusk, since they will be virtually blind during the day."

"How long do you think that will take?" Flint pressed somewhat impatiently.

"It's not that simple!" Perian cried. "There are many things to consider! The troops are in excellent parade shape, but we—they have not fought in battle aboveground, well, ever, during my time in the Thane's Guard, which is more than thirty years.

"He *should* take a fortnight, minimum," she decided at last. Mindful of Flint's grateful nod, she quickly added, "But Pitrick will push them to leave in half that time, maybe less."

He looked at her, seated at his feet on the moss, in surprise. "Fine. We can't possibly be there in less than three days ourselves." He turned to Basalt. "You see, I—we vowed on our honor that we would not leave the gully dwarves, and I will not break that vow. So the Aghar are going to have to come with us. But it will take me at least two days to find some way to get three hundred gully dwarves all moving in the same direction for nearly twenty miles. The thought boggles my mind."

Perian stood and dropped her handful of stones into the pool with a *plop!*, scattering fish. "But if my guess is even nearly correct, that won't give us more than one, maybe two days to build up the town's defenses."

"Or much time to persuade the townsfolk they even need defending!" Basalt chimed in.

Perian dusted moss clippings from her legs. "But why wouldn't they believe us?" she asked, puzzled.

Both Flint and Basalt knew how good their word was in Hillhome, and how enamored the villagers were of the revenue generated by the derro. As Flint pictured himself trying to talk to the hill dwarves, he absently fingered Pitrick's ring. His hand began to tingle strangely, and the uncomfortable sensation spread quickly up his arm to his chest and the rest of his body. He saw Perian wavering before his face, then was distantly aware of her snatching the ring from his finger.

"What were you thinking about?" she demanded. "I could see from your face that you were activating the teleport ring!"

Flint shook away the remnants of the tingling sensation. "You mean someone other than Pitrick can use that thing?" he gasped.

"Of course." She shrugged. "It's just like any other magical item. Pitrick used it constantly because of his clubbed foot. He explained it to me once when he was trying to frighten me. He said all he had to do was grasp the ring and picture as clearly as possible the place where he wanted to go."

Anyplace he wanted . . . Flint remembered his thoughts of Hillhome, moments earlier, and had an idea. He turned to Basalt. "I can't leave the gully dwarves." He looked squarely into his nephew's face. "But you can. You could use the ring to teleport back to Hillhome and give them a couple of extra days to prepare for the derro attack, or at least gather some weapons. They'll believe you, Basalt." Flint took the ring from Perian's hand and thrust it forward. "I know Moldoon will, anyway, and you can start by telling him. He'll rally the rest of 'em."

Basalt recoiled from the magical band as if struck. "You don't understand! I can't tell anyone, least of all Moldoon!" the young dwarf cried, his face wracked with grief. He turned away in shame. "He's dead, and it's my fault!"

Flint shook his head uncomprehendingly. "Moldoon dead? What are you talking about?" Flint clasped Basalt's shoulder and spun his nephew around. "Speak up, harrn!"

Now it was Basalt's turn to explain. Hiccupping with sobs, he recounted the events of the previous evening, just before the gully dwarves had kidnapped him.

". . . then Moldoon stepped between us to stop the fight, and the derro stabbed him, just like that!" Basalt dropped his face in his hands, and his shoulders shook.

Flint was stunned and grieved by the news of the old human's death. He saw the pain in Basalt's face, pictured the casual cruelty of the derro guard. His hatred of the Theiwar burned hotter than ever. It had become a fire that could only be doused with blood.

"Basalt," Perian said, chewing a nail, "it sounds as if this Moldoon was only doing what he felt he had to do. You can't be blamed because he came between you and the derro."

"Don't you see?" Basalt looked up, bleary-eyed. "Everyone has been right about me—I'm nothing but a worthless drunk who can't defend himself! I didn't tell you about the derro patrol that found me outside of Thorbardin after you left. They chased me off like a scared rabbit—didn't even think enough of me to kill me! Gods," he cried, looking upward and shaking his fists, "I wish they had!"

"Stop it" Flint slapped him hard across the face. He saw Perian flinch at what she must have thought needless cruelty. Stunned, Basalt stared at his uncle, wiping away his tears with the back of his hand. Flint waited for him to compose himself.

"Now you've grieved," his uncle said at last, his expression determined. "For your father. For Moldoon. For yourself. Put it past you, because there's something more important at stake here."

The lines in Flint's face softened, and he grasped Basalt by the shoulders. "Prove everybody wrong, Basalt. Starting today, prove everybody wrong by mustering every bit of courage and grit you have to persuade them to believe something they won't want to hear." He shook him, hard. "Do it, Basalt. You must, because it's the only real chance Hillhome has."

"Do you really think I can persuade them?" he whispered.

Flint smiled at him encouragingly. "I know you can."

Basalt looked at the ring in Flint's palm. It was made of two incomplete bands of steel woven together and split at the top, so that the two jagged ends protruded outward. He took it and slipped it tentatively onto the middle finger of his left hand. An unfamiliar sense of energy surged through him, though it came not from the ring, but from the glint of faith and respect in his uncle's eyes. He stood straighter, more sure.

"Go to the family first," Flint advised him. "Under the greed and the pompous protestations, they are Fireforges; show them how you've changed, and they'll give you a chance. You'll see."

"Picture the destination in your mind, Basalt," Perian added, her face a mask of concern for what the naive young hill dwarf was about to undertake.

Basalt nodded wordlessly and began to concentrate on the main room in the family home.

"Tell them everything we've revealed to you, and that we'll be there in three days, four at the latest. We're counting on you to make them believe."

His face scrunched up in concentration, Basalt's image shimmered.

"You can do it, Basalt!" Flint called out as the last traces of his nephew disappeared before their eyes.

Flint and Perian stood alone in the beauty of the grotto, enveloped by the rhythmic pounding of the waterfall.

Chapter 17

Teleporting We Go

Flint threw a cracked wooden shield to the side in disgust. "We aren't going to find enough decent weapons here to equip *us*, let alone three hundred defenseless gully dwarves," he complained bitterly to Perian from atop a six-foot-high garbage mound in the Big Sky Room, across the stream and opposite the Thrown Room tunnel.

They were anxious to begin preparations for the march to Hillhome, and since the first item on Perian's list was collecting weapons, they had made their way back to the Big Sky Room shortly after Basalt had teleported away from the grotto. Across the stream and to their left, the gully dwarves continued to work away at filling the hole that Pitrick's spell and the beast had left in the wall.

As for the beast itself, the Aghar had finished chopping the front half up into little bits. After a stern lecture from their disgusted king about their new game of "beast toss," a number of them had been dispatched to carry wooden crates of the beast out through the crackingrotto, while the rest were now hard at work on the rear.

Up to her hips in odd shoes, discarded pots, leftover food, and other "treasures" on the far side of the mound, Perian was gazing intently at an old axe she'd found.

"Finding anything interesting?" Flint called.

Perian looked up guiltily and, without really thinking, slid the axe into her belt loop, the haft hidden within the folds of her tunic. "What was that? I'm sorry, I wasn't listening."

Flint shook his gray head, climbed off the mound, came around to her side, and stood with his arms crossed dejectedly. "Where are we going to find enough weapons? Are we going to send the Aghar off to war with sharpened dinner forks?" he spat.

Perian slid down the heap to clap him on the shoulder encouragingly. "Don't worry, Nomscul says there are lots more garbage heaps where we may find useful items. Besides, the Agharpults don't really need weapons."

Flint snorted in derision. "Great, then we only need two-hundred Agharpults." He picked up a brown wooden button, the size of his palm, and shuffled it between his hands idly. "We don't stand much of a chance armed against the derro, let alone weaponless."

Perian jammed her hands on her hips in irritation. "Flint Fireforge, if you're not even going to *try* to be optimistic, then—then," she sputtered in exasperation, "then—oh, I don't know why I bother with you! You're the crabbiest hill dwarf I've ever met!"

"And how many hill dwarves *have* you met?" he teased, his eyes twinkling. He enjoyed getting her dander up.

"One more than I like!" she shot back, and though her eyes flashed dark hazel below her curly copper hair, the corners of her red lips were raised in an almost imperceptibly playful smile.

Grinning back, Flint thought, how different she is from the frawls I've met in more than a century of life. He nearly reached up to brush a wayward curl from her forehead, then caught himself. Why do my hands seek excuses to touch her? We both know hill dwarves and mountain dwarves don't mix.

"What, no quick retort?" Perian asked him, suddenly conscious of his stare.

The hill dwarf's bushy mustache turned down in a frown. "We've too much work to do to indulge in verbal jousts," he said irritably, pitching the brown button into the heap again.

Hurt by his sudden mood shift, Perian bristled. "Whatever you say. I'm anxious as well to be done with this Hillhome campaign, so I can get on with things in my own life!"

"There's nothing that says you have to do 'this Hillhome campaign,' " he said coldly.

Perian's hazel eyes narrowed to slits. "You may not understand this, but my sense of honor prevents me from reneging on a promise."

Flint whirled on her. "I never asked for your promise to help."

Perian trembled with anger. "I was referring to my vow to stay with the gully dwarves," she said quietly.

"Oh."

Silence.

"I have things to do." Averting her face, Perian quickly strode across the bridge that spanned the stream and bolted for the tunnel to the Thrown Room.

Flint swore silently. Why all of a sudden had he acted like such a proud, stubborn old fool? Go after her, tell her you're sorry, he said to himself. Tell her whatever you have to to take that disgusted look from her eyes!

"Eeeeeeooooooo!"

Following the echoing cry of distress, Flint's head snapped to the left, where he saw a crew of ten gully dwarves still dismantling the carrion crawler. Hissing smoke rose in small clouds around half of the Aghar, who were doing a bizarre dance of pain.

"How have you boneheads set yourselves afire now?" the hill dwarf groaned, taking the bridge in four strides. He ran the two hundred feet to where they stood around the oozing remains of the giant carrion crawler.

Though surrounded by choking, putrid-smelling smoke, Flint could find no signs of fire. Four of the gully dwarves had drawn into themselves in fear, their big eyes peering now and then over their shoulders at their screaming comrades.

Those five were covered in varying degrees with a black, tarlike slime, which they were frantically trying to fling from their bodies. Each time they managed to toss a globule to the ground, it exploded on contact with a spark and a loud "bang!" then fizzled into a noxious gray cloud.

"It burn my skin off!"

"Black goop make fingers bubble!"

"It like bomb!"

"I all sweaddy!"

"It eat hole to my brain!"

"That your ear," Nomscul informed him calmly, looking closely at the side of one Aghar's head. Nomscul had been supervising the task. His shaman status helped him avoid lapsing into hysteria with the rest of the Aghar.

"Dunk them in the stream!" Perian cried from behind Flint. She had been back by the tunnel when she heard the gully dwarves' screams. Running up to the group now, she propelled two of the injured gully dwarves over to the left and into the gently flowing stream. She held their collars while they flailed in the water, washing away the mysterious black substance. Finally their wails slowed to sobs. Perian hauled them out and was happy to see that the affected skin was shiny pink but otherwise unharmed.

Seeing her success, Flint shoved the other two Aghar in, and soon their symptoms were relieved as well. Teeth chattering, the soaked Aghar clustered around their king, looking like drowned rats.

"Someone had better tell me what's going on here!" Flint demanded of the group. "Nomscul?"

Nomscul's wispy mustache twitched above his lips. "I use my magic bag to stop yelling, but it not work! It *always* work before!" Nomscul's eyes narrowed, shifting the bags underneath them. "You put curse on it, O kingly guy?"

Flint scowled. "Of course it doesn't work—it's just a bag of dir—" He sighed and gathered his patience about him like a cloak. "Nomscul, where did that black stuff come from?"

"That all king want to know?" Nomscul asked. "It beast guts." He pulled Flint over to the remains of the carrion crawler and pointed. "See sack of yuk, there? They chopping like you say, and out goop fly!"

"Must be like a venom sack," Perian suggested. "How are we going to get rid of the rest of this thing without disturbing that exploding organ?"

Flint was scratching his beard in thought. "Hand me your dagger," he said to Perian. Puzzled, the mountain dwarf pulled it from her belt and placed it into Flint's open palm. He bent and stirred it around in the black slime.

"What do you think you're doing with my blade?" Perian demanded.

"Just give me a second here," Flint said softly. Flicking the wrist of the hand that held the dagger, Flint sent some slime sizzling on its way to the dirt floor. A loud clap, like a firecracker, erupted, and then a narrow column of thick, acrid smoke billowed upward. Flint checked the surface of Perian's blade and saw that it was still smooth and unpocked. Apparently, the substance was corrosive to skin, but more durable objects, like metal, and probably glass and clay, were impervious to its caustic effects.

Flint handed the weapon back to the frawl. "How much of this black venom do you figure there is here?"

"I don't know, quite a lot. The abdominal sac is very large—and there could be another venom gland, for all we know. What does it matter?" Perian asked.

Flint was doing some calculations in his mind and did not hear her question.

"You're not thinking of—?"

"I certainly am," he cut in, smiling slyly as he suddenly became aware of her again. "I think, Perian, that we may have found our secret weapon. . . ."

* * * * *

Basalt's right hand curled around the ring of teleportation. His eyes were squeezed shut in deliberation, his thoughts on the main room of the family homestead. Then, for a brief second, an image of Moldoon's inviting tap room flashed through his mind and he could feel his body wavering in midair! In panic, he opened his eyes and saw both the family home and Moldoon's, shimmering and distant. Instantly he clamped his eyes shut again and flooded his mind with thoughts of home, his family, the furniture—and in a brief moment that seemed like an eternity, the wavering stopped and he sensed that he was standing on his own feet. Somewhere.

The air was warm on his freckled cheeks. He opened his eyes slowly, and before him stood his Uncle Ruberik's unsmiling, astonished countenance. The wooden pails in Ruberik's hands clattered to the floor, creating a small puddle of creamy white milk at his feet.

"What's the meaning of this? Where did you come from? What happened to you? You've got some explaining to do, you foolish young trickster!"

"Yes, Basalt," he heard his mother chime in from behind, "besides this bit of nonsense, where have you been since, well—" She coughed uncomfortably. "Where have you been all night? Tybalt's been looking for you, not to mention the rest of us have been worried."

Basalt had not moved since the moment of his arrival, and now he stepped back toward the fireplace to get both of them into view, Bertina in the kitchen, Ruberik at the door. He saw in their faces their usual reaction to him—his uncle's anger, his mother's distress—and he nearly lost his courage. But he reminded himself that there was a good cause for his strange behavior, one far too important to forsake.

"Milk's a-curdlin', so speak up, harrn! You look harder used than an old anvil—where have you been drinking all night?" Ruberik demanded.

Basalt pushed words into his throat. "Ma, Uncle Rubie,

I've got to tell you something," he began, his voice shaking, his eyes darting from one figure to the other. "You're not going to want to believe any of this, but you've got to! Dad didn't die of a heart attack, he was murdered with derro magic!"

Bertina gasped, then bit her knuckles. Ruberik slapped his thigh angrily. "Gods curse you, now you're making up hurtful lies to cover your indulgences! I've tried everything, talking to you, yelling at you, shaming you, trying to help however I could, and this is your response?" He stomped over to Basalt and snatched the young dwarf's wrist. "Maybe a day or two in jail—for running from the scene of a murder—will make you dry out and think about your ways!"

Basalt stood his ground, in spite of his churning stomach and trembling knees, and spoke quickly and intently.

"Please let me explain," he began again. "I'm sorry if I startled you, but the derro are planning to attack Hillhome and we have very little time to prepare."

Ruberik scowled with impatience. "*Now* what nonsense are you jabbering about?"

"Basalt, you're not making any sense, but I've never seen you so earnest," said Bertina. "Whatever's got you in this state, you just take your time and explain it."

Ruberik huffed, "It's obvious what's got him in this state, and I've humored it as much as I care to. It's time to—"

"Rubie," cut in Bertina, "leave it be. Let him talk."

The nervous hill dwarf smiled gratefully toward his mother. "I know I haven't been very responsible lately," he said, ignoring his uncle's snort of agreement, "but I am not drunk now, nor am I lying." He took a deep breath.

"Dad was killed because he discovered that the plows the derro are transporting are just a front for massive weapon shipments to some nation in the north."

"Basalt," his mother moaned, drawing a handkerchief from her sleeve, "how do you know this?"

"I've been with Uncle Flint. They tried to kill him for learning the same thing."

Ruberik slapped his head in understanding. "*There's* a

trustworthy source. My infrequent older brother, the twilight derro killer!"

Basalt frowned. "Uncle Rubie, please let me finish. If you still don't believe me when I'm done, I'll cheerfully hand myself over to Uncle Tybalt and go to jail. It won't matter anyway, because if no one believes me we'll *all* be dead in five or six days," he said ominously. Even Ruberik felt compelled to be silent.

"Flint *had* to kill the derro because he was caught spying in their wagons that night."

It was Bertina's turn to interrupt now. "But what does your father have to do with any of this?"

Basalt rubbed his face. He was exhausted and flustered. How would he convince the town if he couldn't make his own family believe? "Uncle Flint became suspicious and got the idea to look in the wagons when Moldoon told him Father had gone to do the same thing just before he died. Flint sneaked over the wall into the wagon yard and ran into Garth, who thought Flint was Dad's ghost. Garth was frightened out of his wits because he'd been there the night Dad was murdered and saw it all happen. I'm sorry, Ma, but I've got to say this. Garth told Flint how an odd-looking derro had struck down Dad with a bolt of blue smoke . . ."

* * * * *

". . . Perian was a captain of the House Guard under this Pitrick's command until he pushed her into the Beast Pit for trying to save Uncle Flint. She's absolutely certain that Pitrick will follow through on his threat to wipe out Hillhome. . . ."

With the long story finally told, Basalt leaned back in the chair he'd taken by the hearth and stared into the fire. I've done my best, he thought. At least I tried.

Neither his mother nor Ruberik spoke for a long minute.

"So why doesn't Flint come back to Hillhome himself and tell us?" Ruberik asked at last.

"Oh, I guess I forgot that part," answered Basalt, draping the crook of his elbow across his eyes. "The gully dwarves who rescued them have some sort of prophecy that Flint and

Perian fulfilled when they were pushed into the pit. They've been made king and queen of Mudhole, and had to vow on their honor that they wouldn't run away." Basalt's voice trailed off as he realized that, with all the outrageous events in his story, this last part might well sink his credibility entirely. He dropped the raised arm back into his lap. "You don't believe me, do you? If I hadn't seen it, I wouldn't believe me, either."

"That's the most sensible admission I've heard yet," muttered Ruberik.

But Basalt shot up in the chair and extended his right hand. "But I've got the ring! You saw me teleport here— where else would I get something like this? And once I'd got it, why would I come back here just to tell lies? I could go anywhere I want, anywhere at all! Instead, I came back here to warn everyone. Doesn't that count for anything?"

Ruberik rose to his feet and straightened his jacket before addressing his nephew. "When you started this tale, you said you'd go see Uncle Tybalt, whether I believed you or no. Are you ready to go?"

Bertina looked sadly at her brother-in-law. "Would you really turn in my son?" she asked.

"I would if I thought he was lying. But obviously, he's not. Come on, lad. We've some tough persuading ahead of us if we're going to wake up this town."

* * * * *

"We have encountered a new problem," said Pitrick softly.

The thane listened half-interestedly, while his gargoyles leered and flapped their leathery wings behind him. "Yes?" he finally inquired.

"The dwarves of Hillhome are preparing to rise against us," the adviser said. Pitrick used the story he had devised on his way back to the city. He had decided that the hill dwarf's warning was too potentially dangerous to ignore.

"Indeed?" Realgar sat forward and fixed Pitrick with an icy gaze. "What do you intend to do about it?"

"There is but one thing to do," announced the hunchback, his voice an oily hiss.

"The village must be destroyed."

* * * * * *

"What's the next step?" Ruberik asked Tybalt a little later, after they'd convinced the constable of their story. "We're all family to start with, and none of us depends on trading with the derro for our livelihood. But what do you think is going to happen when this story starts getting around? A lot of people are going to get real upset, and the rest are just plain not going to believe it."

"That's certain," agreed Tybalt. "There's just no way we're going to talk people out of the easy money the derro have been throwing around."

The small group of Fireforge harrns and frawls lapsed into silence in Tybalt's sparse office: Basalt, Ruberik, Bertina, and Tybalt. A stout table took up the middle of the chamber. Tybalt, in his sturdy chair, sat with his feet on the table, pipe in mouth. Basalt and Bertina sat on stools pulled up alongside the table, while Ruberik paced between the door and the opposite wall. Despite the tension in the room, Basalt felt a new sense of family unity that he found very warming.

Basalt glanced timidly from Ruberik to Tybalt, then spoke up. "Perhaps if we could get two or three leading citizens on our side, like the Hammerhands or Strikesparks, we would carry a lot more influence. People would listen to someone like that even if they wouldn't believe me."

"The problem with that idea," responded Ruberik, "is that the 'leading families' are almost universally the ones who've benefitted the most from the derro's presence. That's why they're the 'leading families.' "

"No, the people who are profiting won't be willing to risk those profits," stated Tybalt. "Not unless we can demonstrate a clear danger. Then, perhaps, they will admit that dealing with the derro was a bad idea."

Bertina picked up the train of thought. "But as far as I can see, the only way to demonstrate that there really is danger is to get everyone together and have a look inside one of the wagons. When they see that it's full of weapons, how could anyone deny that it's a threat?"

"Precisely," said Tybalt.

"That's just fine and dandy," Ruberik interjected, "but you'll never get anyone to look inside the wagons. They'll all be afraid that we might be wrong. If a mass of townspeople marches up and arrests the drivers and searches their wagons and finds nothing but plows and farming tools, we'll have caused an enormous incident with Thorbardin that could jeopardize the whole trade arrangement.

"No," he concluded, "this town will need to be handed proof—not just evidence—on a silver platter."

Suddenly Basalt grew so excited he nearly tumbled off his stool. "That's the answer, Uncle Ruberik! Let's hand them the proof. They can't stop *us* from searching the wagons.

"If the four of us got into the wagon yard, we could capture the derro inside, search the wagons, and *then* call in the rest of the town and show them what we found. If we find nothing, then the whole affront is our fault and the town can blame it on a tiny group of troublemakers."

Silence reigned once again as everyone considered Basalt's proposal. Finally, Tybalt leaned forward and said, "Here's what we'll need. . . ."

* * * * *

Hillhome was already bustling as the four Fireforges made their way to the wagon yard. They stopped a short way down the street and eyed the open gate.

"Do they ever post a guard?" asked Ruberik.

"One or two of them stay inside, but they don't come out in the sun," Tybalt replied. "Anyone can come or go as they please. But the derro keep a pretty close eye on the entrance because they don't want people who have no reason going inside anyway."

"So we could just walk in?" Basalt proposed.

"Not without attracting a lot of attention," explained Tybalt. "That's where your ring comes in. Remember the plan and what we talked about in my office. Just keep your wits about you and you'll be fine. We'll all be fine. Now, whenever you're ready."

Basalt nodded his head. He peered intently down the street and through the wagon yard gate, concentrating on the forge area. Just beyond the forge was the shop area where tools were kept and the derro slept. To the right of the shop were the stables. Basalt focused mentally on a spot just a few feet from the forge. With his stomach churning slightly, he touched Pitrick's ring and then, with a slight pop in his ears, he was standing beside the forge. I'm really getting the hang of this, he thought with satisfaction.

Guttoral laughter from inside the shop building reminded Basalt of his dangerous mission. He glanced back over his shoulder to see his mother and two uncles standing beneath the trees where he had been only moments earlier, giving him reassuring waves.

Glancing around, Basalt saw the two heavy freight wagons parked to his right, in front of the stables. He spotted a pair of legs moving between the wagons. Quickly he turned back to the door of the forge and flung it open. His keen dwarven eyes adjusted quickly to the darkness. He sighted three derro, bolting from their beds in reaction to the sudden crash and light streaming through the door.

"Wake up, you big-eyed, moss-chewing, parasites. I've brought you some eggs to suck for breakfast!" shouted the nervous hill dwarf. Immediately he turned and ran as the three enraged derro charged after him. The fourth derro raced around the end of the nearer wagon and joined in the pursuit.

As Basalt ran, he picked out a spot along the wall of the wagon yard, directly off to his right. He slowed down, letting the derro nearly catch up to him, before touching the ring and popping across the open ground to reappear twenty yards away, alongside the wall.

The startled derro skidded to a stop, casting searching glances this way and that for the mysterious dwarf. Basalt waited a few moments, then waved his arm and hollered, "Hey, over here, you stinking sewer rats! Are you blind?"

Furious, the derro tore after Basalt again, drawing daggers from their belts as they ran. Basalt watched them come on, at the same time eyeing the top of a barrel standing near the stables. As the derro closed to within a few yards, he touched the ring and instantly vanished, reappearing again atop the barrel.

The derro crashed into the wall where Basalt had been standing, falling over each other and swearing in their harsh language. Within moments they were back on their feet, choking with rage and scanning the yard for their prey. With a yell, one of them spotted him and the pack was on the attack again.

But this time, as they reached the halfway point to Basalt's position, one of them paused momentarily. A dagger flashed in his hand and then, with a ringing "thunk," embedded itself in the stable wall inches from Basalt's left shoulder. Immediately the others followed suit, and another dagger and two hatchets flew toward the hapless hill dwarf. A split-second later they pierced the wooden wall, dead on target, but their target was not there. Seeing the danger, Basalt had grasped the ring and teleported himself next to the forge, back to where he had first landed in the wagon yard.

Basalt realized he was shaking and paused a moment to catch his breath before turning and sprinting toward the wagons. He had taken only a few steps when the derro, bloodlust showing in their oversized eyes, careened around both sides of the stable. Basalt raced scant yards ahead of them directly between the wagons. As he broke past the back ends of the vehicles, Tybalt, who was standing behind one wagon, tossed a gleaming sword to his nephew. Basalt turned in time to see the derro charge straight into the Fireforge's trap; two sturdy spear shafts shot out, knee high, from either side of the passage. Tybalt held one, with his shoulder braced against the wagon's open tailgate, and Ruberik held the other. The derro tumbled headlong over the unexpected hurdles, sliding to a stop in the damp earth.

Seconds later, Tybalt, Ruberik, Basalt, and even Bertina stood over the prone and cursing derro, holding contraband weapons to their throats. "You were right about the weapons and the wagons, lad," puffed Ruberik.

Bertina's face was flushed from the excitement and exertion as she beamed at her son. Tybalt shook his spear at one of the derro, commanding, "Bertina, you run and fetch the mayor and anyone else from the council you can find. Meanwhile, let's get this sorry lot tied up. I've a feeling the truly nasty part of this job's just beginning."

*   *   *   *   *

Hill dwarves from throughout the town quickly gathered as the news of the derro's betrayal spread. Some, such as the pompous merchant Micah, at first objected to the attacks against their partners in trade. Others, including Hildy, the militia captain, and finally even Mayor Holden, recognized the seriousness of their situation.

"It doesn't matter what you think, Micah. This council has made its decision." The speaker, Mayor Holden, stood atop a barrel in the wagon yard, surrounded by the four other members of the council, the village militia master, Axel Broadblade, and a throng of townsfolk. "It's obvious that the Theiwar lied to us and are using our town to prepare for a war. We've all seen the weapons concealed in the wagons and we've heard the testimony from these derro prisoners. The council's vote has gone against you, Micah, and that's the end of that. If you could pry your nose out of all that Theiwar steel you've been collecting, you would see that this is the only decent course of action.

"Now, let's hear from the master of militia what sort of action we can take." Mayor Holden clambered down from the barrel and several other dwarves helped Broadblade, a stocky veteran of many ancient campaigns, up. The militia master was considered the epitome of the military dwarf by the citizens of Hillhome. He always dressed in a clean, green overcoat; a ribbed helmet with hinged earflaps; and thigh-high, hard leather boots with the tops turned down. He also carried a long dagger in a scabbard that hung from his belt in the manner of a human cavalry officer. Cavalry was almost nonexistent in dwarven armies, but the scabbard added a certain panache to the uniform. Broadblade cleared his throat, folded his hands behind his back, and addressed the crowd.

"As those of you who are members of the Hillhome

Militia—and that's most of you, even if you don't show up regularly for drill—are aware, our arsenal of weapons is both small and eclectic, consisting as it does of a mixture of hunting, farming, and carpentry implements. This has proven adequate in the past when dealing with occasional raiding critters and wandering bandit mobs.

"If we are to defend ourselves against the mountain dwarves, however—as we inevitably must, now that their nefarious scheme has been uncovered—we will need quality weapons, of a uniform nature, which can be used in precise formations. Fortunately, a significant stock of such weapons—approximately forty spears, twenty-five swords, and thirty-five axes, or approximately one hundred weapons in all—has just fallen into our hands. Unfortunately, our militia contains just over three-hundred-fifty combatants, leaving us with a shortfall of approximately, uhhmmm, two-hundred-fifty weapons. Some of this can be made up from existing inventory, but a large number of weapons is still needed, desperately."

Broadblade paused for a moment, letting his math settle on the crowd for effect. Then, with a stern face, he continued.

"Two more wagons should arrive tomorrow, according to the usual schedule. We shall seize these wagons and appropriate their contents. Assuming they, too, contain fifty weapons apiece, that brings our total to two-hundred. It would, however, be imprudent to expect any more shipments after that, as the Theiwar will quickly realize that something is happening to their wagons."

"So where do we get another one-hundred-fifty weapons?" shouted someone in the crowd.

"That is the significant question," admitted Broadblade. "The plows and such in these wagons will provide the raw material for a few more, but not nearly enough."

"We can't fight without enough weapons," shouted someone else.

Basalt crowded his way up to the barrel. "Listen, I've got an idea," he yelled as he climbed to the top of the barrel with Broadblade.

The militia master quieted the crowd. "Everyone, this is the young fellow who tipped us off to the whole thing. What's your idea, Fireforge?"

"Two wagons left for New Sea last night. We know that the trip takes two days; they travel all night and then lay up somewhere during the daylight," Basalt explained. "If we start right now, with a fast wagon, we should be able to catch them before dark."

"Use my brewery wagon," offered Hildy. "It's smaller and faster than their big carts, and it's empty right now, waiting for another load."

Broadblade boomed out over the crowd, "We need volunteers to go with Basalt and Hildy to overtake the two wagons. You can draw weapons from the new stock and start immediately. The rest of you, assemble in one hour in the square, ready to start fortifying the town in accordance with the plans Mayor Holden and I will prepare.

"Let's get to work!"

Chapter 18

The Secret Weapon

"Go for big march!"

"Outside time!"

A chorus of shrieks and whoops erupted as the Aghar danced around Flint and Perian, delighted by the news of their impending campaign.

"It's not a picnic!" Flint bellowed. "We're going to war! To fight the mountain dwarves!"

The celebration continued, unaffected by his words of caution.

"Let them enjoy the idea now," counselled Perian, patting Flint on the shoulder. "They'll find out soon enough what we mean."

"I suppose you're right," agreed the hill dwarf. He cast another look at the dancing, scampering Aghar. He could not help but wonder how many of them now cavorted in Mudhole for the last time.

*　*　*　*　*　*

"Come on, Grayhoof, pull!" Hildy barked at the heavy draft horse, her blond braids flying behind her. The steed leaned forward into his traces, straining every massive muscle to pull the wagon up the pass.

Basalt pushed back his red locks and leaned forward on the buckboard beside Hildy, as if he could help the struggling creature with his own forward momentum. Behind them, five more hill dwarves—all young, all armed to the teeth—lay low within the wagon's boxy cargo bed.

"Up, boy! Faster!" The brewer's daughter coaxed and cajoled the grizzled gelding, and the old horse responded by putting every sinew of his massive body into the task. Basalt noticed that Hildy didn't use a whip, yet she seemed able to bring every bit of desperate energy out of her faithful steed. Foam flecked Grayhoof's mouth, and the old horse's flanks heaved with the effort of its labors.

They were six hours east of Hillhome on the mountainous Passroad. The hill dwarves were headed toward Newsea to ambush the derro wagons that had left Hillhome the night before. None of them knew how far beyond the pass they would find the derro waystation. Soon they would be out of the mountains and into the plains just west of Newsea, and that would make for quicker travel. Sooner or later the light wooden beerwagon, with its single hitch, would catch up to the iron-bound freight wagons of the derro, even with their four-horse teams.

The hill dwarves looked anxiously at the sun as it sank into the western sky. They had to reach the derro camp between Hillhome and Newsea by sunset, or else their quarry would start for the sea. A hundred more weapons that could be used to defend Hillhome would then be lost.

"How much farther do you figure it is?" asked Turq Hearthstone, popping his head up from the box behind Basalt and Hildy. A heavily muscled lad, he propped his chin up on the edge of the wagon.

"I don't know," Basalt admitted. "But it's got to be close enough that the Theiwar can get there in one night's travel from Hillhome. We know from Mayor Holden that they get off the road again by daylight."

Another hill dwarf, Horld, also looked up out of the wagon. "How many of the white-bellied scum do you think we'll find there?"

Basalt thought for a moment. "Three per wagon, two wagons coming and two going. . . . My best guess is there'll be about twelve of them."

Horld counted for a moment. "Against seven of us," he calculated.

"We'll have the element of surprise on our side," Basalt encouraged, adding a silent "I hope." Horld settled back, apparently satisfied with the answer.

Basalt saw that the others were looking to him for leadership now. Horld had always been one of the more prominent of the younger generation in Hillhome. In some ways he'd been sort of a bully, and Basalt usually tried to avoid him. Now here he was, asking Basalt's opinions.

"Couldn't you use that ring to go there, find out for sure?" asked Turq, gesturing to the intertwined steel bands on Basalt's finger.

Basalt shook his head. "Magic is strange, I guess. I can only use the ring to go places that I've seen and can picture in my mind. I don't know where the derro stop is; they might take shelter anywhere in a cave or the forest." He shrugged helplessly.

The heavily breathing Grayhoof lumbered through the saddle between two looming hills that marked the summit of the Passroad; it would be downhill from here to the sea. "Giddap, now, boy! Run for it!" Hildy cried.

Sensing the lightening of his burden, the horse broke into an easy trot. The wagon rumbled and jounced behind, and in places Hildy had to rein Grayhoof in a bit just to keep the wagon from hurrying the horse. Traces squealed in protest, wheels and timbers creaked, and the noise of their descent precluded anything less than shouted conversation.

Basalt hung on for his life as they rocketed down the narrow, twisting road. He looked over at Hildy, saw her eyes locked on the horse and the route before them, her face fixed in an expression of fierce, teeth-gritting determination. He thought about the five harrns in the back of the wagon, and began to feel all confused again.

What should we do? They expect *me* to decide—but I'm no adventurer! I can't do this! Now that we are nearing our goal, the whole plan seems hare-brained. *My* foolhardy idea is risking the lives of six others, as well as my own!

Then Basalt remembered his Uncle Flint's words of inspiration. Maybe together he and his comrades could meet these mountain dwarves and best them. They were seven young hill dwarves, all strong, all well-armed. He sneaked another look at the sun. If they were lucky, they would reach the derro in daylight—and gain a significant advantage over their subterranean-dwelling cousins.

Dark pines grew to each side of the rutted track. They passed an occasional farm or forest cottage, inhabited by a few of the hill dwarves who had emigrated over the pass years before. Basalt and Hildy both examined every one of them closely for signs of derro, but saw none. As the lengthening shadows of the trees stretched over the road, Basalt began to fear that he and his crew would be too late to find the derro before dark.

"I see something there!" Hildy whispered suddenly, pointing to a dirt track, deeply rutted, that branched off from the road. At the end of it, some fifty yards away, was a large, dark brown barn of heavy logs. The windowless structure had a large opening on one side, sheltered by an extending, overhanging portion of roof. Four heavy derro wagons, their iron-spoked wheels towering higher than any of the dwarves, stood in the yard. One black-armored derro, standing in the shade beside a wagon, squinted at them as they rolled by. None of the horses was around, and only the single derro was conspicuous, performing a listless circuit of the wagons, obviously bored.

"Stay down!" Basalt hissed to the dwarves in the back. They drew even with the path. "Go past," Basalt muttered to

Hildy, his heart pounding. "Let's not show we're unusually interested."

Without missing a beat, the frawl urged the draft horse along. The small wagon rumbled past the track and was once again surrounded by dark, towering pines.

"Okay, stop here," Basalt ordered after they had rolled several hundred yards beyond the muddy trail. Grayhoof lumbered off the road, pulling the wagon under the thick branches of several overhanging boughs. "Everyone out! Hurry—the sun's already dropping behind the trees."

The six other hill dwarves piled out of the wagon, hefting their weapons and standing in the darkness beneath the trees. For a moment no one moved, and then Basalt realized that they were waiting for him to give the orders.

"Okay," he offered, his voice a hoarse whisper. "We've got to move quietly. We'll sneak through the woods until we get to the edge of their barn. Then we take them by surprise."

Holding their axes and daggers firmly, the hill dwarves advanced in a file through the woods to the left of the barn, Basalt leading the way to the clearing.

Suddenly Basalt squatted. His companions followed suit.

"There's still just the one guard, so the others must be inside," Basalt whispered. "And the horses. I'll get the guard quietly. As soon as I do, rush the barn."

The others nodded acceptance of his plan, and Basalt flushed when Hildy kissed him quickly on his freckled cheek. "For good luck," she said.

He crawled forward until he crouched among the last branches of the pine trees before the clearing, watching the listless derro perform his circuit. Finally, the fellow turned away from Basalt, stepping around one of the wagons and disappearing from his sight.

Instantly Basalt started forward, trying to run in a crouch. He winced with each footfall, but soon reached the wagon where he had last seen the guard. Clenching his axe in both hands, he looked toward the barn. No alarm, yet. No sunlight reached the floor of the clearing, but the sky overhead was still bright. He hoped that would be enough to impair the derro.

Resolutely, Basalt stepped around the corner of the wagon. Before him, with his back to the hill dwarf, was the derro, not ten feet away. Basalt tried to creep soundlessly, but his foot made an audible thunk as he lowered it into a muddy patch of ground.

The derro whirled in surprise. Basalt saw the fellow's wide eyes blink in confusion, and then the mountain dwarf squinted. "Eh?" the Theiwar began. "Is it time, already?" In the bright light he mistook Basalt for one of his own comrades.

"It's time," grunted Basalt. Suddenly all the tragedy, all the frustrations and humiliations inflicted by the mountain dwarves, was focused onto this derro in front of him. Basalt's silver-bladed axe flew forward, biting into the side of the unsuspecting Theiwar's neck. Soundlessly the dwarf dropped to the ground.

For a moment Basalt froze, listening and thinking. He tried to detect some kind of revulsion or horror in himself. He had never killed anyone before; shouldn't he feel some remorse? Yet the slaying of the derro seemed like any other task, difficult and dangerous perhaps, but very necessary.

"That was for Moldoon," he whispered to the corpse. Then he stepped back around the wagon and gestured to the others.

The six hill dwarves rushed from their concealment. Basalt leaped forward to join them, and the whole band charged through the gaping door into the darkness of the barn.

Their eyes struggled to adjust to the sudden change in lighting. They heard the mountain dwarves cursing, smelled the presence of the heavy draft horses.

Basalt could see several derro, who had been squatting around a low cookfire, leap to their feet and snatch up weapons. Several others were still wrapped in bedrolls. Now they struggled awkwardly to escape, taken unawares.

Basalt cracked his axe down, hard, against the parry of a derro's short sword. The mountain dwarf staggered back, thrown off balance. Basalt swung again and again, driving him farther back. He attacked with a reckless savagery that surprised even himself.

This Theiwar wore metal armor and used his blade with skill, striking past one of the hill dwarf's blows to scrape Basalt's leg. But his experience was no match for the hill dwarf's savage onslaught, and in another step the mountain dwarf backed into the wall of the barn.

The derro lunged once more, a desperate stab at Basalt's heart. The hill dwarf skipped nimbly out of the way, and the enemy had no parry for his next blow. The battle-axe sliced into the derro's forehead, driving deep into his brain. Soundlessly, the mountain dwarf toppled forward.

Basalt wrenched his weapon free, whirling to look around the barn. Several other derro lay motionless, and one of the hill dwarves writhed in pain, sprawled on the ground. He saw Hildy driving her heavy sword at another derro, and Basalt sprinted toward her. She ran the fellow through without any of his help, however.

The Theiwar who had finally struggled out of their bedrolls wasted no time in fleeing from the barn, casting frightened backward glances at the hill dwarves. In moments they disappeared into the surrounding forest.

"Let 'em go," Basalt advised when Turq and Horld started after. "We've got the weapons we came for."

Hildy knelt beside Drauf, the wounded young harrn. A chubby lad, he had been cut in the thigh, but the blade had not touched bone. Hildy bound the wound and stopped the bleeding, making Drauf more comfortable. "I'll be okay," he muttered, sitting up weakly.

"Good," Basalt said, clapping him on the back. "Let's be gone from this hole and get back on the road to Hillhome, then. There should be enough moonlight to guide us, but we can stop along the way if we must. We'll take the two wagons that have weapons in 'em. Turq and Horld, go look underneath the boxes." He described the compartment as Flint had related it to him. "We'll leave the other two here."

"If we take all of their horses," Hildy suggested, "then even the wagons we leave are useless to the derro who ran away."

"Good idea," Basalt agreed. They identified and hitched

up the two wagons that still held a great many weapons, tossing out the inferior plows on top to lighten the load. With the eight extra draft horses following along, tied to a single line, they started back to Hillhome.

* * * * *

The rest of Flint's day was spent collecting the secret weapon of explosive sludge into every available glass and clay vessel in Mudhole. More than once, Flint was forced to dive and catch a jug that got knocked over, drag a smoking Aghar to the stream, or haul a frantic subject, kicking and thrashing, from the inside of the carrion crawler's carcass. By the end of the day, his nerves and patience were completely worn out. Even the gully dwarves knew enough to leave him alone that night.

The next two days—all the time remaining to them— were devoted to drilling the gully dwarves in the maneuvers of war. Perian's experience in this regard was invaluable. Unfortunately, the maneuvers and formations used by the House Guard were completely hopeless for the gully dwarves.

"Get in line," screamed Perian. "Get in line!" Eyeing the ragged row of Aghar with disgust, Perian stomped up to the worst offender, who was standing a full four feet in front of everyone else, and walked a slow circle around him.

She stopped in front of him and stared into his eyes.

"What's your name, citizen?"

"Spittul, O great and powerful Queen."

Flint, seated at the end of the line, guffawed.

Perian glowered at him, then turned back to Spittul. "Are you really trying to be a soldier, Spittul, or are you playing games with me?"

Spittul's eyes lit up. The queen was talking directly to him! "Oh, yes, Queen Furryend, I want be a solder real bad!"

"And that's what you're doing, Spittul," shouted Flint. "Keep up the good work." The hill dwarf roared at his joke, and roared twice as loud as the muscles in Perian's neck bulged.

Through clenched teeth, Perian ordered, "Take two steps back and then don't move." She turned and stomped to where Flint lay in the moss, grabbed him by the belt, and dragged him out of earshot of the troops. "How do you expect me to get any kind of discipline into this rabble when you undermine my authority?" she hissed.

"It's hopeless anyway," chuckled Flint, wiping his eyes. "You can't drill these tunnel apes like veterans. They'll never learn. They're just not made to stand in lines."

Perian turned around to look at the assembled group. "So what do you suggest? We herd them into a pack and yell 'charge!' at the first opportunity? They'll fry themselves with their own sludge bombs."

"Probably," Flint confessed. "I think we need some new tactics, something more suited to their ability."

"Be my guest," snorted Perian.

Flint strolled back past the slowly mingling knots of Aghar. "The problem, as I see it," he said to them, "is one of getting close enough to the bad guys to lob sludge bombs into them, without getting beaten up first. It's obvious we can't hope to do it as a big group. Maybe we can do it as small groups. Let's try something . . .

"You harrn over there," Flint shouted, indicating a group of about ten gully dwarves who actually seemed to be paying attention. "I want you to move, all together in a bunch, over to the wall and then back here again."

With a good deal of pushing and shoving, they clomped to the wall, turned, and elbowed their way back to where they'd started.

"Very good," declared Flint. "Now we're going to try it again, this way." He positioned the gully dwarves so that those in front were holding their shields in front and those behind were holding their shields overhead, forming good cover.

"OK, walk to the wall and back, and keep your shields where I put them."

The Aghar stumbled to the wall, turned, and jostled back. By the time they reached Flint, several shields had been dropped and the rest were all askew.

"That was pathetic," Perian announced. "This is a dead end."

Flint shook his head. "I disagree. By the time they returned they were all mixed up, but they reached the wall in pretty good order. I think that with some practice, they could do this."

"Why bother?" Perian shot back.

"I'll show you." Flint turned back to his test group. "Everybody pick up a rock and then resume your positions." General mingling, pushing, rock picking, and swapping broke out until Flint countermanded his order. "Hold it, let's try one thing at a time. Everybody pick up *one* rock.

"Now everybody put your shield where I showed you.

"Now everybody walk toward where the monster came into the cavern and when I say 'throw,' everybody throw their rock at the wall." The Aghar stumbled along a weaving path toward the wall. When Flint hollered, "Throw!" they dropped their shields and pelted the wall with rocks, then fell on the floor laughing, wrestling, and scratching.

Flint turned back toward Perian. "Maybe the hill dwarves should flee now, before it's too late. This is hopeless."

Perian stared at the tangled mob of Aghar on the floor. "Nonsense! I see lots of progress. What do you call that maneuver?" she asked.

Flint sighed. "The wedge."

The wedge—which the Aghar quickly renamed the wedgie—the Agharpult, and general target practice made up the bulk of their drills. Perian was cheered to discover the Aghar were excellent shots with a thrown rock or sludge bomb (a skill developed by stoning rodents for food, she discovered later). The Agharpult they enjoyed, and showed a natural proficiency for distance, if not accuracy.

But the wedgie, Flint was convinced, was their real strength. By the end of their training period they could cross the Big Sky Room in a tight clump at a run, hurl their dummy sludge bombs, and run back, all without being prompted with orders every step of the way.

Still, two days was only two days.

"Why king frown every time when we do our army

stuff?" asked Nomscul. "Him look worse than old gold-funger lompchuter."

Flint only glowered at the gully dwarf shaman. Gritting his teeth, unable to watch the ludicrous marching exhibition for a moment longer, Flint called out, "Listen up you frawls and harrns!" He clapped his hands. After much pushing, shoving, and eye poking, the gully dwarves stood in a mass, at what vaguely resembled attention.

"What you folks need is something to give your work purpose, some driving rhythm that synchronizes and unites you as an unstoppable force." Perian giggled behind her hand, and Flint elbowed her in the ribs. He moved away to pace before them, arms linked behind his back, his eyes on the ground. "That is why I've decided to teach you a very special, sacred, royal dwarven song." A hush fell over the crowd of assembled Aghar.

"King?"

Flint looked up in irritation to see Nomscul waving his hand above his head.

"We know good song," the shaman said proudly.

Nods of agreement fluttered through the crowd. Before Flint could stop them, the gully dwarves launched into a raucous tune.

Big yellow sun,
No spit in eye,
Die all day,
Leafs up in the sky asleep,
Burning bugs,
Gray, gray, gray,
Sleep, old man,
and the trees
call us for eats.
The leafs are on fire,
but so what,
they all gone by snowtime.

"No, no, NO!" Flint roared above their cacophony. He slapped his palm with a thin stick. Eventually their song ground to a halt. "I want you to hear a *real* song. The Dwarven Marching Song is part of your heritage as dwarves. Now, listen up."

Flint cleared his throat and unconsciously straightened his spine. His voice, pleasantly low and rumblingly pitched, began the first strain of the song he had not sung in years, since he had left the dwarves.

> Under the hills   the heart of the axe
> Arises from cinders   the still core of the fire,
> Heated and hammered   the handle an afterthought,
> For the hills are forging   the first breath of war.
> The soldier's heart sires and brothers
> The battlefield.
> Come back in glory
> Or on your shield.

> Out of the mountains   in the midst of the air,
> The axes are dreaming   dreaming of rock,
> Of metal alive through   the ages of ore,
> Stone on metal   metal on stone.
> The soldier's heart contains and dreams
> The battlefield.
> Come back in glory
> Or on your shield.

> Red of iron imagined from the vein,
> Green of brass   green of copper
> Sparked in the fire   the forge of the world,
> Consuming in its dream   as it dives into bone.
> The soldier's heart lies down, completes
> The battlefield.
> Come back in glory
> Or on your shield.

Flint became aware, sometime around "Out of the mountains," that Perian, standing at his side, had joined in the song. Their voices mingled and intertwined, his a low baritone, hers an even, clear alto. When he stumbled over a few forgotten words, Perian was there to fill them in. His heart

was full and near to bursting with pride and passion and
. . . *dwarfness*, as they finished the anthem of their race.
The song had taken on even greater meaning to him with
Perian singing along; he had never thought he shared any
traditions with his mountain cousins. He found his hand in
Perian's, and when he turned to her at the close of the song,
he saw her eyes, brimming with unshed tears, through his
own misty blue ones.

"Quivalen Sath," she breathed, identifying the song's
composer.

"*Is* there anyone else?" Flint asked rhetorically.

"Sing again!" the gully dwarves chanted. "We learn! Sing!
We sing royal song real good!"

Flint and Perian hummed the melody over and over for
the Aghar, then repeated the words of the song with them at
least three times. Practicing, mimicking, stumbling over the
refrains, the gully dwarves stayed with the exercise for at
least an hour. Flint had never seen them try so hard at any
endeavor. A new understanding evolved for everyone. In
the end, when the gully dwarves sang it for the first time in a
chorus, King Flint and Queen Perian did not even mind that
their version came out a bit changed.

> Thunder pills   the fart of the ox
> Erasers for Cindy   these still put out the fire,
> Beated and bammered   the hand thunk a thought,
> The hills are breathing   the fish-breath afar.
> Soldiers hit brothers, sorry
> The battle feels.
> Come back, O glowworm
> And don't forget your shirt.

What mattered was how hard they tried.

Chapter 19

The Best Gift

Thane Realgar of the Thiewar clan strutted before his six hundred House Guard troops, who were lined up in three ranks on the Central Parade Grounds on Level Two of Theiwar City East. His posture was ramrod straight as he stretched to his full height of just under four feet, pearly white hair streaming over his shoulders. He marched rigidly along the line of equally rigid derro dwarves who made up the House Guard.

These troops and their costly barracks occupied the entire second level, just one level below the pinnacle of the city, where the thane and his adviser had their own plush residences. The superior location, away from the smoke and stench of the forges a level below, was a symbol of the military's prestige with its thane.

The dwarves of the guard stood at attention now, conceited about their appearance, smug about their discipline, and haughty over their position in the most prestigious, and only pure Theiwar regiment.

They wore glossy black breastplates of the hardest, most refined steel. Their unnaturally white hair was covered with black helmets of the same metal, with tall, feathered plumes sprouting from the top of each, the color designating a soldier's company, of which there were three. Each dwarf was armed with at least two weapons.

The first rank, denoted by the red plumes on their helmets, were the Bloody Blades, axemen chosen especially for their large size and ferocious demeanor. Among the most savage hand-to-hand fighters on all of Krynn, the dwarves of the Bloody Blades were like machines of death on the battlefield. Each carried a shield and a short sword, in addition to his axe. They were indoctrinated with fanatical loyalty and fanatical zeal in carrying out the orders of their thane. It was rumored that over twenty-five percent of the Theiwar recruited into the Bloody Blades died during training, so rigorous were their preparations. They were forbidden to marry, so they would have no ties outside the unit. Before battle, each would prepare his funeral song, since planning to live through the battle was a sign of weakness.

The second rank of derro, sporting ebony plumes, were known as the Black Bolts. They wielded heavy crossbows, which were slow to load and awkward to fire. But a volley of their bolts could strike with enough force to penetrate steel armor and shields. In fact, most dwarves could not fire one of these crossbows without dislocating a shoulder. Members of the Black Bolts were required to place three out of three shots into an elf-sized target at a range of two-hundred yards. Anyone who failed this test was stricken from the unit.

The third line of Realgar's troops were the Silver Swords, their symbol a tall, swaying gray feather. These derro, while still wearing steel armor, carried smaller shields than the Blades. They were trained in more agile, skirmishing tactics, and could spread out to take advantage of small gaps in an enemy's formation. Individually they were intelligent, motivated, and aggressive. More than once they had won a battle by penetrating the enemy's line and seeking out and killing the enemy general, plunging the opposing army into chaos. They painted their faces with charcoal and ochre before a battle to make themselves appear frightening to the enemy.

Arrayed to the side of these three ranks were the regimental banners, trumpeters, drummers, officers, and signalmen. The trophies they carried from previous battles were both grisly and glorious. They included captured banners, mummified heads, gleaming helmets, monstrous claws, golden spears, and dozens of other tokens and trappings of war.

Actually, there were four ranks of troops, although the fourth was comprised of only six dwarves: the savants. The result of centuries of arcane developments in the deepest bowels of derro civilizations, the savants were the only dwarves who had the unusual ability to cast very powerful spells, ones capable of levitating large objects or even calling down storms of ice. Their skin was even pastier white than others of their race. They wore black like the other House Guard soldiers, though their uniforms were padded robes, not metal armor. Their powers on the battlefield, especially against magicless hill dwarves, could not help but prove decisive.

"Pitrick!" Realgar bellowed, and the hunchbacked dwarf shuffled behind his leader as the thane resumed his inspection. "The troops look splendid! Perian Cyprium obviously excelled at her job before her untimely death." The thane stole a glance at his adviser, suspicious as always about Pitrick's explanation concerning the captain's demise. But the savant kept his face bowed and expressionless. The thane always chose not to press the issue, since Pitrick was far more valuable to him than any frawl captain could be.

"It will please me if you command the House Guard in Perian's stead," the thane said, his tone lazy.

"Yes, my lord," was the adviser's confident response.

"With troops such as these, we can not fail to wipe the little village of hill dwarves from the face of the continent!"

Arms crossed, feet spread wide in a powerful stance, the thane considered his adviser. "The latter is the point of this attack, is it not?"

"Most certainly," Pitrick said quickly. "We shall leave midafternoon this day for the long march through the wagon tunnel, so that we will arrive on the surface at dusk, in familiar darkness. Though I have recently made trips to Sanction, the troops have never been outside the lightlessness of Thorbardin. I am not sure how well their eyes will adjust, so we will travel at night and sleep in caves or under the protection of thick trees during daylight."

Realgar nodded his approval. He, himself, had not been on the surface in many decades, lacking the time or the inclination to go there. "What of snow?" he asked. "Isn't it nearing wintertime above?"

"Yes," Pitrick agreed, "but the wagon crews tell me it is yet early, and the snow is still traversable. I estimate that, encumbered by the mass of troops, it will take two nights of steady marching to reach the dreadful little village. We will attack an unsuspecting Hillhome on the third evening. We can rest the afternoon nearby—out of sight of Hillhome so that our attack will come as a complete surprise."

* * * * *

"What could Perian possibly want in the grotto so late on the night before we leave for battle?" Flint mumbled aloud as he hastened down the final long tunnel leading to the beautiful cavern at the farthest corner of Mudhole. He had been working with Nomscul to pack the explosive sludge into sacks and bottles, as well as clean up some rusty old daggers and sword blades that had been discovered during the searches of the last two days. Nomscul had relayed the message with a giggle: "Queen Furryend say you to meet her at grotto when done. She have big surprise!" With that, the gully dwarf shaman had clamped his hand over his large mouth, refusing to give Flint further clues about the mysterious missive.

At last Flint came to the opening on the right that marked the entrance to the cavern, and he turned down the enclosed staircase, taking the narrow steps two at a time. He paused at the bottom to draw in a breath, then bounded in.

Immediately, he was grabbed by a giggling frawl, Perian's self-appointed "weighty lady," Fester.

"Take off clothes and come with me!" Fester squealed, her fleshy cheeks buckling in a smile as she tugged at Flint's clothing.

"What are you talking about? Stop that! Don't touch me, you silly frawl! Where's Perian?" Flint demanded, trying to shake off Fester's grip.

"I'm right here," Perian called. She came around the corner of a stalagmite and laughed out loud when she saw Flint's stony, red face and Fester's eager tugging. "Stop it, Fester." The frawl Aghar dropped away from Flint, sheepishly regarded the royal family, then scampered up the stairway.

Flustered, Flint gathered the edges of his clothing that Fester had managed to pull down, his face burning. "What's going on here? What have you been teaching her, mugging?"

Perian laughed again. "Unfortunately, she already knew that. Look, I'm sorry," she said, flashing her big, hazel eyes. "Fester must have decided that since I've taken off my usual armor, you would want to as well."

Suddenly Flint became aware that Perian was dressed in a tight-fighting blue-green wrap; his favorite color looked spectacular against her copper hair. She stood silhouetted by the glowing moss behind her near the pool, and for the first time he could really see her shape through the gauzy gown. His eyes traced her form upward, from her surprisingly slim ankles, to her muscular calves, her broad hips, slightly narrowed waist, her ample . . . His cheeks grew hot again, and he forced his eyes back up to the safety of her face.

Perian smiled invitingly and held her hand out to him. "Come, your surprise is getting cold."

Startled, Flint drew back. "What surprise?"

Perian frowned impatiently. "If I told you here, it

wouldn't be a surprise, now would it? You aren't afraid to be alone with me, are you?"

"Certainly not!" Flint huffed, snatching up her hand in embarrassment and irritation. But as he followed her around the stone pillar and into the depths of the grotto, he was not so sure. He forgot his humiliation when he saw what awaited him on the bench before the pool.

Five mismatched pots of steaming food nearly covered the bench and surrounded a single lit candle and two metal plates. Flint clapped his hands and licked his lips as he rushed forward, eyeing the containers.

"What's the occasion?"

"The occasion is our last dinner—a celebration," she said simply, waving him to sit by the plate that faced the pool.

He dropped to the ground on the fluffy moss and slid his legs under the bench. "Celebration," he snorted. "What have we to celebrate? We're leading a ragtag bunch of gully dwarves off to save a village from a powerful, demented magician, and—"

"I know all that," she interrupted with a sigh. "Can't we have just a few last peaceful hours?" She folded her legs under her and gracefully lowered herself to the ground, back to the pool. She took the hilt of an old dagger and stirred it around in one of the pots, then used it to ladle a portion of the pot's contents onto Flint's plate.

"Sauteed white fungus and onions," she said. Pointing from one pot to the next, she rattled off their contents. "There's mushrooms and sprouts, meat—don't ask what kind—in red sauce, turtle soup, and creamed fish."

"Where did you get all this stuff?" Flint mumbled through a mouthful of delicious fungus and onions.

Perian propped her chin up on her hands looking proud, yet a little sheepish. "I'm afraid I risked sending two more Aghar up to the warrens. It took them long enough, but they managed to find most of what I sent them for without getting caught. You'll be happy to know that I did not send them for mossweed—I've broken that habit . . . I think. And also, gully dwarf hands never touched the food during preparation—I made it all myself."

"What a catch—brawn, brains, beauty, *and* she can cook," he muttered unconsciously, busy stuffing his mouth. He listened to his own words and gasped, glancing up quickly, but Perian, intent on her plate, showed no signs of having heard him. They ate quickly and in silence, savoring tastes forgotten in the short week they had been consuming a tiresome catch-all called gully dwarf stew.

When the last bowl was scraped clean, Flint pushed himself back, patting his stomach happily. "Simply marvelous," he sighed.

"I'm glad you enjoyed it," Perian said, standing up. "I hope you like my next surprise as well." She danced past Flint and disappeared behind him into the columns of limestone that ran from floor to ceiling opposite the pool.

The mountain dwarf quickly returned, holding a long, narrow package wrapped in cotton batting and tied shut with twine. Flint watched expectantly, unable to guess its contents.

Perian's head was dipped nervously as she untied the parcel with shaky hands. "I've wanted to give you this for a day or two, but the moment just never seemed right. I wish I could have spent a few more days on it . . ." she mumbled mysteriously as she fumbled with the twine. "Oh, here!" she said, flustered. She flung back the cloth cover and thrust her hands toward him. "A weapon befitting a monarch leading his troops to war."

Curious, Flint peered beyond the wrapping. His breath caught in his throat and he drew no air, his face paling dangerously.

"What's wrong?" Perian asked, concern and dismay creasing her face. "I—I cleaned it up as best I could. I know it's very old, but it's an excellent axe, dwarven-crafted, no doubt. Don't you like it?"

But Flint hardly heard his queen as his eyes focused on the thing in her hands. He reminded himself to breathe, and then he willed his hands forward to grasp the axe.

The haft of smooth oak showed no sign of wear or stress. Polished lovingly, it was without blemish or knots. The wood blended so perfectly into the flawless steel blade that the axe looked as if crafted from one material. The steel blade itself was of that immaculate white-silver quality, and its circumference was decorated with the most delicate, faint tracings. Flint ran his hands lovingly over the familiar dwarven runes, not one bit lighter than when last he had felt them.

For this was no ordinary axe. It was the Tharkan Axe, the weapon he had found, then been given by his brother Aylmar, and then lost again so many years ago.

"Where did you find this?" he said at last, his eyes still on the wondrous axe. Why was it here? Now?

Perian was mightily confused. She had hoped he would like it, but his reaction seemed to go beyond that. He held it like he would a lover. . . .

"I—I found it in the garbage heap in the Big Sky Room, the day we discovered sludge," Perian explained, then chuckled. "You were so sour that day . . . I don't know what possessed me, but the second I saw this axe I knew I had to hide it away and clean it up so I could surprise you with it."

"You didn't know it was once my axe?" he asked, looking from the weapon to her with misty eyes. "But how could you?" he asked himself. "I never told you that story."

"What story? This axe was yours? Did you drop it in the Beast Pit?" Perian was very confused, as her voice rose with her agitation.

Flint shook his shaggy head vigorously, nearly overcome by finding the axe again in, of all places, Mudhole. "No," he whispered softly at last. "My brother, the one who was murdered by Pitrick, gave me the Tharkan Axe on my Fullbeard Day many long years ago. We'd found it together during our dungeon-crawling days, but I lost it in a hobgoblin lair here in the Kharolis Mountains during an adventure several years afterward. I later returned to retrieve it, but it was already gone. The Tharkan Axe served me better than any I've had since." He ran his hands over the haft again, closing his eyes, remembering. "I thought it was gone forever. . . ."

"What a strange coincidence, finding it here," Perian muttered, then shrugged. "Whoever took it from that lair before you returned probably ended up in the Beast Pit, and the gully dwarves just added it to their piles of treasure."

She pressed her fingertips to the runes. "I've made out a few of the words here, but they are in old dwarven. Do you know what they say?"

Flint shook his head, slipping the Tharkan Axe into the loop on his belt. "What with adventuring, I never had the time to have them translated, nor really cared to while the axe worked so beautifully. And then I lost it."

He realized suddenly that he had been so overwhelmed by the present that he'd forgotten to thank the gifter. Flint leaned back and observed her copper head, her peach-fuzzy cheeks, the warm smile on her red lips. He had come to depend on her for so much. . . . "I don't know how to thank you, Perian. This axe is the best present—two presents—" He laughed "—that I've ever received. You've given me hope for tomorrow."

Perian blushed. "I'm just glad you like it, and that it was especially special." She turned away to pour two luke-warm cups of weed tea.

"I have nothing to give you," Flint said sadly, then had a thought. "Wait!" He reached into his tunic and pulled a chain over his head from around his neck.

"I *do* have something for you—it's not much," he said, embarrassed. He did not watch Perian's face as he turned his palm over and held his hand out.

"A leaf!" she cried, setting the cups down on the bench. Perian took the delicate carving, linked to an old, silver chain, and held it in the tips of her fingers, inspecting it, touching it. The spade-shaped wooden leaf was dark-stained on the bottom, and polished as smooth as silk. The top had been intricately carved away until the wood was white. Each leaf vein, big and small, had been etched with precision, creating a work of perfection.

Perian looked up at Flint's ruddy face. "You carved this yourself, didn't you?"

Flint shrugged and wrinkled his big nose. "It's not one of my better pieces—just something I did long ago that I kept for myself because it reminded me of the mountain forests near Hillhome."

"I love it!" Perian said. "Help me?" she asked, holding the necklace up to him.

With frigid, nervous fingers, Flint slipped the chain over her head and watched as she tucked it into her wrap, seeing it rise under the fabric between her breasts.

Flustered, Flint looked away. "You know, the aspen leaf reminds me of you in a way. Aspen wood is strong, but softer than it looks. Each side of an aspen leaf is a different shade of the same color, like black is to gray, and when the wind catches one, the silver side looks like a shimmering vein in a dwarven mine. It is the most beautiful tree in the Kharolis, and it is my favorite anywhere." Flint blushed, realizing the implication of his words.

The mountain dwarf simply stared at him, openedmouthed. She reached a hand toward him.

"Listen, Perian," Flint said, his voice breaking. "I know what I said about a hill dwarf and a mountain dwarf never . . . you know—" Flint gestured vaguely with his hands. "I *still* believe that." He looked at her squarely, seeing the disappointment in her eyes.

"But *neither* one of us is much like our clan, and life is too short—" He gulped at the appropriateness of the phrase tonight. "Life is too short to never take chances. I don't know what will happen tomorrow, or even after tomorrow, but—"

Perian tumbled into his arms and silenced him with two fingers pressed to his hairy lips. "I don't care about any time but now."

His heart pounding in his ears, his vision spinning dizzily, Flint pushed Perian's wrap from her shoulders, and it slipped to the glowing moss. Pulling the beautiful mountain dwarf against his chest, he crushed her moist, parted lips in a kiss that was rooted in his soul.

Chapter 20

The Advance

"Wake up to swords! Wake up to swords!"

The tumbling mass of Aghar spilled into the royal bed-chambers, crawling over and clawing at each other with dirty fingernails in their desperation to be the first to inform their king and queen of the news.

"What's going on?" mumbled Flint, his arm encircling Perian on their mossy bed in the Thrown Room. It was the morning of the fifth day after Pitrick's attack. He and Perian had made their way back from the grotto to the comfort of the moss bed not long before Nomscul arrived. "Stop that!" the hill dwarf ordered, waking up finally.

For a moment Nomscul ceased his bouncing on the edge of the bed nearest Flint, an act that was sending clumps of dried moss flying. "Mountain dwarves marching! Two of them! They go to war, take swords and stuff! Gully dwarves great spies! We see all and tell all right soon!"

"OK, Nomscul, I get the point." Flint was fully awake now. He grabbed the Aghar's bony shoulders to keep him from jumping up and down. "How many were—are you sure it isn't just a patrol?"

Nomscul slammed his hands on his hip bones and sniffed, tossing his head at the insult to his intelligence.

Flint reluctantly rolled away from Perian and pushed himself off the bed. Turning his back, he yanked his pants up to his stomach, stuffing his long blue-green tunic into the drawstring waist.

The mountain dwarf was waking up more slowly. "It can't be the Theiwar troops—it's too early," she protested, stabbing the sleep from her eyes with her fists. "It's only been a couple of days since the attack in the Big Sky Room; Pitrick couldn't possibly have organized the troops that quickly!"

"Tell that to Pitrick and his army," Flint grumbled, stuffing his boots onto his feet. "I just hope Basalt's had enough time to fortify Hillhome. We're coming, whether they're ready or not."

"We can march? Can we?" pleaded Nomscul, thrusting his chest out and stomping about the room to demonstrate his readiness.

Flint ignored the shaman as he finished dressing, his mind on the march ahead of them. He strapped on the Tharkan Axe, his gift from Perian the night before. His fingers lingered over the cool steel blade, while his mind traveled back to the previous evening. Sighing, he slapped some day-old water on his face.

"Tell every gully dwarf in the place that the time has come for the big march. They must get their weapons, their shields, supplies, everything," the king ordered Nomscul. "Gather up the sludge bombs and meet Queen Perian in the grotto. I'm going there directly to have a look outside myself." Nodding furiously, Nomscul dashed from the cavern in the direction of the Big Sky Room.

But Perian shook her head as she crawled over Flint's side of the bed and began to dress hastily. "I'm coming with you."

Flint turned to her in exasperation. "*One* of us has to stay here and see that they get organized!" he objected. "How do we know they won't bring their knives and spoons instead of their swords and shields?"

"We don't," said Perian. "But you won't know which of the thane's forces we face, or how to combat them. I served in his guard—"

"I remember," Flint interrupted.

"—I'll recognize the units, their strengths and their weaknesses. I know the thane's officers! If anyone stays back here, it should be you!"

Flint gruffly assented. He led them down the sloping Upper Tubes, finally finding the entrance to the stairway into the grotto.

They scrambled down the stairway, Flint taking the steps two at a time. Both of them paused to look at the bench by the pool, still covered with the containers of food and their plates from the night before.

"Come on," Flint said at last, following the pool to its farthest corner from the stairway, where a large but low-to-the-ground crack in the granite wall allowed access. A deep channel had been cut in the sandy ground there, and presumably it and the crack had been formed by an old stream bed; now the water left the pool by another, newer channel ten feet beyond the old one.

"This is it." Flint took up Perian's hand and slipped into the jagged fissure, leading the way. Before long they had to walk in a crouch, as the top of the crack loomed close overhead. Flint counted his steps out of habit from his old dungeon-crawling days, and on step ninety-three, they came abruptly into sunlight on a small crest cloaked in pines. The crack was cut slightly at an angle and surrounded by trees, thus it was almost unnoticeable to the untrained eye.

Accustomed to living underground, Perian squinted in pain at the sudden light, made worse by reflections off of early snow. Even Flint blinked at the brightness, having grown used to the darkness below in less than a week. A cold breeze wafted past his face, and the old, familiar sensation invigorated him.

"I have been to the surface less than a dozen times, but it has never looked beautiful to me before today," Perian confessed, shielding her eyes with an upraised arm. "The light hurts my eyes, but I'll grow accustomed soon, because I'm half Hylar." She laughed. "After years of Pitrick's threats, I never thought I would be happy about that."

Flint patted her encouragingly on the shoulder; he had the feeling that a lot of things would change today. The hill dwarf knew that they had emerged in the Kharolis range about a half-day northeast of the tunnel by which he had entered Thorbardin. Climbing up the crest to get a better view, he looked down at a mountain stream that he presumed had its origins in the grotto. Flint shielded his eyes and looked to the east. The sky was crystal-clear, and he could see the shimmering shore of Stonehammer Lake about a day's march away. Looking down the mountain to the west, he could not locate the Passroad, nor see signs of mountain dwarf troops.

"This stream flows down one of the side valleys toward the lake, which meets up with the Passroad," Flint said. "We should come in sight of the road if we follow the stream down."

They moved through an open forest, following the gentle descent of the valley. In less than ten minutes they came around a shoulder of the ridge; across barren, snow-dotted slopes they saw the Passroad, a thick brown tendril snaking its way through the foothills north of Thorbardin.

The road was empty for as far to the west as the eye could see.

Arms crossed, Flint chewed his lip. "Have we delayed so long that they've already passed from sight ahead of us?" he asked, his voice ragged with concern.

"I don't think so." Perian shook her head, not taking her eyes from the general vicinity of the road. "My guess is that they've camped somewhere for the day, out of the sun. They probably haven't moved too far off the road." She scanned the horizon, stopping to examine the edge of a thicket of pines just a little to the west. "See there?" she asked, pointing. "Under those trees? It's nearly at the edge of my vision—they could almost be ants!" She concentrated. "No, I'm sure I saw a red plume waving. It's the Bloody Blades."

Flint shivered involuntarily at the name. "What are the Bloody Blades?"

Perian pursed her lips while she thought. "The House Guard. The Blades are just one regiment of three, each containing two hundred soldiers. The other regiments are the Silver Swords and the Black Bolts. The three regiments always fight together as a synchronized force, complementing their strengths and weaknesses. They form units of heavy infantry, light infantry, and crossbows."

"Could you try not to sound so proud of them?" Flint grumbled.

Perian looked only mildly embarrassed. "Old habits," she said.

Flint whistled through his teeth. "Six hundred dwarves. And against 'em we have a couple hundred Aghar," he groaned. "Why don't we just hand Hillhome over?"

"It could be worse," Perian said, trying to sound encouraging. "The thane has thousands of troops at his disposal, but only the House Guard bear fealty to him alone. The rest defend all of Thorbardin, not just the Theiwar."

"*That's* a comfort," Flint said sarcastically, digging a hole in a snowbank with the toe of his boot.

"You're forgetting Basalt," Perian reminded him softly.

"I'm not," the old hill dwarf said, shaking his gray head. "But we're pinning a lot of hopes on that young 'un."

"Well, we've got to get moving," she said gently. "We'll get ahead of them by a day while the House Guard bivouacs out of the sun."

Flint nodded, shaking off his melancholia. Following the stream uphill, the pair of dwarves made their way back up to the crack in the granite. There they found Nomscul.

"You were supposed to organize the troops," Flint scolded him.

"Rest wait in there, all straight," Nomscul announced,

pointing into the tunnel, "like Nomscul tell them." Suddenly, gully dwarves began popping from the opening—Fester, Cainker, Oooz, Garf, Pooter, and all the rest. They came out in a steady torrent, carrying every manner of weapon: the one hundred fifty Agharpulters with daggers slipped into their robe belts; one hundred Creeping Wedgies with shields tucked under their arms.

The Aghar milled about the tunnel entrance, a steadily growing mob. Flint and Perian circled them like sheepdogs, trying to keep the group together as their comrades emerged.

Last but not least came the Sludge Bombers, carrying their jugs and bottles and big pots of explosive venom. Flint had cautioned them repeatedly about the need to handle the containers of sludge delicately, so they tiptoed, swinging the jugs any which way as they joined their friends in the sunlight on the mountainside.

"Hold those carefully—carefully!" Flint bellowed. "And where are the litters to carry the sludge bombs?" he asked.

Four gully dwarves trooped out of the crack just then, holding the handles of two makeshift litters, old leather vests each stretched across stout limbs. The biggest jugs of sludge, several measuring a foot across, had been set upon the litters for gentle transport.

Flint and Perian began to organize the three hundred-odd members of the army, such as it was, on the mountainside.

"Assemble your units!" Flint barked. "Nomscul, you lead the Agharpults over here; Oooz, get the Sludge Bombers over there; and Fester, put the Creeping Wedgies here, in the middle."

To their credit, the Aghar tried to follow the commands of their king. Several minutes of raw chaos ensued as the gully dwarves charged into a single pile of squirming Aghar, where only an occasional arm, leg, or face could be spotted. Somehow the pile resolved itself into three milling groups, more or less organized by the categories Flint had detailed.

Their king felt compelled to offer up some inspiring words. "Stand at attention for some last instructions!" he bellowed.

Again, they tried to stand at attention, but their habit of facing every which way diminished the military precision of the maneuver. Flint only sighed. "Gully dwarves of Mudhole!" he began sternly, trying to get as many of them to face him as possible. "We embark today upon a great excurs—Ooooz, get back here!—a great excursion, to face in combat an enemy implacable and bold, savage and—what is it, Nomscul?"

The shaman was hopping in agitation, waving his hand in the air and clenching his lips together as if to forcibly prevent himself from speaking without royal permission. "King talk too much," explained Nomscul. "We march now?"

Flint's face flushed, and he aimed a glare at Nomscul that would have transfixed any halfway intelligent subject. Fortunately—for himself, at any rate—Nomscul *was* only halfway intelligent and simply mistook his monarch's stare for a warm smile of congratulations.

"In a moment," Flint growled in exasperation. He turned back to the troops, saw their stupidly eager expressions. "Look, gang, we've got quite a march ahead of us; we'll stop before dark near Stonehammer Lake, then I figure we'll make it to Hillhome midday tomorrow. It's vitally important that we stick together as a group—Basalt and all of Hillhome are probably waiting this very minute for us to come and help them. *Please* try to act like soldiers. Do it for your king and queen."

"Two chairs for King Flunk and Queen Furryend!" Nomscul shouted. The troops responded with resounding screeches and caterwauls.

"Let's go, before they get tangled up again," Perian suggested in a loud whisper, watching them wander from their units.

"Gully dwarves, march!" cried Flint, waving his arm in a circle over his head.

The king of the gully dwarves led his troops, three hundred strong, down the mountainside, heading for the Passroad east of the House Guard encampment below. This would allow him, with luck and speed, to move his force onto the road somewhere ahead of the thane's troops.

The organizing into units represented a masterpiece of military precision when compared to the march of the gully dwarves that ensued. In muttered conversation with Perian, Flint could only compare it to the ridiculous task of herding chickens, though after the fourth or fifth effort at chasing down a wayward column of Aghar and returning them to the fold, he amended his comments to the effect that his comparison did a grave disservice to poultry.

To make matters worse, dark, angry clouds rolled in and it began to snow. At first the storm came as great, feathery flakes, gently wafting earthward. Except for the disruption caused by gully dwarves breaking file to catch particularly choice snowflakes with their tongues, the light precipitation caused no problem for the hardy Aghar.

But then the wind rose and the big, friendly flakes grew small and hard, turning into hail. Blustering out of the north, the weather drove stinging needles of ice into their faces, considerably slowing down the progress of the Aghar force. And as the day progressed, the dwarves became more widely scattered, forcing Flint and Perian to cover three or four times as much ground as their charges, constantly running back and forth along the column.

Still moving into the teeth of the storm, they finally descended into a small valley that gave them protection from the worst of the wind.

"I think we'd better stop for a short rest," urged Perian.

"Why don't you go ahead and look for a place big enough to hold all of us?" suggested Flint. "I'll collect the Aghar and bring them up."

Perian headed away toward a grove of tall pines that was barely visible through the storm. Nomscul came up quickly with his comrades of the Agharpult, and Flint directed them toward the grove. Next came Oooz with the Sludge Bombers, and he urged them in the same direction.

Flint waited behind for Fester as the last of the sludge bomb team disappeared after Perian. The Creeping Wedgies had been bringing up the rear, but even for the Aghar they seemed unusually far behind. Flint's concern grew as several more minutes passed.

Full darkness had settled, giving the late autumn wind a sharper bite, yet there was still no sign of Fester and the Creeping Wedgies. Flint peered fruitlessly into the darkness, seeking any sign of movement, but all he saw was the frigid expanse of blowing, drifting snow. There was no denying the fact, now: Fester and the Wedgies were lost, or even dead, buried in the snowfall.

Flint thought about backtracking, but he sensed that the task would be futile. Instead, he turned and plowed his way through the snow toward the grove. He would have to inform Perian of the grave news that before they had even met the enemy their army had been tragically reduced by a third.

Only with difficulty did he locate the copse of trees, so completely did the weather cloak them. Finally he stumbled into a small clearing, surrounded by dense pines, giving the area shelter.

Perian sat atop a snow-covered log near a small, unfrozen pool of water. "Where's Fester and the Wedgies?" she asked at once, noting the look of concern on Flint's face.

"They're lost—or worse," he said glumly. "And I'm afraid we'd be running the risk of weakening ourselves still further if we set out to look for them in this snow."

"We'll just have to hope that they find their way to us," Perian said, thinking fondly of Fester, her "weighty lady." The other Aghar seemed not to notice the disappearance of their comrades. They focused instead on gaining the most comfortable sleeping spaces in the damp, snowy grove.

Calculating that the derro soldiers would stay in their own camp only until darkness, Flint and Perian decided to take a chance and wait for more than an hour. Still there was no sign of the missing Wedgies. In that hour, though, the storm began to abate. The wind that had made traveling difficult was now blowing the storm clouds away. Though visibility was not great, they could see a vista of complete whiteness. The peaks and ridgelines gleamed under their pristine frosting, and the whole region was revealed as one of astounding natural beauty. A small, frozen waterfall hung suspended like a great icicle at the head of the valley of their camp.

"We've got to get moving," urged Flint after the hour had passed. "Break time is over." He stepped among the bundles of gully dwarves, discovering that his subjects had collected in groups of four to six. Sharing body warmth, albeit with a great deal of pushing, shoving, pinching, and biting, the Aghar had managed to remain warm.

Blinking, stretching, and enjoying an afternoon nosepick, the Aghar gathered in ragged bunches at the edge of the clearing. Here the pool of water, fed by a hot spring, remained clear of snow.

"Come on, you gullies!" Flint bellowed at them, trying to get their attention. "Fall in—no! I mean, line up!"

But it was too late. For once the gully dwarves responded to a command with alacrity, dropping into the pond like a mass of scattered tenpins.

"Great Reorx! Get out of there this minute!" roared the king from the edge of the pool. Suddenly the snow bank beneath his feet gave way and he, too, plummeted into the warm water.

For a few moments Flint stood stock-still in the waist-deep water. Realizing that the eyes of his subjects were fixed upon him, he desperately stifled his terror. With supreme willpower he held his tongue, fearing that once he began to scream, he would never be able to stop. Slowly, with great deliberation, he dragged himself out of the pool. He pulled the hem of his tunic out of his pants and wrung the water from it, only to find his clothing already freezing.

"This is going to be a long campaign, even if it's over this afternoon," he groaned to Perian, who was dabbing at his face and soaked clothing with one of the rag bandages from a supply pack.

Slowly, after more frolicking and splashing, the Aghar hauled themselves from the pool and finally stood, dripping and shivering. "We've got to get them moving before they freeze to death," Perian urged, trying vainly to dry their heads.

The deep snow encouraged the Aghar to remain in file. Flint and Perian took turns forcing a trail through the soft powder. When they became exhausted from the grueling task, some of the more trustworthy gully dwarves rotated the duty, though their trails tended to zigzag more often than not. Throughout the long afternoon the file of Aghar waded through the snow, skirting the highest elevations along the route Flint judged the most likely shortcut to the Passroad.

The heavy pace of the march served to keep the Aghar warm, however, and the hardy gully dwarves showed a remarkable resilience to the cold.

They had crested a low rise, Flint again in the lead, when he heard sounds before him and hastened his steps to reach the summit. In moments he stood atop the low hill and saw a wide, snow-filled valley stretching before him. The brown strip running through the valley was unmistakably the Passroad. On the far side of the road the valley floor dropped steeply away, a long, descending slope that finally reached Stonehammer Lake, below and perhaps another mile distant. But what Flint saw on the Passroad made him groan audibly.

"We're too late," he mumbled, dazed, then turned to Perian. "I thought you said they'd stay camped until dark."

The mountain dwarf was standing next to him. She colored, and her voice was taut with bitterness. "Pitrick must have decided to take advantage of the cover the storm provided."

"I'm afraid so." Flint could only look helplessly at the scene in the valley below.

Three colors of plumes—red, black, and gray—waved in martial precision, as the thane's guards moved past them far below, perhaps two miles ahead. The three companies of mountain dwarves maintained distinct formations, but the whole column was a tight, disciplined military grouping.

The gully dwarves would never be able to catch them now, no matter how hard Flint drove them. Admitting defeat was bitter medicine. It took all of Flint's willpower not to collapse dejectedly in the snow. They had come too late and lost a third of their army in the first day. How had he ever been so foolish as to think they could win?

Perian elbowed him. "What's that?" she asked.

"What?" He was barely paying attention.

"Look—something's moving in the snow down there!" she said, pointing in the general direction of the amassed mountain dwarf troops. "Your eyes are better in this light than mine—tell me what that fuzzy blob is that's on this side of the road near the base of the mountain?"

"What?" Flint, despite his dejection, had his interest piqued. He, too, squinted down the distant, snowy fields toward the road. He saw a length of rippling snow, a shimmering movement. Was that a leg I just saw? he wondered, baffled. Was that a pack of snow-covered animals moving down the slope?

Slowly the mass of movement became visible as many small, individual forms. Flint saw a tightly packed group of creatures, each snowy white on top. The snow, he finally realized, was carried atop each of the creatures upon a shield carried over his head.

"It the Wedgies!" Nomscul shrieked suddenly. Jumping up and down in his excitement, he slipped on the snow and toppled to the ground. "It old trick," he said offhandedly, picking himself up. "They hide under shields and creep at enemy!"

"But they'll be slaughtered out there alone and we're too far away to help them quickly!" Flint exclaimed, clenching and unclenching his fists in helpless frustration.

"Wait." Perian put a calming hand on Flint's arm, never taking her eyes from the events below. "The Wedgies have a chance. The derro don't seem to notice them yet, what with the snow covering them and the glare."

Stunned, king and queen looked on from a distance with two-thirds of their troops, as the Creeping Wedgies, now a rippling mass of shield-and snow-covered Aghar, continued to eke slowly forward. The Wedgies reached the Passroad just as the last company of Theiwar marched by, sporting gray plumes, some thirty feet behind the black-plumed rank. Total disorganization suddenly swept through the gray plumes, as the Wedgies infiltrated them.

Fully erupting from the snowy surface like jack-in-the-boxes came a multitude of white, diminutive figures. Their appearance in the middle of the Theiwar company had thrown the unit into disarray, but swords rose and fell, and crimson stains appeared on the distant snow.

In confusion, the last company stopped and fell back from the other two regiments, who continued on, unaware of the distraction.

"It's the Silver Swords," observed Perian bitterly, "the thane's light infantry. If they can gather their ranks, the Wedgies *will* be cut down."

"We've got to try to help them!" Flint cried, though he knew it would be hard to reach them in time. He started to run down the slope toward the distant road. "Come on, gullies! Charge!"

"We go, too!" A wave of gully dwarves started down the gentle, snowbound slope.

The king kept his eyes glued to the battle as he advanced. Suddenly he saw a change. The Aghar of the Creeping Wedgie had turned and bolted from the road, disappearing on the far side of the thoroughfare, over the slope that led down to Stonehammer Lake.

"Good, they're saving themselves!" Flint cried. "They didn't have a chance of stopping the mountain dwarves, anyway."

"But, look!" pointed Perian. "They're giving chase! Perhaps the Wedgies have accomplished something after all."

Before Flint's astonished eyes, the Silver Swords, now far behind the two other ranks of derro who had continued blithely up the road, abruptly started down the slope after the Aghar. None of the mountain dwarves, hampered by their vision, seemed aware of Flint, Perian, and their troops thrashing their way down the snowy slope above.

"Shush!" Flint ordered his giggling, whooping charges in a harsh whisper. The retreating Aghar had disappeared by now down the steeper slope beyond the road, and the pursuing Theiwar had all followed.

After fifteen minutes of frantic plowing, Flint and his followers set foot on the Passroad. Without even stopping for a breath, they rushed across and down the next slope after the Creeping Wedgies and the Silver Swords, unconcerned about detection now.

Their charge gained momentum as they slid down the steep bank toward the remaining Wedgies, who were gathered now with their backs to the lake. The Theiwar had formed a contracting half-circle around them, and they were tightening it swiftly.

Overconfident, the Theiwar lunged in for the kill, and a number of the Aghar dropped lifeless into the snow. But others of the fleet-footed Aghar managed to dart away and pop up behind the heavily encumbered mountain dwarves. Fighting dwarves swirled chaotically about the field. Shocking crimson blotches appeared on the white snow.

Minutes later, when Flint and the rest of his troops reached the lakeshore, the situation had reversed: the mountain dwarves were enclosed in a semicircle of howling, growling gully dwarves.

"Get lompchuters!" Without waiting for a command from Flint, Nomscul quickly formed his Agharpults. Flint charged forward, suddenly aware of gully dwarves soaring above him, crashing into the Theiwar beyond. Pooter screamed past, knocking three of the enemy into the river before he lost altitude and plunged into the water with a splash.

The rest of the Aghar smashed head-on into the line of Theiwar at the riverbank, ignoring the weaponry and armor of their foes in a courageous effort to follow their king into battle. Steel weapons cut cruel wounds into the loyal Aghar. Flint snapped the neck of a Theiwar captain and he looked around for another target, reaching this time for his magnificent Tharkan Axe.

Suddenly he felt the very ground shift under his feet. Apparently just an overhanging shelf of snow and ice, it broke off from the shore with a sharp crack under the extreme weight of the combatants. Hill, gully, and mountain dwarves were thrown into the deep, wintry waters of Stonehammer Lake. The ice floe drifted away from shore, breaking into smaller pieces that bobbed in the gentle current.

"Whee!"

Chapter 21

Eye of the Storm

ONLY AN OCCASIONAL BEAM OF SUNLIGHT FILTERED through the thick canopy of dark pine boughs. Still, the forest floor seemed an uncomfortably bright place to the dwarves of the Theiwar army. They made camp before full daylight, fortunately finding a dense patch of woods where the pale-skinned, underground-dwelling derro could all but avoid the direct rays of the sun.

The ground lay beneath a blanket of snow, and the sticky, straight trunks of the trees seemed to merge overhead into a solid blanket of needles and snow-covered branches. The dampness and chill of the camp seemed a small price to pay for its chief virtue: that same thick canopy that provided a blessed escape from the light.

Many of the Theiwar veterans now tried to rest, having scraped the snow away from the small patches of ground that served as beds. A damp chill sank into their bones from the still, cold air.

One of the dwarves made no attempt to sleep, however: Pitrick paced between several large trunks, following the tracks of his previous pacing, where he had worn the snow down to bare ground. His hands were clasped behind him, and the throbbing pain in his foot put him into a foul temper. Perversely, he would not sit and rest that foot, even though the dwarves would be on the march again as soon as night fell.

"Where are they? Where's Grikk and his party?" he demanded, turning to look at a nearby derro, not expecting an answer. "They should have reported back by now!"

The hunchback peered anxiously between the trunks. "They've deserted—that's what they've done!" He sneered at the imagined treachery. "I send them to find the Silver Swords, and instead the miserable cowards have likely fled back to Thorbardin! They'll pay for this! By all that's mighty, I'll see Grikk flayed alive, slow-roasted! I'll see—"

"Excellency?" A sergeant approached him tentatively.

"Eh? What?"

"Grikk's coming, sir. Returned from the search."

"What?" Pitrick blinked, confused by his own tantrum. "Very well—send him to me at once."

The scout, Grikk, a grizzled veteran with a patch over one eye and a beardless cheek that had been permanently scarred by a Hylar blade, clumped up to the adviser. "We searched the valley along this whole shore of the lake, Excellency. There is no sign of the Swords—at least, nothing that we could see."

"Then go back and look again!"

"I'm sorry, sir." Grikk drew himself to his full height, his unpatched eye staring into his commander's face. "But we can't. We were blinded out there—I lost one of my scouts in the lake, simply because he couldn't see a drop-off under his feet!"

Pitrick saw that Grikk's exposed eye was puffy and

bloodshot. He knew that the sun reflecting off the snow created an impossible brightness. Frustration gnawed at him. His body shook with tension, and he made little effort to bring himself under control.

"Excellency," Grikk said. "Perhaps we could go back and search tonight. It would only mean delaying the attack on Hillhome for one day."

Pitrick's thoughts immediately turned to that nest of insolent hill dwarves, little more than a mile away. His decision was easy.

"No!" he cried. "Tonight we attack Hillhome! Nothing can be allowed to delay our vengeance!" He stared through the woods, in the direction of the village filled with those loathsome enemies, the hill dwarves.

"When the sun rises tomorrow, it must shine upon Hillhome's ruined remains."

* * * * *

When they finally crested a low ridge and Hillhome lay before them, Flint and Perian anxiously looked for signs of smoke or massive destruction. To their relief, they found neither. Instead, they saw that a large earthwork had been erected along the south border of the town—right across the Passroad, Flint noted with satisfaction.

"So that's Hillhome," Perian breathed, picturing a young Flint in that setting. She squeezed his hand reassuringly. "It would appear they're expecting an army."

Flint let his arm fall around her shoulder for a moment, pride making his eyes sparkle. "The young harrn pulled it off. Basalt actually did it. *We* did it.

"Double time, you bug-eating, belching bunch of Aghar!" Flint bellowed, using their favorite pet names, and they started down the long ridge.

At the bottom of the slope, the gully dwarves, sensing the importance of the moment, marched in the precise military formation Flint had dubbed the "mob of chaos." Its success could be said to be achieved when the majority of the gully dwarves were moving rather quickly in approximately the same direction.

This was easily accomplished now because the Aghar were universally fascinated by the small community before them. They climbed over each other and pushed one another in their haste to enter Hillhome.

For all of the Aghar, this was their first experience with a hill dwarf community, or any above-ground community for that matter. As they approached Hillhome, they stared to the right and left, awestruck by the architectural marvels around them.

"What in the name of all the gods is this?" said Mayor Holden, witnessing the gully dwarf stampede as he stood with a shovel at the outskirts of town. "Oh, it's you, Fireforge," he added, recognizing Flint at the lead. He cast a scornful gaze at the whooping gully dwarves. "What are those slugs doing here, and at a time like this?"

Flint grabbed the mayor, whom he had never really liked, by the lapels. "Nobody calls my troops slugs except me! Show some respect to the Aghar who are willing to give up their lives protecting *your* town!"

"Uncle Flint!" cried Basalt from nearby, throwing down his shovel and racing toward his uncle. Flint released the mayor, who muttered some sort of apology as he skulked back to his digging.

"You really came through," said Flint. "I'm proud of you, pup." He gestured at the wide earthwork, the bustling dwarves extending it to either side.

"We've gathered some weapons, too," said Basalt, his pride obvious in his voice. "A couple hundred, anyway— enough for half the town."

"You mean four hundred hill dwarves are willing to fight for this old town?" Flint said, honestly surprised.

"Yup!" Basalt was clearly proud of his kinsmen, and Flint enjoyed the change in his nephew. "And even the ones who can't fight are busy sewing leather right now. They're making padded leather breastplates for as many of us as they can."

"Excellent," Flint pronounced. "But what'll they do when the fighting starts?"

"We've got provisions stored in some caves, up in the

hills. At first sign of the mountain dwarves, the old folks and youngsters will head out of town," Basalt explained.

Tybalt, Ruberik, and Bertina joined them, together with an attractive young dwarf maid whom Flint recognized as Hildy, the daughter of the town's brewer. They greeted him warmly, and even Ruberik unbent his spine—just a little, for a brief moment—to nod his respect toward his brother. Flint, in turn, introduced them to Perian, who stood at his side. Bertina gave her a scrutinizing glance, but was satisfied enough with the mountain dwarf to give her a cheerful hello.

"What about the mountain dwarves?" asked Tybalt. "Basalt told us that they're on the move already. How far have they gotten?"

Flint looked to Basalt in surprise and the young harrn held up his hand, showing the steel-banded ring or. his finger. "It was easy, with this," he explained. "I teleported down the road until I saw 'em marching toward the shore of Stonehammer Lake. That was early last night. I was afraid they'd attack this morning, before you could get here."

"Hey—cut that out!" At the sound of the irate voice, Flint looked around to see another young dwarf chasing a pair of Aghar who had snatched his shovel while he rested from the rigors of excavation. "Give that back to me, you little runts, or I'll rip yer ears off!"

Somehow, Flint wasn't surprised to find gully dwarves at the other end of the rebuke. If the Aghar were ever going to work with the hill dwarves, some ground rules had to be established.

"Limper! Wet-nose! Stop that right now!" Flint bellowed. Each of the gully dwarves actually stopped to look at him before they went on to make insulting gestures at their pursuer with their feet.

Groaning, Flint turned back to his comrades. "The mountain dwarves, yes. We lost sight of them before dawn. For all I know they could be coming around the bend of the valley in ten minutes."

"I don't think so," Perian disagreed. "I'm sure they won't be moving during the day. We have till at least sunset to prepare, but I'll be surprised if we don't see them right around then."

"Well, that's something, anyway—a few hours," said Flint, pleased both at Hillhome's farsightedness and the fact that his Aghar had marched considerably faster, over rougher country, than had the dwarves of Pitrick's army.

Basalt took the arms of both Flint and Perian. "Why are we talking in this dusty street? We'll be here by need soon enough. Let's go to Moldoon's—Turq Hearthstone is running it now—to discuss the details."

Everyone agreed. Admonishing Nomscul to behave and make sure his fellow Aghar did the same, Flint and the rest set out through the village and past the brewery to the north edge of town, where Moldoon's Inn beckoned invitingly. For a moment the dwarf almost believed that his old companion would come to the door of his inn to greet them. The truth brought a thick lump to his throat, and he made a silent vow to avenge Moldoon's death tenfold.

It was early afternoon, and Flint and Perian were famished. Turq brought them heaping plates of fresh, buttered bread and stew. The innkeeper noted their noses wrinkled in distaste.

"The bread's great, Turq, but have you something other than stew?" At the dwarf's puzzled expression, Flint held up a hand and shook his head ruefully. "Don't ask; it's too complicated and not worth the bother to explain. But some meat would be most welcome, if you have it."

Turq brought two steaks back within minutes. Flint and Perian dug in like starving dwarves, while the bulk of Flint's family looked on, waiting for them to finish. The pair ate with great relish, with much smacking of lips and licking of fingers. The steak, Flint swore, was the best food he had ever eaten. Finally, some time later, Perian pushed back her chair. "I'm stuffed," she admitted. "And one of us had better check on the Aghar." She quickly got up to go.

"Mmmph," Flint agreed, still shoveling in the tender meat.

Only after Flint popped the last bite into his mouth did he even stop to notice where he was. Something about the inn felt different than the last time he'd been here.

"I know what's changed!" he cried, slamming his fist to the bar. "No derro!" Flint nodded his approval. At the same time, he realized how much he missed Moldoon, and his earlier melancholy returned.

"The ones we caught are still in jail," Basalt explained. "Maybe we'll let 'em out after the battle."

"Yeah," Flint agreed, suddenly serious. The few hours of peace remaining to Hillhome could be counted in the low angle of the sun to the horizon. "Well, I'd better check on Perian," he said.

The others accompanied him from the inn, and they started back toward the earthen wall defending Hillhome. From some distance away they heard Perian castigating her charges, and Flint unconsciously picked up his pace.

"No! *Higher*! Make the wall *higher*!" Perian shouted. Her voice came out as more of a pale croak than a command.

"But look, Queen Furryend! We make nice notch right here!" A dirt-caked Fester protested, indicating with pride the deep cut the gully dwarves had gouged in the earthwork. "Pretty soon road go right through, no problem!"

"Yes, problem—*big* problem! Road go—damn! Look, if the road goes right through, then the mountain dwarves can go right through. Do you understand?"

"Sure!" beamed Fester. "No problem!"

"We don't *want* the mountain dwarves to go through. We want to *stop* them here, stop them with the wall that used to cross the road!" Perian felt her temperature rising, and was frustrated that the woeful state of her overworked voice did not allow her more effective vent of her displeasure.

"Oh," said Fester, crestfallen. For a moment she looked at the pile of dirt they had moved, then turned back to Perian. "Why?"

The queen had been trying to supervise the gully dwarves while they learned the art of military fortification. In the few short minutes she'd been at it, she had decided that it was an unrewarding pipe dream.

She was spared the further rigors of instruction by the arrival of Flint, Hildy, and Basalt. Flint chuckled in sympathy, taking her hand.

The hill dwarf turned his attention to the growing earth-work project. "Looks impressive," he complimented. Indeed, the redoubt was now a great, curving wall, shaped roughly like a horseshoe, with western Hillhome protected by its dirt shelter. It averaged perhaps eight feet high, though of course with gully dwarf craftsmanship there was no excess of precision.

"We'll have about four hundred hill dwarves and three hundred gully dwarves. At least the thane's troops won't have us outnumbered too badly."

Flint's heartiness seemed forced. The disciplined ranks of Realgar's elite guards, with their metal armor, deadly cross-bows, and well-practiced combat formations, were a more formidable force than the rabble of armed, but unarmored, unpracticed, and wholly undisciplined Hillhome folk and gully dwarves.

"What's the plan?" Mayor Holden called to them as he approached from the center of town. They turned to see Turq and the mayor climbing the wall.

Holden seemed eager to inspect the fortification. Now that the evidence of mountain dwarf treachery was inescapable, Flint reflected sourly, the mayor had become a devout patriot to the cause of Hillhome. Perhaps I'm being unfair, Flint chided himself. The mayor only reflected the consensus of the majority of the hill dwarves. The dwarves of Hillhome had simply grown comfortable in their good life. Anyone would be reluctant to rashly reject his prosperity when confronted with claims of an unseen, secret enemy.

And, Flint reminded himself, when the fact of the enemy had been made plain finally, the dwarves of Hillhome had jumped to the defense of their community. The four hundred harrn and frawl who had taken up arms ranged from young adults to venerable grandfathers, and all were strong and dedicated. And those who were not physically capable of battle had been busy, too.

"Splendid, splendid!" crowed the mayor unnecessarily, looking around the graceful curve of the earthen wall. "Now, what is our strategy?"

Flint, Perian, Basalt, Hildy, and Turq looked at one an-

other over the stupidity of the question, as if they were di-
viding up for a game of luggerball. But the mayor had inad-
vertently revealed one thing: they had not officially
appointed a commander over their force.

"I suggest that Flint Fireforge be given the task of assigning the plan of defense," proposed Turq Hearthstone quietly.

"Aye," echoed Basalt and Hildy.

"Yes," piped up Perian.

Flint looked around at his companions. He tried ration-
ally to consider the alternatives. Basalt and Hildy were too
young. Mayor Holden was not a harrn of action. Perian was
an outsider—a mountain dwarf, to boot—though it did not
matter to him in the least. She would fight loyally for the
town's cause, but she was not the choice to be its champion.
Tybalt, Ruberik—his brothers—he now sensed, looked to
him for leadership.

"We'll meet them here," Flint began, indicating the wall.
He looked self-consciously at the others to gauge their reactions, but when he saw that they listened unquestioningly,
his confidence rose, and so did the strength of his voice.

"I'll manage the Sludge Bombers right in the middle," he
decided. "That should break the cohesion of their attack.
Then, we'll try to hold them . . . where?" He looked at the
line, evaluating the ground and finding what he desired.
"There." He pointed at the right side of the horseshoe, where
it curved almost to the bank of the river.

"Basalt, you'll command a small company of hill dwarves
over there, enough to stop them when they try to climb the
redoubt. Perian can back you up with the Wedgies."

His followers listened attentively. He and Perian had already explained the gully dwarf formations, and indeed the
Aghar had demonstrated the creeping wedge and the
Agharpult. They had come dangerously close also to ac-
quainting the hill dwarves with the dread sludge bomb, but
fortunately Perian had come upon the bombers in the nick
of time.

"Then, over here," Flint continued, turning to the left,
where the wing of the earthwork extended into a field beyond the Passroad. Perhaps a hundred feet beyond the end

of the barrier began the tree line, but there was no time to carry the redoubt that much farther. "Tybalt and Hildy will take the rest of the hill dwarves and the Agharpults."

He surveyed the expanse of the line, satisfied. "Then, when the enemy line is broken by the bombs and half of them are occupied over here, Tybalt and Hildy, you charge forward and attack with your company of dwarves. With luck—and lots of that—we can carry half of the thane's forces away before sweeping around to catch the others in the rear. With those trees blocking them from too wide of a movement, we might have the chance to hit 'em hard, cause them some real confusion.

"Now, Ruberik," he said, turning to his brother. "Are you still a dead shot with that crossbow?"

"I've been keeping my hand in," the farmer admitted.

"Good. I have a job for you." Briefly he explained another idea he had, and Ruberik gave his hearty approval. Flint's brother headed into town, seeking the two large, clay jars he needed to put the plan into operation.

"Now, we'll need some bonfires out there in the field. That'll at least give us a picture of where they are when they're advancing." He stopped to think while Tybalt and Hildy organized a score of hill dwarves. The group gathered dry wood and quickly started to form several large piles in the field before the redoubt. These bonfires would be lit as soon as the derro came into view, providing the hill dwarves some view of their advancing enemy.

Soon Flint turned to the others. "Now, how are we fixed for straw? Can we get fifty bales? A hundred would be even better."

Tybalt nodded.

"Good. And lamp oil? How many kegs do you have in your store?" he asked Mayor Holden.

"Well, there's not, that is, it's my most expensive item! I can't. . . ."

Conscious of the stares of all the other hill dwarves, the mayor stopped speaking and flushed with embarrassment. "Well, I guess I've got a couple of kegs. But what on Krynn do you need them for?"

Flint explained his plans, assigning dwarves to gather the necessary ingredients and make the required preparations. Slowly, the various elements of Hillhome's defense came together.

The defensive strategy sounds good, Flint realized with satisfaction.

Even as they were speaking Flint noticed that it grew steadily darker. The sun dipped beyond the western hills, and twilight settled over the town and its valley. They've got to be coming soon now, he told himself.

"If they break the line here, everyone fall back through the town," he added, developing a contingency plan. "We'll make a final stand in the brewery, if it comes to that." Hildy had already offered the building—the largest structure in Hillhome—for that purpose.

"Look!" cried Perian suddenly, turning toward the south. The others squinted into the distance. The movement along the Passroad was painfully obvious to them all, even in the fading light. A long column snaked its way through the mud.

The armored mountain dwarf troops of Pitrick's legion.

"They must have started right at sunset," Basalt guessed. "And they're coming fast."

"They'll be here in an hour," Flint judged, "maybe sooner if they hurry. That doesn't give us a lot of time. Everybody spread out!" Flint ordered. "Pass the word through the town—every dwarf with a weapon should get down here. The rest should take shelter in the hills if they're not gone already!

"Basalt, Hildy—get your crews out there and light those fires. I want them blazing high by the time the Theiwar get down to the field. And then hurry back—remember, the battle's to be fought here, not out there!"

Basalt grinned as he trotted off with the fire brigade. The others, too, turned toward the stations for the imminent battle.

Perian turned to leave, and Flint caught her by the shoulders. "Not you," he whispered hoarsely. "Not yet." Flint clasped her to him, and tucked her face into his throat beneath his beard.

He smelled of salty perspiration and soap, an honest, good scent. Flint's scent. She nuzzled him for the first time since they had left Mudhole.

"Don't tease me, you heartless wench!" he growled, gathering her up tightly. He pulled back abruptly, taking her face in his thick, callused hands. "I've grown quite fond of you," he grumbled. "For Reorx's sake be careful!"

Perian tilted her head back slightly and gave him a lingering, bittersweet kiss that was salty with tears. "I'll be careful—but only if you promise that you will, too." He nodded somberly, and she kissed him on the nose this time, reluctantly wiggling out of his arms.

Perian gave him a playful pat and a smile. "Mind you remember that promise." Then she was gone to her assigned post.

Flint watched her go, and then got caught up in the frenzy of activity that swirled across Hillhome. Dusk settled over the town. Looking to the field, Flint saw one fire, then another, then several more spark to life.

And the Theiwar troops marched onward to Hillhome. Twilight faded to night as Basalt, Hildy, and the other hill dwarves kindled the bonfires laid in the field before the redoubt. These blazes crackled quickly upward as the dry wood ignited, sending pillars of sparks into the dark sky.

These dwarves scurried back to the safety of their companions as Pitrick's forces neared the town. The bright yellow firelight soon reflected off of rank upon rank of black-armored, steel-tipped death.

Darkness grew as the mountain dwarf wave started forward again, marching inexorably toward the confrontation with their dwarven kin on the dirt embankment.

In the next instant, as if from a single throat, Pitrick's legion raised a hoarse cry. With a clash of their arms against their shields, they surged forward into a charge.

Chapter 22

Fire in Their Eyes

*The din of the Theiwar charge crested over the de-*fenders in a wave of sound. The mountain dwarves voiced hoarse challenges; they beat their swords and axes against their shields; and they pounded the ground with their heavy, rhythmic tread.

The sound rolled forward from the darkness, though the bonfires spotted throughout the field gave Flint and the others a rough idea of the derro's location. Flint saw the flames glinting from steel axeblades, and dark, shiny shields. Even at this distance, the horrid eyes of the derro seemed to catch and reflect the light. Flint thought, incongruously, of fireflies glimpsed across a summer meadow.

For a moment he wondered if the volume of sound alone

would be enough to sweep the defenders from the breast-work, but a quick look around showed him that the hill dwarves were ready to stand firm. The gully dwarves actually contributed to the din, most of them sticking their tongues out or shrieking insults.

Flint looked nervously over his shoulder into Hillhome, now sheltered behind this semicircular barrier of earth. The darkened town seemed lifeless under the overcast night sky, especially in contrast to the fires scattered about the field. The town, in fact, was virtually abandoned. Some three hundred and fifty of its citizens stood with Flint, Perian, and the Aghar along the redoubt. The others, almost one hundred and sixty hill dwarves—the very old, very young, and otherwise infirm—had retreated to caves in the hills, waiting fearfully for the outcome of the battle.

"Ready the sludge bombs!" cried the king, turning back to the charging Theiwar. The Aghar in the center reluctantly ceased their rude noises and took up the small, glass and ceramic vessels that contained their weapons.

"The torches, too," Flint added. "Light them now!" Several dozen hill dwarves touched matches to the oil-soaked torches they had prepared. "We'll give the little grubs a surprise when they get close enough," he remarked to his brother Ruberik as the farmer came up to him. Ruberik nodded grimly as they stood silently for a moment, peering into the darkness.

The thane's ranks swept closer. The charge, begun at several hundred yards distance, swiftly closed the gap. Now, in the glaring light of the bonfires, Flint could discern individual derro. He saw faces distorted by battlelust, eyes squinting murderously, seeking victims. Most of the derro advanced at an easy trot, their shields on their left arms while their right hands held axes or short swords.

Some of the fires vanished from sight, trampled by the dark line in its implacable advance, but closer pyres now illuminated the army. Flint wished for a rank of longbow-men, or a catapult—any kind of missile with long range. The sludge bombs, unfortunately, would only carry the distance of an Aghar toss—anywhere from one to fifty feet—

and he wouldn't risk the gully dwarves in the Agharpult until he was ready to attack.

"Stand firm, there!" Flint bellowed at a nearby pair of young hill dwarves who had started looking anxiously over their shoulders.

He heard Perian shout similar encouragements on the right flank, where she stood with Basalt and a small company of hill dwarves, supported by a reserve of Creeping Wedgies.

Flint cast a quick glance to the left, where Tybalt stood with the majority of the hill dwarves, concealed behind the wall. Somewhere in that group, Flint knew, were Hildy, his brother Bernhard, and his sister Fidelia. He thought briefly of Bertina and Glynnis, who were both persuaded over their loud objections to help supervise the young dwarves who had been sent to safety in the hills.

Tybalt gave him a casual wave, and Flint chuckled at the constable's cool and easy demeanor. It surprised him to notice the warm feeling he got from having his family near during these hours of crisis. They're a good bunch, he told himself with not a little pride.

"How soon?" Flint turned as Ruberik asked the question. The farmer was still standing beside him atop the wall of earth.

"Close," Flint replied. He looked at the large crossbow in his brother's hands. The weapon's hilt, of weatherbeaten oak, was smoothed by long usage. Its steel crossbar did not shine, but nevertheless tensed with unconcealed strength. It had once been their father's weapon. "You ready?"

In answer, Ruberik raised the heavy weapon and held it firm, drawing a bead on his target in the field—a target that was not the charging derro, but instead a large clay jar in the Theiwars' path.

"Can you see well enough?" inquired Flint, dubiously peering into the darkness. Flashes of yellow light rippled across the ground, but quickly died back to shadows. "This seemed like a better idea in the daylight."

"No need to worry," grunted Ruberik, squinting in concentration. "I *did* manage to learn a little of what Father thought most important—weaponry." The farmer crouched, as immobile as a rock, and waited for his brother's command.

"Another few seconds," Flint said, his voice taut. He saw the target, standing motionless in the path of the charge. The derro swept closer. "Wait a minute . . . wait . . ."

"Now, shoot!"

With a sharp crack, the crossbow released its steel-headed shaft. The missile flashed into the night, then was lost in the darkness.

But in the next instant a sharply defined cloud—a billow of smoke that was so dark it showed clearly against the moderate blackness of the night—erupted from the clay jar.

"Nice shot!" shouted Flint, clapping his brother on the back. Ruberik paid no attention, already concentrating on the laborious recocking of his powerful weapon. He loaded another shaft, sweat popping from his brow as he quickly turned the powerful crank.

Flint growled, unconsciously voicing his delight, as the sludge smoke spread across the field. He saw the rank of the derro split and waver as the dwarves stumbled away from the noxious fumes. He couldn't see their reactions in the darkness, but he took savage pleasure in imagining their discomfort. The derro swept around the growing cloud, but their advance had been temporarily interrupted.

"Ready the torches!" Flint cried as the Theiwar swept closer. "And the sludge bombs!" Nearby, Ooz and Pooter hefted their small vials and shook them vigorously.

"Careful!" Flint warned. All we need is to have one of those pop open back here, he thought with a shudder. The battle would be over before it began.

Behind the wall, several dozen hill dwarves held burning torches. They kept the flames hot, but held them low, out of sight of the advancing derro, awaiting Flint's command to put them to use.

Ruberik finally raised his weapon, taking aim at the second of the great pots. This one was much closer than his first target. With another sharp thunk, the weapon fired and the bolt shattered the jar, releasing another cloud of the noxious sludge smoke.

The derro were less than a hundred feet away. Now Flint and Ruberik could see the wrinkles in their grotesque faces, the links of their chain armor.

Flint turned to the Aghar gathered to either side of himself. "Sludge Bombers, throw!" he cried.

"Eat sludge!" Ooz cried as he tossed his vial up and outward. It crashed to the ground among the first rank of derro troops and broke, releasing a smaller cloud of the stinking black smoke.

With a volley of exuberant cries, the Aghar in the center of the line pitched their sloshing missiles. The jars were small and the hurlers enthusiastic. As they had practiced, each gully dwarf cocked back his arm and then flung the jar as far as he could in the general direction of the attacking derro. Some could not help but tumble forward from the momentum of their toss.

Several of the vials plopped right on the front of the earthen barrier before rolling into the ditch at the bottom, between the attackers and defenders. Most of the bottles sailed a couple of dozen feet, and some had the forward thrust to soar through the air and burst among the feet of the first rank of approaching Theiwar.

Instantly a thick, black cloud rose from the exploded vessels. The smoke burst upward from the force of its explosive release, then it hung thickly in the air, a moist, oily blanket of vapor. Some of this smoke rolled up and over the breastwork, and Flint caught a whiff of it before he could duck out of the way. Instantly he doubled over, gagging and choking. He tripped and rolled to the bottom of the sloping wall, the Tharkan Axe bouncing heavily against his thigh. There he lay, helplessly, retching.

"King not like sludge bomb," Ooz said, looking sadly down from the redoubt. Some of the smoke had drifted around his boots, rising to tickle his face, but the gully dwarf merely wiped his nose and blinked a few times.

Flint crawled from the last vestiges of the mist that had seeped over the wall. He shook his head a few times to clear it, praying that the derro found the sludge bomb effects as obnoxious as he did.

Indeed, most of the smoke had spilled against the redoubt, and rolled back into the onrushing wave of the Theiwar. It crept like a living thing along the ground, clutching at skin, pouring into boots and clothes, forcing its way into every available crevice.

Flint's reaction to a small whiff of the sludge bomb, in fact, was mild when compared to the extreme effect of the gas upon the Theiwar. The derro caught the full brunt of the oily, noxious mist. The vapor was so heavy that it spread in a cloud barely higher than the head of a tall dwarf, flowing like liquid across the battlefield.

The first rank in the center of the charging Theiwar dropped like felled pigeons. The next rank staggered and stopped as the sludge gas enveloped it; the dwarves stumbled and fell, senseless, coughing and retching.

The gas dissipated the farther it spread, and its intensity diminished. But it reduced any Theiwar luckless enough to be caught within its oily folds to paroxysms and gagging. As Flint had intended, the noxious mist spread into a wedge in the center of the Theiwar formation. By the time the king climbed back up to the redoubt—now clear of the heavy gas—he could see that the thane's forces had been split in two by the creeping stench.

Many of the derro stopped, looking around anxiously. Others behind them stumbled to a halt. Through the darkness, Flint saw the neat formation of the Theiwar dissolve into a collection of surprised, confused soldiers. The charge had been effectively delayed.

"Flint—over here!" He heard Perian's urgent cry, and saw her running in his direction. He quickly raced along the wall to meet her.

"Pitrick's savants!" she said, pointing to a half-dozen derro that had worked their way forward from the far rank. "We're going to get hit by magic in a minute or two."

Flint saw the savants, clearly illuminated by a nearby bonfire. Their hair seemed bleached almost to white, but it flashed red as the fire flared upward. They wore long dark robes that seemed strangely incongruous among the gleaming black armor of their fellows.

Flint considered the savants. "Here come the fireworks."

"I've got an idea," Ruberik mused. "The torches are ready. What do you say we wait till the derro get a little closer, and then give them something to look at?" He gestured to the oil-soaked bales of straw before the breastwork. Privately, Flint hoped that the idea he had had during the calm of the afternoon would prove as effective as he'd imagined, now that it was the dark of night amid the raging chaos of battle.

"That's a great idea!" Perian exclaimed, clapping Flint's brother on the back. Ruberik blushed.

"Let's hope it works," said Flint.

"Of course it'll work," Perian replied, her tone surprisingly jaunty. For the first time, Flint became aware of just how much of a warrior this frawl was. "When that light flares up in front of them, they'll be blinded for a long time. They'll find that more frightening than facing cold steel and close range!"

Flint looked at her quietly for a moment, noticing again the curl of her auburn hair, the smooth softness of her cheek. By Reorx, he wished this battle was done with! She sensed his look and turned, surprising him with a soft blush.

Then they heard derro sergeants barking commands, and saw the derro ranks gather again. The foot soldiers surged forward behind the spellcasting savants, the whole mass of derro approaching the ditch at the foot of the earthwork.

"Torches, now!" Flint shouted.

Dozens of hill dwarves raced to the top of the wall, pitching their blazing torches down the other side, onto the bales of hay that had been thoroughly soaked with lamp oil and placed along the edge of the ditch.

With a loud rush of air, each oil-soaked bale erupted into a high column of flame, an explosion of bright yellow light in the darkness.

With howls of agony, the savants clutched their eyes and stumbled backward. They rolled on the ground, shrieking and moaning, their wide, full-pupiled eyes temporarily blinded.

The savants closest to the blaze had been most seriously

affected. But the warriors behind them blinked in uncomfortable surprise, forced to turn away from the painful glare. Once again Flint heard the sergeants cursing and growling, and the derro started slowly toward the middle of the hill dwarf line.

"I've got to get back to my post at center!" he called, and Perian ran back to her own position by Basalt. "Good luck!"

The towering columns of fire marked the entire periphery of the semicircular redoubt. In the center, the black sludge smoke still obscured the field, preventing any derro advance. To Flint's left, the mountain dwarves hesitated in disarray and confusion, but to his right, where the savants had led the way, the Theiwar officers whipped their savage troops forward.

Flint scrutinized the lightly held right flank. Perian and Basalt had a thin force—barely one hundred hill dwarves, and half that many Aghar. But all they had to do was hold, since the steep river bank beyond the breastwork blocked the derro advance to that side. The wall of the earthwork itself would then force the Theiwar to attack upward, and give the defenders a significant advantage.

The first rank of black-armored mountain dwarves reached the ditch at the foot of the redoubt. The Theiwar ranks quickly scrambled through the shallow trench. The glowing piles of the haybales, mostly consumed by now, collapsed into cinders, but even so the derro were forced to march around the hot coals. They were armed with two-handed battle-axes, but they held the weapons in one hand, using the other to help them scramble up the steep breastwork.

Flint saw Perian leap forward and drive her axe down through the iron helmet of a Theiwar. Basalt, too, swung his blade and sent an attacking mountain dwarf tumbling backward into the ditch. All along the line, the dwarves stood atop the low wall, hacking and chopping at the derro coming up beneath them.

The Aghar of the Creeping Wedgie surged along the top of the redoubt, bashing their shields onto the heads of climbing Theiwar, causing more confusion. Weapons struck, and blood flowed. Flint's heart lurched as he saw several defending hill dwarves fall and lie still.

The king of Mudhole held his breath, wondering if the line would hold. He saw a derro scramble over the wall, but then Basalt cut him down with a swift blow to the neck. Perian led a band of dwarves in a sharp counterattack, battering and smashing the Theiwar, knocking them off the wall.

He heard her hoarse battle cry, saw the hill dwarves leap to follow her. She attacked like a banshee, laying about with heavy blows, darting away before a return blow could land. Flint's heart faltered as a derro struck at her back; she sensed the attack with some kind of prescience and whirled to cut the leering Theiwar down.

Finally Flint exhaled, seeing the hill dwarves not only hold, but continue to drive the mountain dwarves back into the ditch. Disorganized, confused, and dismayed, the Theiwar crowded together at the foot of the redoubt.

"Smoke's still keeping 'em away from here," grunted Ruberik, indicating the oily fog in the center of the battlefield. Flint looked at his brother in surprise, sensing disappointment in his voice.

"You *want* a chance to shoot a few of 'em, don't you?" Flint asked.

Ruberik cleared his throat, nodding. "I guess I *would* like to personally see that a few of 'em don't get back home."

The brothers turned their attention to the left, where the mountain dwarves had resumed their advance. They were swinging wide of the redoubt through the open field. Because of the black cloud that still lay across the center of their line, these mountain dwarves could not see their compatriots who had been halted on the right flank.

"Keep an eye on things here!" Flint barked at Ruberik.

"Wait! What do you mean? What should I—" Ruberik shouted as Flint darted away.

Privately, the king felt misgivings about leaving his brother in charge of the rambunctious Sludge Bombers. A quick look at the black smoke gave him assurance, however, for it seemed like it would linger for some time, blocking access to the middle of the redoubt.

Flint ran along the top of the breastwork until he reached Tybalt, who stood among a group of hill dwarves on the left wing of the semicircular barrier. They looked down as the charging Theiwar suddenly veered away, turning and running past the front of the breastwork instead of trying to climb it. The open end of the wall beckoned out in the field, offering its easy route past the defenders.

Around the hill dwarves crowded Nomscul and the gully dwarves of his Agharpult wing. They hopped and jumped, attempting to observe the enemy over and around the slightly larger hill dwarves.

"Agharpults, get ready!" Flint shouted as soon as he was in earshot.

"For what?" asked Nomscul, turning to his king in puzzlement.

"To shoot, you numbskull!"

"Me Nomscul!" beamed the Aghar. "You king!"

Flint restrained his tongue for a moment, and then was pleased to see Nomscul and his crews quickly spring into action; they even remembered which way to aim!

"Good, good!" he encouraged them, slightly out of breath as he reached Tybalt.

"They're sweeping around quickly," said the constable, with just a touch of alarm.

Flint looked across the field and saw the mountain dwarves advancing at a fast march past the redoubt from right to left. Soon they would be in position to turn and charge into the rear of the fortification, past the end of the wall.

"We can't waste any time!" snapped Flint. He saw that the hill dwarves were ready for the counterattack.

"Agharpults, shoot! Shoot two times!" That command, he hoped, would keep them launching until they ran out of Aghar. Then he turned back to the enemy.

The pyramids of the Agharpult tilted atop the earthen wall as the lone gully dwarves who served as missiles sprinted up the sloping inner side of the barrier. Vaulting onto their comrades, the whole mass of dwarfdom toppled forward, momentum hurling the topmost Aghar into the teeming ranks of the Theiwar. They struck like balls crashing into tenpins, knocking the derro formations asunder, toppling dozens of mountain dwarves to the ground.

"Hill dwarves, charge!" Flint raised the Tharkan Axe above his head as he shouted, and then stopped in surprise as a cool white light suddenly sprang from the axe, washing over the field. It spilled brightly across the derro ranks, and the mountain dwarves, to a harrn, turned their faces from the painful brightness. Flint stared at the axe for a moment, surprised by the rush of power. Around him the hill dwarves raised a hoarse cheer.

"To victory!" bellowed Tybalt.

With a ragged roar that almost matched their enemy's challenge in volume, the hill dwarves swarmed down and into the side of the mountain dwarf force. Flint saw Hildy, her face a mask of grim determination, race down the earthwork. His brother Bernhard and his sister Fidelia were also charging with the frenzied mob, though he didn't know exactly where they were.

"For the Great Betrayal!" howled Turq Hearthstone. The big hill dwarf flew past Flint and crushed a derro skull with his heavy iron hammer.

The charge came so quickly, and was such a stunning surprise, that the advancing Theiwar quickly broke in confusion. Desperately, in ones and twos and threes, the mountain dwarves met the rushing hill dwarves. A confused melee erupted as weapons clanged against shields and dwarves cried out in the tumult.

Overhead flew the bodies of many brave, tightly bundled gully dwarves. The Agharpults were being launched with remarkably accuracy after the days of training, and the Aghar were crashing effectively into the tight rows of Theiwar soldiers.

Flint was surrounded by the mysterious circle of light as he led the onslaught of his kin. He wielded the Tharkan Axe with brutal force, striking to his right and his left as he waded into the Theiwar army. His blade smashed a dent into the black steel of a mountain dwarf's breastplate, felling the fighter in one blow. He parried a barrage of assailants, dropping two more with crushing blows that split their helmets and shattered their skulls.

A derro screamed and ducked away, his eyes seared by the brightness of the blade. Others squinted and rushed forward, faces twisted by hatred. But they had trouble facing the light, and Flint killed those that did not turn and flee.

The great din of battle rang in his ears, a constant dissonant clash of metal against metal, mixed more and more with the shrill screams and dull groans of the wounded. Flint saw a dazzling array of bristly-headed derro around him, their faces a constantly shifting pattern of cruelty, hatred, and fear.

He caught a glimpse of Fidelia, wearing an old shirt of leather armor and wielding a long pitchfork with deadly effect, pinning a squirming derro to the ground by driving the makeshift weapon through his stomach.

Around him he felt the weight of the hill dwarves cracking the precision of the mountain dwarves' ranks. In the growing confusion Flint surged ever forward, dragging, as if by the force of his will, those hill dwarves who fought beside him.

He heard Tybalt's throaty roar as the constable slashed to the right and left with a huge two-handed sword. Almost unconscious of the sound, Flint, too, howled a battle cry and jumped forward to drive another Theiwar back. Flint noticed that his axe glowed as brightly as ever, and now the steel haft had begun to grow warm under his palms. The blood of dead mountain dwarves darkened the blade.

He came upon Garf, one of the Agharpult missiles, sitting on top of an unconscious mountain dwarf and rubbing his head.

"Hard shirt!" complained the Aghar. He thumped the metal breastplate of the warrior to show where he had landed after being fired from his weapon.

"Hard head!" Flint pointed out, patting the courageous gully dwarf on the back and indicating the fallen Theiwar.

Suddenly Garf's eyes widened in surprise. "No!" Flint cried, seeing the bloody tip of a sword emerge from the Aghar's chest. Stabbed from behind, Garf fell and Flint stared into the wide, maddened eyes of the sneering derro who had slain him.

Those eyes widened farther as Flint leaped forward, driving the still-glowing axe through the mountain dwarf's forehead. The enemy fell across the body of his small victim, and Flint blinked back tears of anguish and anger.

Then a mountain dwarf surged at him, and Flint barely had time to parry the blow. He left Garf's body as he slashed and then backed away, thrown off-balance by the savagery of the axe-wielding Theiwar's assault.

He heard Hildy cry out beside him, but he couldn't break away from the aggressive derro. A small handaxe flew past Flint's head, embedding itself into the derro's skull. A hill dwarf suddenly stood beside Flint, and he turned to nod his thanks at his brother Bernhard. He turned to help Hildy, only to see that she had dropped her opponent with a sharp stab of her sword.

But the derro pressed all around, and he felt himself backing up to keep from being surrounded. Bernhard and Hildy fought beside him, desperately holding the renewed derro attack at bay. From somewhere, a swordblade bit into Flint's forearm, and he shouted in pain. Two more derro lunged, their faces twisted by cruel grins.

Before Flint could raise his axe, another form stepped between them. He saw Bernhard drop one mountain dwarf with a sharp blow to the neck, but then his brother's weapon stuck in the armor plate of his victim. Desperately Bernhard struggled to pull the axeblade free, but the other derro was too quick.

Flint stared in horror as Theiwar steel sliced into his brother's throat. Blood—more blood than Flint could have imagined—spilled down Bernhard's chest. The hill dwarf spun, giving Flint a look of uncomprehending surprise, and then he slumped to the ground.

"Bastard!" growled Hildy, lunging at the still-grinning derro. The mountain dwarf raised his blade, deflecting her attack, but he could not guard against two at once. Flint, his whole body trembling with rage, attacked. The Tharkan Axe flashed, and the Theiwar's head flew from his shoulders.

Through his shock, Flint sensed a change in the tangled melee; the elite mountain dwarf fighters were recovering their equilibrium.

"Back!" ordered Flint. "Back to the wall!"

The order was unnecessary because the defenders of Hillhome were being forced back to the breastwork through no choice of their own. Soon, as the mountain dwarves pushed their renewed attack, it was all Flint could do to prevent their fallback from becoming a rout.

The hill dwarves desperately scrambled back up the wall and into their redoubt, but the mountain dwarves followed their advantage aggressively.

"Hold at the top!" shouted Flint, turning and bashing one more of the mountain dwarves. Once again his axe crushed metal armor, killing the foe without penetrating the rigid barrier of his steel plate. His victim tumbled back down the breastwork, knocking two of his fellows over as he fell. Flint noticed that the still-glowing Tharkan Axe was growing uncomfortably warm to the touch, and the blood of his enemies now sizzled on its blade.

Along the crest of the wall, Tybalt and other hill dwarves stopped their retreat. Gasping and panting from the exertion of the combat, the defenders nevertheless stood firm.

The Theiwar, exhausted from their long charge, still disorganized by the disruptive attack, suddenly fell back from the wall to catch their breath and regroup. Flint sensed the near-collapse of the hill dwarves around him and knew that the respite had come none too soon.

Then he looked over his shoulder and saw disaster.

Chapter 23

The Last Bastion

"Damn your filthy cowardice!" Pitrick exploded at the two sergeants who stood before him.

At first, things had seemed to develop fairly well. His regiments had formed with parade-ground precision, and their advance had proceeded with apparently irresistible momentum. It seemed certain that the hill dwarves would be overwhelmed by the first rush!

His eagerness for battle had increased with a conclusion he had gradually drawn over the preceeding day's forced encampment. He had brooded and cursed and schemed, still tormented by Perian's existence, out of his reach. But the more he thought, the more he believed that she would be here, in Hillhome, once again within his grasp.

After all, had she not dwelled in Mudhole with the very hill dwarf who, to Pitrick, embodied the pestilential stubbornness of Hillhome? And would not Flint Fireforge be certain to race to his village's defense? It therefore seemed very likely that Perian would be here, too, and this added heat to Pitrick's hatred, made him more determined than ever to wipe out the town and all its inhabitants.

But the first wave of his assault had been thrown back, and now these two craven warriors stood before him, stammering their pathetic excuses.

"Do you mean to tell me that you were beaten by *hill dwarves!*" the hunchback continued, turning his savage, penetrating gaze on each of the frightened mountain dwarves in turn. Good, he thought. They face the odds of battle willingly enough, but when *I* speak to them, they are still afraid.

Pitrick paced back and forth before the cringing derro. He limped awkwardly on his throbbing foot, and the pain momentarily distracted him from the matter at hand. He shook his head to clear it.

The Theiwar commander trembled with rage. Angrily he looked at his shaking hands, too unsteady to bear a weapon or cast a spell. Every nerve in his body screamed that he should kill these two failures before him, vent his fury upon their miserable lives.

But he could not do that. Pitrick faced the fact that this battle would not be so easily won. Slowly, he brought his anger under control, until he could speak normally. Then he turned back to the pair of veterans who had led his first attack against the breastwork.

Around him, the bonfires set by the hill dwarves had mostly burned themselves out. The darkness, thick and protecting, settled around his army again, broken only by the hot piles of red coals. Many derro stood in small groups, gathering around their sergeants, waiting for further commands. Others tended their comrades who had been overcome by the vile gas. The night was a blanket of protection and security back here, away from the defenders.

Before them, however, in the ditch along the fortification,

the great, oily bundles of hay still smoldered, glowing with painful brightness in the cool night. The bales had been soaked with oil, Pitrick recognized, and their ignition had been a cruelly successful trick. But, very soon now, the hill dwarves would pay for their cleverness.

The stench of the black smoke wafted past his nostrils. He grimaced at the cloud, which still blocked the center of the hill dwarf defenses. No matter, he would break them to the left and to the right. He would destroy them!

His ambitions called his mind back to the two black-plated derro who stood before him. They watched his face anxiously, contorted as it was by his all-consuming rage. Hesitantly, one of them opened his mouth.

"But, Excellency," stammered the grizzled battle veteran. "They fight like demons, madly possessed! They have weapons and discipline. You, yourself, have smelled the noxious gasses they cast—and they hide behind that wall, out of our reach!"

"And the fires!" chimed in his comrade. "The savants were totally blinded—and the rest of the troops suffered great pain!"

"You fools! I will tolerate no further delay! Attack again!" Pitrick sputtered, his voice a shrill scream.

"But—" A sergeant opened his mouth to object, then shut it when he saw the look in his commander's eyes.

"*No* delay," Pitrick said, his voice dropping to a sinister hiss. Unconsciously, his hand grasped the five-headed iron amulet than hung at his chest. Blue light seeped between his fingers, and the eyes of his sergeants grew wide with terror. The light seethed like thick smoke in a growing cloud around him, slowly reaching toward the cringing figures of his warriors.

Pitrick's vision vanished in the red blur of his hatred. He clenched his teeth, his breath coming in hissing gasps, as he again struggled to retain his self-control.

"We attack now, Excellency!" stammered one of the sergeants. They turned, stumbling in their eagerness to escape their maddened leader.

Pitrick took a pace after them, still tempted to sizzle one

of them into nothingness as a lesson against the consequences of failure. But that single step sent throbbing arrows of agony darting up his leg, and he winced, forgetting for the moment his recalcitrant subcommanders.

By the dark powers, his foot hurt! He screeched his agony, a sound of fury that frightened those troops within earshot. Then Pitrick limped after the two sergeants. He would find the savants, speak to them himself. Then they would know the folly of retreat!

He located, after long and painful minutes of walking, the six robed figures of his spellcasting savants. They squatted on the muddy ground of the field, pressing cold compresses of slushy grass to their seared eyes.

"Fools! Idiots! Morons!" he shrieked, walking among them and kicking the startled derro to their feet. "You can't stop now! The enemy strikes us a blow, then we must strike him back—*harder!*"

"But, Master," screeched one, groveling on his knees and holding his eyes downcast. "Our eyes . . . we can barely see!"

"Damn your eyes if you don't get up and attack!" sneered the hunchback. "Come with me! We will lay them low with fire and sorcery! Stand up, you blathering idiots—we must lead the attack!"

Slowly, reluctantly, the savants rose. They followed Pitrick as he limped forward, forcing his way over the muddy ground, closer to the hill dwarf redoubt.

As Pitrick marched, the pain in his foot became worse, a driving, pounding awareness that threatened to overwhelm every other sensation. But the hunchback used that pain, turning it into a kind of brutal example to show his men the true measure of their race. He marched harder and faster, intentionally punishing himself, sneering at the weakness of those around him.

His own vision suffered from the flaring fires across the field, but he forced himself to look past those, toward the enemy on top of the low, sloping wall. He saw a long rank of motley hill dwarves there, and growled inwardly at the thought that these puny specimens had repulsed an attack of the vaunted House Guard.

They would not do so again.

As he approached, Pitrick saw the struggle that was raging on top of the wall. The Theiwar were advancing in small groups, rushing up the sloping wall, only to meet the sharp weapons of the resolute hill dwarves when they reached the top. Each attack broke as the derro died atop the wall, survivors forced backward to fall, roll, or run to the ditch at the bottom.

"Now," Pitrick snapped, his shrill voice calling for the savants' undivided attention. "I will *show* you how to attack! Without mercy—without hesitation!"

He grasped the iron amulet and looked along the top of the redoubt, trying to identify the hill dwarf leader. The battle raging between the charging Theiwar and the staunch hill dwarves made it difficult to see. Once again he watched some of his elite troops thrown back, pushed physically from the top of the wall by the tenacious enemy.

Still, he only needed to find their captain. Then he would cast a single, very potent spell, and all cohesion would vanish from his enemy's formation.

Suddenly he froze, his eyes locked on a long-haired dwarf near the center of the enemy position. He blinked, but then he looked again, growing more and more certain of his identification. He saw that it was a frawl, and that she chopped about her with an axe, savagely skillful. Her auburn tresses burst free to swirl past her face.

Perian Cyprium!

"She *is* here!" Pitrick cried aloud, uncaring of the surprised looks from the savants behind him. Instantly he raised his hand, pointing his index finger right at her. He could almost taste the effect of the fireball spell on this frawl he had come to both desire and hate so much.

But something stayed his hand. The savants waited expectantly as he stared at her. The yearning for her was once again surging through his pain-racked body.

Pitrick reached a decision. He would not burn her—yet. A fireball seemed too fast, too impersonal a way for Perian to die. Far better she saw that it was he who took her, and that death should come slowly . . . afterward. There was even the chance she would yet come to appreciate him, and for a moment his mind thrilled to the image of Perian, on her knees, begging for mercy. A part of his mind began to imagine his response. Suddenly, violently, his attention turned back to the battle.

"Sound the fallback!" he shouted to the bugler, and, to his savants: "Prepare your spells!"

The brass notes of the horn sounded across the field, and the derro atop the earthwork quickly fell back to the relative safety of the ditch at the bottom of the wall.

At the same time his eyes flickered to Perian again. Later, he told himself. Later I will have her. I will find her and, by magic or might, claim her.

"Now!" cried Pitrick. "Destroy them!"

His hand clasped the medallion. Blue light spilled forth, illuminating the hunchbacked derro with a chilling outline as he launched his spell.

Violent magic exploded.

* * * * *

Basalt stood atop the redoubt on the right side of the position, raising his axe, bashing the mountain dwarves, standing firm. The battle had lasted less than an hour so far, yet it felt as though his life had always consisted of this same muscle-aching combat, the ringing cacophony of pain and death.

At first, terror had consumed him, and every blow he struck had been a matter of insuring his own personal survival. But, with each victory over an individual derro, his confidence had grown, and with it his rage. Now he struck with cold, deadly anger, slaying to avenge his father, Moldoon, and all the other unnamed dwarves that he knew were dying around him.

Perian fought nearby, astonishing the young hill dwarf with her skill and tenacity. She shouted hoarsely at her former comrades. The black-armored mountain dwarves who recognized their former captain hesitated for but a moment before they tried to close with her. But their hesitation was crucial. Swinging her axe with bone-crushing force, she managed to fend off all their attacks.

Basalt saw a mountain dwarf gain the top of the rampart between himself and Perian. The warrior raised his bloody axe and turned toward the frawl. Basalt twisted to his rear and swept the Theiwar from the breastwork with the savage cut of his axe.

"Fine work!" said Perian with a grin. Her face, flushed with exertion, showed a glow of exhilaration at the intensity of the fight.

Suddenly a bugle sounded, and the mountain dwarves fell back from the breastwork. We stopped them again! Basalt cried inwardly with relief. But Perian spotted six figures moving forward through the ranks of the thane's troops. Then, beside them she saw the dark, twisted figure of her worst nemesis—it could only be Pitrick. She stared, momentarily uncertain of the threat, but then she saw the wash of blue light and her panic galvanized her into desperate action.

"Get down!" Perian cried, throwing herself flat on the rampart.

"What?" grunted Basalt, even as he, too, flattened himself to the earth.

He squinted into the night, seeing a tiny globule of flame drift slowly through the air. It danced forward, toward the redoubt, to a place just to the right of Basalt's and Perian's position. Basalt thought that the tiny ball was rather pretty, though that instantly struck him as incongruous.

But nothing could have prepared him for the horror that happened next.

The dot of fire drifted onto the top of the breastwork among a huddled group of dwarves. Then it instantaneously erupted into a huge, globelike inferno of death. Basalt felt the heat from the nearby explosion singe his skin and hair. He heard screams of terror and pain, yet saw nothing for precious moments against the brightness of the fireball.

But then the fire faded, and he stared in dull shock at the charred bodies of the hill and gully dwarves who had been unfortunate enough to be within the fireball's killing zone.

The stench of burned flesh carried past him on the breeze, sickening him. He could not bring himself to believe that those blackened, stiff shapes had ever been living dwarves. The corpses looked like statues carved from charcoal.

Then Basalt saw more sparks, more light, explode from the dark-robed dwarves. The hill dwarf looked up in shock as crackling bolts of energy hissed and exploded over his head. With horror he saw a pair of hill dwarves—lifelong neighbors—fall lifeless, slain instantly by the strike of the magic. Screams erupted from the line, and Basalt sensed panic arising in his own heart.

The savants chanted a new sound, and hail erupted from the clear skies overhead to pummel those on the breastwork. Basalt clapped his hands over his head and pressed his face into the dirt, waiting for this nightmare to end.

Large round stones of ice hammered his body, smashing against his skin, numbing his hands, pounding a savage cadence of pain into his skull. He cried out with agony as a large ice ball cracked his elbow, and when another pounded him brutally in the kidney. Holding his breath and gritting his teeth, Basalt struggled to maintain consciousness, knowing that he could not stand another minute of this punishment.

The unnatural storm ceased as suddenly as it had started. For a moment a low, rumbling stillness fell over the field— not exactly silence, for many Aghar and hill dwarves groaned in pain along the ice-hammered redoubt. Basalt winced as he struggled to his knees, seeing other dwarves slowly climbing to their feet. We've got to hold them off, he told himself.

"Wait!" hissed Perian, pushing him back down.

Now the hill dwarf heard the sharp clunk of heavy crossbow fire. Metal bolts raked the top of the breastwork where many battered, exhausted hill dwarves gasped for breath. A few, like Perian and Basalt, had dropped to the ground in time. Most still stood, fully exposed to the lethal volley.

* * * * *

"To the brewery!" shouted Flint, Tybalt, Hildy, and everyone else who knew the plan. The stone walls of that structure would provide a last bastion of security, though they all realized that it meant leaving the town in the hands of their rapacious enemy.

Flint stopped in the center of town, watching the hill dwarves stream past. Small bands of gully dwarves scrambled along with the larger brethren. Perian and Tybalt joined him while Hildy and Basalt went to organize the defense of the brewery.

"Damn!" the constable cursed. "I thought we were going to hold them!"

"We tried," said Flint. "Now it's up to the stone walls of the brewery. We've got to stop them there!"

"Basalt all right?" Tybalt asked Perian. The blossoming fireballs and hissing magic missiles had been clearly visible to the other hill dwarf defenders.

"Fine—he's getting the defenses organized at the brewery," she replied. "The magic really raked us on the right, though. I'm afraid we lost two score or more." She turned to Flint as Tybalt started off to join the defenders at the brewery.

"That many, maybe a few more, fell on the other side," said Flint, trying to keep his voice level. The picture of Garf's surprised look and Bernhard's valiant charge lingered in his mind.

Perian's soft smile showed that she understood. "And you, with that axe! I could see you clear across the wall, swinging it like you were blazing a trail."

"Wasn't I?" Flint asked, grimly.

"Yes. But so many of our own have fallen, too," Perian observed quietly as most of the rest of their force moved past.

The last few hill dwarves trotted by. Up the road, Pitrick's marching Theiwar could be heard plainly, still an interval away but resolutely advancing through the defenseless town.

"Let's get to cover," Flint suggested.

"Wait," said Perian. "I want to check for more of the Wedgies—I saw Fester leading a group into the village."

"There's no time!" Flint objected, groaning. Yet he knew they could not leave their charges in the village, exposed to the Theiwar attackers, if there was any chance of getting them to safety.

"I'll just be a minute," Perian said. "Keep the gate open for me."

Swallowing his further objections, since they would just waste time, Flint said, "Hurry!" Then he watched as she darted between a pair of buildings toward the direction taken by Fester. With an anxious look up the road, he was mildly relieved to see no sign yet of the advancing mountain dwarves. Flint broke into a run, and soon rounded the curve in the road that took him toward the brewery.

The stone wall of that enclave now loomed ahead, the last battlement of the defenders of Hillhome. But a strong bastion it might prove to be; only one gate provided access to the courtyard within that wall, which was six to eight feet thick at its base. The brewery consisted of three buildings: a barn, the vat house, and an office and storage building. Each of these three structures was placed inside the compound, against one of the courtyard's four walls.

At the gate he found Ruberik and Tybalt, together with a dozen armed hill dwarves. This group waited in the street, holding the gate open while they tried to ascertain that all the defenders had passed inside.

"The vat house windows are blocked," reported Tybalt. "There's a hundred of us in there, with swords, spears and pitchforks—and also, the Wedgies. I don't think the derro'll be coming in that way."

"Is everyone inside now?" asked Flint.

"This is most of us," said Ruberik as a dozen more hill dwarves, led by Turq Hearthstone, sprinted around a corner and joined the group at the gate.

"I didn't see anyone back there," Turq gasped. "I think everyone's gotten away—at least, everyone who could still walk," he added grimly.

"I'll stand at the gate," said Flint. "We can hold it open for another minute. At least until we can see them coming." Hurry, Perian, he urged silently. "Can you go into the vat house?" Flint asked Tybalt and Ruberik. "See how Basalt and Hildy are faring. We've got to be ready for an attack from behind."

The two Fireforge brothers nodded at Flint. Each of them clasped one of his hands and for a moment they stood together in silence. "You and Basalt have given Hillhome a chance," Ruberik said quietly to Flint. "And whatever the outcome, we're all grateful for that."

Flint cleared his throat awkwardly and winked. "What do you mean, 'whatever the outcome'?" His brothers smiled at his forced joviality, then turned to pass through the gate.

Looking up at the high stone wall, Flint thought that his village just *might* have a chance. True, they would be surrounded, cut off from escape or food supply. But the mountain dwarves would have difficulty attacking them. If they could hold the Theiwar off for a while—though how long such a while might be, he had no idea—they might outlast their dark-dwelling foe.

Then Flint turned and looked up the street. He heard sounds of the enemy approaching, but as yet he could see nothing in the distant darkness.

Where was Perian?

* * * * *

Darting around the corner of an old warehouse, Perian looked up and down the side street. When she saw no sign of Aghar, she didn't know whether to be relieved or worried.

Then she heard a sound coming from the open door of a darkened greengrocer's shop. Crouching, she slipped across the street and looked into the store.

"Hi, Queen Furryend! Get food for fort!" Fester beamed at her, looking up from her efforts at collecting bacon, pickles, and other provisions. The Aghar's mouth was outlined in white sugar—apparently some of her supplies would be transported internally—but her apron bulged with food. Other gully dwarves moved forward from the shadows at the rear of the store, laden with pork, cheese, bread, and melons.

"Good, Fester—that's great! But you've got to hurry, now! Are there more of you near here?"

Fester nodded her head. "More get hungry and get food."

"Good! Now, run to the fort as fast as you can!" Perian barked the command sharply.

Fester looked momentarily puzzled, but then dashed for the door. The other Aghar, nearly a dozen in all, raced behind the "weighty lady."

Perian followed them from the store, looking anxiously up the side street. She heard the tromp of heavy footsteps to the west, though the derro were still some distance away. With relief, she saw Fester and her companions disappear in the direction of the brewery.

Were there any more stragglers? She looked around, her sensitive eyes seeing well in the darkness; she spotted no Aghar. The sounds of armored dwarves on the march came closer on Main Street, but still there were no derro on this side avenue.

Pivoting smoothly, she turned toward the brewery. The structure was visible at the limits of her vision, its tall, featureless wall offering protection. The gate lay just around the corner, and there she would find Flint. A quick, low dash, and she would reach the shelter of that fortress before the attacking Theiwar.

A blue wash of light spilled through the street, and Perian knew that Pitrick was near.

"Come!" The lone word echoed through the night out of nowhere. She heard the savant's voice as she tried to break into a run, but something in the power of his voice—in the power of his word—held her step.

Perian whirled to face him, ready to shriek her hatred and revulsion. Instead, she took a step toward him. Gaping in astonishment, she looked down at her feet even as she took another step toward the repulsive hunchback.

"I knew I'd find you!" he crowed.

Perian tried to articulate a challenge, or to raise her axe in defense. But her mouth clamped shut, beyond her control, while her arms hung slack at her sides. She felt, but could not stop, her axe slipping from her numb fingers. The weapon dropped to the ground.

Again that blue light surged, and she saw its reflection in Pitrick's eyes. He leered at her, all but licking his lips, as she stumbled forward another step. Perian thought of the walled fort, of Flint waiting for her at the gate. The knowledge halted her advance as she resolutely planted her feet, ignoring the compelling power of Pitrick's spell.

But the derro raised his hand and curtly gestured her forward. Once again she took a step toward him, fighting the impulse with every ounce of her will, but helpless against the grip of his power. Perian stared at the hideous figure, cocky in his deformed stance, the grotesque hump pressing him into his forward-stooping posture. His huge eyes gleamed at her, glowing like dire beacons in the night.

Flint! She wanted to cry his name, to fall into his arms, but instead there was only the grinning apparition of Pitrick before her, growing larger with each inevitable footstep. The hunchback planted his fists on his hips, sneering confidently as Perian stumbled closer still. In moments she would be within his reach; he seemed to take a perverse pleasure in bringing her toward him, while he remained immobile, waiting.

Her attention riveted to that hateful face, Perian felt as though she and Pitrick were the only beings in the world—a world that had become very forlorn indeed. Blue light seeped from his amulet, and it was the only light she knew. Blindly, helplessly, she stepped toward him again, and once more.

A few more paces would take her to his side. She struggled to speak, to cry out, but her mouth remained slack, her arms frozen at her sides. Only her feet moved in that slow, doomful cadence.

"Come, spiteful wench. Come, and feel the touch of your master! Come, and meet your death!" Pitrick threw back his head and laughed into the night.

Perian took a final step and then stood before him. Waves of despair tormented her soul. Pitrick reached forward with a clenched, clawlike hand, raising his fingers toward her face.

He touched her cheek.

Pain flashed through her skin as he made contact. His caress was like a shot of vile sickness, far worse than the clean wound of a steel blade. Sheets of agony wracked her body, bringing hot tears to her eyes.

And, finally, the pain broke the thrall of his magic. With a groan, Perian crumpled to her knees, clasping a hand to the cheek he had touched. She twisted away from Pitrick. She was free.

"You disgust me!" she spat, leaping back to her feet.

Pitrick stepped backward in momentary surprise. At the same time, blue magic erupted from his amulet, but the light diffused through the night, out of its master's control.

"Stop!" he cried, groping for his axe.

But Perian, too, was beyond his control now. She felt for her own weapon, remembering that her axe had fallen from her hands. The march of the advancing derro sounded around her, and she knew that the Theiwar would soon come to their commander's rescue.

Desperately, her fingers reached toward her belt and closed about the hilt of the small knife—her only weapon. She raised it and slashed wildly, feeling a grim satisfaction as the blade drove into Pitrick's hastily raised forearm. He screamed and slumped backward, tearing the blade from her grip.

Perian jerked away and saw the charging forms of black-armored mountain dwarves in the darkness beyond Pitrick. Some animal instinct in her wanted to stay, to keep striking him until he was dead, but her rational side told her there wasn't time.

She turned and sprinted toward the brewery, hearing the savant's hysterical shrieks of hatred. She did not see him reach for his amulet, though the blue light flared before she could dart around the corner. Lightning crackled through the night.

* * * * *

"Hurry!" Flint cried, overcome with relief as Perian stumbled toward him. The Theiwar troops advanced down the road behind her, but he swept her into his arms and together they tumbled through the gate. Other hill dwarves slammed the heavy portals shut and dropped the bars to lock them.

"You made it!" he grinned, gasping for breath and rolling over to look at Perian. "I was so worried!"

She smiled weakly and took his hand in hers. He was surprised to see that it was covered with blood. Then his eyes widened in horror as he saw the deep wounds, blistered by hot magic, in her back and along her left side.

"Perian!" he cried in disbelief.

Her smile slowly faded.

Chapter 24

When Gods Collide

"She's—they're getting away!" Pitrick's voice exploded in a shrill screech of outrage. "Incompetent fools! You're letting them escape!"

Watching Perian slip away, the hunchback limped into the main street, his hand clasped over the wound in his arm. His hatred of Perian and all that she stood for flared to new heights, causing him to tremble beyond control. Flecks of spit drooled, unnoticed, from his lips as he raved. Her escape only served to inflame him further. Through the smoke of the lightning bolt he'd cast, he had seen that she was mightily wounded. Despite this knowledge, Pitrick could think only of total, mindless destruction.

"Excellency, please!" pleaded one of his battle-weary sergeants. The leader of the derro looked up at him, smoke and grime smeared across the white skin of his face. His bristling beard and hair had many scorched patches, singed during the battle.

"The hill dwarves have gathered in one large building—they have not gotten away!" The warrior spoke quickly, fearful of his commander's wrath. "They are trapped there, waiting for us to draw tight the noose!"

Pitrick dropped his fist, a thin smile creasing his grotesque face. "Trapped? *All* of them?"

"All that we could see, sir. It's a stout building, with a heavy gate. But I think we can bash it down."

"Good. Very good." The hunchback abruptly sat down on the street, thinking. His face lightened still further as an idea occurred to him.

"Let the hill dwarf scum sit and watch while we burn their village!" Pitrick ordered, springing to his feet. "Put the torch to every building, every barn, every pile of hay in Hillhome!" He imagined the conflagration consuming the town around him, and the thought gave him much pleasure.

"Excellency, I have a suggestion," said the sergeant, with unusual courage.

Pitrick looked at him suspiciously for a moment, then gestured for the derro to speak.

"It will be dawn soon—no more than an hour to first light, and in another hour the sun will drive us under cover. I urge that we attack the hill dwarves immediately, destroy them now, while darkness still surrounds us. Then we can destroy their town at our leisure.

"But, if we stop to burn now," the sergeant continued, knowing he risked his life by daring to suggest a plan counter to the idea of his temperamental commander, "the sun will rise before the battle is concluded, and we will have given the hill dwarves another day of life."

Without pause, the sergeant rushed on. "The hill dwarves have already proven resourceful and treacherous. Who knows what they will do while the sun shines and we are at the disadvantage. Excellency, we are on the verge of a great victory! I urge you to finish the fight now, while this victory is within our grasp!"

Pitrick grew suddenly, ominously calm. Then he spoke. "Very well. We will destroy the enemy first. Now, where is this building that shelters them?"

The derro sergeant, concealing a sigh of relief, described the brewery to the adviser as they walked up Hillhome's deserted Main Street. Pitrick knew that his savants had expended their most potent spells against the earthwork, and would be of little use in the next battle. They would need to spend many hours studying their spellbooks before they could again cast the volleys of magic missiles or storm of hail that had proven so decisive on the wall.

And Pitrick, too, had employed most of his spells already. One or two might prove useful in breaking into the fortress, and then there were several he saved for his anticipated confrontation with Perian and the insolent Flint Fireforge.

Unconsciously, Pitrick fingered the dark battle-axe at his side. He had not yet used it, but he looked forward with cruel anticipation to the chance to drive it into a hill dwarf body. Perhaps even Flint Fireforge would find himself tasting the bitter steel of that Theiwar blade.

They came to the brewery, and Pitrick quickly took in the formidable nature of the position. The gate was the obvious vulnerable point, but he would also send his forces against the walls, using makeshift ladders, poles, and whatever else they could find. He had no doubt that they would quickly break into the last-ditch fortress.

His subcommanders gathered around, waiting for his orders. "We will take them here. Attack from all sides.

"And as for the gate," Pitrick said to his sergeant. "Make a battering ram."

*　*　*　*　*

The derro hurled themselves at the stone-walled brewery, assaulting it from every side. They scrambled up the steep wall, they bashed against the gate, and they pressed hard to break through the barricaded windows along the back wall. Everywhere the defenders stood firm.

Some of the Theiwar laid long poles against the top of the wall, and slowly inched up these crude ramps in an attempt to force their way over the barrier. Others found ladders in nearby barns and shops and used them to climb the walls more directly.

But the top was several feet wide, and this made a good platform for the defenders. In several places, mud-slick piles of earth from inside the compound had been used to bolster the walls. The sloping surfaces of these served as easy routes to the top, allowing many hill and gully dwarves to scramble up.

The defenders fought resolutely. The Aghar of the Creeping Wedgie, organized by Nomscul and Fester, found a new use for their shields, conking the derro on the head as the enemy reached the top of the wall. The hill dwarves, inspired by Fidelia Fireforge and Turq Hearthstone, used pitchforks, shovels, and spears to strike at the derro climbing the ladders. They learned to knock the poles aside and drive the ladders toppling to the ground.

To the rear of the compound, more Theiwar hurled themselves with savage abandon against the barricaded windows. They hacked the wooden barriers to pieces, flinging themselves through the narrow openings this created. But, within the vat-house, Basalt and Hildy directed an equally savage defense. Each attacking derro no sooner squirmed through the entrance than was impaled by the weapons of a half-dozen hill dwarves. Soon the bodies of the attackers piled up, creating an additional obstacle to the Theiwar.

The gate was the weakest point of the defense, though behind it stood a sturdy company of hill dwarf fighters. Tybalt Fireforge stood with these, watching the creaking gates. The portals swung farther with each crash of the ram, and the cracking of the beams became more and more visible as dawn's light diffused through the courtyard.

Then, creaking and splintering, the gates began to collapse.

*　*　*　*　*

Flint barely noticed the heavy pounding at the gate. He

held Perian's limp form in his arms. She was unconscious, her breathing shallow and weak.

He had enlisted Fidelia's and Ruberik's help to carry her into the storeroom, where he tried to make her comfortable on a bed of hay and blankets.

Ruberik stayed with him. He brought water in a tin cup, though Perian was not aware enough to drink. He stood awkwardly to the side, not wanting to intrude on Flint's grief, yet offering any help that he could.

Finally, Flint looked up at his brother, after trying to stem the bleeding as best as he could. In his heart, he knew there was nothing more he could do.

The brothers' eyes met in a pain-filled gaze. "You'd better get out there," Flint said hoarsely. "I'll be . . . following along." He could say no more, dropping his head to hide his tears.

"I'm sorry, Flint," replied the gruff farmer. Ruberik shuffled wearily out the door.

Flint turned back to Perian. She looked as beautiful as ever to him. A few strands of coppery hair curled across her forehead, but the skin below that hair was so pale, now—so horribly pale. And at Perian's too-white throat Flint saw the aspen leaf necklace.

Suddenly her eyes fluttered open, and Flint's heart leaped. She smiled at him weakly, and her hand closed, ever so faintly, around his. Her lips parted slightly, but she didn't have the strength to speak.

"My Perian . . ." Flint said, choking the words around his tears. Her hand tightened once more, breaking his heart.

And then she was gone. Flint held her long afterward, still unaware of the battle outside. His grief threatened to tear him apart. He felt as though he never wanted to leave, to do anything again.

But as the chaos of the battle grew to a crescendo, his pain slowly changed, burning its way from his heart to his soul. And as it moved, his mourning became anger, developing into a hot, blazing rage that at last compelled him to return to the fight, and to kill those who had slain Perian.

The gates of the brewery splintered open, and even from

within the building Flint sensed the urgency of the fight. He reached for the axe Perian had returned to him back in Mudhole, cursing with surprise as the weapon's haft burned his hand. The white glow of the Tharkan Axe had become tinged with red, as the metal itself heated like an iron bar in a smith's forge.

Without thinking, Flint looked around the storeroom, quickly spotting a pair of leather gauntlets. He drew these over his hands, and then picked up the gleaming weapon. Its razor sharp blade gleamed clean, ready to drink again.

Flint charged the door of the storeroom and threw it open, looking upon a scene of mass confusion in the courtyard. The derro had smashed open the gate with a heavy battering ram and now poured into the enclosure, where they were met by a sturdy line of hill dwarves.

He concentrated his gaze, looking for one hated form. Finally Flint saw the hunchback, limping along behind the leading mountain dwarves.

"Pitrick!" he bellowed, charging into the courtyard. The force of his voice carried even above the din, and several of the mountain dwarves, including the thane's adviser, turned toward him.

"Come and die!" Flint challenged. He raised his axe, and though its unnatural light was somewhat mutted in the growing illumination of dawn, it drew the derro's eyes like a hypnotic token.

"Fireforge," breathed Pitrick, watching Flint's advance for just one moment. Then the hunchback seized the five heads of his iron amulet, and that cold blue light poured from the magic token.

"Reorx curse your cowardly skin!" Flint growled, sprinting toward the savant. He knew he would never reach him before Pitrick cast his spell. Oddly, he felt no fear of his own death; just an overwhelming sense of sadness that so much other killing would remain unavenged.

Pitrick's sneer was all the answer he spared for his victim, then the derro barked the harsh command for his spell. A bolt of lightning suddenly sizzled from his hand, exploding toward Flint in a blast of magical death. The hill dwarf howled his rage, squinting against the blast of approaching magic, but not faltering in his charge.

Then the Tharkan Axe blinked brightly, and a white burst of light overpowered the pale dawn and caused Pitrick to close his eyes, crying out in pain. The axe shone as the lightning bolt crackled into Flint, and suddenly the spell was gone, inexplicably snuffed. Whatever the reason, Flint dimly realized it had something to do with the axe.

"*Now* you'll fight, scum!" hollered Flint in savage exultation. For reasons he did not stop to contemplate, the axe would protect him from Pitrick's magic!

Other mountain dwarf troops stepped in the way. Suddenly one of these was bashed away by Tybalt. Then Ruberik stepped to Flint's side, knocking back another of the savant's protectors.

"Face my blade, you miserable coward!" called the king of the gully dwarves, until only one guard stood between Flint and Pitrick. He was charged by Fidelia, who cut him down with a blow.

"A hill dwarf will never best a mountain dwarf," Pitrick said, his tone threatening, challenging. Trembling with both fear and joyous anticipation Pitrick raised his axe finally, knowing that he could not defeat this hill dwarf with his spells. Flint raised the Tharkan Axe and the weapon lit up the courtyard.

Resolutely, the two leaders hammered their blades together. The hunchback was surprisingly strong, and both dwarves staggered back from the impact of their combined blow. The ringing noise filled the courtyard, and the hill dwarf found a savage satisfaction in the clash.

Flint pressed quickly forward, feeling the heat of his own weapon through his gloves. They clashed again, and once again fell back from the resounded collision. Scowling in concentration, Flint focused all his strength, his skill, and his hatred against the repugnant derro before him. Again and again he raised the blade high, driving forward with earthshaking blows that Pitrick somehow deflected.

Flint sensed the fight around them stopping, as derro and hill dwarf alike paused to watch the duel between their leaders. A hundred individual combats waned, forgotten in the periphery of this fight to the death.

Flint and Pitrick raged back and forth, axes clashing, fine steel meeting steel, backed by muscle and fury. The thane's adviser attacked with bestial savagery. Suddenly he flew forward, unleashing a storm of lighting-quick blows. Flint fell back, desperately deflecting the mountain dwarf's cuts. The Tharkan Axe blocked every assault, the haft growing hotter and hotter under his palms, until even his gloves could not protect him. Ignoring the searing pain, Flint held his axe tighter—he would cling to it until death or victory freed his grip.

Suddenly Pitrick lurched away. The quick retreat caught Flint off guard, and he instantly crouched, watching his opponent warily.

Again the savant seized the iron amulet that hung at his neck and raised his fist toward Flint. With a sharp hiss, like hot rocks dropped into water, a line of blue sparks erupted from the Theiwar's hand. The embers seemed to hunger for Flint's flesh as they rushed toward him. Swirling like living things, the sparks formed a ring around him.

Desperately the hill dwarf raised the Tharkan Axe and stumbled backward. The gleaming blade bit into the blue fire as if the flame were a solid body, striking true with the keen, avenging steel. Once, twice, and again Flint chopped, each time with growing force, breaking through the circlet of magic, knocking the stream of sparks to pieces. Slowly the pieces settled to the ground, and the arcane magic of the amulet lay as twisted ringlets of harmless smoke on the ground.

Both dwarves sprang at the other, and once again the fight became a test of physical strength and endurance. Blinking his eyes to clear the sweat away, Flint ignored his fatigue. He saw only the hateful face of his enemy before him, and his own hatred coalesced with Pitrick's to form a cocoon of berserk rage around them. The derro smashed his axe again and again against Flint's blade, but suddenly the hill dwarf saw his opening. Ducking backward before the Theiwar swung, Flint waited until the derro's attack swished harmlessly past his face.

Then he stepped in, putting every bit of the strength in his toughened muscles behind the blow. All his hatred and fury, all of his overpowering grief came together, focused by the driving power of his weapon. Pitrick tried to twist away, to turn or parry the punishing blow, but in his last instant he knew he would not succeed. Finally, for a brief second, Flint saw those mad eyes grow still madder, this time from stark terror.

It was a sight he would savor for a long time.

The Tharkan Axe cut a silver streak through the air, meeting the savant's neck below his helmet and above his breastplate. The blade made a clean cut, severing the heads of his amulet, then his skin and muscle.

The blade finally came to rest near Pitrick's heart, jammed tightly into his collarbone and breastplate. The Theiwar commander staggered backward, tugging the weapon out of Flint's hand. Pitrick's blood soaked the once shiny blade of the Tharkan Axe, sizzling and scorching from the fiery heat of the metal. As he watched in disbelief, Flint saw the blade grow cherry red.

Pitrick's body twisted, then sagged to the ground. He dropped to his knees with a groan, looking in disbelief at the blood that spread in a growing circle around him. Finally he collapsed on his face in the mud, the pool of his blood growing ever larger.

And the world went mad.

The first rays of sun crept over the eastern ridge, spilling light into the town. Flint scarcely breathed as he reached to retrieve his weapon. The Tharkan Axe in Pitrick's chest, nestled against the remains of the five-headed amulet, glowed red, so hot that Flint could not even touch it through his gloves.

Suddenly it burst into flames. White smoke billowed from the fire. The cloud hissed forth, snaking upward and rapidly spreading into the sky.

Simultaneously, the severed heads on the amulet began to writhe like snakes, hissing, spewing a great cloud of black smoke. This dark vapor, too, poured into the air, growing like a living thing, writhing and twisting its way upward. The two clouds met, spuming around each other, but each remained separate in a shocking contrast of light and dark. The dawn sun reflected from the white smoke with a bright glare, but the black vapor seemed to absorb the light, sucking the energy from the air and giving nothing back.

Flint stumbled away from the clouds, stunned by their sudden incarnation. The sight frightened him in some subconscious fashion with a terror he could not articulate but that chilled him to his soul.

The warring dwarves in the courtyard watched in amazement and backed away in fear. The dense trails of smoke, both white and black, grew larger and larger and began to coalesce vaguely into the shapes of humanoid heads: a beautiful, dark-haired human woman with blood red lips and almond-shaped eyes; and a gray-bearded, fierce-looking harrn dwarf, his eyes radiating anger. The two foggy shapes hovered above the brewery.

The clouds writhed together and apart, almost as if in combat—though an eerie, silent, and ephemeral battle it was. They grew still larger, filling the sky above the entire town. At the base of the intermingled black and white clouds, the amulet and the axe crackled with white hot fire, an arc of hissing power sizzling between them. The heat drove Flint still farther back, though he could not avert his eyes from the spectacle.

Suddenly, there came a terrific rumbling sound, and then slowly the earth beneath the dwarves' feet began to shake and tremble. The ground rippled like water, shaking stones loose from the brewery walls, knocking Flint and every dwarf in view off of their feet. Many of the wooden buildings began to fall like matchstick shelters.

Wisps of the black smoke trailed through the town, touching off fires where they struck the dry timbers of buildings whole, or ruined. In moments the flames roared upward, and Hillhome became a nightmare of hungry, crackling blazes.

The dwarves in the courtyard of the brewery scattered in fear, trampling each other to get through the gate first. The

Theiwar were the first out of town, running through the wreckage for the hills. Not a living one of the derro remained to face the rage of the vengeful hill dwarves.

The earth shook again, a convulsive tremor that wracked the town from one end to the other. Great cracks appeared in the ground, exploding outward from the white fire of axe and amulet. Flint watched, still stunned to immobilty, as these fissures erupted to either side of him. He saw hill and gully dwarves disappear into the cracks, and he could not move to help them. The stone walls of the brewery crumbled and split, collapsing into heaps of gravel.

Screams of panic shrilled through the air. Mad stampedes erupted, as hill and gully dwarves scrambled through the ruins, seeking an escape from the convulsions that wracked the world around them.

Flint shook off his numbness.

But before Flint could gather his family and escape, the trembling of the earth stopped. The black and white smoky forms cast one more stony glance at each other and then dissipated into thin wisps in the morning air. The hissing fire between the two artifacts slowly faded. There was no sign of Pitrick's body, nor of his amulet.

Flint's attention fell upon what remained of the Tharkan Axe. It was now a thin sheet of fragilè foil in the shape of the axe. Of the weapon's original form, onlỳ the runes remained.

"The Tharkan Axe," said a soft voice beside him.

He turned to look at Hildy's blood- and dirt-streaked face in surprise. "How did you know it's name?"

"My father taught me the Old Script," she explained, pointing to the runes. Flint nodded dumbly, watching as the runes themselves started to fade.

"The Axe of Tharkas, it says," repeated Hildy. "Crafted by the god Reorx in honor of the great peace among dwarves. Its magnificence shall last—" Hildy looked softly at Flint, sympathy welling in her eyes before she concluded, "—until it is used by a dwarf to shed a dwarf's blood."

In the courtyard, now full of the stillness and death that follows war, the sheet of foil caught the wind and fluttered away.

Epilogue

Hillhome became a ghost town in less than a week. What the battle had left standing had been leveled by the earthquake. Not a single family had escaped losing at least one member in the Battle of Hillhome, and most of them wanted to start anew elsewhere in the hillcountry, where the memories would fade more easily with time.

Diehards, like the Fireforges, whose families had been in the village since before the Cataclysm and whose homes had been at least partially spared from the devastation, chose to stay around and rebuild their town as best they could. Though her brewery was destroyed, Hildy stayed behind with Basalt and the promise of a life together.

And so with much dignity and tears the Fireforge family

buried its dead, among them brother Bernhard, the valiant Aghar Garf. And Perian.

After the short service offering their souls to Reorx, Flint had wandered alone with his thoughts to a small crest overlooking Stonehammer Lake to the west and the remains of Hillhome to the east. The sky seemed too blue, the early winter air too crisp and . . . *ordinary* for a day when his heart was near to bursting, His memories of Perian were few but sweet; he prayed they would not fade with time. Suddenly he became aware of shuffling behind him.

"Old queen gone," Cainker said sadly, coming up behind the gray-haired dwarf, a tear dripping down his filthy cheek. In his grief Flint had lost track of his subjects and was now reminded that they were likely waiting upon him for the direction of their lives.

"Yes," Flint said softly. He looked with affection at the gully dwarf, but then he thought of something. "*Old* queen?" he asked.

"Sure. New queen Fester, she just fine!" Cainker bobbed his head enthusiastically.

"Hi, kingly guy!" said Nomscul as he joined them. "Good fight!"

"Thanks," Flint muttered, growing more confused. "What's this about Fester being queen?"

"Yup. She my queen! Me new king, you know."

"New king?" Flint was too surprised to immediately do the sensible thing, which was to heartily endorse the idea.

"Sure. Now that you got no queen, it good idea." Nomscul sighed, apparently with real regret. "You one nice guy, though," he amended. "But just not work out as king. *Real* nice guy, all right!"

Flint chuckled, feeling a lump growing in his throat. He wanted to laugh aloud, and he wanted to cry, so he just stared in bemused wonder at the new king of Mudhole.

"Just not work out," Nomscul said with a shrug.

* * * * *

The general stood high upon the temple platform, looking over the still-smoldering city. Sanction was not so empty as before, as thousands of ogres and human mercenaries gathered. Legions of hobgoblins formed vast camps on the ashen slopes around the city.

Across the valley, beneath the seething Temple of Luerkhisis, the rest of the general's army was born— draconians, hatched by a corrupting process from the secretly hoarded eggs of good dragonkind.

The draconians pleased the general greatly, gathering as they did in well-disciplined companies of savage warriors, eager for bloodshed and war.

Indeed, his army grew daily, and this made the matter of armaments all the more vexing. One day, the shipments to the hidden cove had simply stopped, and they had never resumed. All of his attempts to contact the grotesque Theiwar, Pitrick, had failed, and the general disliked failure. He would not fail his Dark Queen, the five-headed dragon-goddess, Takhisis.

Yet the preparations would go on. He had enough good steel to arm many of his troops, and the rest would find other sources for blades, and shields, and armor. Still, the general knew, his army would be strong.

And soon, it would be ready.

FOR THE BEST IN PAPERBACKS, LOOK FOR THE

In every corner of the world, on every subject under the sun, Penguin represents quality and variety – the very best in publishing today.

For complete information about books available from Penguin – including Puffins, Penguin Classics and Arkana – and how to order them, write to us at the appropriate address below. Please note that for copyright reasons the selection of books varies from country to country.

In the United Kingdom: Please write to *Dept E.P., Penguin Books Ltd, Harmondsworth, Middlesex, UB7 0DA*.

If you have any difficulty in obtaining a title, please send your order with the correct money, plus ten per cent for postage and packaging, to *PO Box No 11, West Drayton, Middlesex*

In the United States: Please write to *Dept BA, Penguin, 299 Murray Hill Parkway, East Rutherford, New Jersey 07073*

In Canada: Please write to *Penguin Books Canada Ltd, 2801 John Street, Markham, Ontario L3R 1B4*

In Australia: Please write to the *Marketing Department, Penguin Books Australia Ltd, P.O. Box 257, Ringwood, Victoria 3134*

In New Zealand: Please write to the *Marketing Department, Penguin Books (NZ) Ltd, Private Bag, Takapuna, Auckland 9*

In India: Please write to *Penguin Overseas Ltd, 706 Eros Apartments, 56 Nehru Place, New Delhi, 110019*

In the Netherlands: Please write to *Penguin Books Netherlands B.V., Postbus 195, NL–1380AD Weesp*

In West Germany: Please write to *Penguin Books Ltd, Friedrichstrasse 10–12, D–6000 Frankfurt/Main 1*

In Spain: Please write to *Alhambra Longman S.A., Fernandez de la Hoz 9, E–28010 Madrid*

In Italy: Please write to *Penguin Italia s.r.l., Via Como 4, I-20096 Pioltello (Milano)*

In France: Please write to *Penguin Books Ltd, 39 Rue de Montmorency, F-75003 Paris*

In Japan: Please write to *Longman Penguin Japan Co Ltd, Yamaguchi Building, 2–12–9 Kanda Jimbocho, Chiyoda-Ku, Tokyo 101*